DANGEROUS DEFIANCE

Chester Thornton had almost persuaded himself
that his daughter Betty was safe at home when he
saw her.... Wrapped in his wife's fur-trimmed
velvet cloak, Betty stood out against the neon lights
almost regally, like an angry princess.

"Well, Chester, what do you seem to think you're up
to now?" Her voice was cold, like showers of icicles
aimed at her father's heart.

He tried to speak, but no sound came from his
parched throat.

Betty stepped coolly out of the light.

"Come on, Dud, let's go back and have another
dance."

A laugh of triumphant defiance broke hoarsely
from the young man. But suddenly Chester's fury
was set free. With a quick blow under the chin, he
sent the young man sprawling. Betty whirled
furiously on her father. There was a look in her eyes
that Chester was to remember long years after, a
look like a blow that left a scar...

Bantam Books by Grace Livingston Hill
Ask your bookseller for the books you have missed

Grace
Livingston Hill

THE PRODIGAL GIRL

BANTAM BOOKS
TORONTO · NEW YORK · LONDON

This low-priced Bantam Book
has been completely reset in a type face
designed for easy reading, and was printed
from new plates. It contains the complete
text of the original hard-cover edition.
NOT ONE WORD HAS BEEN OMITTED

THE PRODIGAL GIRL

A Bantam Book/published by arrangement with
J. B. Lippincott Company

PRINTING HISTORY
Lippincott edition published 1929
Bantam edition/October 1979

ISBN 0-553-12809-4

Published simultaneously in the United States and Canada

Bantam Books are published by Bantam Books, Inc. Its trademark, consisting
of the words "Bantam Books" and the portrayal of a bantam, is Registered
in U.S. Patent and Trademark Office and in other countries. Marca
Registrada. Bantam Books, Inc., 666 Fifth Avenue, New York, New York 10019.

PRINTED IN THE UNITED STATES OF AMERICA

Chapter I

As soon as the letter came that practically promised the contract for which he had been bending all his energies for the past six months, Chester Thornton sat back in his chair and let his mind relax.

For the first time in a year he took a deep breath without a tremble of anxiety at its finish. Now he could look things in the face and know that instead of a gradually increasing deficit there would be a good profit. This new connection would mean the backing of half a dozen of the best firms in the country; it would mean prestige and widening interests, unlimited credit and respect. It spelled Success in large letters and filled him with an ecstasy such as he had not known since he was a carefree boy and went a-fishing.

He stared across at the letter files unseeingly and tried to think what it would mean to his home and family! Why, they could even buy a new house, a palatial place up on the Heights, and choose their own place in the world. In three or four years the firm would be one of the wealthiest in its line in the country; they might even open up a foreign office—!

He drew himself sharply back from day dreams into the present. It would mean right now that he could do a lot of things that had needed to be done for a long time, little repairs to the house—not extensive of course if they would be moving in a year or so, but enough to put things shipshape and liveable again until they could look about them and choose just the home that they wanted. They might have to build. Why, of course they would build, that was the idea—*build,* and have just what they wanted! And in the meantime, whatever he had to do to their present home would only enhance its value for sale.

Then, too, Christmas was coming in a few weeks!

For the first time in his life he would be able to purchase real Christmas presents, gifts that were worth something, and not just scrimped necessities. He really had never enjoyed giving Betty that wrist watch, platinum though it was, and set with some good little diamonds, because he had to lie awake so many nights planning just how he could make up for having spent that money on it. But Betty was the dearest daughter in the world, she deserved all that he could give her. Then his thoughts turned to Eleanor and his soul swelled with joy,—now he could buy that string of pearls he had wanted for so many years to give her and never dared. It wasn't expensive as those things went, not the one he wanted, very simple and lovely, not a long string, for Eleanor liked quiet things—

A lover-like smile hovered over his lips for an instant at thought of the gentle-faced woman who was his wife. Then his released ambitions leaped forward.

Well,—Betty could have the car now that she had been coaxing for for over a year. Of course she was a little young for a car, only a trifle over seventeen, but all her girl friends had them, and it would relieve the situation for Eleanor wonderfully if she could have the family car free for herself, and not have it continually off with Betty and her friends.

Of course Chris would be sore about Betty's having a car, but Chris could wait another year or two. A boy wasn't really fit to own a car till college age, though of course some of them did. But there were other things for Chris and his time would come later. And there was Jane,—and the twins! Oh, it would be rare to buy Christmas gifts this year with no grim spectre of Want hovering behind to restrain his every impulse!

Thornton left the office at three o'clock that

afternoon for the day. Things were in good shape and he really could not hold himself down to work he felt so happy. It seemed as if he must do something about it.

Following out this desire, he went at once to the showrooms of the new Mermaid eight. If he was going to get that runabout for Betty by Christmas it was high time he was looking into the matter. It ought to be ordered at once.

The Mermaid eight proved to be far more fascinating than he had been told, and it was almost time for the five thirty train to leave the station when he came puffing into the last car and dropped into a seat by the door.

He sank with a sense of satisfaction into a comfortable position, cast a quick furtive glance around hoping there were none of his close acquaintances near to whom he must talk, and unfurled the newspaper which he had bought from habit as he dashed past the news stand. He did not want to talk to anyone just now. He wanted to enjoy this new sense of freedom from care, and think over his afternoon's experience.

Which one of those three Mermaid eights would Betty rather have? The yellow one was out of the question of course, entirely too loud for a young girl. Perhaps it would be better to let her choose,—but no, that would spoil the joy of the surprise. This first real gift that was really worth anything he would choose just as he wanted it to be. And he knew in his heart that the deep rich green like the heart of the woods would be his choice. Of course the blue was good, too, but blue was so common now. No, that green one with the sporty little gray top, and the nickel trimmings was distinguished enough for any girl. Yes, he would get the green one. Perhaps he would not even tell Eleanor about it. He would just surprise them all.

His gaze wandered from the newspaper which he was not reading to the window with its lights flashing past. How beautiful it was out there with the river far below surrounded by lights clustering along its banks, little red lights like red berries on the barges tied up at the empty wharfs. Smoke billowing softly, cloudily from the tall stacks of factories, more lights in clusters, stars above, stars below. Why, how beautiful it was! What a world to live in anyway, when even the river bank down by a factory could appear beautiful at night. Someone ought to write a poem about it. The beauty of a city at night. Perhaps someone had. Perhaps others had noticed this beauty, he never had. It took an easy mind to just sit down and see beauty. He must remember this and get more time to look around him, see the beauty in the world before he got old!

It certainly was good to feel that great load of anxiety gone that he had carried now for ten years. Success in sight and writ large! His heart swelled gratefully.

It was then that the words struck him. They hurled around his protecting paper, and got him by the throat like so many demons taking him unaware to destroy him.

He had heard those two young voices; boyish, silly, vacuous, he had unconsciously labeled them when their conversation reached his averted consciousness. He had heard without knowing what they were saying, until suddenly his daughter's name was mentioned! followed by a loud nasty laugh, the kind of a laugh a demon from the pit might give after a dastardly deed of depredation.

Instantly the father's senses were alert, stung into horror, unable to believe his ears. If the two youths who were so frankly talking over their conquests could have seen his face, could have known who was sitting behind them listening to their depraved confidences they would have flung themselves with scant delay from his neighborhood. But in cheerful ignorance of his proximity, and with confident casualness, they proceeded, in no hushed voices, boastfully comparing experiences—and girls!

"Little rats! Little dirty rats! Vile dirty devils!" A voice from Thornton's soul away off in the distance seemed to be crying, "Throttle them! Choke them! Rub their faces in the dust of the earth! Strangle them! Pull out their tongues by the roots! *Exterminate* them!" The words seemed tumbling over and over in his brain, while his

4

heart turned cold with horror and anger, and his brain seethed with helpless phrases. For a moment he knew how a murderer felt. He must kill them. Of course he must kill those vile creatures who had presumed to speak of his white precious daughter in such vilely intimate terms.

And yet when he tried to throw down the paper and rise, his hands trembled and had no power to release the sheet from his hold! And the power was gone from his feet! He could not make his muscles move to bring him upright. He could not move his eyes to see those two who were blaspheming his child in his hearing. An icy hand had his throat by a terrible grip and something was binding his heart with fearful pressure so that it seemed as if the very veins in his temples would burst. Was he having a stroke? Was this paralysis that held him hand and foot from dragging those low-lived youths the length of the car and flinging them from the platform into a passing field?

Gradually his heart beat more steadily, and he could think a little. His eyes which had been staring so blindly began to see the larger letters on the sheet before him, although he did not comprehend their meaning. He was groping, reaching out, trying to steady himself. Perhaps he had been overdoing lately. Those blinding headaches to which he had been subject the last few months were a result of overwork and worry, and now that the pressure was relieved somewhat he was feeling a reaction. Surely he *must* have only fancied that he heard those awful words, the loathsome laughs that were like crawling serpents coming toward him, menacing the one he held so dear. What had they said anyway? He recalled the words, forced himself to bear again the shock of their meaning. Surely, surely they were lying! Boasting to one another! Trying to outdo one another, the dirty little vermin! Surely, they only chose his daughter's name to accompany such boasts because she was so high, so pure, so far above any possibility of a breath touching her reputation that the boast was all the greater! Of course it could not be true,—his *daughter!* Betty! Why—*Little Betty! They must be made to suffer for this!* It was not true! He must do something about it though! He must take them out when the train stopped, take them somewhere—perhaps to the garage, and put them through a grilling and then wallop them till they were sick. Would that be sufficient for such a hellish offence? He must control himself. He must remember his daughter's fair name. He must not bring her into the public eye by attacking the criminals here in public. He must put a hold upon himself.

He was startled at the strength of the fury that had been unleashed within him,—righteous fury!

Yet there he sat frozen in his seat, and those boastful boy-voices were speaking further of his Betty, setting forth her personal charms with a frankness that was more than revolting, comparing her exquisite intimate loveliness to that of some other girl whom they called Judy! Why did he not reach forward now and grip that boy by the throat! Call the conductor and have him taken in charge—! What was it that held him this way from making a single move?

Was it—? Could it be that he was afraid lest Betty—? No! But—*had* Betty been—*indiscreet?* Could she have allowed intimacies without realizing—meaning to? Innocently of course. Oh, no,—impossible! His Betty! But,—yes,—that must be what held him back!

He thought of her exquisite rose-leaf body lying softly in the white blanket when he and Eleanor had looked at her alone together for the first time, almost to worship her, so fresh and sweet she was from God, like a bud dropped down to earth from heaven. It had seemed a sanctuary just to stand and look at her. Her father's heart had turned to God more closely at that moment than ever before, when he realized that God had trusted him with such a flower of perfect life to love and train. It had made him feel that he must somehow purify his own life to be worthy of so great a trust. And through the years when she had been growing up he had always felt this more or less whenever he looked at her glowing beauty. He felt almost like worshipping her, giving her reverence for her exquisite purity and beauty.

And now, these swine dared to joke about her charms as if—

He paused and stared about him as the train came to an abrupt halt at his home station and neighbors arose all about him swarming out.

He let his paper fall from his numb fingers, and tried to stand upon his feet. The two youths in front of him were noisily dragging one another up, laughing irresponsibly. The one who had spoken those first terrible words caught at the falling newspaper and restored it to Thornton's nerveless hand. The father lifted his stricken eyes and recognized the youth as the son of a neighbor, a classmate of Betty's in High School. Thornton's face was ashen but the boy was not looking at him. He was still employed in a whispered line of jokes with his companion, his eyes following a girl who had just come down the aisle. The little swine! He had not even known that the father of Betty had heard what he had said! Would he have cared if he had noticed?

The stricken father stood there dazed, filled with loathing of life, trying to think what he should do. He seemed to lack the power to move out of that car. Yet he knew that when all the others were out he must get out quickly and go after those boys and— What should he do? What could he do that he would not have to explain and thus bring his Betty into notoriety! Oh, he understood now why men sometimes became murderers!

But when he had gone out to the platform and the train had passed on its way he seemed dazed by the dark. He tried to look around for those boys, but they were gone. Presently everyone else was gone and he was left standing alone on that platform with the rows of lights, and the sound of the station agent slamming the late baggage into the baggage room, getting ready for the next train down to the city.

He dragged his heavy feet across the track. He had the feeling that his heart was a great burden that he had to carry home, and that his feet were too frail for the task. His head, too, bothered him. He could not think. He could only hear those awful words about his Betty beat over and over in his brain, and he could not decide what to do. Should he go to the house after Dudley Weston,—ask

7

for Mr. Weston senior,—and demand—what should he
demand? What was adequate for a young girl's name and
intimate sweetness defamed even in thought?

He knew of course that there were stories being told
about the frankness of youth, the lengths to which they
would go, the orgies, the debaucheries— But these were
not young people like his own. Such a thing could never
touch his family, reared in refinement, guarded and
taught the right from babyhood; with such a home and
such a mother—! No, of course not! Betty would never
allow intimacies! And yet these boys had dared—! Had
said that she—!

He would get to that point and every time would
halt and recall the boy's words, phrases,—what Betty had
said, what Betty had—Oh, God! Could there be any
punishment for desecration like that?

Oh, yes, the boys and girls had stolen kisses when he
was young, and thought it smart, had held hands on a
sleigh ride or a straw ride, or coming home in the
moonlight. But nothing like *this!*

Petting parties! Was that what they meant when
they mentioned in the papers and magazines the doings of
young folks? And referred to them lightly! It could not be
that the writers understood! Oh, it could not be that a
thing like this, a loathsome cancer, could steal into the
heart and life of a rose of a girl like his Betty and defame
it!

Yet all the while in the back of his mind was that fear
growing as he dragged his heavy feet along the path, the
fear that Betty had inadvertently been a party to the whole
thing. Giddy and pretty, fun loving, daring, she might
have led her companions on unwittingly—He got no
further than that. Yet it was something that might bring
shame on her sweet self if brought to the light of
enquiry,—and what was he to do?

He groaned aloud so that a passer-by hurrying
down to the next train turned and looked after him and
wondered if he ought to offer help.

And now the necessity for getting home and seeing
Betty rose within him like a frenzy. One look at her sweet

flower face would of course dispel these groundless fears, and give him strength to go out and bring vengeance on her maligners. He felt sure that all he needed to set his spirit right and give it the accustomed strength to act, was to look in his Betty's eyes and see her sweet pure smile. His little daughter Betty!

And then he came within sight of his home, a comely stone dwelling with welcoming windows set with shaded lamps, and a glow of firelight into the cheerless night.

He paused a moment to look at it all once more and think how dear it was before he stepped within and learned the truth.—Before its charm could be shadowed by anything that could sadden the beautiful life they had lived within. Why had he thought they needed another home? This one had been so gracious, so wonderful, so satisfying. Even if he came to have millions why should he change such a home as this for the fairest mansion earth could offer?

There was Eleanor standing by the fire one foot resting on the fender, and Doris hanging on her mother's arm. Jane was playing something on the piano, a dashing little jazzy melody that rang out cheerily through the closed window. Chris was seated in the window reading the sporting page of the evening paper, and John was working away in the corner with his radio. Thornton saw all this as he stepped up on the porch and hungrily looked in the window. His home! Why hadn't he been more mindful, more grateful for having such a home?

And they were all waiting for him. He must be very late! It seemed ages since he had got off the train and started to walk home. He could see through the open door beyond that the table was ready. The pantry swing door opened a crack and the maid looked in crossly and out again.

But where was Betty?

His heart contracted sharply and he hastened to open the door and step within to dispel that spectre fear again.

Betty was just coming down the stairs as he closed

the door and looked around. She was dressed in a little rosy taffeta, slim and straight to her narrow waist, and then hooped on the hips and flaring out like the petals of a lovely flower. Her exquisite head with its sleek gold cap of close-cut shining curls was tilted delicately as if she knew her power, and her slim white lovely arms and neck gleamed against the darkness of the staircase as if they were also of the texture of the rose. She poised on her little high-heeled silver slippers, fussing with a spray of silk roses on her shoulder and called crossly to her father where he stood staring by the door.

"Well, is that you, Chester, come at last? You better cut this out! *I've* got to go out this evening and I can't be kept waiting all hours! We were just going to eat without you! I didn't see any sense myself waiting all this time. Come on Eleanor, he's here at last and you better give him a dose of medicine. He looks like a stewed prune. Do get a hustle on, I can't wait all night!"

Chapter II

The lovely little daughter pirouetted lightly on the lower step of the stair till the light over her head showed full upon her loveliness, accentuated here and there,—a touch of carmine on the pouting imperious little mouth; a soft blush on the cheek that he had always called her lovely complexion; a darkening of lash and brow; a shadow under the great blue eyes that somehow wore a dashing look of boldness and impertinence tonight that he had never seen before. It seemed that the hall light was cruel. Those overhead lights were always trying. When she got out to the table he would see her as she really was, and then this horrible fear that was gripping his heart now so that he could scarcely breathe, would leave him forever.

Just let him get a good look into her dear eyes, and see her smile. He wished she wouldn't call him Chester in that pert tone. It didn't sound respectful. When she had first taken it up playfully it had been a joke, but to-night— Well,—to-night it hurt!

The spectre stepped nearer and gripped him by the throat. He must drive this awful thing away. He must get to the dining room quickly! Perhaps he was going to be sick! He must swallow a cup of coffee. That would make it all right of course. There was nothing in all this. Of course there was nothing at all—nothing at all!

Seated at the table he passed his hand over his eyes and looked about on them all, trying to focus his eyes on Betty's petulant face. It was plain that Betty was displeased with him. Yet somehow her face did not look quite so disturbing here as it had under the weird light of the hall chandelier. It was better blended, less suggestive of paint and powder. Of course he was quite accustomed to the ever present powder puff that all girls nowadays played with in public, but it had never entered his head that his daughter wore anything like what people called "make-up." That was low and common to his thinking, and quite unbecoming a girl of respectable family.

Chris broke in upon his thoughts with a sudden request for money.

The father tried to summon a natural voice:

"Why, Chris, you had your usual allowance and it is only ten days into the month. What do you want of more money?" he asked feeling that his voice sounded very far away and not at all decided. His mind really was on Betty.

But Chris seemed almost to resent his query:

"Well, I *want* it!" he said crisply, as if his father had no right to ask the question.

"What's the matter with your allowance? You'll have to give an accounting. What have you done with it?"

"He-he-he's lost it playin' pool!" chimed in Johnny joyously with a grin of triumph toward his older brother.

"Shut up! You infant! You don't know what you're talking about!" said Chris angrily.

"I do so! I was lookin' in Shark's window with Bill

11

Lafferty when you lost. I heard Skinny Rector tell you he's goin' ta tell our dad if you didn't pay up tanight—!"

Chris shoved his chair back noisily.

"Aw, bologny! Dad if you're gonta listen to an infant I'm done! *Keep* yer money. There's plenty of places I can get money if you won't give me what I want! Other boys don't get this kinda treatment in their homes— Wantta know every nosey little thing, and listen to a n'infant—!"

He had complained all the way through the hall in a loud voice and the front door slammed on his final word.

The family sat in a perturbed silence for an instant till the mother broke it in a worried voice that had a hidden sob in its texture.

"He hasn't eaten a mouthful, Chester."

"Well, what can you expect?" reproached Betty. "You can't treat a young man as if he was a three year old. If Chester wants Chrissie to stay at home he'll have to shell out a little more liberally from now on. Chrissie's almost grown up, and isn't allowed anything compared to other boys. Why, we're the only two in our set that haven't got cars to come to school with, and I think it's scabby! I'm getting ashamed to go out of the house."

"That'll be about all from you, Betty!" said her father in a cold voice that was so new to him that he felt frightened at it. Was he actually talking to his little Betty this way?

"On second thought, you needn't go out any more until we've had a thorough understanding on this subject and a few others," he added.

Betty stared at him in astonishment for an instant and then burst into a mocking laugh:

"Try and do it!" she sneered. "How do you get that way, Chet? It isn't in the least agreeable."

"Now Betty," began her mother anxiously, "don't hurt your father. You know he didn't mean—"

"He better not!" said Betty imperiously.

"We gotta boy in our school ut says ya don't havta obey parunts," broke forth ten year old John. "He says 'What they gotta do about it?' He says they ain't got any

12

more right ta say what ya shall do an' what ya shan't n'we
have. He says we all got the same rights—"

"John, leave the room this minute!" said his father
sternly.

Johnny looked up aghast, his well loaded fork half
way to his lips. He was not used to hearing his father
speak like that.

"Go!" said Thornton.

Johnny hastily enveloped the forkful.

"But I was just gonta tell you about the club we got.
It's called 'Junior Radicals.' We—"

"Johnny, your mouth is too full to talk," besought
the distressed mother.

"Go!" there was something in his father's voice that
Johnny Thornton had never heard before. He made sure
of another forkful of chicken stuffing and reached for a
second hot biscuit as he rose reluctantly from his chair,
but his father's hand came out in a grip like a vise and
rendered his small sinewy wrist utterly useless. The
biscuit dropped from his nerveless fingers dully on the
table cloth and Johnny Thornton walked hastily toward
the door, a little faster than his feet could quite keep up,
propelled by a power outside his own volition. He had
never known his father could be so tall and strong.

"Great Cats!" remarked Betty contemptuously as
the dining room door closed sharply. "Chester must be
crazy! I never knew him to be so off his feed before! I'm
going to pass out of the picture before anything more
happens. Tra-la-Eleanor. I wish you joy! You better beat
it yourself till the weather clears."

"But Betty! Your father said—" began Mrs.
Thornton.

But Betty was gone out through the kitchen and up
the back stairs to her room. Her closing remark as she
sped through the swing door into the pantry was:

"Applesauce!"

The door upstairs into Johnny's room was heard to
close firmly and a key to turn in the lock. Then Thornton's
steps came slowly, unsteadily down, almost haltingly, his
wife thought. Could Chester have been drinking? But no,

13

of course not. He hated the stuff. He never touched it. It must be business. She ought to have told Betty to be more considerate.

When he opened the dining room door again his face was white as a sheet and his eyes were staring ahead as if he saw a spectre. He marched sternly to his seat and sat down, but he made no attempt whatever to eat. Instead he looked around his depleted dinner table.

"Where is Betty?" he asked in a voice that was husky with feeling.

"Why, I think she's gone up to her room, dear," said his wife placatingly.

Thornton's face did not relax, and Jane who had been biding her time silently, mindful of the fig pudding which was her favorite dessert, decided to leave while the going was good. But when she slid stealthily from her seat to go out her father's voice recalled her.

"Sit down!" he said severely. "And don't leave the table until dinner is finished."

Jane stuck up her chin indignantly:

"I was just going up to my room," she said defiantly, "I've got some 'mportant studying to do."

"Sit down!" thundered her father uncompromisingly.

Jane slid into her seat sullenly.

Mrs. Thornton looked at her husband almost tearfully and explained in a low voice to the sulky girl:

"Daddy comes home tired out and doesn't want to be worried. He isn't feeling well I'm sure. He wants it to be quiet and orderly and not everybody jumping up and running out—"

"He went out himself," said Jane impertinently—

"Hush!" said the mother with a fearful glance at her husband. But little Doris diverted the attention suddenly, contributing her bit to the conversation, having been turning over her mind for a suitable topic ever since her brother's summary exit. It seemed the dramatic moment for her to enter the limelight also.

"We got a new book in school to-day. Our teacher read it to us. It's a story about a lady that lived in a tree and could do things with her toes just as well as with her hands. And bime by she got to be a real lady and came down outta the tree, and lived in a house. She was one of our Aunt's sisters, the teacher said."

"You mean *an*cestors," corrected Jane coming out of her sulks with a giggle to correct the baby of the family.

"No, Aunt's sisters!" insisted Doris. "She 'estinctly said Aunt's sisters."

"What does all this mean, Eleanor?" said Thornton looking at his wife. "Do you mean they are stuffing that kind of bosh down babies?—in *school?*"

"It's her science class," asserted Jane importantly. "They're just starting to learn about how the earth began, all gases and things you know, and how everything developed of itself, and then animals came, and some of 'em turned into men—. We had it all two years ago, but now they're beginning it in First Grade."

"What utter nonsense!" said Thornton angrily. "It's all well enough for some highbrows to think they believe in evolution if they want to, but they have no right to stuff it down children's throats, not *my* children anyway. And in the *Public* School. Eleanor, haven't you taught these children *any* of the Bible?"

"Why, of course, Chester," quavered his wife soothingly, "They had all the Bible stories read to them. You know about Adam and Eve, darling. Why, Jane, you got a prize once in Sunday School for telling the story of Creation. How can you let Daddy think that you don't know—"

"Oh, of course I remember all that, Mud," said the thirteen year old, "but that's all out of date. Didn't you know, simply *nobody* believes the Bible any more? My teacher said the other day, simply *nobody* that really knows *any*thing believes it any more. She said there were some places in the New Testament that were true to history but the rest was all fanciful, kind of legends and things, especially all that about Adam and Eve. It was just like mythology you know. Didn't you and Daddy *know* that? I suppose you haven't been paying attention to what went on since you stopped school you know, but my teacher says almost *nothing* in the Bible is true any more. It isn't *scientific*—! Why even the children in the Grammar School know that—!"

"That will do!" thundered Thornton furiously. "Eleanor, this is unspeakable! Why haven't you known what kind of bosh our children were being taught? Where are the rest of them? I want to sift this matter out and know just where we stand! This is *awful!* Send for them all to come back! I want to see them right away."

Mrs. Thornton looked distressed. She had been listening to Betty's tiptoeing feet overhead and now she knew they had ceased. She was even sure she had heard the creak of the back stairs, and the opening of the kitchen door. Therefore she temporized.

"Suppose we go away from the table, anyway, Chester," she suggested, "so that the maid can clear away. You've scarcely eaten a thing. Jane, you and Doris take your pudding up to the sitting room while your father finishes. He is all tired out and ought not to be disturbed while he eats. Take another cup of coffee, Chester, dear. Your nerves are all worn out. You must have had a hard day to-day. I'm afraid things haven't gone as well as you hoped at the office. But never mind, dear! Don't let it worry you. Whatever comes we've got each other. Remember that and be thankful."

"Got each other!" exclaimed Chester strickenly. "But *have* we?"

"Of course we have," cheered his wife. "Now dear, drink that hot coffee and you'll feel better. Come, and then we'll go into the library and you'll lie on the couch and tell me all about it. Then by and by when you are rested I'll call the children and you can talk to them, or perhaps tomorrow morning. You know you are in no frame of mind to talk calmly to them, and in the classes I've been attending about child training they say it is simply fatal to talk excitedly to a child, that it arouses antagonism, and that really is the worst thing we can do. You know really they are human beings like ourselves, and have to be given a chance to express themselves— They won't stand for radical discipline such as you and I passed through. Really Chester, the children of to-day are quite *quite* different from a few years ago. You know things have changed, and young people have *developed*. There is a more independent attitude—"

"Stop!" cried Thornton. "Stop right there! Eleanor, if you have swallowed that rot whole and are going to take that attitude I shall go mad. *Express* themselves! I feel as if the whole universe has gone crazy."

"But Chester, dear, you are overwrought—!"

"I should say I was overwrought. Eleanor, you don't know what you are talking about. Listen—!"

"Well, drink your coffee," she said soothingly. "At least drink your coffee before I ring for Hetty, and then we'll go into the other room and you shall tell me everything. You poor dear, I'm afraid you are going to be sick!"

"I don't want any coffee! I can't eat! I tell you Eleanor, I must see the children! I must see *Betty* first! No, I can't tell you anything till I have a talk with Betty. It is too dreadful! I want to understand the whole thing better before I tell you. Come, quick! Get Betty. I must see her at once."

She tried to persuade him to lie on the couch and let her cover him up before she called her daughter. She poked the fire into a blaze and stalled for time by turning the hall light out so it would not shine in his eyes, but he pranced back and forth and refused to even sit down.

So at length she went upstairs to call Betty.

But Betty's room was a whirlpool of garments, little silk dewdabs, trailing negligees, powder puffs, with an eddy of diminutive high-heeled slippers in one corner and a strapped pile of school books submerged in a chair under a torn evening frock. But no Betty!

It was as her mother had expected. Betty had made good her escape.

Mrs. Thornton passed through the confusion with deft hands, picking up and straightening as she went, hanging the flimsy little inadequate rags her daughter called clothing on the hooks in her closet, sweeping the clutter of ridiculous shoes into a quiet bag on the door,

17

smoothing the bed, tidying the bureau. She stalled again for time. If only Chester would fall asleep he would be more reasonable. He would not blame the children. Something terrible must have happened in the business world that he should come home like this. He was usually so fond of the children, so interested in all that they had to tell about school life, so proud of Betty's looks, and Jane's music.

Probably the deal that he had hoped for so long had fallen through and she knew that that meant a great loss of money. But he would pull out of it. He always did. And he was yet a vigorous man, young for his years, and keen in business ability, beloved and respected. All would be right. All she had to do was to soothe him now for a little while. If he would only fall asleep—!

She heard his voice calling her impatiently:

"Where is Betty? Why doesn't she come down at once?"

The mother hastened down with a placating air:

"Chester, I'm afraid she's gone, but she ought to be back before very late. Suppose you just lie down here and tell me all about it. You know that always makes things better—"

But he interrupted her:

"Gone? Where is she gone!" There was alarm in his voice and in the startled eyes he turned on her.

"Why, you see Chester, she had an engagement this evening—"

"Yes, I believe she told me so," he shouted, "but I told her at the table that she was to stay at home!"

"Hush, Chester, the maids will hear you! Let me explain. You see, Chester, she really *couldn't* stay at home. It was an engagement of two weeks standing—She had promised!"

"*Couldn't!*" he said, his voice still loud with alarm and excitement. "Couldn't obey her father? Well, I'd like to know why not?"

"Why because there were other people involved. Chester, you really didn't give her any chance to explain

18

you know, and it was getting late. You remember you kept us waiting for dinner—!"

"Involved? Who else was involved? Where has my daughter gone? I want to understand this thing perfectly. Where *is* Betty?"

"Why, Chester!" said his wife aghast. She had not seen her husband so roused in years. He must be losing his mind.

"Listen, dear, she has only gone to a little High School dance. She'll probably be home before long now. They don't usually stay very late."

"But why should that be more important than obeying her father?"

"Because she had promised to go with one of the boys, one of her classmates, and she couldn't leave him without a partner."

He wheeled on her.

"*Who* has she gone with?"

"Why Chester, how strangely you act! Just one of the boys she has known all her life."

"*WHO?*"

"Only Dudley Weston, our neighbor," said the mother complacently, sure that the name would cool her husband's heated temper. But his eyes fairly blazed.

"Dudley Weston!" he cried and his voice was like a moan. "That little *viper!*"

"Why, Chester! Now I'm sure you must have a fever or something. It is only yesterday you told me he was growing into a fine manly fellow, and said how handsome he was as he went down the street."

The man groaned.

"Well, I don't think so any more. Betty might as well have gone with the devil from hell."

"Now, Chester, you are swearing! I never heard you swear before. Oh, what shall I do?"

But he paid no heed to her words. He was searching behind the hall table for his hat that had fallen on the floor.

"Where *is* that dance?" asked Betty's father.

19

"It is at the High School hall," said Mrs. Thornton. "Oh, daddy! What are you going to do? You are not going *after* her? You are not going in public to mortify our daughter! Our little Betty! Oh, Chester! She will never forgive you! She won't come! I'm sure she won't come. She is very angry at you already. If you do a thing like that you will alienate her forever. Chester, you *mustn't!*"

She was crying now, great tears rolling down her cheeks, though she seemed unaware of them. She caught hold of his coat and held him with all her slender strength.

Something in her frail sweetness and agony touched him even in his wrought up state. He looked down at her, and for a moment his eyes softened with deep pity and tenderness.

"Listen, Eleanor, you don't understand. You must trust me in this. I know what I'm about. And our Betty is in terrible danger. That boy is rotten! I heard him talking to-night in the train! About our Betty! Saying unspeakable, loathsome things about her! Oh, I would have saved you this if possible. He was boasting—I can't tell you all, not now anyway, there isn't time. I must get Betty before it is too late. Where is Jane? Call Jane. I want her to stay with you.—*Jane!*"

He sprang up the stairs and flung her door wide, but there was no Jane there. He turned to his wife who had come stumbling up the stairs after him, the tears still flooding her face.

"Where is Jane?" he asked now with that strained white look about his eyes returning.

"She has just gone over to Emily Carter's to study her lessons. She asked me if she might go. They often study together. She'll be home by nine o'clock."

He glanced at his watch.

"Nine o'clock! Why, it's past nine now! I'll just step around and bring her back. I don't like her running around the streets at this hour of the night even a block. She's too young, and there are too many devils abroad. Besides, I want her to stay with you."

Then with sudden tenderness he stooped and kissed her:

"Don't cry, Eleanor. I didn't mean to be harsh. But you didn't understand. It was pretty bad, and shook me a good deal, but we'll pull out of this somehow."

Then he was gone out into the night leaving his wife with the worst alarm in her heart she had had in all the years of her married life. What would Betty do now? And what might not Chester do, when he found that Betty would not obey him in public? She recalled all the recent lectures on Child Training and sat weakly down on the lower step of the stairs and wept again.

Then out from the little front room near the linen closet at the end of the hall where Johnny had his haunts there arose a raucous voice singing from Johnny's radio:

> *"I'm a little boy,—!*
> *And I love a little girl!"*

And the mother on the stairs wept and wondered what the child trainer would tell her to do under the circumstances.

Chapter III

The Carters lived half way down the next block.

Thornton reflected that he had better take the car to save time. He could explain to Jane on the way home that her mother was feeling worried about something and he wanted her to stay up with her till he returned. Then he could drop her at the door and drive right on to the High School.

But when he stopped at the Carters' door he was surprised to find the house all dark, both upstairs and down. Probably the children were up in some back sitting room studying, or in Emily's bedroom. He frowned anxiously as he rang the bell, and waited impatiently. It seemed terrible to think that Betty had gone off with that unspeakable boy! And how was he to go about it to explain to her? He would probably have to let her mother do it. It would be such a humiliation for his delicate minded Betty to hear the foul words that had been used about her. Perhaps a hint from her mother would be sufficient without having to humble her by having her father tell his awful experience. That would have to be her mother's part. His was to deal with the lad.

He brought his mind back from his unhappy reflections to ring the door bell again. Surely these people had not retired at half past nine! And if so what had become of Jane?

He rang a third time, this time prolonging the pressure until he could hear the distant whirr of the bell from the front steps.

A window was pushed up slowly above his head, and an African voice called casually.

"Who down dar? What you-all want? Ain't nobuddy hum 'cept jes me an the baby."

"I'm Mr. Thornton," explained Chester, "I've come for my daughter Jane. Won't you tell her to come right down? I'm in a hurry."

"Her ain't hyear no moh! Her 'n' Em'ly went out som'ers. Said they wuz goin' down t' the drug sto' at the cohneh fer a soda. Reckum they'll return d'reckly. But you cawn't nevvah tell. Mistah Cahteh an' his wife don' gon' ta town ta the *thee*-a-tre, an' Em'ly she gene'lly does as she please when dey out. I can't be bothahd! You jes' try the drug sto' ef yoh wants yoh gal in a hurry. Mebbe yoh find her! I gotta go back. The baby's cryin'!"

The window went down with a slam.

A sudden sense of fury descended upon Chester Thornton. Why did all these things have to happen to him at once! Just when things were looking up and everything was hopeful! Here was life in a terrible mess! Little Jane too! Just a baby! Wandering around the streets at night with another child. He never did like those Carters. They were common! *Common!* That's what they were! Or the girl would know better than to take another child out alone at night—

He climbed wrathfully into the car and stepped furiously on the gas, startling a furtive cat into a streak of shadow.

Now, where should he look for Jane in case she was not in the drug store? But perhaps Jane had already gone home. Yes, of course, that was it. Jane wouldn't go to corner drug stores alone at night. Jane knew she was to go home. That was the explanation. She had been told to return at nine o'clock. She was not common herself, even if she did like to go sometimes with a common child. Probably it was not in the least necessary for him to hunt further; of course she had gone home and he had missed her in the dark. Nevertheless, now he was here he would make sure.

He parked his car hastily in front of the brightly lighted store, and leaving the engine going he sprang out to look in the window.

There was a crowd in the drug store. The soda fountain was always popular of course at this hour of the evening, even in winter. The near-by College and Prep school supplied a continuous flow of patrons.

Thornton stopped at the window, lowered his head to look under a pasteboard image of a bold miss advertising a new brand of cigarettes, but the crowd inside the window was too close for him to get a good survey of the entire store. He went up the steps and flung open the door, and just as he did so the crowd parted to let out an elderly woman with a large bottle and an anxious air of haste. For an instant Thornton got a glimpse of an open space beyond the crowd, and a young delicate little face strangely familiar, whirling giddily before a circle of admiring spectators.

Almost instantly the crowd closed up again, and a noisy cheer followed. Several rough young voices called out familiarly:

"Go to it, Kid!"

"Give us another of those high kicks, Jane!"

With strange premonition Thornton pushed aside

23

the crowd of college fellows that stood in his way and brought himself inside the circle of onlookers, unmindful of the resistance of the youths who blocked his way.

"Say, what's your haste, old gent!" one flung up at him as he elbowed his way to the front.

And there was *Jane,* his little child Jane, with her brief kilted skirt tucked up like a ballet girl, her delicate features aflame with excitement, a bold abandoned challenge in her big blue eyes, her close cropped dark curls quivering, her bare childish knees above their rolled down stockings flashing white against the dark background of the mahogany show case. Jane, dancing in solo, to the clamor of a jazzy radio in some unseen depth of the store's recesses. Jane, dancing for the amusement of a score of lustful-eyed youths who watched her all agog, and cheered her on with none too delicate phraseology. Seemingly regardless she danced on light as thistle down, yet vulgarly suggestive in a dance that might have had its origin in the slums.

As her father entered upon the scene Jane was in the midst of an intricate whirl of arms and legs, white knees all mixed up with rippling skirts and flying arms, white hands fluttering, one dark lock of hair longer than the rest, waving like a crest over the pretty forehead. Her vivid little face with its forward impudent smile flashed back and forth so rapidly that for an instant Thornton did not know his own child. Then, as the shaft of bitter assurance entered his soul she finished with several high kicks and a lazily graceful hand-spring, coming upright with shining eyes and glowing cheeks, and a little saucy tilt of triumph, openly aware of the admiration of her audience.

The irreverent onlookers broke forth into coarse jest and cheer once more; raised neglected cigarettes and quickly wove a blue haze of smoke about their favorite; gathered closer about her, reaching for her with bold intimate hands.

Suddenly they fell back and a hush came over them all. Jane had seen her father!

Jane's delicate little features grew suddenly drawn

and mature. Jane's big dark eyes stood out in her little white face, the color ebbed away, and a kind of panic of fright spread over her face. Even the shell pink ears, so carefully uncovered by the barber's shears, so boyish in their bareness, were white as if they were dead. Jane stood and stared at her father, for she had never seen such a look on his face as she saw now. Not at least since the day in her babyhood when she had put her mother's diamond ring down the sewer pipe in the street, and her father had taken her to his study and given her the soundest spanking she ever remembered to have had. Jane stood still in her tracks and watched him come, felt a sudden leadenness in her knees and hands, and wished for a nice convenient hole to open through that tesselated marble floor and let her down anywhere, she did not in the least care where.

Emily Carter, standing at the soda fountain counter with a young man almost twice her age, sucking soda through a double straw, watched him come, and giggled excitedly. The crowd of college boys with a sprinkling of prep boys, away without leave to purchase cigarettes, saw the fright in their favorite's eyes, and a long low murmur like a young menace swept among them; but Chester Thornton came on with two long strides and gripped his daughter by the arm.

Without a word he led her out, her boyish head held high, a side sweep of frightened grimace on her face turned toward her erstwhile audience.

One or two of the bolder boys tried to step in his way and protest against the removal of their entertainer, but Chester Thornton swept them aside as if they had been made of card board, and took Jane out to the car.

"Get in!" he said sternly. His voice sounded like a knell.

Jane tried to summon a natural voice.

"I've left my coat and hat behind," she said as if it were quite a natural thing to have done in a corner drug store at ten o'clock at night. "I'll have to go back and get them, Daddy." Her voice had reached almost a cheerful tone now.

"Get in!" commanded her father.

"But Daddy! It's my best hat and coat!"

Thornton shoved his daughter forcefully into the seat and slammed the car door shut.

Jane began to cry. She was angry at herself for crying, but she could not keep the tears back. She had never seen her indulgent father act like this. It must be true as Betty had said that Daddy had gone crazy.

"I'm cold!" she chattered.

He paid no heed to her.

As the car turned around she saw Emily Carter come to the door to watch her with an awed, sober look; then she heard a jeering laugh ring out from one of the boys, and her face grew crimson with mortification. He had no right! Her daddy had no right!

"I've got to stop at Emily's and get my books," she said as they whirled down the block. "I've got very important lessons to study for tomorrow."

"You should have thought of that before you went down to display yourself before the loafers of the town," he said curtly.

"Why, Daddy, I only went down for a minute. Emily had to get some tooth paste her mother had sent her for this afternoon and she had forgotten and then the boys asked me to give the dance we are going to have in our school play!"

Thornton was silent and grim, driving hard. They flashed past the dark Carter house and Jane put a detaining hand on his arm.

"This is the house, Daddy! I really must get those books. I'm going to have to sit up late now to get done. There's a test tomorrow—"

"You're mistaken!" said her father crisply. "The test was tonight! And you *have* failed! You needn't worry about your books. You'll not need them any more. You're done with that school forever!"

"Daddy!"

Jane sat frozen to silence, trying to fathom the horror of what had just been said to her. Did it mean that Daddy was so angry he was going to send her away to boarding school? She would like that! It would be a regular lark— But what if he were to have her taught at home! That would be unbearable!

They stopped abruptly at home, and Thornton took his daughter by the arm firmly, almost painfully, and escorted her to the house.

Eleanor was still sitting on the lower step of the stair weeping. She looked up anxiously as the door opened; hoping, half expecting Betty,—almost afraid to look at her face. But instead there stood Jane, with a sullen, defiant, frightened look and tears on her face, rolling slowly, heavily down from wide eyes.

"Why, Janie, dear, you didn't go out on a night like this without a coat, did you?" her mother asked, springing to her feet anxiously.

"No," said Jane fiercely. "Daddy wouldn't wait till I got them on and I'm all in a shiver."

"Why, Chester, that was dangerous!" said his wife turning worried eyes on him.

"So was the place I found her in," said Thornton grimly. "Eleanor, put her to bed, and *watch* her till I get home. It isn't safe to let her out of your sight."

"Why, Chester! You frighten me!" said his wife, her hand fluttering to her breast. "Where did you find her?"

"I'm sorry," said Thornton gravely, "but it was necessary to frighten you. I found her in the corner drug store 'expressing' herself for the benefit of a lot of lewd fellows who were cheering her on and calling out dirty remarks."

Mrs. Thornton's eyes sought Jane's sullen ones in horror:

"Janie!"

Jane's eyes went down to the toes of her small slippers, and she shrugged her shoulders indifferently.

Thornton looked at Jane in a kind of helpless despair.

"Now, I'm going out to hunt our other daughter," he said in a choking voice. "Goodness knows what I'll unearth this time. We seem to have run amuck."

He paused and looked at his wife compassionately, as if he would like to say something comforting, when there wasn't anything comforting to say. Then he turned toward the door.

"Well,—" with a tone that had a choking sound, "I must go—"

"Don't you think, Chester, don't you think maybe you'd better wait?" began his wife anxiously. "Betty will be sure to be home soon now—"

A look of finality came quickly into his face.

"No!" he said and was gone, then opened the door again to say:

"If Chris comes in tell him to wait up till I get back. I've *got* to see him!"

Five minutes later Thornton parked his car in a long line that stood around the athletic field of the High School and took his way up the broad steps to the Assembly Hall where the dance was being held.

"Strange!" he said to himself. "*Dancing* in a school! When I was young they used to say such things detracted from the studies, and made the student unfit for work the next day."

The stairs were bordered with couples seated close together holding hands, giggling, eating candy, smoking a furtive cigarette. He thought he saw a girl's delicate fingers toying with one,—but of course he was mistaken. Not a High School girl, openly like this. Not in Briardale, anyway. They might do it out in the world, but not in Briardale!

He scrutinized the faces as he came slowly up the stairs, which somehow seemed to be a mile long and very steep.

Of course Betty would not be sitting out on the stairs. Her mother would have brought her up better than that. And yet, young people were thoughtless. He might find her there. He remembered when he and her mother used to slip out and sit on stairs, and talk. There was nothing terrible in that—unless—unless she was talking to that young hound of a Weston! He couldn't bear it if he found her with that boy! She must be made to understand that she must never speak to him again. He was like pitch. It was a desecration to even think of him!

28

The sound of jazz from the High School orchestra led him on. He reached the door of the Assembly Hall, with difficulty, through the giggling, rough-housing crowd of boys and girls, and looked about anxiously for Betty. Several couples were dancing in the centre of the great floor, dancing in a way that brought disgust to the father's heart. Was that the kind of thing his Betty had been going out for! Did Eleanor know how they danced to-day? He drew a deep breath and took a resolve. If he ever got Betty out of this—!

But he got no further for he heard a furtive whisper just behind him:

"Oh, there's Betty Thornton's old man! Won't she be furious! I'll bet he's come spying on her! Great Cats! If my dad would try to put anything like that over on me wouldn't I kick!"

He turned and looked in the speaker's face, a pretty, painted, bold face, coarse in its bravery of cheap taffeta, flimsy tulle and lengthy earrings, a girl who lived two doors above his home, and whom he had known by sight for several years.

She met his gaze defiantly, coldly.

"Can you tell me where to find Betty, Clara?" he asked, hating himself for having to ask her, yet not knowing where else to turn.

"Betts? Oh. Why she must be round here somewhere," answered the girl carelessly. "Did you see Thorny anywhere, Jim?" she called to a young man who was ambling past with a tray of ice cream dishes.

"I sure did," grinned the boy. "She and Dud just passed out. Dud said it was too slow here and they were going up to Todd's Tavern where they could get something real."

Something familiar in the set of shoulders held Thornton's stern glance as the youth passed with a leer nimbly on among the dancers. It was the other boy from the seat in front on the evening train!

He watched him for an instant as some strong lion in a temporary cage might have watched his prey, and then turned to go down the stairs. It became apparent to him that a group of young people were watching him and snickering openly. He held his head haughtily and compelled himself to walk steadily down the stairs, although they seemed to have become insecure and to rise and fall with each step. He was conscious of holding the words of the lad in abeyance, as if they were something like a missile flung to hurt him, which he had caught just in time, but which had come nigh to wounding him fatally. It was as if he had yet to sense the import of their meaning, though the words had been going over and over like a chime of horrid bells in his brain keeping time with his every move.

When he reached the outside steps he stood still looking up to the quiet stars overhead trying to steady his mind and understand. Repeating the lad's answer over now alone with the stars he took home the terrible truth. Betty was out alone with that filthy youth, Dudley Weston! Todd's Tavern! They could go to no worse place in the whole region round about. It bore a reputation that stood for all the modern sins!

He had just sense enough left to hope that Jim Harkness might have been trying to pull over some kind of a sickly joke. From the tone of his conversation earlier in the evening, and from the leer on his face when he was asked where Betty was, he could easily judge that a joke of just that kind would appeal to Jim Harkness. In fact, wasn't Jim the kid that used to carry Betty's books to school a couple of years ago? Perhaps there was a tinge of jealousy in the affair.

With momentary relief from his fears he drew a deep breath and pressed his white lips firmly.

Nevertheless there was no time to be lost. If Betty had gone to a place like that she must be rescued before she could step foot inside it. Fortunately he had a car that bore the reputation of being able to outdistance anything on the road, though he seldom had occasion to put it to the test. But now as he climbed into it, he threw in his clutch with a determination that made the engine jump.

Out at the school gate he came to a sudden halt and

accosted a row of grammar school boys sitting on the curb smoking in the dark.

"Did you see a car drive out here a few minutes ago?"

"Yep! A Knowland Six! One eye on the blink. Tail light no good either!" they responded definitely.

"Which way did it go?" Thornton asked as if life and death hung on the answer.

"Out de pike!" was the prompt answer.

Grimly Thornton gave rein to his steed.

Chapter IV

The car shot forward like a race horse suddenly put to track. It curveted around the next corner and dashed into the pike at fifty-five, barely escaping a darkened bus on the through line from Washington, threaded a precarious way between two Fords dizzily driven, and an old fashioned coupe piloted and passengered by elderly frightened women. He careened down the long hill by the Plush Mill, across the trolley tracks as if they were hurdles, and rocked up the hill beyond the bridge crazily. If he had seen another man drive as he was driving he would have said he was out of his mind. And perhaps he was, he thought, and strained his eyes to see ahead, watching for the fluctuating wink of a red tail light.

Occasionally as he fled along through the darkness, leaving the town behind and penetrating further and further into the country district, he wondered vaguely what had happened to the satisfaction he had felt as he entered the evening train on his homeward way that night? Surely, all this was a bad dream! Surely he would waken soon and discover he was still on his train, dozing,

31

and hear Briardale called out, and hurry home to tell Eleanor about the car he was going to buy for Betty.

But no. The memory of the scene at the dinner table queered that. It passed before his mind like a panorama. A series of catastrophes, each one in itself enough to lay a burden on a father's heart. Even the twins seemed to have suddenly sprung into activity with their rationalistic talk. He must look into that school at once. Some fool teacher was likely amusing herself teaching such truck to the babies. Some half baked little country girl who had gathered a few wild ideas in college which she thought were higher education. He would find out who it was and have her fired at once. What was the school board thinking about? But of course they did not know. He would see that they were informed before another day dawned. He probably ought to have accepted that nomination as a member of the board last spring instead of pleading that he had no time. Well, this was his punishment. But if he *had* accepted the position he would have done his work better than the others seemed to have done. Nobody who taught things like that would have got by him.

These ideas served to take his thoughts for a few minutes from the awful fear that was growing in his mind about Betty, as he plunged on in the darkness, yet each time he sighted a blinking red light ahead his heart would fail him again and a smothering sensation between horror and fierce anger would rise and almost choke him. The blood seemed to be all in his head and beating through his eyes, as if he were on his own feet running a race. His heart could not keep up and felt as if it would burst. He wondered if perhaps he might be getting a stroke of apoplexy. But he must not, he must not, not till Betty was safe.

He overtook three different cars ahead, only to find them filled with staid elderly couples, or family parties sleepily jogging home.

He had almost persuaded himself that Betty was safely at home by this time instead of driving off across the country with a wild youth. That was it of course.

Dudley Weston had been taking Betty home. Betty would never consent to go to a place like Todd's Tavern. Betty was too well bred for a thing like that. Of course she would not know what kind of a place she was being taken to, but she would understand that it was too late at night to go off on a drive anywhere with a young man. It wasn't respectable. Betty would have made him take her home of course. Eleanor had said she would be there pretty soon. Eleanor had seemed very sure. He was a fool of course to have taken this long jaunt on a chance word of a jealous boy who wished to put something over on him.

He had reached this point when he came in sight of Todd's, set far back from the road in the midst of a lonely grove on the top of a little hill, in a wild and lonely countryside. There were no lights anywhere in sight in any direction on hill or valley, save the fringe of red and yellow glare that edged Todd's Tavern. They blared through the night with a garish lure that sent the shudders down Thornton's back. That *his* child should be taken to a place like that even against her will was unthinkable! He would *somehow* have that Weston fellow arrested!

His car plunged on through the night, over ruts and humps without regard to its going, till he came at last to the high arched gate with its single bright globe streaking across the dark of the road in a great gash of light, above the dark winding drive that led by devious ways up to the Inn.

Then caution suddenly seized him. He backed down into the shadow, parked his car as silently as possible and proceeded on foot. As he trod the dry grass at the edge of the gravel making his footsteps as inaudible as possible, he began to think that it was going to be awkward to appear in that house and search for his daughter, *HIS DAUGHTER!* Supposing she was not there? He must let no one suspect that he even thought she was. He would have to be searching for someone else if he had to account at all for his appearance. He shrank inexpressibly from the ordeal. And yet it must be gone through with. If only he were sure whether she were really there he could enter with more dignity. Perhaps there was a window unshuttered where he might look in and make sure, and possibly save being seen at all. It might be those High School children were entirely mistaken. Dudley Weston had perhaps taken some other girl to this abominable place, and his Betty might be even now at home asleep in her own bed. He must proceed slowly. It would not do to let even people who came to a place like this know that he feared Betty was here.

He dragged his heavy feet up the winding way, till he came out on the level and was suddenly aware of a long line of cars parked in the dark edges of the drive. Somehow the sight of them brought a premonition. Was that—Could it be the Weston car? The last one in the line, parked boldly quite near the drive way?

Carefully, silently, he stole nearer, peering through the darkness. Yes, that was a Knowland, the same lines at least, and the tail light was out. So were the headlights. But he was sure about the car. He was used to seeing it go by his house every day. Perhaps he had better step up close to be positive. That would give him something to go on. Perhaps it would be well just to boldly go up to the door of the tavern and ask for Dudley Weston.

Thornton had taken the precaution to bring his flash light from the car before he left it, and now as he stole toward this dark car his hand gripped it ready for use when he should get close enough to see. One flash would make it plain. Besides, if he remembered rightly the Weston initials were on the door.

With the flash light drawn and his finger on the spring he crept close, and raised the little lamp, but even as he did so he became aware of strong cigarette smoke and two red sparks glowed at him like two eyes from the tonneau of the car.

It was too late to retreat, for the fingers had obeyed the order his brain had given, and his big search light blared out full in the faces of the two occupants, discovering to Thornton's horrified gaze his daughter Betty lolling in the embrace of Dudley Weston and puffing away at a cigarette.

The flash went dark and there was an angry stir in

the back seat of the car. Two glowing sparks of lights sped through the darkness like fireflies and were extinguished in the grass on the far side of the car. Then two angry young people issued forth and confronted him, Dudley Weston and his daughter Betty!

There was nothing about his daughter to show either that she had been lured into the present situation against her will, or that she was a penitent sinner brought to overwhelming judgment. Wrapped in a fur trimmed velvet evening cloak which Thornton recognized as his wife's, she stood out against the blaring background of Todd's illumination almost regally, her slim body drawn to its tallest, her little sleek head held haughtily, like an angry princess. She surveyed him, and her voice was cold like showers of icicles as her words buried their sharp points in her father's heart:

"Well, Chester, what do you seem to think you're up to now? It strikes me somebody had better take you in charge. I'm about convinced that you've taken leave of your senses! What's the little old idea anyway?"

Then, suddenly confronted by her unbroken morale, Chester Thornton could think of nothing to say in reply. He even flashed his torch upon her again, with an aimless idea that he had made a mistake somehow and this was not his Betty, his little girl, talking that way to him, not ashamed at all of what she had been doing! She bore the scrutiny of the light and his searching, pitiful, gaze without flinching. Her eyes were cold and hard and her lips were scornful.

He tried to speak, and no sound came from his parched throat.

Betty stepped coolly out of the spot light and laid her hand on her companion's arm:

"Come on, Dud, let's go back and have another dance," she said nonchalantly. "If Dad thinks he can pull anything like this he's got another guess coming. Let's go!"

A laugh of triumphant defiance broke hoarsely from the young man as he turned to obey. But suddenly Chester Thornton's senses were set free, and fury arose within him. Was this young reptile to defy him and lead his daughter away while he stood by? He had not forgotten the tricks he learned in college, and a quick well directed blow under the chin sent young Weston sprawling on the hard bare ground to the utter astonishment of Betty who whirled furiously on her father, a look in her eyes that was not good to see. It was a look that he was to remember long years after, a look like a blow that left a scar.

But Thornton was alert now, and keyed up to the fighting point. He picked young Betty up in his arms as if she had been a feather and strode off down the hill.

Betty struggled furiously at first and then was still for an instant in sheer astonishment. When she began to struggle again silently he held her like a vise.

"Look here, Chester, you needn't think you can treat me like this. I won't stand for it!" she defied him when she saw she could not get away.

But he strode on through the night without a word.

"I'll scream!" she said threatening, "and then what will they think of *you*. There are plenty of people in that house and they will come out and laugh at you. A silly old parent that thinks he has just come out of the ark!"

Still Thornton strode on down the hill. It was taking all his breath, between his anger, and helplessness, and the weight of his daughter which he had by no means been training for during the years.

They were almost to the car, and Chester Thornton was wondering whether he could hold out, when Betty dealt her final blow.

In a cold, hard, matter-of-fact tone she said:

"Well, I *hate* you, and I'm *off* you for *life!*"

The impact quivered through his trembling flesh like an actual blow. He realized that here was another thing with which he would have to live out the years, and never forget!

Betty! His little Betty! His first baby girl!

There was an instant's struggle again as they reached the car. Betty was determined not to be carried home ignominiously. But he held her fast.

"Will you get in quietly, or shall I have to tie you?" he asked in a strange panting voice that somehow startled her in spite of her hardness.

"Oh, have it your own way," she said relaxing suddenly into indifference, "I'm getting terribly sleepy, anyway, and might as well go home." She summoned a casual yawn.

How had the universe got turned around! *This* was his Betty! The child for whom he had but a few short hours before been planning an expensive Christmas surprise and exulting in her probable delight in it. How had all this awful change come about?

He tried as he drove along through the night to think of a wise mode of approach, for he must have it out with her before he reached home. He would have to tell her all those awful words that that foul mouthed boy had said. There was no way to spare her from it. She ought to know the truth. Her humiliation would have to be complete before she could be brought to her senses.

Betty was leaning back, feigning sleep.

Very gently, very tenderly, with the deep hurt love in his voice and words chosen from the depths of his suffering heart he began:

"Betty, it is because I love you—" he started in a voice she used to love.

"Rot!" said Betty sleepily. "Save your breath, Chester. That kind of mush is out of date."

Appalled, he summoned new words, sharp with truth and began to tell her what he had heard in the train.

She listened through to the finish and then her scornful laugh rang out like a flashing knife:

"Oh, is that all you've got on your chest?" she scorned. "I thought you were off your nut. But you've only got a Victorian complex after all. Poor dad, you'll recover, but you've lost out as far as I'm concerned. I thought you had an open mind!"

"Betty! What do you mean? Don't you—Aren't you—?"

"No, I don't think Dud is a beast! No, I'm not shocked nor humiliated, nor any of the other things you want me to be. This is an enlightened age, and things have changed since you were young. I have my doubts whether they were so very sanctimonious as you try to make out even then, but of course you want me to think they were. But as for Dud, he's all right. He's no worse than all of the rest of us. We're just frank and honest. All the boys talk like that. That's nothing. We're just living our lives in the new free way; that's all. You lived your life and it's our turn now to live ours as we please, and there's no use in thinking we're going to be tied now by any antiquated whims that people tried to kid themselves into a century ago, for we won't do it."

"My child!" he said sadly, "Right and Wrong do not change. God is always the same. There are certain laws—"

"Oh! Applesauce!" broke in Betty. "You don't really believe that. That's all Bologny!"

Appalled at last he gave it up, and silently drove her to her home. There was nothing left to tell her, nothing to say, because she did not care for any of the standards he set up. She had torn them down with a laugh, and flung them to the breeze. She had declared her inalienable right to do as she pleased, and flouted the idea that there *was* such a thing as right and wrong.

He groped for the right word and wondered what it had been in his youth that had held him back from many things. Sin—that was it, a sense of sin. Why, *she seemed to have no sense of sin* at all!

He spoke the word as if it were a talisman, a sword that he had mislaid and was glad to find again.

"Betty, it is *sin*—" he said.

She laughed.

"What is sin?" she said pertly imitating his voice as he pronounced the word.

An old answer came from out his past, learned back in the years of long dear drowsy Sabbaths, with a smell of spiced cookies and gingerbread in the air, and his mother's sweet face as she sat in the rocking chair by her window on the old farm and read her Bible while he learned his catechism:

"Sin is any want of conformity unto or trangression of the law of God," he said.

Betty stared and laughed again.

"Where did you get that, Chet? Sounds like some highbrow lawyer. Whatever it is it's moth eaten. What right would God have to make laws for us? If He put us here on the earth and made us live whether we wanted to or not, it's up to us to have as good a time as we can, isn't it? If there *is* a God—" she added mockingly.

He was silent with the shock of it, the humiliation.

He had never taken time to live by them himself, but he had all the doctrines thoroughly defined, laid carefully away in a neat napkin in his mind ready for any time of need. He was an elder in the church! A warm advocate of all things orthodox and Biblical! And his child was talking like this! This was rank Atheism!

He was silent as he drove up to the door, on his face such a look of haggard despair that Betty turned, in a kind of hard pity, as she got out of the car:

"Listen, Chester," she said with a bit of fine condescension in her voice, "you needn't worry about me, really! Dud isn't as bad as he seems to you, and anyhow, *I* know how to take care of myself. *All* girls do nowadays!"

With that she was off into the house and the door closed lightly behind her.

He sat in the car for a minute more staring at the house, staring through the dark at the door where she had passed, hearing over again the awful things she had said to him,—actually *said* to her father!

He moaned, and leaned his weary head down against the wheel for a moment. Then laboriously he started his car again and drove slowly into the garage.

His wife was waiting for him when he came in. She had hot coffee and a nice little tray with delicate chicken sandwiches, and a cup custard in a china cup. She had stirred the fire when she heard him come, and his chair was waiting drawn up before it with the tray on a little table at the side, and only a dim shaded light at the far end of the room. She knew how to do all those exquisite little comforting things so perfectly. Just her presence was a rest.

But tonight, he waved her aside. How could he tell her? Betty's mother, pure as the snow! How could he tell her that Betty's lovely lips had uttered words of perdition, and that the very breath on which they were borne to his ear was rank with stale tobacco smoke, and a tang of something stronger! Betty's little rosebud lips! Betty's baby lips that had been so pure and sweet and wonderful!

He sank into the chair by the fire with a groan and covered his face with his hands. He shook his head when she tried to press the coffee upon him, and groaned again. How could he tell Eleanor? And yet he must. This was something they must bear together, work out together. Could he make Eleanor understand the horror of it all? And if she did understand, would it perhaps *kill* her?

Into the midst of the turmoil of his mind and the distress of his wife, there came the sound of a key turning cautiously in the lock, a key that was unsteadily fitted into place, and turned reluctantly. At last the door opened, and Chris lurched into the hall. In his clumsy attempt to be quiet about it he knocked over a vase of flowers that stood on the hall console, and then tried to mop it up with his hat, muttering that it was all right. No place for weeds anyway!

Something thick and unnatural in his voice caused both father and mother to look at him with startled eyes, and his father drew himself sharply out of the comfortable chair and went toward him:

"Chris!" he said and his voice was like an electric current. "What is the matter with you? Where have you been?"

"Th'as none o' your business!" replied the boy trying to straighten up and look steadily at his father, his dripping hat back again on his head, "You refused to gimme the dough I needed, an' I went where I knew I could get it! Th'as all! Whas that t'you? Got m'debts all paid an' three dollars lef' over. Pretty good, what? You ain't got a single kick comin'—"

40

Chris's voice trailed off suddenly in a kind of choking sound as a strong hand seized his collar.

"That's enough!" said Chester Thornton authoritatively. "Don't say another word in your mother's hearing!"

He threw the boy's hat off, pulled off his overcoat, and taking him firmly by the arm propelled him up the stairs to the bathroom, his face sternly white, the boy dragging back and protesting.

"Wha's yer hurry, old soak?" Chris asked his father blearily, "Got all night, ain't we? I know I'm half stewed, but wha's that? It's happened once or twice before—!"

The bathroom door slammed over the last words, and Eleanor Thornton listening in horror at the foot of the stairs heard the water turned on furiously in the bathtub.

As if he were assisting at some horrid rite Chester Thornton helped his son to remove his clothing, and then against his most earnest protests plunged him into a tub of cold water.

Minutes later, sobered, ashamed, well rubbed down and arrayed in dry warm pajamas, Chris crept to his bed, and Chester Thornton came slowly, heavily down the stairs like an old old man.

"Eleanor!" he said gropingly, as she came toward him from the darkened parlor and stood beneath the hall light, "Eleanor, I—"

It was then that everything went black before his eyes and clutching for the stair railing and missing it he fell and struck his head against the newel post. Then all the world fled away from his consciousness.

Chapter V

Her mother's scream brought Betty to the head of the stairs calm, superior, in a hastily assumed kimono. But when she saw her father lying at the foot of the stairs with blood on his forehead and her mother kneeling beside him wiping his face with her handkerchief, and endeavoring ineffectually to lift him to a sitting posture, her assurance fled, and a white scared look took its place. For angry as she was with him she adored her father.

She flew down the stairs taking command as she came.

"Now Mums, you keep cool," she said, "I'll call the doctor. How did it happen?"

"He fell," said her mother reproachfully, "I think he was dizzy—He—Your brother—*You*—! He's been—"

But Betty was already giving the doctor's number at the telephone, and waiting for no orders proceeded efficiently to the kitchen for water and ice and pieces of old linen.

The doctor arrived almost at once. Betty had caught him just as he came in from a late call before he had retired.

They laid Thornton on the couch in the living room, and Betty stirred the fire and put on fresh wood. She brought glasses and spoons and blankets, and hovered silently in the shadows of the room until the quivering eyelids opened at last and she saw her father's searching glance go hurriedly around the room, heard his deep profound sigh as returning consciousness brought back his problems. Then she stole silently up to her room and lay down in the dark with her door open, listening. She was frightened at the white look of her father's face, but angry too. It didn't seem quite square of Chester to collapse this way just because he had discovered a few trifles about his children that he hadn't known before. He had no right to be so far behind the times that he would

expect them always to be infants! When he got better she
would have to take him in hand, bring him up to date and
open his eyes to a few facts. Times were changed of
course, and Chester hadn't realized it, but she had never
expected him to show weakness, physical weakness, just
because his whims were crossed. Whims! They were worse
than that. They were antiques, wished on him by a former
generation. How could he have been so blind as not to
have seen before this that the world had outgrown them?

Yet she lay and quivered at the thought of her father
ill. Dad had always been so strong, so ready to give her
anything she wanted.

She stole out to the hall and listened when the
doctor talked in a low tone to her mother, straining her
ears and trying to hear what they were saying. She could
not sleep until she knew he was out of danger.

Then she heard her father call to the doctor. His
voice sounded weak, strained, yet insistent.

The doctor went into the living room again and
Mrs. Thornton came slowly upstairs. Betty could see that
she was weeping even before she lifted her tear stained
face.

"He's all right now, I hope, dear!" said the mother.
"The doctor wants him to get to sleep. I'm going to put a
hot water bag in the bed, and get his things out. The
doctor doesn't think the bruise was serious."

There was a quiver in the end of her voice that gave
Betty a strange uneasiness.

"It's not like Chester to pass out!" said Betty with a
half return of her habitual flippancy.

The mother shrank visibly from the words.

"I wouldn't, Betty dear," she said in a half apologetic
tone. "Your father doesn't like you to call him that. It
doesn't sound respectful—"

"Rats!" said Betty inelegantly, "are *you* trying to be
an old stiff too?"

"Betty! Really! Your father is very sensitive just
now, and the doctor says we must be very careful. He says
he is in a very dangerous state. He says this has been
coming on for a long time—"

Betty gave her a startled look.

"For what reason?" she said and pinioned her mother with her glance.

"I'm afraid it's business," she said with a catch in her breath. "He's been lying awake at nights, oh, for weeks, and perhaps longer. I don't know. He didn't tell me till recently. And then this tonight—!"

"Business? What's the matter with business?" asked Betty sharply.

"I'm afraid things are in a very bad way."

"Whaddaya mean, bad way?"

"Well, I'm not sure, but I'm afraid your father has failed. I'm afraid it's just as bad as it can be. I know he was expecting something to happen yesterday which would turn the tide either way. And just now when the doctor asked him if he couldn't get away from business and take a real rest he said, 'Oh, the business doesn't matter any more!' just like that as if everything was all over. And I think that he is kind of desperate about it. I feel that we shall have to do everything we can to make him happy, and make him understand that it doesn't matter whether we have any money or not if he only gets well. The doctor said that this was a warning— He didn't say just what, but from the questions he asked I'm sure he was afraid of apoplexy, or paralysis, or some of those terrible diseases. Betty, we must be *awfully* careful not to worry your father— But there! I believe the doctor is persuading him to come up. Get that other pair of pink striped blankets and lay them on the radiator. We might need them. He said he was so cold—"

Betty eyed her mother keenly. Evidently Dad had not told her yet. That was decent of him. No need in stirring mother up.

Betty flew around efficiently, helping her mother, thinking her keen stubborn young thoughts, trying to look a new situation in the face, and rebelling furiously at having her young life upheaved by any financial catastrophe. It wasn't like her dad to go fluey and leave them all in the mud. He must have done something awfully foolish to get things all in a muddle. She couldn't keep a kind of resentment out of her thoughts as she worked.

Yet when she caught sight of her father's white face again, as the doctor helped him up the stairs, while she stood in the darkened back hall and watched, her heart failed her. Poor Dad! Poor Chester! He had always been such a good scout! Perhaps he would pull out of it! He had got to. He would have to *borrow* money or something till times got all right again. Of course, that was it. He would borrow money. Everybody did nowadays anyway. It was old-fashioned to worry because you couldn't pay your bills right on the dot. Oh, Chester would pull out of course. She couldn't think of them as settling down to be *poor*. Of course not. It wasn't to be borne!

And so, comforting herself, she crept back to her bed, and having heard the doctor go down stairs and out the front door, she composed herself to sleep.

Mrs. Thornton tiptoed around her room putting things in order for rest, laying her slippers and warm kimono on a chair by the bed for possible sudden need in the night, switching on a night light in the hall just outside her bedroom door, switching off the brighter light. She slipped softly into bed, making the least movement possible that she might not disturb her husband.

She curled down gratefully under the blankets, let her tired head sink into the pillow and closed her eyes, for the evening had been a long hard one and the culmination had been appalling. She had done a good deal of weeping which was always exhausting, and her senses were almost benumbed with the various shocks they had received. But the things that had happened during the last hour had left the earlier events somewhat in the background. The unpleasant scene at the dinner table, and the incidents of Jane and Betty seemed comparatively unimportant in the light of later developments.

What, for example, had been the meaning of Chris's strange actions and his father's unexampled treatment? Could it be possible that Chris was growing wild? She could not get away from the memory of the smell of liquor about him when he came into the house. She shuddered

45

involuntarily as she thought of his unsteady step, and incoherent speech! Chris! Her first little son, Chris, scarcely grown out of childhood, just coming into strength and beauty. Chris of whom she had always been so proud! Her first man child! Chris gone wrong so early! And gambling! Could it be true? Surely it was someone else's fault, not Chris'. Why Chris had been brought up to respect himself and his family! And that family had always stood for temperance and right living! His father an elder in the Presbyterian church, too! Surely Chris would not have knowingly disgraced his family!

She tried to think who Chris could have been going with that she might have someone else beside her son to shoulder the blame. That Harold Griswold, very likely. He had an expensive racing car, and all the pocket money he wanted, and Chris had been possessed to be in that car every waking minute out of school. They tore by the house forty times a day like a mad torpedo bound for destruction, and Chris' mother had formed the habit of catching her breath and closing her eyes in a quick prayer whenever she heard the screech of the Junior Griswold car, for she was always certain that her own son was clinging somewhere about its rigging, if he was not actually driving it. She fully expected to see him flung white and lifeless across the pavement some time from mere momentum, as the reckless bunch of wild youths hurled by. Several times she had been on the point of appealing to Chris's father about it, only she knew that her husband was already overburdened with anxiety, and she kept hoping that Chris would find some new attraction and it would not be necessary to worry his father with it. She did so hate to have Chester blame Chris for anything. He seemed at times so hard on the boy. As if he did not remember being a boy himself.

But now, surely, this Griswold boy was the one who had led Chris astray.

Having settled this matter, and made up her mind to suggest this to Chester the first thing in the morning, so that he would not blame Chris so severely, she turned to other troubles.

46

Chester. The doctor had said he was nervously run down and needed a change. The nerves around her heart gave sick sore thrills of anxiety as she recalled the doctor's warning. Assuredly it must be managed and at once. If only Chester would be reasonable and see the thing as it was.

It would be fine if he could take an ocean voyage. The Batemans were going on the Mediterranean trip. It would be great if Chester could go with them! Of course he would demur at going without her, yet he would not want to leave the children alone, especially after what had happened tonight. And of course it would be cheaper for Chester to go alone. He might even balk at any expense on his own account, but expense was not to be considered where his health was at stake.

Poor Chester, he must have had an awful day at the office, worn to a thread! And he had been so hopeful in the morning! Probably that was the explanation of his being so excited over Betty and her affairs, and even the children at the table, and poor little Jane. Jane was only a child. She had sobbed herself to sleep. She hadn't an idea she was doing anything out of the way to show the boys her little school dance when they asked her, just a few of the college boys who had been friendly. But of course she must be made to understand that it wasn't nice to have done what she did. She must give Jane more attention, let her invite her little friends home, and have parties, so that she wouldn't be continually asking to go with the Carter child. Probably it was all the fault of the Carter girl. She was ill bred. She ought not to have allowed Jane to become so intimate till she had had time to get to know her mother. But she had been so busy! Those Club Meetings, and the Child Training class had been one straw too much. Yet it had seemed important to know the latest discoveries in Child Psychology.

Suddenly from out the still darkness came her husband's voice:

"Eleanor, are you awake?"

How did he know? She had not stirred. She was alert at once, a pang of fear at her heart.

47

"Yes, what is it? Do you feel worse?"

His voice sounded as if it came from far away, years ago; as if a great many things had happened since they last talked. He ignored her question as if it had not been.

"Eleanor, would it crush you entirely to give up our life here, in this house, in this town?"

He asked it anxiously, apprehensively, as if he knew he were asking a great thing, and yearned over her to have to answer such a question.

Fear gripped her heart, and for an instant all speech left her. It had come then! Chester had failed. In spite of his bright hopes all was lost. They were going to be *poor!* Somehow she had never considered that possible. Poor Chester! How terribly he must feel!

Then her brave heart rose to the occasion and she summoned a cheer that she was far from feeling.

"Why, of course not, Chester. I wouldn't think of letting a thing like that crush me. If you are only well we can make a lark out of anything else. If that's what you are worrying about, forget it, and go to sleep. It's really most important that you get your sleep. The doctor told me so. Now just put everything aside and try to relax. We'll talk everything over tomorrow and fix up some nice plan."

"You don't understand, Eleanor," he said almost sternly. "This isn't something that can be put off. We've got to act, at once. It is imperative! Eleanor, we've got to begin our life all over again! I haven't told you everything—"

"Don't try to, dear," she said eagerly. "Just let it wait. I'm ready to do whatever you think best of course, but you really must get some rest."

"I can't rest until this is settled," he said decidedly, "I've got to act immediately, the first thing in the morning. There isn't an hour to lose. I've been thinking it over in every detail and there's only one thing to do. But I've got to have your hearty coöperation or it will be a failure."

"Haven't I always coöperated, Chester?" she asked half tearfully, feeling a premonition of even more than she had feared.

She leaned toward him and her hand stole within

his. He gripped it feverishly, eagerly, as if it were something strong and comforting to hold to.

"You certainly have, dear, always. You're a wonderful woman. That is why I shrink from putting this all upon you, especially just now when I had so hoped that I was going to be able to make life beautiful and easy for you from now on. But I see no other solution for our problems."

Bravely she rose to the occasion as she always had for lesser troubles:

"Then, Chester, let's accept it and get a good time out of it somehow, as we always have."

"Bless you my dear!" said Chester folding her hand closer and giving it a firmer clasp.

"Well, then, wonderful little woman, how soon can you be ready to start?"

She caught her breath with the thought of all she was going to give up. Their lovely home into which they had put so many comforts and sweet memories. Their host of friends! The good schools—all the things that were so superior and had brought them to Briardale in preference to any other suburb. It came over her like a great shock. She had never thought it could come to this. She had expected possible economies, but not to have to go away.

Then she rallied her strength and forced her voice to be steady.

"Why, let me see, the dressmaker is coming next week—"

"You'll have to cut that out. It won't be necessary anyway, now."

"Oh," said Eleanor, with another shock, "perhaps not." Poor Chester! "Why, I can't tell without thinking. There'll be a lot of packing and sorting to do you know."

"Not much!" said Chester crisply. "We'll only need to take the barest necessities, of course good warm things, and bedding."

A new fear gripped her. Then the failure must have been complete.

She was still for a minute trying to take it all in and

then her voice trembled back to steadiness as she asked:

"But what will we do with the house—and—and the things we are leaving behind? Won't we have to sort—and—and—pack—"

"No," said Chester quickly, "I'd thought of that. Hannah will be here, and she knows where everything is, and we can send for anything we may have forgotten. There are professional packers you know, if there is anything Hannah and John can't manage. There won't be anything like that to hinder."

Appalled she considered again. At last she asked falteringly:

"Why, how soon did you think we could get off, Chester?"

"About noon tomorrow," he answered crisply as if it were the greatest relief in the world to have the announcement made.

Chapter VI

"Tomorrow!" she gasped, "Why, Chester, it is tomorrow already, and you haven't been to sleep yet! You know the doctor wouldn't possibly give his consent to your travelling tomorrow!"

She said the last in a soothing tone as one would speak to a sick child who demanded cake and ice cream.

"The doctor has nothing whatever to do with this," he said impatiently, "it is something you and I have to settle. As a matter of fact, if it comforts you any, I mentioned it to the doctor that I might be going away on a long trip tomorrow, and he seemed to think it would be the best thing I could do."

She lay still, growing cold at the thought of the

inevitable, unable for the moment to take in all that had befallen her in one short night.

She was still so long that he thought she had gone to sleep.

"Eleanor," he asked cautiously, "you're not asleep? Why, Eleanor, you're not crying are you?"

"Nn-o, Chester," she managed with a little catch of her breath, "I'm just—just—thinking! It's been rather sudden you know."

"You poor darling! yes, I know. How I wish I might have saved you all this. It seems as if I couldn't stand it for you—I—!"

But Eleanor roused to protest once more:

"Don't think of it, Chester. It's not a bit harder for me than for you. And so long as we bear things together they won't get the better of us."

"You were always brave, Eleanor. But I'm afraid this is going to be particularly hard for you. Going away from comfort and convenience into comparative primitive living. I'm not sure you will be able physically to stand it. And yet I can think of no other way at present."

Primitive! She turned a startled look at him in the dark.

"Where—had you thought of—going, Chester? Had you any plan?"

"There is only one place. The old farm in Vermont. It's ours you know, and I've always meant to remodel it some day,—make it liveable for a summer home. There are associations of my boyhood that I've always clung to. But now it seems like a haven, and I guess we'll have to put up with it as it is for a while, till we can get on our feet again and know what to do."

Eleanor's heart sank. Vermont! And he talked as if it was to be permanent! It must be that he was already out of the firm, or he would not think he could run away at a moment's notice this way. He must be really down and out. She had never seen him give up like this. How terrible!

She roused to her maternal tone.

"Nonsense!" she said briskly. "It will be a lark! I've

always wanted to go there, and we never seemed to get around to it. Don't worry another second. Go right to sleep now. If it isn't comfortable we'll make it so, somehow. And it will be good for us to have to go without some of the luxuries we've been surrounded with so long that we don't really have sense enough to be grateful for them. What do you think I am? A butter-fly? A peacock?"

"But there's no running water, Eleanor—" he explained anxiously.

"Well, there's likely some kind of water, isn't there? And we can do the running ourselves." She actually summoned a gay little laugh. "The twins will just enjoy carrying water."

"And no electric light or gas—" went on the sad honest voice.

Eleanor was appalled, but she only hesitated a minute.

"We'll make a bonfire then," she flashed at him. "Now, will you go to sleep?"

"And you are willing to start tomorrow?" he asked anxiously.

"If you feel well enough in the morning," she promised. "Come go to sleep quick or I can't get up in time to get ready!" and she deliberately turned over on her pillow and pretended to settle down for sleep.

"It will be very cold up there, Eleanor. You'll need all the warm clothes you can get, and blankets."

"All right!" said Eleanor briskly to hide the plunk of a great tear that was rolling down her cheek.

"You'll have to wear flannel, *real* flannel you know. You can't get along with flimsy silk stuff such as you wear down here."

Eleanor was still a minute over a new thought.

"Hasn't that house been shut up for several years? Won't it be very damp? Do you think it will be safe to go in? We might all get sick!"

"There's been a caretaker living in the back part until a month ago. His son-in-law got hurt and they went down to Albany to live with the daughter and help her

52

out. It can't be so very damp. And there are stoves. It won't take long to rustle a fire."

There was almost eagerness in his voice, a yearning toward the scenes of his boyhood.

Eleanor's heart sank again. Rustle a fire! What mysterious thing was that! She had never made a fire in her life, nor come any nearer to it than to set a match to the fire in the fireplace, or stir it up and put on a stick. What was this new life going to mean? Surely, surely, it couldn't last. But she must be brave. Something would turn up to lighten the burden! When Chester got better he would be back in business again, and would soon right their fortunes. At least the change would not be bad for him now. She could see he was almost attracted by it. But the children! How would they take it? Such a shame to take them from their schools where they were doing so well and were so attached. Suddenly she voiced her trouble.

"You don't think, Chester, that maybe there would be some way to—well to hold it off a little till the school year was up? Or maybe leave the children here with friends to finish? It's going to be so embarrassing for them not to get their credits for the year's work when they have been doing so well. Helen Winslow would take Betty I'm sure, and maybe Jane. Of course it wouldn't matter so much about the kiddies. They are young yet. But Chris and Betty ought to finish the grade and not miss a whole year or even six months."

"Eleanor!"

Chester Thornton sat up abruptly regardless of the bandage on his head.

"Eleanor! You don't understand! I wish you didn't have to either, but you must. No, don't try to stop me. I'll have to explain now. Do you know where I found Betty to-night? Up at Todd's Tavern at the side of the road, in a dark car, lying in the arms of the foulest mouthed boy it has ever been my fate to hear speak, and she was smoking a cigarette!"

"Oh, Chester!" cried Eleanor as if he had stabbed

her, the tears flowing unguarded down her cheeks now. "Oh, Chester! Surely, surely you must be mistaken. Isn't that *awful!* Oh, but at least—I cannot think it was Betty's fault—! Someone else has—"

"I'm not so sure!" said Betty's father grimly. "Do you know what she said when I remonstrated with her? She called me an antique, and said I had a Victorian Complex! And when I tried to tell her what that little viper had said about her in the train she only laughed and said he was no worse than any other boy of their set, that *every* body talked 'frankly' nowadays. People didn't have foolish reserves the way they used to, and it was a great deal better. She even hinted that she thought that you and I had probably indulged in the same indecencies when we were young. And she added quite significantly, that I needn't worry, that she *knew how to take care of herself!*"

Eleanor gasped and sobbed broken heartedly for a minute then pleaded sadly:

"But Chester, really, Betty wouldn't have *meant* all those things. She really *wouldn't.* You know that kind of talk is a kind of fad nowadays. The girls affect that sort of thing, but they don't *really mean* it all."

"Eleanor!" said Chester Thornton, and his voice was sternness itself. "Is it possible that *you* can excuse a thing like that?"

"Oh, no, no, of course not," said Eleanor quickly, stifling the great sob that seemed to engulf her. "No, I wouldn't *uphold* it, of course not! Only really I don't think *Betty* had an idea of meaning all that. She must just have been copying some of the other girls—"

"Well, we'll put her where she won't have any of that kind to copy then," said her father firmly. "Eleanor, where have we been? What have we been doing? Sleeping? That this thing could have burst upon us full fledged? Do you know our eldest son came in drunk to-night? Positively drunk? Do you know he had been in one of the lowest places in this city all the evening gambling? He told me so. He was drunk enough not to realize what he was revealing!"

"Oh, daddy! daddy!" said Chris' mother. "*Surely*

someone else was to blame for that. Someone gave it to him without his realizing what he was drinking. I'm sure he wouldn't drink—not *really drink*—our *Chris!* Or if he did I'm sure he never did it before—"

"I'm afraid not," said the father sadly, "I found a flask in his pocket with his initials on from some fool of a girl, and it was not a new flask either. It had a last Christmas date on it. It was nearly empty. Chris knew well enough what he was doing, Eleanor!"

Eleanor crumpled down into her pillow and felt as if the world had come to an end. How could all these awful things have come to her in one brief evening!

"And little Jane," went on the father, as if he were but thinking aloud. "Little Jane. If you could have seen her, leering, making eyes at those fellows, flinging her legs around in the most indecent way for those great loafers to watch her. I won't repeat the words that passed between them. It was too disgusting. Where have we been, Eleanor, that our children could have got away from us this way? Oh, we have been asleep!" He groaned aloud.

"Oh, don't, Chester?" begged Eleanor, "I can't bear you to take it like that! I *have* been worried," she confessed. "They've told such terrible things at the Child Training class. Really, you'd hardly believe—"

"After to-night I can believe *any*thing!" said the father grimly.

"But they warned us not to oppose the children—" Eleanor hastened to explain. "They said this was a new generation, and we must deal with them carefully, and not antagonize them. They said it was a phase that would pass, a phase of adolescence!"

"Poppycock!" Chester snorted. "Poppycock! And *you* swallowed that? Eleanor, I'm surprised!"

"Well, no, I didn't exactly swallow it," said Eleanor mopping her hot weary face with a soppy handkerchief, "I thought about it, and I've been very careful. Of course I've always tried to put *positive* thoughts, good suggestions forward, and not negative ones. They say you must not say 'don't' any more, that it merely rouses antagonism—"

"Bosh!" said Chester angrily. "They all need a good

sound spanking! A lot of them! We've been all wrong, Eleanor! We've been too easy! I see it now—And those women in that Club, Eleanor,—they need to be spanked too! They weren't spanked enough when they were young. They are fools! Eleanor. What in thunder did you ever see in a bunch like that! I declare, I shall go crazy, *insane,* if I don't get out of this town before tomorrow night!"

"Of course," said Eleanor, suddenly rousing to remember that her husband was sick and the doctor had warned her that he must be kept very quiet and not get excited. "Chester, if you will just lie down and go to sleep now, I understand it all, and I'll get ready to go. I'll be ready whenever you say—! There dear! Do lie down! It's all right now, I understand. It'll be *all right*—!"

Chester Thornton lay down suddenly feeling very weak and tired, and murmured:

"Eleanor, you're the best little woman a man ever had for a partner!" and in spite of all her troubles Eleanor Thornton somehow felt her heart warm, and knew that *every*thing was not quite lost.

She laid a soft hand on the hot forehead of her husband, and was rewarded in a few minutes by hearing his low steady breathing and knew he had fallen asleep.

But she herself lay down in a daze, and could not even close her eyes.

Over and over again she heard the awful words of arraignment of her children. Over and over she rehearsed certain sentences of Chester's which she took to relate to his business affairs, and her heart sank lower and lower, till there seemed no glimmer of light at all.

But so curious a hold has money and the things of this world on a human heart, that strangely enough the loss of the money loomed almost as large in Eleanor Thornton's scheme of things as did the misdemeanors of her children. Not that she did not hate sin as much as her husband, and shrink from having it come near her own, but that she simply could not believe that things were as bad as Chester had said. Chester was excited and weary and had seen things writ large. Chester would learn later that the children were not quite gone to perdition yet.

They had only been experimenting a little, and would soon come to their senses. In a healthy atmosphere these things would pass off. And of course in a way there was some advantage even in hiding themselves in a desolate Vermont farm house for a time.

But the morals of her children did not deeply trouble her as much as the immediate problem of how they would take their father's failure, and what she was going to do herself about many little embarrassing details that were going to arise in the morning if Chester carried out his program of leaving the city at once.

There for instance was her Civic Committee. It was supposed to meet with her tomorrow, and the Psychology class immediately following. The little cakes that she would serve with tea and bonbons were even now reposing in the tin cake closet, each one perfect in its snowy icing.

There was her bridge club the next day, and her old friend Genevieve Whitely just back from Japan and coming! And there was the Committee for decorating the Church at Christmas. It was to meet that Saturday night, and the plans were all made. She was chairman! She would have to write out the directions fully. No one else would understand, and the greens were all ordered. They would wonder why she had bought so many yards of laurel unless she drew a plan for the festoons. And there was the dressmaker! She would be annoyed, because she had changed three customers to give her these special days next week. There was Chalkley's bill she had promised to pay at once. She must not forget to make out the check the first thing when she got up.

So heavily did all these things weigh upon her that she almost contemplated getting up at once and beginning, only that she knew it would be sure to arouse Chester, and he really must get his sleep. By and by when he was surely sound, she would just slip out and make out some lists, so that she wouldn't forget anything.

There would be all the children's clothes to pack, for they wouldn't have sense enough to select the right things. Betty would want to take all her party dresses of course, and right then there would be a conflict, if she tried to explain what kind of a place they were going to. They would all rebel at flannels, and woollen stockings. Thank goodness there was a whole trunk full of things like that stored away in the attic, packed safely in camphor, and all clean and mended. She had intended to get them out and send them in some missionary box pretty soon. They were put away one spring before it was certain that flannel was taboo for the rest of time. She foresaw that she must pack such things without the knowledge of the children or they would manage some way to throw them out. Then there were the goloshes. They all had new ones, but she must not forget them.

She began to enumerate the list on her fingers, "Notes, telephone, checks, flannels, goloshes—" trying to relate one to the other in such fashion that she could remember them. If she only had a pencil and paper.

She reached stealthily out in the dark to see if she had left her little note book on the bedside table, and was rejoiced to identify it under a magazine. Carefully she drew it toward her. Yes, the pencil was inside.

She turned to a back page of the book where she knew nothing was written and began to set down the items, writing as well as she could by sense of feeling, hoping it would be readable in the morning. At last when she had written all she could think of, she put the book back on the table with a sense of relief and closed her eyes. It was a mountain of work to be accomplished in one short morning, but she thought she could do it if it was thoroughly systematized.

She decided to get up as soon as daylight came and go up to the attic while the household still slept, filling the old suitcases with flannels, old sweaters and woollen stockings, and thus escape any chance of argument on that score. Then after breakfast she would make the children—No, that would entail constant argument if they did it. Better get them out of the way. That was it. She would arise *before* daylight and write her notes, write the ladies of the committees, and the Bridge club, and a supply for her Sunday School class, that she had been suddenly called away. Write her checks, and write as many notes instead of telephone calls as she could possibly get done before the children awoke. Then she would send the children with the notes and get them out of the way, leaving a free time for her to select the things that were to go along. She could rush it through by going through every closet and bureau drawer systematically.

She meant to keep Chester in bed till the last minute possible.

She was just trying to decide how to tell the children of the sudden cataclysm that had befallen them, or whether to let Chester do it, when most unexpectedly she fell asleep. And when she summoned her thoughts and opened her eyes the sun was streaming broad across her bed, and Chester was not in the room!

Chapter VII

She sat up in a panic and called him, but there was no answer. The whole house seemed to be most silent. Oh, she had overslept! And Chester had escaped!

She looked at the little clock on the bureau, and behold it was quarter past eight! With sudden premonition she sprang up, threw her kimono about her shoulders, slipped her feet into slippers, and went down the hall to find the escaped invalid. But there was no one in the hall or bathroom. The children's doors were all open and no one answered her call.

She hurried down stairs to the dining room but there was no one there. The table showed signs of a few hurried breakfasts, but no one answered when she called again.

She went out to the kitchen and Hannah was just emerging from the back kitchen, her arms full of milk bottles and fresh loaves of bread from the baker's cart that usually passed about this hour.

"Oh, are you ready for your breakfast, M's' Thornton?" asked Hannah, quite in her every morning usual tone.

"Why, Hannah, where is Mr. Thornton? Did he come down stairs? I must have overslept!"

It began to seem to her that she must have dreamed all those awful things that had happened last night. Probably none of them were true. Probably they were not going away to Vermont this morning, and all was as usual.

But Hannah broke that illusion.

"Yes, ma'am, Mr. Thornton was down at half past five. I was up because I'd forgot to put the note in the milk bottle to leave that cream for whipping. I give him a cup of coffee right at once and he went down to the office. He said he couldn't wait, but I made him eat some bread and butter and scrambled eggs, and while he was eating he told me I was to put up a lunch, a good big one, so I got the sandridges all made, ham, an' chicken, an' jelly ones. I used that half a roast chicken was left from last night. You all didn't half eat yer dinners an' there was plenty. I got some little blackberry tarts in the oven now, and I've made a sponge and a nut cake. I guess you'll do. And there's some o' that spice cake left too. Mister Chris he likes that—An' I'm boilin' the eggs now fer hard boils—!"

"Oh, Hannah!" cried the frantic mistress, "you're an angel! And to think I overslept when I was so very anxious to get down before anyone else."

" 'S awright!" said Hannah indulgently, "the mister said I wasn't to disturb you till half past nine. He said you was all tuckered out an' needed the sleep."

Eleanor gasped.

"Oh, he ought to have waked me up! I don't see how I'm ever to accomplish everything. Hannah, do you know where the children are?"

"Why I rackum they've went to school," said Hannah placidly. "I didn't say nothin' to 'em. Miss Betty she come down late as us'l an' drunk two cups of coffee an' beat it. Jane she was down furst off, soon's her pa got outta sight, said she had some lessums to study an' she'd lef' her books over ta Nemly's."

"But didn't they see their father, didn't he tell them—"

"I guess not, Mis' Thornton. They didn't come down till he was gone. The twins come down just after Jane, and I scrambled 'em some eggs, and they went. Come to think I don't know if Mr. Chris come at all. I ain't heard him—"

Eleanor caught her breath and did some swift thinking.

"Oh, all right, thank you Hannah," she said and turned back up stairs.

Perhaps it was just as well that the children were out of the way for the time being. She would get a lot done toward the packing before they knew, and forestall *all* contention. Of course she would have to do the work single handed, but perhaps that was easier. And if worst came to worst she could cut out the telephone calls and send telegrams on the way saying she had been suddenly called away.

She dressed hastily, and fairly flew up to the attic.

It took but a few minutes to sort out the woollen things and dump them into the suitcases that stood close at hand, to pile a few extra blankets and coverlets at the head of the stairs ready to be taken down. She added a roll of old linen and sheets. If they had to return to the primitive life they would need old rags.

She resurrected several old travelling rugs, and sweaters and a thick coat or two, and began to wonder how all these things were to be carried in one seven passenger car that would have seven full sized passengers in it when they were all in. The trunk would have to be reserved for their wearing apparel, and would scarcely be adequate even then. But perhaps Chester meant to pack a box and send it by express. At any rate the things were there, ready to put right in somewhere.

She went down stairs with a feeling of relief that the worst item of her list was finished.

Betty's room was the first to attack. Betty would be the worst to deal with in case she came back soon. Perhaps Chester had sent her to school to get her books and say good-bye.

She went through Betty's things hurriedly, worriedly. It would seem that there was not much of Betty's apparel that was suitable for an occasion like this. A couple of rather expensive sport dresses, one a silk and wool jersey, one silk pleated skirt with an exquisite angora sweater, whose only claim to going along was that the sweater was warm, and a gay little knitted dress for which she had just been wheedled into paying a fabulous price. Betty was wearing her most sensible dress, to-day, a rich soft brown. That was well, for she needed something warm and dark for the drive, and it would have been a struggle to make her put it on perhaps if she hadn't chosen it herself.

As she reasoned she began to be aware that she was almost afraid of Betty, of what she might say and do. That was not right of course. Perhaps she ought to have been more firm with Betty. In spite of the Child Training class, she might have made a mistake. Betty used to be a tractable little girl.

There was scarcely any underwear among Betty's garments that was suitable for a winter life on a northern farm, but mindful of the goodly stock in the attic she packed a few of Betty's most sensible underthings, added a couple of pairs of silk stockings for dress up—although what dress up could there possibly be for poor Betty out on that dreary farm? Was Chester doing just the wisest thing? Would not Betty and all of them in fact rebel at such summary tactics? However, it might not last. Chester might find some other way out. Perhaps it would prove to be merely a nice Christmas vacation for them all, and there would be a way out of their catastrophe in a little while.

She folded Betty's things neatly and laid them in piles on her bed, trying to put everything into as small compass as possible. Shoes, warm gloves, hair brush, comb, toilet articles. None of those ridiculous bottles and

jars of cold cream would be needed. She need not bother
about ornaments either. A little dose of simple life would
do Betty good.

She discovered as she went toward Jane's room that
the three big suitcases that fitted into the automobile
trunk were standing ready in the hall. Poor Chester,
himself ill, yet thinking of all these things, even telling
Hannah about a lunch! Oh, would he get through the day
without breaking? She sent up a swift prayer for him and
hurried on with her work.

It did not take so long to lay the neat piles into a
suitcase. There was going to be more room than she
feared. She even in pity stuck in a string or two of Betty's
beads. The child would feel utterly lost without something
of the sort.

Jane's garments were less of a problem. Jane still
wore gaudy woollen stockings with fancy tops on
occasion. Jane wore kilts and sweaters. Jane had several
warm pretty dresses. She made short work in there. Also
the twins were no problem at all. They had their good
sensible clothes. Betty would have her new fur coat of
course and her old one which she was supposed to wear to
school—and seldom did now because she liked the new
one better. The old one would do for Jane.

She worked swiftly. By half past nine she arrived at
Chris' door, suddenly remembering that Hannah had said
she had not seen him that morning.

There he lay deep in sleep, and the hard lines of his
young face, the weak sag of his handsome mouth, startled
her. Chester had been right. They needed to get away at
once.

Eleanor went swiftly from drawer to closet, working
with frenzied fingers, the tears running down her face, but
Chris lay sound asleep and did not stir.

After she had packed the things she thought he
needed, leaving out those he would have to wear, she
turned toward him and laid her hand on his forehead.

He stirred uneasily, and drew away from her touch.

But this was no time for sentiment. The minutes
were flying and she needed Chris' help.

"Chris!" she called clearly, close beside him, but Chris slept on.

At last she brought a cold wet cloth and washed his face. It would not do for his father to come back and find him sleeping while his mother was doing all the work alone.

He started awake angrily, furious at the cold water, not sparing his mother any rudeness that came into his cloudy mind.

"Chris," she said firmly, "you'll have to get up at once! I need your help. Your father has been very sick and we have to go away. The doctor thinks it's imperative!"

"What the deuce!" said Chris flinging himself back on his pillow and blinking at her. "Dad was all right last night. I'll say he was. What's he trying to put over on us?"

"Chris, that's not the way to speak of your father. And you must get up at once and get to work. There is a great deal to be done and your father is a sick man. He's gone down to the office for a few minutes but he may be back any minute, and it would be dreadful if he were to find you still in bed. It's half past eleven. Chris, your father has been going through a terrible time. I'm afraid he has lost all his money,—everything! You'll have to be very gentle and helpful! Hurry! I've several important errands I must send you on. Don't waste time, get up at once."

She left him, closing the door and going at once to her own packing of which she made short work, folding into the remaining suitcase, her own and her husband's plainest garments.

Hannah came up while she was doing it.

"Now, M's' Thornton, wha' kin I do? I got the supper packed in the hamper, an' I got a pot a soup on fer you all ta eat. What you want I should do after you all leave?"

She began as she spoke to smooth up the bed, and tidy the room with a deft touch here and there that made it much easier to sort out things and pack.

Mrs. Thornton could hear Chris splashing about in the bath room and knew that in course of time he would appear, so she gave Hannah a few directions and sat down to write some of the notes that she felt were imperative to send before she left. If Chris got ready in time he could take them, if not she would leave them for Hannah to deliver.

But Chris when he appeared was not minded to deliver notes.

"What's all this about going away?" he asked his mother, frowning as he stood imperiously in the door of her room and stared around on the suitcases and the general air of devastation the packing had wrought in his mother's usually neat room.

His mother was finishing an important note and did not answer at once and Chris further addressed her:

"I want you to jolly well know that *I'm* not going along! I've got important things to do here at home. If dad's broke I've got to get some money somehow, even if I have to accept a job somewhere! And you can just take my things outta that suitcase! I'm staying at home!"

His mother looked up sorrowfully, and it seemed to her that she had not really noticed before how her boy had changed. He seemed to have been suddenly transformed in a night, or was it that her eyes had suddenly been opened and she was awake now?

"Chris, there probably won't be any home here to stay in," she said sadly, the enormity of the situation sweeping over her anew, and the tears coming unbidden into her eyes and rolling down her cheeks.

"Whadda ya mean?" demanded Chris furiously. "No home. Whadda ya mean?"

"I mean just that. We're going to have to leave here. I have not had time to talk with your father beyond a few minutes of planning for the immediate future, but I feel positive that the business has been swept away, at least so far as your father's part in it is concerned. Your father has been going through a terrible ordeal, and the doctor told me last night that unless he gets immediate relief from the strain he will have a stroke of paralysis or something terrible like that. So, you see, that if you make it any harder for him you may be responsible for his life!"

"Great Cats!" said Chris irreverently. "Has Dad been speculating? I thought he had some sense! He had no business to let things get into a mess when he had us to take care of! A man has no right—!"

"Christopher!" said his mother. "A mere boy has no right to criticize his father! Don't let me ever hear you speak of your father like that again! You ought to be ashamed—!"

"Aw well," said Chris, walking into the room with an air of a young prince. "Looka here, Muth. This leaves me in an awful fix. I'm broke. D'ya understand? And I've practically promised to buy Hal's automobile day after tamorra. I swore I'd have the first payment for him, an' a fella can't let a thing like that go fluey. I ask you, cannee?"

"Chris, you don't mean that you have bought an automobile without telling your father? You know what he said about not allowing you to drive yet—"

"Oh, now come off, Muth, don't begin that! This is an nofful good bargain. I could fix it up and sell it fer fifty or a hundred bucks more'n I paid, see? It would give me something steady to do outsida school, see? Dad's always harpin' on my being employed. As if a fella oughtn'tta have a little fun now an' then."

"Chris, for pity's sake don't let's talk about such things now. I want you to go up in the attic and bring down the large leather trunk over in the corner, the one with Grandfather's initials on it. Bring it right away quick! I'm in a great hurry. And then go back and bring down that pile of blankets at the head of the stairs."

"Awwright, Muth, only waitaminute! I wanta ast you something. Say, Muth, this is very important to me. How much money have you got, Muth?" he lowered his voice anxiously. "B'cause if you lend me some—about two hundred say, I'll pay it up soon's my allowance comes in, I mean in reason of course, I'll pay half of my allowance every month till it's all paid. Honest I will, Muth—!"

"Chris!" said his mother looking at him with blanched face. "What are you talking about? What in the world could you possibly want with two hundred dollars?

And you know what your father said about borrowing from me or anyone else. I couldn't lend you any money if I had it, and I haven't got it. I've just made out checks for bills we owe, which takes all but a dollar or two of what I had in the bank, and I don't know when your father will be able to give me any more. You don't seem to understand that your father is financially embarrassed. Now, will you get that trunk?"

"But Muth, I *gotta* have it! Right now, I gotta have it."

He looked at her pleadingly, his miserable eyes piercing her very soul. She felt as if the earth beneath her was reeling. What had Chris got into now? At another time, even the day before, if Chris had come to her with eyes of anguish and pleaded like this she would have turned heaven and earth to get the money for him. She would have covered it up, and thrown some kind of a sop to her conscience for helping him evade his father's law about borrowing. But her eyes had been opened, at least half way. She began to suspect that there was something wrong, something more than just what Chris put on the surface.

Down stairs the twins had come bursting into the house, home from school for luncheon, and Jane's voice could be heard outside calling gaily to her companions.

"Oh bother!" said Chris. "Oh *Heck!* Muth, I simply *gotta* have that money 'fore night! I'm up ta my eyes. My *honor's* at stake!"

"*Your honor?*" said his father's voice in the doorway behind him. "Your *honor!* Just what is it you call your honor, Chris?"

Chris turned as red as a beet. His eyes drooped and he wheeled and faced his parent like a thing at bay. When he lifted his glance to see how angry his father was his eyes fell again as if they had been struck.

Eleanor came forward anxiously, her eyes on her husband's white face:

"It's nothing you need bother about, Chester," she said. "It's just a little matter between me and Chris. You needn't worry, I'm just as firm as you are when it comes to things like this. You go and lie down and let me deal with this."

Chester's eyes looked at her sadly, and then he turned back to the boy again, who had already brightened under his mother's tone.

"Just a little matter of two hundred dollars," he said as if it were a sword that he had held back from doing damage.

"Chris, step into your room for a few minutes. I have something to say to you."

"Why, I can't just now Dad, I promised to get a trunk down for Muth," said Chris with a show of haste. "She's waiting for it."

"Very well," said Chester, "I'll wait."

Chris tugged the empty trunk down the attic stairs, with many a thump and a snort as if it were very heavy indeed, and then went back for the blankets while his father waited at the foot of the stairs courteously, until the task was completed.

"Now, if you're quite ready, Chris, we'll step into your room," said Chester.

When the door closed behind the two Eleanor Thornton sank back into her chair again and buried her face in her hands. She was so tired and frightened and worn out with various emotions that it seemed to her she must just sink down on the bed and cry.

The clamor below stairs roused her. Jane was tantalizing the twins, or they were tantalizing Jane. It didn't matter which. There was sound of breaking crockery and Hannah's sharp voice remonstrating. This was no time for weeping. She had promised to be ready.

She hurried down stairs and started the children to eating. Jane was clamoring that she must hurry back. They had a rehearsal of the play fifteen minutes before the afternoon session. She begged that she might have bread and butter and plum preserve and go right back eating it on her way.

"Sit down, Jane. You're not to go back to school to-day. We're going away!"

"Going away?" screamed the twins in chorus. "Gee! Where? Can we go too?"

"Yes, we're all going. Now eat your lunch. There isn't time to talk. There's a great deal to be done. Jane, sit down! Didn't you hear me?"

"Mamma, I can't go anywhere to-day," said Jane assuming Betty's best manner for the occasion. "I think it's the limit for you to go away somewhere when you know I can't go. You know the rehearsal lasts all this afternoon—"

"Jane, sit down, and I'll explain. You are not going back to school. We are going away. They will have to get along without you at the rehearsal."

"But they can't, Mamma," said Jane with her mouth full, "I'm in every scene. I'm really the *star!* It wouldn't be *honorable* of me to go away and leave them in a hole—"

Honorable! There was that word again. What a strange sense of honor her children seemed to be suddenly developing!

Eleanor essayed to explain.

"Circumstances have taken a most unexpected turn, Jane. I haven't time to explain to you now. But your father or I will see that your teacher is notified. It isn't as if there wasn't plenty of time before the play to supply your place,—and you told me yourself that at least two of your classmates were both eager and able to take your place, so we shall not be seriously inconveniencing anybody."

"Do you mean that you're not going to *let* me be in the play at all!" asked Jane aghast.

"We will not be in town, Jane. We are going away this afternoon."

"I won't *stand* it!" Jane shouted with a quick burst of angry tears. "I won't, I *won't!* You *shan't* do a thing like that to me! I'll run away! I'll—I'll—I'll stay at Emily Carter's." She paused in her outburst and brought out a tempestuous little smile with a tilt of her small chin, and a toss of her curly head. "*That's* what I'll do, Mamma, I'll stay at the Carters' till you come back,—or—or—till after the play's over."

"Under no circumstances will you stay at the Carters', Jane. And your father is quite unwilling that you shall either act or rehearse in that play even once more. He saw quite enough of your part last night. If I had known what it was that you were doing, if I had understood—"

"Why, Mamma, it wasn't like what I did last night. I changed it just for fun. There's nothing you couldn't like about the play, really—If you'll just come over and watch me rehearse, Mamma. Please—"

"Jane, sit down!" said her mother severely, "Sit down and eat your lunch. We have no time for further discussion. I'll explain everything later. As soon as you are through go up and change to the dress that is lying on your bed, and be quick about it!"

But Jane in a storm of tears dashed into the living room and flung herself upon the couch to howl.

"Jane, you must stop this noise at once," said Eleanor following her. "Your father has been very ill and you will make him worse."

Jane wept on, growing louder.

John appeared on the scene, his face smeared with plum jam and a blackberry tart in either hand:

"Aw, cut it, Jay," he called. "We're goin' to have a corkin' time. Hannah says we haven't any money any more an' we're goin' away off to live on a farm where they have pigs and cows and a hay mow to slide down, and ponies and a wheelbarrow."

Jane sat up and looked at him. She made a face at him, and then she went on crying.

"I—shan't—g—g—g—go!" she sobbed out tempestuously.

About that time the door of Chris' room opened upstairs, and Jane heard her father's footsteps, heard his voice in grave tones. She remembered his grip of her arm last night and got up from the couch. She came slowly back into the dining room, mopping her red nose and eyes, and catching her breath in broken sobs as she slid into her seat at the table.

The dining room became very quiet. Even the twins were still, eating tarts and drinking more milk.

70

Chris was walking down stairs behind his father.

"Yes, sir!" they could hear him say in a subdued tone.

"Yes, sir. I will."

They came into the dining room silently and took their seats. Chris did not look at his mother. He sat down and began to eat from the plate Hannah gave him. He asked for coffee, but he did not look at anybody. His eyes were down upon his plate as if he were ashamed, or afraid, his mother could not tell which. Her heart began to quake with new fears.

Chapter VIII

"Where is Betty?" asked Chester Thornton looking with troubled gaze around the table.

"She got off to school before I woke up," said Eleanor apologetically, "and I haven't had time to send word for her to come home."

"But she ought to be here by this time," said her father looking at his watch.

"She ain't comin' home," volunteered John, "I saw her go into the cafeteria with some kids fer lunch. She told me to tell Mamma she wouldn't be here."

"I had better telephone for her," said Eleanor rising anxiously.

"No!" said Chester sharply, "just get her things ready and we'll stop for her on the way. We haven't time to wait for her to come home."

Eleanor sank back into her chair once more, finished the coffee, and took one more bite of her bread and butter, but she felt as if she could hardly swallow anything.

"The truck will be here soon," said Chester.

"There'll be room for a trunk or two, and all the blankets and pillows you need to take. How soon will you be ready?"

"Oh!" said Eleanor feebly. "Why, yes. Very soon."

"Chris and I have an errand to do," announced Chester. "It may take us fifteen or twenty minutes, and when we get back I'll be ready to start whenever you are. I noticed you had my things pretty well packed."

Eleanor marvelled at the restrained voice of her husband. He seemed deathly white, and she feared for him. She wondered what was the errand that was important enough to take him away even for fifteen minutes. She looked keenly at Chris, but he went on eating with his eyes downcast. Her heart seemed heavy like lead. She swallowed the scalding coffee and rose without attempting to eat anything more.

"I'll go up and put the last things in," she said. "Jane, you had better come with me."

Jane looked at her father.

"Daddy!" she said with a quiver in her voice, "Daddy, do I have to go?" Her question ended in a wail.

"Yes!" said Chester looking at the little girl with a reminder of last evening in his eyes, until she quailed.

"But—Daddy—" her lips were quivering with the pretty pitiful plea that had always won her what she wanted, "Daddy, I can't leave my teacher in a —h-o-o-ole!"

"I will explain to your teacher," said Chester Thornton. "Jane, your mother needs you upstairs."

Jane arose slowly, reluctantly, sobbing into her handkerchief despairingly, but her father and Chris went out without noticing her. Chris walked as though he were about to face an ordeal.

When they had gone out the front door Jane returned to the dining room to retrieve the last tart from the twins, and went slowly upstairs, emitting crumby sobs occasionally.

"Jane, sit on this suitcase while I fasten it," called Eleanor, and Jane discovering her old last year's sweater and cap grew suddenly interested. She looked around and discovered the other suitcases and the big trunk. Somehow the affair took on proportions of moment. There might be going to be something interesting in it all, even if one didn't get to act in the play. There would be other plays, and they would likely be coming back some day. It was rather fun after all to be taken out of school and go off on a mysterious trip.

Chester and Chris did not come back in fifteen minutes. Eleanor watched the clock anxiously, not because she cared how late they started but for fear of what might be unearthed of Chris' misdoings.

Then Michael and the truck arrived and she had her hands full getting the right things loaded in. Of course having the truck come made things a thousand times easier. She could just wrap a lot of things in an old quilt, and have it piled into the back, without bothering to pack.

During this episode Jane disappeared, and was discovered just turning the corner of the street. It was Michael who ran after her and brought her back.

"I was only going to get some things I left at Emily's and then run around and say good bye to the school," she explained sulkily.

Eleanor set her to work scrubbing the tart off the twins, and searching in the hall closet for all the goloshes.

"I don't see what we need these for," said Jane. "We're going in a car aren't we? Where are we going anyway?"

"To a nice place where Daddy used to live when he was a boy," explained Eleanor. "We're all going off to have a good time, because Daddy is all tired out, and needs a rest."

Jane eyed her keenly. She had a lurking suspicion that the migration had something to do with her performance at the drug store, but she said nothing.

Then Chester arrived with a subdued looking Chris. Eleanor tried in vain to read from their faces what had happened, but could not in the bustle of leaving.

Hannah came down to the car to take last directions, and there was no more time. She had to count up the suitcases, run back to look through all the rooms and make sure that nothing important had been left behind.

Then they all piled in, Eleanor in the back seat with Doris in the middle leaving a place for Betty; Jane, still sulky, and John too excited to sit down, in the middle seats. Chris was in front, with Chester driving.

Chester slammed the door shut and put his foot on the starter. Hannah came running with the other thermos bottle of chocolate for the twins, and an extra milk bottle, and Eleanor looked back at the home she so loved, and wondered if she would ever see it again.

The twins were excited now and were talking.

"Daddy, will there be plenty of pigs?" asked John.

"Cut it!" growled Chris importantly, and then subsided again as if he suddenly remembered.

The car started and went down the street. Jane looked hungrily toward the Carter house, and twisted her neck to get a last glimpse of the drug store on whose steps lounged two prep boys, smoking illegal cigarettes. She gave them a grimace with her tongue in her cheek, which was not unmarked by her mother, and then settled down to the excitement of going on a journey. Jane was not at the stage of life where an impression had very deep hold. A new one could easily erase it.

They turned down the street on which the High School was located and suddenly Eleanor's heart gave a thud of fear. There had been so many that day. Now, what would Betty do? Make a scene, probably. What would that Child Training Teacher have suggested in a case like this? But then of course that Child Training Teacher would never have allowed things to go as far as this. She would likely have said that the children had a right to express themselves. They had their own lives to live and if they did not want to live them as their father and mother wanted them to do, they should not be forced into it. Bah, what foolishness it all was. Something was wrong. Why had she not seen it all before? It was a wrong basis to start out on. Expressing themselves! What were "themselves" anyway when they didn't know what it was all about yet?

Chester stopped the car and got out. He walked

briskly up the steps of the High School and disappeared within the great doors. Jane had a satisfying reflection that Daddy would meet his match in the superintendent. Perhaps there was still hope that they might not have to go anywhere until school was over. What a lark it would be *then* to go off on a mysterious journey to a new place!

Betty was applying lipstick to her pretty mouth, carefully, thoroughly, vividly, behind her largest study book propped up on her desk.

Her seat happened to be at the back of the room, and as the teacher was busy with a class in the front of the room she was not likely to be discovered. It was counted a misdemeanor to apply make-up in school, especially so in that teacher's precincts, but Betty felt a little pale, and the class meeting to be held immediately after school was one of the places she liked to be particular about her appearance.

Betty never attempted anything but the faintest make-up around home. She knew her mother did not count it good taste and her father could not endure it, so she always went early to school and paid a good deal of attention to patting her face into order behind the door in the cloak room before she went into her class room. It was annoying to have to plan, and be stealthy, just to be decent. A pity one's parents were so behind the times!

She was thinking about it as she put the finishing touch to the gory little cupid's bow she was making of her mouth, her lips pursed up like a cherry, when she heard her name called, and felt the searching eyes of Miss House come down and pierce behind her Latin Grammar.

Lipstick and mirror went down like a flash. Out came a small white handkerchief and gave a quick polish to her chin while she assumed an interested manner and lifted innocent eyes to her teacher's call.

"Miss Elizabeth Thornton, you are wanted in the office at once!"

Betty arose, annoyed. Surely Miss House wouldn't send her down to the office just for brushing up her lips a little, all so quietly in the back seat with no one sitting near to watch her. She had waited till the Psychology class came in to recite before she even started, and it hadn't taken her but a minute.

Betty went down to the desk haughtily to protest, but Miss House waved her toward the door.

"Some one in the office waiting to see you. Professor Morley said you were to come at once!"

Wondering, yet somewhat relieved she took her way down the hall.

Some one to see her! Who could it be? Surely Dud hadn't taken this way of communicating with her. He wouldn't dare openly. He would likely call up and make an appointment in code sometime late in the afternoon. But who on earth could it be?

As she turned the knob of the door there came a sudden thought of her father like a sharp little pain going through her heart. Perhaps something had happened to her father! Perhaps he was worse and her mother had sent for her! How terrible if one's father should die, as Hattie Blaine's father had done last week!

Then girding herself up and lifting her chin a little haughtily she entered the door and stood face to face with her father.

She stared at him, half relieved, half frightened. Had Chester gone crazy, tracking her around this way? What could have happened? She forgot entirely the vivid color which she had just applied to her lips and could not understand the startled stare her father gave her for an instant before he spoke. Then his voice sounded harsh and stern as he said:

"Get your hat and coat, Betty, and come with me! Professor Morley understands your going, so you need wait for nothing but to get your things. Hurry! I will explain it all to you on the way. We are late already!"

Betty's face darkened ominously, and her little red lips went thin and hard with determination.

"I couldn't possibly think of it," she said. "Wherever you're going, Chester, you'll have to go without me. I've got dates all the afternoon, and I haven't a minute to

76

spare. I've one more recitation before three o'clock, and I'm not quite ready for it."

"You are excused from recitations, Betty. I have arranged all that."

"But I have a class meeting and an important report to give. I couldn't possibly go if it were a trip to Europe. And we have basketball practice this afternoon—"

"That has nothing to do with it, daughter. Something far more important has come up, and you will have to come with me at once! If you have any message to send to anyone I am sure Professor Morley's secretary will take it for you."

He turned to the girl at the desk who was discreetly making out index cards.

"Will you kindly let my daughter's friends know that she was suddenly called away by her father and will not be able to be at her class meeting this afternoon, or her basketball practice?"

Betty bit her red lips hard, she was so angry with her father for mortifying her this way. She tried to think of some way out but he stood waiting for her and she turned, slowly, reluctantly, and went across the hall to the cloak room, looking eagerly either way in hopes of seeing some of her special friends that she might send a hasty word of explanation to one of the boys who had asked her to take a ride in his new car that afternoon. She had really been planning to slip away from basketball. But no one whom she dared trust came by, and she had lingered as long as she dared in the cloak room with her father standing just outside the door. She finally had to come out and follow him down the steps.

Once outside the school she made another stand.

"See here, Chester, what's all this about? I simply *can't* go away anywhere to-day. I really have things that I must do. You don't understand what a responsibility a girl in my position has. I'm class president, and we've just found out some of the class are trying to put something over on us. Trying to influence the faculty to say we can't wear anything but plain white muslin dresses at

77

commencement, and a lot of folly like that, and I've simply *got* to go back and put a stop to it. If the vote goes their way it will make us no end of trouble. We'll have to get up a school strike to undo the mischief."

Chester Thornton took his daughter's arm, firmly, but with a friendly touch:

"You'll find it won't affect your future in the least, Betty," he said in a kindly voice. "There are several things you do not yet understand, and I will have to explain, but the main one just now is that you are to come with us *at once!*"

"Us?" said Betty with a sudden quick glance down the walk at the car which she had merely taken for granted before. "Us?" incredulously. "Really, is this a family picnic? It is a poor time to choose," she remarked coldly. "Thanks, I don't care to attend."

And she stopped short in the walk and looked defiantly up at her father.

He looked down into her face with eyes that were sharp with the pain of disappointment. There was even a look of disgust about the glance he gave her, and his voice sounded entirely unlike the indulgent father she had always known.

"Betty," he said, "I am quite capable of taking you up and carrying you to the car as I did last night. But, there are several young people up at the window over the front door. They have evidently recognized you. Do you wish to leave the school house in that manner, or will you walk down and get into the car in the usual way?"

Betty looked up startled, recognized the boy of whom she had been in search, talking to a girl she disliked, gave a quick nod and a gay wave of the hand to them, and tripped down the walk to the car, vanishing into the place left for her in the back seat with much the same manner that an arrested man dives from the patrol wagon into the door of the court house when a crowd is standing around watching.

Chester was in his seat almost as soon, and the doors slammed shut, John pulled down his little middle seat, and off they went.

As soon as they had turned the corner Betty sat up, her cheeks flaming brilliantly under the generous coat of white she had applied to them a few minutes before, and her eyes flashing like two naughty stars.

"Well!" said Betty with the air of a royal princess kidnapped, "I should like to know what possible explanation there can be to this extraordinary performance?"

She fixed her mother with her eyes, but her tone was loud enough to reach easily to the front seat.

Eleanor busied herself with folding back the sleeve of Doris' sweater that had come down below her coat sleeve, and did not pretend to try to answer. Chester was threading his way carefully through traffic, going in the opposite direction from home. Betty grew angrier with every second.

"Is somebody dead? And are we all going to the funeral?" she asked contemptuously. "I'm sure I don't know who it could possibly be that would demand our instant presence before the afternoon session of school closed. Now, I shall lose my marks on my report, and every mark counts from now on whether I win the College scholarship or not."

But no one answered. Chester was too much preoccupied in getting through a snarl of vehicles at the railroad crossing to be expected to reply, and Eleanor had stooped to recover her hand bag which had slipped to the floor of the car.

"I'm perfectly furious!" said Betty sitting up the straighter and looking angrily at first one parent and then the other, and then around the ring of brothers and sisters.

"So we all observe!" said Jane quaintly, settling back sanctimoniously. Having suffered herself it was good to be able to watch some one else take a grilling. Besides the affair had begun to take on the proportions of an adventure in Jane's eyes. She was already forgetting what she had left behind in the joys of what might possibly be before. Jane was still half a little girl.

But the road wound on out of Briardale, down

GRACE LIVINGSTON HILL

toward the city and finally turned into the state highway. Still nobody had answered.

When the car dashed out of Briardale and toward the City Line, Betty turned to her mother.

"I insist on knowing where we are going," she said in a tone that made Chester feel like slapping her. When did Betty develop into such a little minx? He hadn't noticed it coming on.

"Your father will explain presently," said Eleanor in a gentle tone. She was still engaged in settling some of the little bags and boxes that had been tossed into the car just as they started. She had avoided her daughter's eyes because she could not bear to see the fury in them, and so had not noticed her make-up.

"Gee!" said John turning around and suddenly getting a good look at his oldest sister. "Gee! You look like Lily Whiffletree!"

Now Lily Whiffletree was a maiden of uncertain age and unsavory character who lived with her blind and deaf old father on the outskirts of Briardale, and her daring costumes and notorious deeds were the talk of the town.

Chester and Eleanor both turned suddenly and looked at Betty, Chester with open annoyance, and Eleanor with horror. Betty became suddenly aware of herself, and sought her scrap of a handkerchief in her coat pocket. Her mother's reproachful "Oh, Betty! How could you be so common?" only served to anger her the more.

"I'm going to get out!" she said and burst into passionate tears.

"Yes," said Chester, "you're going to get out, right down there by that brook on the edge of the Willowvale Golf Course, and wash your face!"

80

Chapter IX

He drew up at the side of the road and opened the door of the car.

"Get out, Jane," he ordered.

Jane got out with a leer on her elfin face.

"Get out, Betty!"

Betty resisted, but her father reached in and drew her out.

"Now, go down there and wash your face! You can get some of the flour off at least, and if the red doesn't come off with water we'll stop at a drug store and get some acid or something to take it off. I'm not going through the world with my daughter looking like a bad woman."

"Doesn't she look funny, Mamma?" laughed Doris. "Doesn't Betty look funny, all red and white like a circus clown! Why Mamma! You're crying. What'rya crying for, Mamma? Are you crying cause Betty looks like Lily Whiffletree? Mamma, *say!*"

"Aw shut up, can't ya!" growled Chris suddenly entering into the conversation. "Such a *life!*"

Betty returned with her father from her trip to the creek, looking several shades more life like, and climbed into the car indignantly.

"I never heard of a girl of my age being treated this way in my life!" she remarked as she settled back and turned her face toward the window of the car with an air of withdrawal from the world.

Chester Thornton climbed back into the car and slammed the door shut. He waited an instant with his hand on the wheel and then he turned around and faced his little family, a yearning look on his tired drawn face that went to his wife's heart.

"Now," said he, "we have quite a journey to take before night, and we haven't any time to waste in talking. There are things that I intend to explain to you when we get to a place where we have leisure. At present it is enough to say that it is your own doings that have brought this journey about, and that your mother and I feel that it is for the best in every way. Now you know, however much you may pretend that you are your own masters and mistresses, that that isn't the case at all. You are all *our children,* and in the eyes of the law—you are still under age and therefore under our control. Also, you have a moral obligation, whether you own it or not, to obey me as long as I am supporting you, whether you like it or not.

"I am taking you on this journey because I feel that it is for your own good, and I shall go into no more detail at present. There will probably be some unpleasant things, and hard things in what is before us, and I expect you to be good sports and take them as all in the day's work. If you do this you may find that the journey will be a pleasant one. It will be, of course, just what you make it. We shall also incidentally discover who of you are loyal to the family. That's all. Now, shall we go?"

"All set!" rollicked out John joyously. It was plain that John had no objection to the family flight.

Chester stepped on the gas and the car shot forward into the clear cold winter afternoon.

For an hour or more no one spoke save John and Doris who eagerly watched every car they met, counting how many of the different makes they passed, and discussing their various qualities. Their chatter reminded Chester of his happy errand about this time yesterday hunting a Mermaid Eight for Betty, and planning his Christmas presents. Now, what would Christmas be? Had he done right to bring them all off into a desolate place just as the holiday season was arriving?

But a glance in the mirror showed him Betty's hard angry face, fierce in its concentrated fury. Betty was by no means subdued.

He recalled her struggles the night before, and her resistance at the school house. Betty was a problem indeed.

Chester was very tired. He had had scarcely any sleep for twenty-four hours, had eaten almost nothing since noon of the day before, and suddenly he felt the strain. His weary eyes longed to close and his body to relax. His heart seemed to go slower and slower and the tensity of the atmosphere among his family was almost more than he could bear. Yet he knew he had been right to come. It seemed as if there had been some one leading, choosing this way for him, almost as if he had no choice in the matter.

Eleanor was terribly weary. She longed to put her head back on the cushion and cry, yet she knew she must keep a steady front. It would not do to break down. She felt Betty's presence like a stranger, as if she had suddenly become an enemy. Her own little girl! It wrung her heart.

And Chris sat slumped beside his father, his eyes down, or out of the window, with a strange embarrassment upon him. What could have happened to subdue him so? He did not even make any display of more than a passing interest when they came upon the wreck of two cars at the turn of a hill. There was a little group of people standing about it, and a state constabulary taking names and asking questions. There was no need to stop and Chester drove straight ahead. Betty seemed frozen to ice. She never moved a muscle, and kept her unseeing eyes fixed out the window, as if she had withdrawn to another universe and had nothing in common with any of them. Jane too was sullen and unhappy as if she would like to cry but wasn't sure it would do any good. She had a kind of frightened look about her self-willed little mouth that reminded her mother of the time five years before when she had run away from her call, straight into a mortar bed in front of a new house, and got into liquid lime to her waist. It was a frightened defiant look.

To judge by their looks there did not seem to be an over amount of loyalty in any member of the party.

It was Doris who finally voiced the question that was trembling on all their lips and brought their thoughts to a climax:

"Well, anyhow," she said after a long silence in which not even John had spoken, "anyhow I gotta go back by next Friday. We have our party then, and Miss White wants me to speak a piece. I know it all now, and I've got to have a new dress to wear. They are all gonta

83

have new dresses. Mine has gotta be red. I'm a holly berry!
Say, Daddy, when are we goin' back? I gotta get ready for
the party."

"I can't answer that now, Doris. I'm not sure that we
shall ever go back," he said gravely, sadly.

A new consternation settled down upon the group.
Betty's face grew even harder to read, as her mother
glanced furtively toward her. Chris seemed to slump
further down in the seat. After that not even Doris spoke
any more, and presently Eleanor found that the tears were
rolling down her cheeks silently. She drew the little girl
into her arms and patted her.

"Don't cry, darling," she whispered. "I think we'll
have a nice time where we're going."

"But—I—wanta—be—a—holly berry—" sobbed
the little girl.

"Well, perhaps we'll find some real holly berries
where we're going," whispered her mother summoning a
smile, and wiping Doris' tears away.

Jane still sat sullen and thoughtful, as the car rushed
on through little towns and big ones, out on the great
highway, detouring into byways now and then to avoid
traffic near a town, and back again to the highway.

Suddenly Chester broke the tension by turning to
Chris:

"Want to drive a while now, Son?" he asked in a
kindly tone as if nothing had happened to precipitate a
cataclysm in the family.

Chris accepted with alacrity, almost embarrassed,
eager to be of service. Chris liked to drive beyond
everything, but his father seldom allowed him to do so.
They stopped and made the change and something tense
in the atmosphere seemed to break away. Chester gave a
few suggestions about keeping to a certain spot in the
road and avoiding the rough edge. The boy warmed under
the kindly tone, and seemed to feel his self respect
returning. It relieved Eleanor to see them more like
companions again. Chris was only a boy yet!

But Betty still wore her air of offended princess,
resolved to have nothing further to do with the family.

Jane was wriggling restlessly and at last she announced:
"I'm hungry! When do we eat? Aren't you going to stop somewhere pretty soon?"

"We can't waste daylight stopping," said her father, with more of the old fatherly tone than he had used since the evening before. "I guess mother has a snack along somewhere if you are hungry."

That was the signal for a general sigh of relief.

"Right there in the hamper at your feet, John. Hand it up here. There are special packages for to-night. Hannah has it all systematized."

She opened the hamper with John's eager assistance and began to hand out sandwiches, all neatly wrapped in wax paper, delicate chicken and ham between wafer-like slices of bread and butter, a tang of mayonnaise, or was that a spiced pickle? Appetizing egg sandwiches and cookies that would melt in your mouth. Jane bloomed into good nature at once and filled both hands and her mouth eagerly. Doris and John accepted the little tin cracker containers that held their portions, and promised to be very careful not to drop any crumbs. Chris folded his lips about a whole small sandwich and went on driving with a look of feeling great responsibility for the car. Even Chester swallowed gratefully the cup of steaming coffee his wife poured from the thermos bottle. Only Betty refused to have part nor lot in the general good cheer. She would eat nothing. She would not drink any coffee, and she scorned the cup of milk from the other thermos bottle that Doris offered her. She sat with haughty mien, staring out at the gathering dusk, a princess in exile, chafing at her bonds.

When the hamper was all packed away again everybody seemed to feel better, everybody but Betty. One would almost have thought Betty was not there, so still she sat, so cold, so angry and immovable.

As it grew dark the twins got sleepy. Jane began to laugh and call attention to houses they passed, and then to tell something funny she had heard that day and the atmosphere cleared visibly.

Chester offered to take the wheel again, but Chris

said in a grown up tone, quite as if he were used to saying what should be done:

"No, Dad, you're all in! I'll drive carefully. You rest!" and Chester relaxed into the seat and watched his boy, watched also, furtively in the mirror, the dark hard little face of his Betty and sighed, wondering if it were too late for little Betty. His Betty!

It was about this time that Chris discovered that a Ford truck was following them, had been for a number of miles, had turned whenever they turned, stopped a good distance behind them whenever they paused at traffic lights, and when they bore out on the lonely highways, came steadily on with them, as if it belonged.

"If I didn't know we were miles away I'd say that was Mike sitting on the front seat," said Chris important-ly, eyeing the dark car that came on like a distant shadow.

"It is," said Chester, "Michael and his brother."

"No kiddin'?" asked Chris in amazement. "Are they going with us?"

"They are bringing up some supplies," said Chester, and opened his lips as if he would have said more, but closed them again.

The children grew silent again thinking what this might mean. It would look as if this were even a more serious business than it had at first appeared, this being kidnapped by one's father. There seemed to be no nonsense about it. They were really going into exile. It occupied them fully for a little while, this thought of what it might mean for them if it were really true as their father had said, that they might never be returning.

Doris crept into her mother's lap, presently, and went to sleep, and John stuffed the lap robe between his seat and Jane's and camped down with his head in Jane's lap. Jane herself rested her head against the upholstery of the door, and drowsed off, and then it all grew silent again save for a word now and then between Chris and his father.

Eleanor's arms ached and her head swam, but she made herself fairly comfortable in her corner with Doris in her arms, and she too fell asleep. But Betty maintained her stiff hard gaze out of the window, hungry and weary, but refusing to rest or to eat.

About midnight they came to a halt beside a long low old-fashioned building that looked as if it might have been a country tavern sometime back in the seventies. It was neatly painted and its wide low-browed verandas, the lower one level with the sidewalk, gave it an appearance of being centuries old. Betty frowned out at it in dismay. What could her father be thinking of to stop at a place like this? They had just passed a quite modern looking brick hotel a couple of squares back, and here Dad had chosen this out-of-the-world, impossible looking place! It was disgusting! It was all of a piece with the rest of the crazy expedition. Dad must have gone out of his mind. But what could Mother be thinking of to allow this farce to proceed?

Chester got out and went into what seemed to be the office, though it was little less than a wide hallway with a big desk. He had a few words with the proprietor and then came out accompanied by a boy who began to take out suitcases.

Chester opened the car door and said "Come!"

Jane shook John awake, and he stumbled out, more asleep than awake. Chris got out at his mother's direction and helped Doris out, making her stand on her feet, and helping her into the great wide parlor where she collapsed into sleep again on a convenient couch.

Eleanor gathered up some of the little things that had been stowed about her, and followed. Betty was last. Her father waited patiently and then turned the car over to Michael who by this time had driven the Ford truck up behind them.

The parlor into which they had been shown while Chester went through the formalities of registering, was a strange quaint place, very long and spacious, but low of ceiling. The floor was covered with beautiful old oriental rugs, and the room was furnished completely and luxuriously with some of the finest old pieces of mahogany that Eleanor had ever seen. She could not help stopping to exclaim over their beauty, tired as she was.

Three great davenports of priceless pattern, gate legged tables, leaved tables with lyre pedestals, rare old chairs covered with real needle point, and carved by an expert's hand, a whole dozen mahogany straight chairs all perfect, and all matched! How had they been preserved through the years! Some fine old engravings were on the wall, and a few oil portraits that bore the unmistakable hall marks of a master's brush.

"Chester! Where did you find such a place? How did you hear of it?" exclaimed Eleanor with the true connoisseur's delight in the antique and the precious.

"Gartley told me about it this morning. Said it was worth a trip just to stop here over night," said Chester looking around with eyes that seemed rested already. "I wasn't sure just what it would turn out to be."

He cast an anxious eye toward Betty who was standing in the doorway with curling lip. Nothing could be more out of harmony with Betty Thornton's present mood than this quaint bit of yesterday in the guise of a hotel. She swept the long lovely room with a scornful glance and turned on her little high heel with a shrug of her trim shoulders.

Chris was standing in the front door looking out disconsolately on a deserted square in the midnight, its bare cobbled surface as empty as if it had been swept. On the opposite side were nothing but warehouses, softened by tall willows standing at intervals along the curb.

Betty took a quick step and was at her brother's side, speaking low.

"For heaven's sake, Chris, give me some cigarettes! I'm just ready to pass out!"

"Same here!" said Chris gloomily.

"Do you mean you haven't got any?"

"Not a one," said Chris, "and not a red cent to get any if this dumb dump had any place to buy 'em. I tried to get Mike to give me some, but he said he had only a pipe and he wanted that himself, and his brother don't smoke. Whadaya know about that? A full sized man and don't smoke. But say, Betts, what's tha matter of you lending me some money? I'll go fifty-fifty."

"I left my purse in my desk," said Betty sadly, "I hadn't an idea there was anything like this being put over. Dad wouldn't wait a minute for me to go back."

"Tough luck!" said Chris. "Guess I'll have to part with my class ring. I don't see going without."

"I've nothing but a vanity case," said Betty frowning. "I can't spare that. I'd stand a fat chance of getting another, and I'd be a fright to go anywhere if I ever get out of this."

"Come Betty," said her father just behind her, so close his voice made her start. How much had he heard of their conversation?

Chapter X

"Come, Son! The rooms are ready, and I guess we're all ready for bed," urged Chester.

"Think I'll take a little walk around and see the town," ventured Chris suddenly, with a swagger that was a trifle overdone.

"Not to-night, Son," said Chester, laying a firm hand on the shrinking shoulder of the boy. "We've a hard day's ride before us tomorrow, and it's high time to turn in. We've quite a mileage to our credit so far already. Come!"

There was nothing for it but to turn their reluctant feet and walk upstairs. Well, perhaps there would be a chance to get out a window or something after the family had retired. Betty tried to convey the idea to Chris with her eyebrows as they straggled behind the others, but when they reached the second floor, behold there had been unexpected arrangements made. Only two rooms were available, the larger one with two double beds, the other containing a double bed and a cot. Each had its private bath and both were clean and quaint and altogether attractive.

"Eleanor, you and the girls had better take this room," said Chester looking around appraisingly at the larger room. "The boys and I will get along famously in the smaller one. Turn in now quickly and don't waste time. I want to get started at least by eight o'clock, if you feel that will not be too early."

"Are you sure it will not be too much for you, Chester, to start again so early? Remember, you had hardly any sleep last night, and you've been on the dead jump all day. You are a sick man, you know."

"Don't you believe it!" said Chester giving Eleanor a wan smile. "We're off for a lark, and every hour that passes rests me. I feel that we've left all care behind."

It was maddening! Betty turned away with a sick empty feeling at the pit of her stomach and every nerve in her crying out for the stimulant to which she had been for months accustoming herself.

But in turning she caught sight of the little tin box of sandwiches which Eleanor had taken the precaution to bring in, and swiftly, while her mother was still talking with her father she reached for it, and sneaked out several, hiding them in the folds of her coat, and slipping into the bathroom to eat them behind a locked door.

When she came back into the bedroom again her temper was by no means improved, though her stomach was not quite so empty.

"I'm sure I don't see why Dad picked out such a perfectly poisonous place to stay all night," she growled bitterly. "What was the idea of herding us all into one room as if we were so many sheep? Why couldn't I have a room to myself? I'm not a baby."

Eleanor refrained from telling her that she was acting like one.

"Why, we thought this arrangement would be better, dear. You see we don't like to put the twins in separate rooms, they are so young to be in a hotel alone, I asked Daddy to fix it this way on their account. And then, too, you know it's much cheaper to have only two rooms."

"Oh, Hen!" said Betty inelegantly. "Is it as bad as that? Are we really poor?"

"I'm afraid we are, dear!" said Eleanor, a pathetic note stealing into her voice. "Do, dear, try to be pleasant. Your father has a great deal to bear already—"

"Well, what did he let himself get into such a heck of a mess for then?" said Betty. "I'm sure I think he was to blame!"

"Betty!" said her mother, "hush! Don't speak again to-night! You are unbearable!"

Betty slid out of her dress, and declining the sensible night array that Eleanor had selected for the journey, flung herself into one of the beds in the brief flimsy silk affair that she was pleased to call underwear. She turned her back on a dreary world, resolved that she would find a way back into her own life again, somehow, even if the rest of the family had to go on and be poor. She felt that life owed her a good time and she meant to have it, and no stuffy old father and mother were going to do her out of it.

As she closed her eyes she resolved not to sleep a wink, and to be the first one out of the room in the morning. She simply had got to manage a smoke somehow or she would go to pieces.

But in spite of her resolves sleep took her unawares, and she was the last one to awaken in the morning.

Jane was poking her when she finally struggled up to face a bitter world once more.

"Wake up, Betts! Dad says we must be down to breakfast in five minutes."

Eleanor felt refreshed. In spite of the rebellion of her children, and the approach of poverty, her heart somehow was lighter. They were all together. They were on their way—somewhere, and Chester seemed almost happy, as he knocked at their door and asked how near ready they were. There was the old glad gay lure in his voice that there always had been when they all went off anywhere for a frolic. The journey that had been begun in gloom and sadness, might yet end in victory, and a reasonable amount of comfort. She resolved to enjoy it while she could. If Chester had sad news to tell her tomorrow when he had settled down to face the future, she would try to bear it sweetly, and help him in every way she could. It would be good to have this one more day together to look back upon just as if nothing had happened to interrupt their glad life.

And, too, there was a sense of security about having the children all there together where she could be sure what they were doing and what they were not doing. All the fears of the day before, all the awful happenings that had made her afraid to think about her children, seemed to have vanished with this morning's sun, and not even Betty's glooms as she arose, and donned her brief apparel at her mother's command could quite put her back in her wretchedness.

Breakfast was a dream.

A wide lowbrowed room with a great open fireplace at one end, high enough and wide enough for one to stand within its enclosure, the fire leaping over great back logs as if it loved them, as if it were a part of a happy pleasant place. The walls were painted white, with sheer white ruffled curtains tied back from the small-paned old-fashioned windows. The floor was wide old boards scrubbed to glistening white and sanded. The tables and chairs were painted apple green, and the linen that dressed them was glistening white and immaculate. It was as if they were guests in a comfortable old farm house where everything was ordered for beauty and peace. The neat maids in simple print dresses and white aprons brought oatmeal that would put to blush its sister cereals in other stopping places; brought rich yellow cream in fat little apple green pitchers; brought sausage and fried potatoes so crisp and well seasoned that they seemed some lordly dish; brought golden brown wheat cakes, light as a feather, and coffee fit for a prince to drink. There were plates of golden honey in the comb, and willow baskets filled with deep purple grapes. The children ate and ate, and could not bear to leave a crumb.

Betty drank two cups of that strong delectable coffee, and felt better. So did Chris. They had eaten of everything, even the despised oatmeal, until they were ready to burst, and when they finally gathered their effects and packed themselves once more into their car in the wide cobbled square, they were reluctant to leave the queer old-fashioned inn. There was in their general attitude more of the spirit of holiday than any of them had felt the day before, and they rode away into the morning with a certain feeling of adventure that was almost enjoyable. They had almost forgotten that they were being kidnapped.

The sun was shining when they drove away. The bare brown branches were picked out against the sky like brown lace. The little streams they passed glistened in the sunlight. The brightness flooded everything and made the meanest home they passed seem cheerful. There was a briskness in the air that brought a smile to the faces of people on the street.

The sun was still shining fitfully as they skirted New York to avoid the heaviest of the traffic, though deep blue clouds the color of ink stains were looming on the horizon.

Chester eyed them anxiously as he speeded on every clear stretch of road, and pressed on long after the others had owned they were hungry.

"We're going to have some bad weather, I'm afraid," he said once when they came to a long detour that was bound to delay them.

They had a late afternoon luncheon at a small smug town hotel, not half so well cooked as their breakfast had been, nor nearly so intriguing in its menu. Underdone chicken and heavy biscuits, elaborate salad on wilted lettuce, elaborate desserts, ice cream and pie and pastry, but it did not satisfy as the morning meal had done.

Chester hurried them out to the car again, paused to give a few careful directions, and point out something on the map to Michael, then, with another anxious look at the sky he put Chris at the wheel and they started on again.

The sun was making no pretense of shining now. It seemed to have erased itself from the heavens. The sky was overcast with thousands of cluttery blue-black

fragments of cloud, hurrying busily here and there at
cross purposes, some lazing and blocking the way for
others. It gave the sky an uneasy, unrestful appearance.
The whole family felt it. Doris and John fidgeted, and
wanted to get out and walk, wanted to stretch out full
length and rest, wanted to ask innumerable questions.
The whole little company began to have a breathless
feeling as if they were running a race, and even Eleanor
began to look out at the clouds anxiously, and finally
suggested timidly that perhaps they ought to find a place
to stop for the night if there was going to be a storm.

Then suddenly they came upon a forest, standing up
before them in serried ranks, like beautiful soldiers in
battle array, lifting dark lovely arms of fir and balsam,
and pine. Spires of white birch were etched delicately
against the plumy branches of the evergreens. The road
was covered with pine needles, hushing their going till the
way seemed almost weird.

Down into a narrow dirt road they dashed, amid the
winter grandeur, a moss-banked brook at the side, with a
sudden bridge across it made of great logs put corduroy
fashion, rumbling like thunder as they flew over; a road so
narrow that two cars could not pass. They wondered what
would happen if another car came in sight. But none
came.

A casual railroad leaped across in front of them in
an occasional break in the woods, no sign of its being, no
voice of engine or warning word, no hint of station or
possible train to travel it, just a shining track left there
alone in a great crack in the vast forest. It seemed like
some forgotten toy of a forgotten generation.

Now and then they came out of the forest for a mile
or two to skirt some gleaming lake, its waters like the
polished sheen of gunmetal in the gloom of the cloudy
winter afternoon; then into the forest again, and on,
through the narrow quiet road that seemed to wear an
eerie light of mystery. The tinkling brook was much
farther below them now, and at the next turn, close below
them, they saw a great stone covered with vivid moss and
lichens in the midst of a tiny torrent.

"Oh," the children exclaimed, "oh, Daddy! Let us get out and climb over on that stone!"

"Yes, Daddy! Stop! I never saw a stone like that!" cried Jane.

"There will be other stones," said Chester. He was looking up at the clouds.

They began to climb upward, and still the serried ranks of trees seemed climbing with them. But when they came out into the open again, across another casual railroad that ambled through the wilderness, there were slow lazy flakes drifting down through the leaden air, and the sky overhead seemed to hold a menace.

It was not half an hour before the few lazy flakes had become millions, great fat wide flakes, like small blankets, hastening, blurring and blotting the landscape from sight. They clung to the windshield and when the windshield wiper slushed them off they froze again in a fine blur over the glass and made it almost impossible to see the way ahead.

Eleanor was almost glad when the road wound into the woods again because here the snow was not so thick, being held off by the branches overhead; and yet, there was a kind of feeling of insecurity about it all that made her apprehensive. She began to wonder if it had been wise to come off like this in the dead of winter into a strange wild place where they knew nothing about anything, or anybody. She eyed her husband anxiously, but though his face was grave, he did not look worried, more as if he were eager.

They were passing few villages now, although there were lakes with summer cottages circling about them. But in the gathering dusk they made desolate cheer with their boarded up windows. There were no stars and the moon seemed to have been blotted off the heavens.

Chester had taken the wheel again himself during the last hour, and was driving ahead as if he saw a definite goal not far away. He seemed to be well satisfied at each small landmark, never hesitating which way to turn at a crossing.

"Are you sure you know the way, Chester?" Eleanor

ventured at last. "It looks so all alike," she added fearfully.

"Positive!" said Chester cheerfully. "I knew every twig and stone for miles around this region when I was a boy."

"It would be some stunt for you to get lost in a dump like this!" sneered Betty.

The children looked at their father wonderingly, and stared out into the dark night again. Somehow he seemed unfamiliar. It had never been a reality before to them that he had been a boy. Chris stared out at the murky shadows and grew thoughtful. He wondered what it would have been like to have been a boy with Dad. He was a pretty good scout sometimes. He would have been a peach of a kid.

"Didya go a fishing?" suddenly called out John, who was supposed to be asleep.

"I sure did," said Chester. "Remember that great boulder we saw down in the creek below the log bridge this afternoon? I used to sit on a boulder like that hour after hour and fish for trout. I'm not sure but that boulder may be there yet. We'll take a look some day."

"Gee!" said John sleepily, and dozed off again.

It began to seem as if the last forest they had entered was interminable, but suddenly they came out upon a fairy scene,—the dull sheen of dark water, set in white velvet, and lit by the clustering constellations of a little town on its farther bank.

"There she is!" exclaimed Chester excitedly, almost as John might have said it. "Right across there. That's the town where I used to go Saturdays to buy things for mother; shoes, and sugar, and corn to feed the chickens!"

Betty sat up and stared coldly at the few bright lights.

"Is that all there is of it?" she asked contemptuously, and relapsed into her corner again as if she had no further interest.

They drove through the little country town that lay snugly under its new white blanket of snow. The roofs were blanketed and hung with festoons already, and the streets looked deserted. Only a few houses showed lights in the lower floors, for the hour was growing late for country folks. The stores were closed and shuttered. To all intents and purposes it was midnight in the main street of Wentworth.

Chester slowed down the car, and looked eagerly about him, driving as if he loved it all. Even under the snow it looked clean and good and homely to his weary eyes. If only he could find his mother waiting at the journey's end as he used to in the boyhood days! If only he might take Eleanor to her, and his children. She would have known what was the matter with his children. She would have told him what to do with them! Had he drifted away from her teaching that he did not know himself what to do for them?

At the end of the short street Chester made a sharp turn to the right, up a hill, and was presently plunged once more into midnight darkness, with the tall forest on either hand.

Eleanor's heart sank.

"Don't you think, dear," she said leaning forward and speaking hesitantly, "wouldn't it be a good idea to just go back to that little town and stay at the hotel all night? You are so tired—we all are tired."

"Hotel's closed this time of year."

"Well, then, somebody must take strangers. Couldn't we enquire?"

"No, Eleanor, it wouldn't do. You know I telegraphed to Jim Hawley to expect us. He has the key and I told him to have the fires lighted and the lights going. He might wait up all night for us. It's only a couple of miles farther now."

The children began to stir restlessly, breathing on the windows and trying to peer into the impenetrable darkness. Eleanor's heart grew strangely heavy. What was coming next? She was so weary it seemed as if she could bear no more strain.

A few minutes later they stopped at a little shanty of logs, where a lantern was slung out over a rude porch.

Chapter XI

A woman opened the door as the car stopped and came out shading her eyes with a worn hand.

"Is this Mrs. Hawley?" asked Chester lowering the window and speaking into the snowy atmosphere. His voice sounded strange and shut in as voices sound when children play under a tent of quilts.

"Yes. I'm Jim's mother. And this'll be Mr. Thornton. I remember you when you was a little kid."

"Jim got my telegram then?" asked Chester impatient to be gone. "Is he over at the farm?"

"Yes, he got the telegram, leastways I did. Murdock brought it over this morning on his way back from his milk route. But Jim he's broke his leg, Mr. Thornton. A tree fell on him, and busted him all up. He's flat on his back fer a spell I guess. Don't 'spose he'll be much use till Spring now. Yes, he's awful sorry he couldn't do nothin' fer ya, Mr. Thornton. Yer Ma was allus so awful good to him when he was a little kid and sickly like. But you'll find plenty o' wood. Jimmy he stowed it up in the wood shed thinkin' it might be needed. An' I managed to git up there myself to-day an' dust around and lay a few fires. You ain't got nothin' to do but touch a match to 'em. Sorry I can't take you all in, but we ain't got a fire only in one room, and the rest o' the house is cold as charity. You'll be more comfortable in yer own place. But I kin make ya a pot of hot coffee ef you'll wait—"

"No, Mrs. Hawley," protested Chester, "we won't wait for that. We've plenty of coffee in our thermos bottle, and we'd better be getting on. Thank you just the same. Have you the key?"

"Yes, I'll get it—"

She hobbled back into the house and they noticed that she was lame.

"To think she should have taken all that trouble," said Eleanor with compassion. "Chester, that was dreadful!"

"Yes, she is a good woman," said Chester, and then reached out for the key which the old woman had brought.

"Mrs. Hawley," he said, "we feel it keenly that you should have felt it necessary to leave your own work and go to the farm. I wish I had known. I'm very sorry to have put this on you when you had enough trouble of your own."

"Oh, that's all right. It give me a change to run over, and Jim he was that fidgety till I did. I couldn't get nothin' else done."

"Well, we're deeply grateful, and we'll come over to see Jim and shall hope to be able to return your kindness, as soon as we get ourselves straightened around."

They started on again leaving the old woman holding the lantern high over her head, peering after them through the snow.

"Oh, Chester! What are we going to do? Won't the house be fearfully cold?"

"We'll soon have it warm if the fires are laid. She's a faithful soul. Fancy her toiling around laying fires for us! I'm sorry it turned out this way, Eleanor, for your sake. I wanted you to see the house first under pleasant circumstances. But it can't be helped now, and we are lucky to get here before the snow gets any deeper I guess. I've been rather worried the last hour or so."

With that he turned the car with a lurch suddenly straight to the right and plunged into the deepest darkest road that Eleanor had ever experienced. There seemed no opening in the thick growth of trees. She wondered how her husband knew where the trail was.

The headlights of the car picked out the white pathway foot by foot and discovered a little brown rabbit standing startled right in the way. The children came to life at this, and even Betty thrilled with the thought of being out there in that dense woods in the snow, stretched her neck to see the little creature of the wild. It was like attending personally the scene of an educational movie.

"For Pete's sake, where are we going?" asked Betty at last roused to a shivering idea of discomfort. "What's

99

the little old idea, anyway, Chester? Do you want us to freeze to death? It looks to me as if you were trying to see how far you could go before you finished us all. And you call this a lark!"

Chester's lips shut in a thin firm line but he did not reply. He was driving carefully over ruts a foot deep, and the car lurched from side to side and wavered on like a foundering ship at sea.

It seemed hours that they were ploughing along in that narrow dark trail, though in reality it could not have been more than five minutes, before they suddenly emerged to a wide clear space, deep with snow, the air thick with great flying flakes. It was like coming to the top of the world and looking out on winter. Gradually as they hitched along more slowly yet, there emerged from out the thick whiteness an outline of a low rambling building, dark, and snow crowned, like an old woman hunched into a shawl with a heavy wool hood over her eyebrows.

Chester drew up at the side of this building, and shouted to Michael to pull in also. They all looked out in dismay. It seemed terrible to think of getting out into that whirl of driving blinding snow.

Chester, with his flashlight in his hand, got out and unlocked the door. He went inside and they could see the bobbing of the flashlight through the doorway and the windows, as he went into another room. Then there flickered up another light, yellower, steadier.

They sat and waited, and in a moment more another flare lighted up the room, wide and yellow and cheering, and the long low old farm house came alive. Chester had touched off a fire in the great old fireplace, and welcome leaped out to meet them.

Chester appeared at the doorway again, an eager smile on his tired dirty face.

"Come!" he shouted through the blizzard. "It will soon be warm in here! Chris, help your mother and the girls out while I light the other fires. We'll have a warm house in no time!"

Chris clambered out stiffly, and helped out his mother and Betty. Then he went back and carried Doris in, dumping her on a couch, and going back for wraps and bags.

Michael and his brother had already backed up the truck and were unloading boxes and bags, great packing cases of canned stuffs, and the trunks and bales of blankets.

"They all came through in great shape," smiled Michael to Eleanor, as he threw down the last bale of blankets.

Betty was walking about disdainfully studying the rooms. She felt that prison walls were about to close in upon her.

Eleanor was busying herself pouring out hot coffee from the thermos bottle for the two men, Michael and his brother.

"It seems dreadful, Chester," Eleanor was saying, "to let them go out in this storm again to-night after driving all day."

"I'm bound to get down that mountain, ma'am," said Michael smiling, "afore this snow gets any deeper. There's goin' to be drifting before morning, an' I'll feel easier if I get beyond the pass before I sleep. Jim an' I'll be all right ma'am, don't you worry, an' I wantta get back where I can telegraph my wife, fer she'll be that worried if she don't hear."

"Of course," said Eleanor sympathetically. "But are you sure it's safe to go back now in the dark?"

"Perfectly safe, ma'am, while the snow lies still, but if a wind should come up, an' she might any minute now, it wouldn't take long to put that pass twelve or fifteen feet deep. O' course there's other roads, but not so quick, and Jim and I figure we'll get down the mountain, and beyont the pass now while the goin' is passable, and then we'll take our rest. Good-bye ma'am, an' I hope you find everything all right, and get along fine—"

Betty and Chris listened as though they heard the keys to their cell turning in the lock. So, Michael and Jim were going back! Then who was going to do things for them? Were there servants in this strange desolate place to which they had been brought?

101

Chester stayed out in the snow with Michael and Jim for a few last words, but Eleanor shut the door and came over near the fire.

"Isn't this wonderful!" she said cheerily, though they could see she was terribly worn and tired. "I've dreamed of a fireplace like that! I was beginning to be chilled clear through."

"I'd much rather have a hot water radiator!" said Betty contemptuously.

"We'd better undo these blankets at once and spread them out to take the chill off them before we start to make up the beds. Come Betty, get to work."

Betty reluctantly drew off her gloves, and Chris without being asked untied the lug ropes that bound them together.

"I can't see what was the idea of prancing off here to do all this hard labor," said Betty. "Why not stay at home and work if it had to be? Is it just a gesture, or what?"

But nobody answered her. Eleanor was spreading out the blankets in front of the fire.

"Isn't it funny having no electric light!" giggled Doris waking up to look around.

"Look out, Doris, don't go near the table. A candle is a dangerous thing. We'll have to get the lamps in shape as soon as possible." Eleanor lifted the candle and set it on the high mantel.

"Lamps!" said Betty aghast. "For Cat's Sake! You don't mean kerosene lamps? I draw the line at that. You can count me out if that's what you have in mind. I never saw such folly! It's perfectly *poisonous!* Chester must have gone crazy!"

"And now," said Chester coming back, stamping the snow from his feet, "isn't this cosy?" He beamed about on them with almost a happy look on his tired lined face.

"I'll say it is," said Betty contemptuously. "Cosy as the tomb! I should have thought you could have found a cemetery nearer home, but perhaps this one is cheaper!"

Chester looked at her as if she had struck him, an ashen shadow stealing over his face, but Eleanor, deliberately cheery, blithed forth:

"Yes, dear, it is wonderful! I'm going to love it, I'm sure. Now Chester, we need some more light and let's see how many beds we can get ready in a jiffy. These children need to be put to bed, they are too cross to live with."

"Yes," said Chester, "I have five pounds of candles here—" He picked up a box by the door. "If I remember rightly there are candle sticks in every room. We'll touch off the fires in the air tight stoves, and you don't know how quickly you will have nice comfortable rooms, everywhere. Old-fashioned stoves beat the furnaces for quick heat every time."

He led the way up a quaint staircase leading from a large hall covered with old oilcloth in tesselated gray and black blocks. The stair rail was mahogany, and the rises were painted white.

Eleanor followed Chester, urging sleepy little Doris. The other children remained huddled in the big living room where they had arrived looking about with alien eyes.

"Some dump!" commented Chris slumping into a grandfather's chair that would have been almost worth its weight in gold in a New York antique shop.

"Isn't it perfectly poisonous!" responded Betty turning from a survey of a snow plastered window pane, "I've a notion to go out and sit in the car."

"You can't," said Chris shortly. "It's gone!"

"Gone? What do you mean? I mean our car."

"Well, I say it's gone."

"But how could it go?"

"Jim drove it. Whaddaya 'spose he came along for?"

"You don't mean we're stranded in this desert without a car?"

"I said it."

"Chris Thornton! I shall go raving insane!"

"Good stunt!" responded Chris. "Might enliven the desert."

"Chris, did you manage to get anything?"

"Not a red."

"I'm just ready to pass out."

"Same here."

Jane eyed them knowingly.

"You needn't be so terribly mysterious. I know what it is you're talking about. Cigarettes. I'm not dumb! I guess I've smoked cigarettes, too!"

"Shut up you baby! We were speaking of chocolates. If you go blabbing what we say you'll get what's comin' to you, that's all," threatened Chris.

"So will you if you call me baby any more," said Jane impishly. "I'm going upstairs and choose the best bed!" and she vanished into the hall.

The big old farm house had a hall running through the centre upstairs, with rooms on each side, and then down three steps from the top of the stairs, rooms rambling off again over the back wings of kitchen and sheds. They seemed vast chambers with their great old four-poster beds, and their fine old mahogany chests of drawers. Eleanor, tired as she was, could not refrain from laying an admiring hand on the rare old wood, and exclaiming over some particularly fine old specimen of a chair or little bedside table.

She chose the right-hand front chamber for Chester and herself, with the room connecting just back of it for Jane and Doris. Betty was assigned to the room across the hall from her mother's, and Chris and John in the room back of that. There would be plenty of room for each of the children to have separate quarters later if it seemed feasible, but to-night the main thing was to get everybody to bed as comfortably and quickly as possible. There were air tight stoves downstairs with drums in the two back upper chambers, and a gradual warmth was beginning to penetrate the whole house, though it still felt damp and chilly.

"Chris," called Chester, "you and John come with me and bring up several armfuls of wood. We've got to keep fires going all night."

"We can't go out in all this snow and get wood," growled Chris.

"You don't have to," laughed his father. "Come this way. If I'm not much mistaken you'll find the kitchen shed full. Come on, you wouldn't make much of a pioneer."

"I should say not!" responded Chris disgustedly. "I think the world has got beyond that stage. There's no sense in living the primitive life in these days!"

He flung a meaningful glance at Betty with whom he had just been discussing their father's failure in merciless terms. They both felt that he had no right to fail when he was responsible for them. They felt that he was taking their discomforts in altogether too blithe a manner and needed reproving.

Chester carried a candle and set it on a high shelf in the kitchen and put another in the kitchen shed. Chris came slowly after him. He stared about at the great rambling shed with its rough floor and high rafters, unlike any room he had ever looked upon before, reaching out into weird shadows of seemingly illimitable proportions. It might have been a barn or storehouse, a warehouse perhaps, but what a peach of a gym it would make! His mind wandered to basketball vaguely. Perhaps if one worked things rightly there might be some fun left in the desert after all, that is provided there were any natives near enough in the wilderness to make up two teams.

Along the entire length of one wall was a huge pile of wood, neatly cut in stove lengths, and fireplace lengths, and over it the one candle shed the weirdest play of light and shadow. Chris reluctantly consented to carry an armful of wood into the living room, and slowly returned for another, while John, fully awake now, and delighted with the kitchen shed carried three.

Betty and Jane meantime had been requisitioned for bed making, and the house took on an atmosphere of liveliness, with cheerful voices calling back and forth, and candles flickering in every room. The old house had not seen the like for almost twenty years. Chester came up the stairs with an armful of wood humming an old tune, "We'll stand the storm, it won't be long, We'll anchor by and by—"

Unconsciously he had chosen an old favorite of his father's. It seemed somehow to have been a part of his childhood waiting for him in the old house, come to his heart to welcome him. As he went down the stairs for another load he began to hum and the old words came back to him unconsciously:

> *"Should earth against my soul engage,—soul engage,*
> *Should Earth against my soul engage,—soul engage,*
> *Should earth against my soul engage, and fiery darts*
> *   be hurled,*
> *Then I can smile at Satan's rage,*
> *   And face a frowning world. We'll stand—"*

"Listen at Dad!" said Betty with a wondering look on her face as she paused in the flinging of a warm sweet smelling sheet across her great grandmother's bed to Jane who was supposed to be helping make the beds. "I never heard him sing like that! Never!"

"*I* think it's going to be *fun!*" declared Jane, catching the sheet and vigorously tucking it in on her side.

Betty suddenly froze into a frown.

"Help yourself!" she said bitterly. "Not me! I'm not accepting things like this when they're wished on me."

"What'r ya going to do about it?" mocked Jane.

"I'll find something to do, mighty quick, and don't you forget it, Janie!" affirmed Betty mysteriously.

"Well, if you want my opinion, Betts, you're a fool not to take the fun while it's going. All us here together like this, and Dad and Mother playing along with us, I think it's going to be great."

"It's poisonous, Jinny, just perfectly poisonous! And you'll find out quick enough. Just wait till you have to fill a lamp, precious! I've heard about lamps. They smell to heaven, and you never can get your hands clean afterward. Sort of a Lady Macbeth act, darling. Not all the rain in the sweet heavens and all that sort of thing. You know you've had that in school. Only in this case it would be snow of course. Did you ever see snow like that? I ask you. Look at the window panes, perfectly obliterated, and there's a pile of snow on every window sill! Will you look? Isn't this the grandest dump for the Thornton family to be arrived in, caught like rats in a trap."

"I think it's fun!" said Jane stoutly.

106

"Help yourself!" yawned Betty, "I pass."

"Betty dear," called Eleanor, "come down and get something to eat."

"Thanks! Nothing doing!" shouted Betty rudely. "I'm going to bed."

So Eleanor climbed the stairs once more and brought Betty a long thick night dress with long sleeves that she had just unearthed from the old attic trunk.

"What! Wear that thing?" refused Betty. "Not while there's life left in me to protest! I'd never expect to emerge if I once put on that antique. That's one that Noah wore in the ark, Mums."

"You'll be glad of it when you find out how cold it is here," urged Eleanor earnestly.

"Then I'll wait till I'm glad, but I think you've guessed wrong. I'll never be glad, and I think I prefer to die to the cause of suitable garments for sleeping. So if you find your little Elizabeth frozen stark in the morning you can lay it to bringing her up to the North Pole against her will, and not to the lack of Grandmama Noah's best nightgown."

"Never mind, Eleanor," said Chester coming by the door just then. "She'll come to it. Let her find out for herself. That's the best way."

Betty cast him a gleam of hate and resolved that she would freeze solid before she ever put on a thick nightgown.

At last they were all stowed away in their beds, most of them glad to get the thick garments from other days, and the hot water bottles that Eleanor had tucked in beside them. There were heaps of blankets and eider downs over all, and piles of wood by every stove. The house had lost its freezing atmosphere, and was filling with a healing warmth, and only Eleanor's teeth were chattering as she crept in at last to a well earned rest, and put her tired head on the pillow. Too weary she was to realize that it was less than forty-eight hours since she had lain and worried about this trip, and now here she was! Just glad to lie down and be warm, and know that her brood were safe for the night at least. There were thousands of things that might happen tomorrow of course, but for the night they were safe.

The candles left in the hall burned down to the sockets and blinked out. The house lay dark and still. The fires banked down, stopped crackling, and all the family slept. While outside in the wide wild night the soft flakes continued to come down, wilder and faster as the night wore on.

And the next day was the Sabbath.

Chapter XII

When the morning dawned it was scarcely perceptible, the air was so altogether filled with the beating, flying, drifting snow. Snow from above, snow from below, snow from all sides, out and over and under, a new white world, such as the children had never seen before. The old rambling farm house seemed almost snowed under, and only the smoke from the big mouthed chimneys gave any signs of life.

They slept till nearly noon, and when they awoke the whiteness prevailed over all the earth, and the air. It was as if they had been let down, house and all, to the bottom of the ocean, and were there amidst the drifting hurling eddying deep, only that the water was white, white snow in tempestuous motion. They were as isolated as if they had been wrecked at the bottom of the ocean. They stood at their various windows and looked out with varied feelings.

Chester's face was almost exultant. They were here! They were *all* here! And none of the terrible things that had attacked his children could get to them! Not for a while at least. So far they were safe.

If they had waited a day later they could not have

made it up the mountains. The drifted snows would have shut them out, and perhaps he would never have been able to manage it again, never have been able to save them from the world, the flesh, and the devil. But now they were here and God had shut them in with His snow and His terrible cold.

It was curious how old phrases from the Bible kept continually coming to him and fitting in with things. Was it just because he was here where these walls had so often echoed to the reading of the scripture, and where his father's and mother's voices in prayer had so often been heard? Had these things perhaps lingered in the atmosphere, and some undiscovered arrangement of his soul had become a human radio to set them vibrating once more? He had read that some one was trying to perfect an instrument so delicate and so far reaching that we might sometime be able to hear the voices of Moses and the prophets, of Jonah and Paul, and Washington and Lincoln again. Well, perhaps some such thing had happened here. He turned from the window with a reverent look in his eyes and called:

"Eleanor, come and see the world! We must have slept till Christmas!"

Eleanor's first word was an exclamation of anxiety:

"Chester, what can have happened to Michael and Jim?"

Chester's face sobered.

"I think they are all safe," he said. "An hour would have got them down through the village and over the pass. After that it was all clear sailing, just a big snow storm. They reached a good hotel and were fast asleep probably before we got to bed last night. Michael said there was no risk whatever. Besides, remember it is high noon, twelve full hours since they left us. There weren't three inches of snow in the pass when we crossed it, and it did not start to blow till after daylight. I was up putting more wood on the sitting room stoves and I heard it commence."

Eleanor looked up at him and found to her surprise that he did not look as worn as she had expected.

"I believe you are enjoying it, Chester," she said

wistfully, "I believe it was the very thing you needed."

"Is it going to be so very hard for you, dear?" he asked with sudden anxiety.

"Oh, no!" she said veiling her apprehension, "I believe it is almost interesting. This is such a fine old house, and there is so much to see. And we haven't been all alone together like this without anything coming between or anything we had to do, since the babies were little."

"Do you feel that too, dearest?" he said and stooped to kiss her.

Across the hall Jane was wriggling into her clothes underneath the bedclothes to keep from having to stand on the cold floor, and Betty was protesting at being waked up.

"For Pete's sake, get out of this bed!" said Betty crossly.

"Mamma says to get up. It's time to get dinner. Did you know we had slept all the morning, Betts?"

"I don't care if I sleep all the afternoon too," snapped Betty. "Go away and let me alone. There's nothing to do in this dumb dump but sleep. I don't care if I never wake up."

"Oh, but Betts! You wanta wake up and look out! It's grand. The sky and the earth are all mixed up and you can't see anything. Not anything but just snow!"

"Well, I'm sure I don't see what there is nice about that. I think it is poisonous! Just perfectly poisonous!"

"Oh, but it's going to be fun! It's going to be wonderful!"

"It isn't my idea of fun," growled Betty, and turned over to sleep more.

The twins however were overjoyed at the snow later when Jane had succeeded in rousing Betty and they all sat down to a belated meal which was neither breakfast nor lunch. Chris began to ask questions about coasting and skating.

"Oh, for the matter of that," said Chester, "there is a place only a few miles from here where they ski. It's one of the famous hills where they have the big contests. Some record jumps have been made by the great ski champions there, both Canadian and American."

"Really?" said Betty surprised out of her gloom.

"Absolutely!" said Chester with something of his old twinkle in his eyes.

Betty remembered her rôle and relapsed into silence, but Chris began to ask questions.

"Have you ever been to one of those contests, Dad?"

"I sure have," said Chester, his eyes taking on a pleasant look of reminiscing. "It was the last time I was up here in winter. I went over with your Uncle Clint. Let me see, that was, I'm not just sure what year. Surely I've told you about it before."

"Oh, gee! why weren't we along?" breathed Chris.

"It must have been the winter Mother had you all down in Florida, the time Betty was so sick. I thought surely I' would have told you about it though. It was wonderful.

"You know the whole course up there is outlined with evergreens, and strung with a perfect blaze of pennants of all colors. It looks like a vast border of flowers against the whiteness of the snow. People come from all around to see one of those meets. Perhaps we'll find a way to get there sometime ourselves. They come in sleighs and automobiles from miles away. It is a great affair. Bing Anderson made his big record leap that day of 190 feet."

"Gee, I've seen 'em in the movies," said Chris greatly excited, "but I never realized they leaped that far."

"Oh, yes, I've read that Nels Nelsen several years later leaped over two hundred and forty feet!"

Chris edged his chair nearer.

"I certainly would like to see that!" he exclaimed excitedly. "I don't see how it's done—!"

"We'll go over some day and look at the track. There's always somebody over there practicing. You know how the course is built, don't you? It's like this— here's the take-off, here's where they gain their first momentum—"

Chester took knives and salt cellars and laid it all

111

out, with greatgrandmother's Wedgwood sugar bowl for the starting hill, and crumpled napkins for other points.

"This is an iced groove—" Chester tilted a silver knife against the crumpled linen hill. "Here is a tower for the judges," he drew toward him a bottle of olives that Betty had set on the table, "and the bystanders are all along here. Why, at the carnivals I'm told even amateurs do some pretty high jumping."

"Oh, boy! I'd like to get in on something like that!" remarked Chris wistfully. "Any chance for a fella that isn't in their clubs?"

"Why, I don't know," said Chester thoughtfully, looking interestedly at his son.

"I've seen *girls* in pictures doing that—" said Jane pointedly.

"It might be that there'd be a chance for you all to try skiing somewhere around here. We'll enquire when we get settled," said her father. "That depends—" But he did not say what that depended upon.

There was a distinct silence while the children thought it over, got a thrill from just the idea of going out and skimming through space.

"It's like what I dream sometimes," said Jane thoughtfully. "I think I'm walking along on the street, and suddenly my feet somehow rise up a little off the ground and I go along just the same sort of walking on the air, getting faster and faster, only when I go real fast I have to be awfully careful not to lose my balance or I go up higher than I meant, and it kind of scares me, and sometimes I'm afraid my feet will get up over my head, they go so fast, like when you're in the water you know—"

"Why, I've dreamed that!" said Betty forgetting herself once more, and then went hurriedly on with her eating.

They finished the last of the sandwiches—only stopping to make coffee.

"We must clean out the lunch box first and not waste anything at all," said Eleanor, "for there's no telling how long this storm will shut us in from getting fresh supplies."

"Don't worry about that," said Chester, "I called up the grocer and told him to pack canned goods and groceries to last for some time. I think also there are a lot more things that Hannah put in the truck. You better investigate, some of them might not keep."

"I have," said Eleanor. "There is a pair of roasted chickens, and a great beautiful baked ham. I'm sure I don't see how she managed to get it all done in so short a time without my knowing a thing about it. There's a great big tin box full of doughnuts, too."

"M-m-m-m-m-m-mmm!" said the children in chorus.

"Well, Hannah went out before seven o'clock and got the things as soon as the stores were open," said Chester, "I just gave her a little hint that we might be needing them."

"It is really wonderful what you accomplished," said Eleanor, "We shan't have to cook for several days, and that will be nice. We shall have a chance to get acquainted with our house, and put things away."

Betty cast a frowning look at the imprisoning snow.

"How long do they keep up storms like this?" she asked at last, "I think it is perfectly poisonous to have it snow this way. I don't see how on earth we're ever to get away from here. How deep does the snow get?"

"Sometimes six or eight feet when it drifts. In fact there have been times when we have had to tunnel through worse drifts than that. When I was a boy I remember a storm that began just like this, and lasted for three days and nights—!"

"Oh, murder!" said Betty under her breath casting a frightened look toward the window.

"We don't often have such blizzards. That was the worst I ever remember. When it finally stopped snowing we could hardly get the door open. There was a drift all across the front of the house, away up to the top of the first story windows. You had to go upstairs to see out! My, but it was a beauteous sight! I remember we all went up to the attic to look out and see whether our neighbors were snowed in. It looked like velvet, spread everywhere,

and all the valleys and ugly rocky places covered. It was
like fairy land. The trees—But there! You'll see for
yourself when the sun comes out."

"I don't think it's ever coming," said Betty
disagreeably, but Chester went on with his story.

"We cleared the way from the back door to the well,
and out to the cow yard and barn. That was comparatively sheltered, and it didn't take long with all us boys
working. There was John, and Sam, and Clint, and
father; and I was almost eleven years old and did a good
share myself—"

The children sat back from the table and looked at
their father trying to think of him as only eleven years old.

"Gee!" said John and grinned toward his mother.

"Then we started to clear away the drift in front of
the house, and it was some drift! In places you could reach
the top of it from the second story windows."

"Ohhhh!"

"It was Clint that suggested we had better find out if
anybody else needed help before we began fancy digging
around the place, and he was the one that first thought of
going up to the attic to look."

"How could you tell up in the attic?" asked Chris.

"Why, you could see most of the houses in the valley
from there, and you could easily tell if anybody was
snowed under."

"Why didn't you telephone?" asked Jane.

"They didn't have telephones then, silly!" said
Chris.

"Yes, the telephone had been invented, but it hadn't
penetrated these parts then," said Chester, "and if it had
we couldn't have afforded to have one. People were poor
in those days. We got our living from the soil. But when
we looked we could see smoke coming cheerfully up from
most of the houses, showing that they had fires, and in
some places we could see that the men were out digging
paths around the houses. But there was one house, just
below the brow of a windswept hill, that seemed to have
been utterly obliterated. There wasn't even a dark streak
where the chimney ought to have been, and not a wisp of
smoke in the air above it."

"How did you know there was any house there at all?" asked Doris eagerly. She was sitting on a little old-fashioned stool by the fireplace now, her cheeks red as roses, and listening with all her might. Doris loved a story.

"Oh, we knew every house in the neighborhood of course, just as you know every one who lives on your own street. And besides, that special house was where Letty Cameron and her mother lived alone, and they were very poor. Mr. Cameron had died the year before after a long illness and Letty and her mother had had a hard time getting on. They took in sewing and Letty taught in the district school over on the other side of the hill. Letty was a pretty girl, and Clint had been going with her more or less, taking her to singing school and going over there to cut wood for them sometimes. And when there wasn't any sign of smoke coming from the chimney, I could see Clint was very much disturbed, and so was Father.

"He asked Clint how much wood he had cut the last time he was there, and Clint said 'Plenty.' They talked about it a minute or two, and then Father said we must go and see. They got out the old bob-sled and hitched up the horses, but the drifts were so deep they had to keep stopping to shovel themselves out. I remember Mother didn't want me to go along, but Father said, 'Oh, let him go! He's got to learn to be helpful and he's getting a big boy now.' I was so proud to be allowed to go along. But it was a long time before we got down to the road. By that time they had got out the old snow plow down in the village, and part of the way the road was broken. We stopped and got some other men and boys to go along, and then struck into the back road that led to the Cameron cottage. It was an exposed road and terribly drifted. I remember wishing several times that I had stayed at home, my hands got so cold, and my feet felt as if they didn't belong to me. But there were eight or ten men with us by that time, and at last we reached the Cameron house. But it was all snowed under except one or two windows on the second floor.

"When we shouted, nobody answered, and when at last we tunnelled through to the side door and knocked, nobody answered. The men talked about it a minute or two and decided the Camerons had gone to somebody's house to stay till the storm was over, but Clint insisted that we ought to go in and see, and so at last Father put his shoulder to the door and wrenched it open.

"I remember how solemn we all felt just as if we were house breakers, as we went marching solemnly in. Father told Clint to go ahead as he was kind of a friend and was often there, and when they got into the kitchen where they lived mostly, they saw why there hadn't been any smoke from the chimney. There was plenty of wood piled around the hearth, as if they had brought it in from the shed to be ready for cold and storm, but the fireplace was completely smothered in snow, and snow lay away out over the floor for a couple of feet. You see, the stone that is put across the top of the chimney to keep things from falling down, had blown off in the storm, and the snow had come down and put out the fire, probably fallen down in great quantities. The Camerons were unconscious, almost frozen to death. They were huddled in each other's arms in the bed, with all the blankets they had piled over them, but it was bitter cold and the wind and storm had been rushing down the chimney for hours.

"I don't think either of them ever quite recovered from the shock. Mrs. Cameron had pneumonia the next winter, and Letty was never strong after that. My brother Clinton married her a few weeks later and went to live down at their house. He seemed to have aged during that day. I never saw anyone work so hard in my life as Clint did, digging that tunnel to the house. He was all bound up in Letty."

"Was that my aunt Letty that died?" Jane asked with awe in her voice.

"Yes, she only lived about five years after their marriage, and Clint has never got over it. He can't seem to settle down, just travels from one place to another, doesn't care to have a home any more."

Betty got up suddenly and walked to the window blinking out at the deep white lace of the snow on the pane.

"I think this is a *terrible* place!" she said in a choking

voice, "I don't know why anybody would stay in it, *ever!* It's perfectly *poisonous!*"

"Aw, cut out that poison business, Betts. You've overworked that word for two days now!" declared Chris gruffly.

"Well, now," said Chester with compunction in his voice, "I'm sorry I've given you that feeling, little girl. I was just reminiscing. It didn't occur to me that it would be depressing. This really is a lovely place and I want you to grow to like it as much as I did."

"I never shall!" said Betty violently, "I hate it! It's just like a prison. It's perfectly poi—"

"There you go again, Betts, with your poison!" interrupted Chris. "You're a pain in the neck, you are! If we can't have a little holiday, sort of a vacation—"

"Holiday!" uttered Betty witheringly. "Do you call this a holiday? A vacation? Come out here to smother under a blanket of snow! The worst of it is there won't be anybody to dig us out when the storm is over if it ever is!"

Chester cast a look of despair on Eleanor and sighed heavily.

Eleanor laughed, although she was far from cheerful herself.

"Well, you know, Chester, that wasn't exactly a cheerful story you told about people freezing to death. Come, let's do something pleasant. Betty, why don't you look over those books. Perhaps you'll find something really interesting to read. There ought to be some rare old books in a collection like that. I confess I'm curious to see them."

"There wouldn't be anything among those fusty old-fashioned things to interest me," said Betty with her nose in the air and a fine contempt sitting on her shrugged shoulders.

"Yes, there would, Betts, here's the very thing. Suits you just down to the ground. Fox Book of Martyrs. Come and try it!" said Chris holding out a faded old volume with tattered edges to its yellowed pages.

"I think you're all perfectly horrid!" said Betty bursting into tears and rushing up the stairs to her bed where she was heard to fling herself down and weep.

Chester started to follow her, his face full of distress.

"Let her alone, Chester," said Eleanor. "Let her cry it out. She's all strung up. You must remember you never crossed her in anything before in her life. It is hard for the child."

Betty cried herself to sleep, and did not come down again until night had settled over the world, and a pleasant smell of something cooking came luringly up the stairs.

Chapter XIII

There were lamps burning brightly in all the rooms, and a great fire of logs in the fireplace in the living room. Now and then a spit of snow came down the chimney to sizzle in the fire as a reminder that the blizzard was still in full force outside, but the house had a cheerful look.

They had all been at work getting things into order. The suitcases were gone from the living room, the packing boxes had vanished from the dining room, the canned things were standing in neat rows on the big old pantry shelves on clean newspaper shelf covers, and the two roasted chickens were in the oven sending out a delicious smell every time the oven door was open. There was really something like a regular dinner set out on the table. Bread freshly cut from the loaves that Hannah had providently wrapped in double wax paper, a plate of butter, a dish of preserves, another of olives, potatoes roasted in their skins, a corn pudding just out of the oven. Really they had done wonders for their first real meal in the house. Betty slid into her vacant chair and when she had eaten looked less forlorn.

118

"Now," said Eleanor when they had finished, "we'll all work together putting things away. Jane, you and Daddy may put the food away in the closet we cleaned. You know where everything belongs now. I will wash the dishes, and Chris and Betty may wipe. Thank fortune we have plenty of dish towels. Hannah remembered to put them in. I never would have thought of them. Here, Betty, put this apron on. You mustn't get that dress dirty. There's no cleaner here to call every Tuesday and bring things back Friday. We'll have to look out for our cleaning ourselves. John, you and Doris wash your hands and be ready to carry the dishes to Jane to put in the cupboard."

It didn't take long when they all worked, and though Betty did not enter into the affair with any degree of heartiness, she yet managed to do her part, and in a very short time the kitchen was cleared up and the table set for breakfast the next morning.

"Now," said Betty dismally, consulting her little wrist watch. "For Pete's sake what shall we do? It's only seven o'clock and a long evening ahead!"

"Not so long, Bettykins," said her father gently. "People go to bed at nine o'clock in the country you know."

"For Cat's Sake, what for?" said Betty.

"Well, because they have to get up in the morning, I guess."

"I don't see how they exist!" moaned Betty.

"Come on," said Eleanor coming in from the kitchen rolling her sleeves down, "we're going to have a sing now. Jane and I found the old melodeon this afternoon and Chris mended one of the reeds so it goes pretty well. Where are those old singing books you said you found, Chester?"

"Right here on the shelf," said Chester eagerly. He was pleased as a boy at the prospect.

"Oh Heck!" groaned Betty, but accepted the book and slunk down on the corner of the old sofa that Chris had drawn up to one side of the fireplace.

"Try number ten," said Chester eagerly sitting down

near a lamp, "we always used to begin with that every Sunday night. Father liked it. He had a good deep bass voice and Clint always sang tenor."

Jane went to the melodeon and pumped away vigorously at the pedals.

> "On Jordan's stormy banks I stand,
>   And cast a wishful eye,
> Toward Canaan's fair and happy land
>   Where my possessions lie."

they sang; only Chris gave Betty's foot a brotherly kick and loudly substituted Briardale for Canaan with a meaningful look at his sister.

"How perfectly torturous that instrument is!" said Betty as they finished the seven verses and began to turn pages over in search of another.

"Torturous is good!" said Chris, "only don't overwork it like you did the poison."

"Shut up!" said Betty, and curled up disconsolately in one corner of the sofa again.

They sang "The Lord's my Shepherd," "Rock of Ages," "Just as I am," and then they sang "Happy Day," and "Happy Land" for the children, and Chester's face looked so rested and happy as he sang the old tunes to the cracked accompaniment of the old melodeon, that even Betty refrained from further contemptuous remarks.

"We always sang in the evening," said Chester, when they were quite hoarse with singing. "It's a pleasant custom. I wonder why we never kept it up!"

"I don't see how you got time," said Betty sarcastically.

"What did they have to do?" said Jane. "They couldn't farm in the night time."

"Oh, we had plenty to do," said Chester. "There was wood to cut and pile in the woodshed, and if we stayed out skating after school we had it to do after supper. There were lessons to get, and we all sat around the table with the big student lamp in the centre and studied till nine o'clock. Then Father always got the big Bible and drew up to the table, and we children scattered around the room,

Emily by mother's side, and the boys around the room, and we sang first, two or three hymns."

"Who played?" asked Jane quickly.

"Nobody," said Chester. "We just sang. The melodeon was an importation of later years, bought for Emily to take lessons on. She got so she could play for worship about the time I went away to college and I only remember that when I came home at vacations."

"Aunt Emily was the one that married a missionary and went to Africa, wasn't she?"

"Yes," said Chester, with a sad note in his voice. "We never saw her again. She died of jungle fever after she'd been there about five years, but she was a dear little sister. Pretty too. She looked a good deal like Betty. I remember the last worship we had before her wedding. Father read the ninetieth psalm, and I shall never forget his prayer that night."

He was silent for a moment, and Eleanor spoke, as if for the moment she and her husband were alone together.

"Yes," she said thoughtfully, "I've often missed it. We always had family worship in my home too, you know. I never cared so much about it when I was a girl, but after I went away I really missed it sometimes. It is strange how sweet home grows when we once get away from it forever."

"I don't know why we never had it," said Chester. "I've often thought I'd start it some day. It seemed the right thing to do, especially since they made me an elder in the church, but somehow the time never seemed to come."

"Yes, I know," said Eleanor, "I don't see how we could, with school so early, and you having to rush off to business meetings at night so much. But it would be nice. The children don't realize what they've missed—"

Betty looked bored, and Chris began to whistle a tune from the hymn book, although it sounded much more like the jazzy thing they sang in the pool room the night he played his last game than it did like any conceivable hymn.

"Of course we could have it here," said Eleanor hesitantly.

There was a long pause. Chester looked a little startled. At last he said:

"I suppose we could."

He rose and went over to the old bookcase that ran from floor to ceiling on both sides of a corner of the room and selected a large old worn book. He came slowly back, turning the leaves.

"Here's the old family record," he said. "'Emily, born April 7th, 1880; Clinton born November 10th, 1885; Esther,'—that's the little sister that died when she was only a month old. My! How this carries me back! There, Mamma, you read something to us!"

He laid the old Bible down in Eleanor's lap and retreated to his chair, sitting down with his hand shading his eyes. The children watched him curiously, embarrassedly. This was not the father they knew, who joked and kidded them, and bought them grand ·presents, and humored them, and went off to business most of the time. This was somebody they would have to get acquainted with all over again.

Eleanor opened the book hesitantly, studied the record for a moment, then turned the leaves aimlessly.

"Where was it you said your father read the night before Emily went away?" she asked fumbling among the leaves.

"The ninety-first psalm."

Eleanor found the place and read:

"He that dwelleth in the secret place of the most High shall abide under the shadow of the Almighty. I will say of the Lord, He is my refuge, and my fortress: my God, in Him will I trust. Surely He shall deliver thee—"

The words sounded strangely to the children as they sat wondering, shy, wishing it was time to go to bed. Yet the words fitt?d the strange setting of the quaint old room, lovely with furnishings of the past, flicker of firelight, candle glow, and the wild dark storm clashing at the window panes.

A sudden gust shook the kitchen door and set it banging, and John tiptoed to shut it, glad of the relief from sitting still so long, wishing he might find a mouse in the pantry, or a strange dog in the kitchen to break the monotony.

When he came back his mother's voice was still reading:

"There shall no evil befall thee, neither shall any plague come nigh thy dwelling. For He shall give His angels charge over thee to keep thee in all thy ways."

It seemed comforting to the twins. They stopped wriggling and began to listen. Somehow the storm did not seem so powerful after those words. Only Betty was not listening. Betty was pulling a hair out of the old horsehair sofa. She felt out of place.

When Eleanor's voice ceased and she closed the book Chester sat for a moment and then took his hand down from his face.

"Well,—" he said looking about on them with a look that was almost shy. "Well,—I suppose we should pray next."

He waited a moment and no one spoke. Then he rose and knelt beside his chair, and Eleanor too knelt, swiftly, as if she were accustomed. The children looked around startled, hardly knowing what to do. Jane followed her mother's example first, then Doris, half giggling, got down upon her knees and covering her face with her hands peeped through her fat fingers. John slid off his chair tentatively, to one knee. Finally Chris, his eyes suddenly raised to a swift survey, as if he had but just realized what was going on, got himself casually to his knees.

And now only Betty was left, curled up on her sofa staring at them all with hostile eyes. What did they all want to do that for? Were they all gone nutty together? It was the storm had got them. Well, no wonder, but she would not go crazy too!

She sat bolt upright while her father seemed to wait for her, or was he hesitating for words? It was a strange unpleasant experience. It was almost as if she were alone facing God who stood out there in the middle of the room somewhere and looked at her. Not harshly, only gently, as if she were doing something impolite to Him.

Then suddenly Betty too seemed to melt down into her sofa, head on the arm, body reclined, one knee half on the floor, a sort of a compromise between kneeling and sitting, her eyes shut to keep out the feeling of God out there in the room watching her sitting up and declining to yield to family worship.

It was a new thing for Chester Thornton to have to search for words. He was the one of all others who was always being called upon for an extemporaneous speech, in his business club, at banquets, or on social occasions in the church. Yes, and he was a standby to be called upon to pray at meetings of Presbytery, or session, or on the few occasions of late when he had found it convenient to present himself at the mid-week prayer service. As the church janitor aptly put it: "Mr. Thornton certainly can compose a handsome prayer!" And it was the general opinion of the whole church.

Yet, behold, Chester Thornton upon his knees in the old home of his childhood, surrounded by sacred and precious memories and only his wife and children present. Every word that he had ever known seemed stricken from his vocabulary.

But at last the habit of later years came upon him as he struggled and sought for words, and he opened his mouth and let habit guide it:

"Oh, Lord, we thank thee that we are permitted to meet here to-night—"

What was he saying? That was the way he usually prayed at prayer meeting after a longer absence than usual! He paused and hesitated—tried to get back to the beginning again—"Oh Lord—" and he an elder in the church! What would his children think of him! How was he to get out of this? What was it he was struggling after, that he had come up here to find? Why had he actually walked into this worship? Why, because he was longing to get for his children what his father and mother had given to him in his childhood, something clean and fine and strong that would anchor them—

"Oh—Lord—*Father!*" with a desperate ring to his voice, "Show us all what to do—! Amen!"

There was a moment's tense silence and then they all rose, awkwardly, in the garish candlelight, blinking because their eyes had been closed, and there had been near-tears behind their lashes.

Only Eleanor had an exalted look upon her face.

Betty had stolen away silently, while a log in the fireplace fell down in a shower of sparks and made a soft lush sound of parting ashes. Stolen up the stairs so quietly and swiftly that no one noticed her going. She might not have been there at all that evening for all they were aware of her.

Upstairs she was undressing, swiftly, silently, in the dark; creeping into bed, that she might not seem to have been present at that strange solemn ceremony downstairs, so disturbing, so somehow humiliating. She could not bear to think of her father kneeling there silent, ill at ease, in that ridiculous posture, humbling himself before an unseen Being that was not there! Of course it was all tradition, this God business. Nobody believed in it anymore. Why did her father want to make himself ridiculous with such performances! Just because it was the fashion to have what they were pleased to call family prayers when he was a kid!

Betty crept under the blankets shivering and pulled them up over her head with a dry sob, swallowed instantly. She pressed her fingers hard upon her eye balls trying to shut out the memory of her father kneeling there in the firelight with the flicker of a candle wavering back and forth in weird shadows across his head and face. But the more she tried to hide from the memory the clearer it became, until the thought of that One, whom she thought of as God, standing across the room and looking at her, became intolerable. Then she flung back the bedclothes and said aloud to herself:

"I *won't* let this get me! I'll go nuts too if I do!"

When they all came up to bed Betty was apparently fast asleep.

Some time in the night the wind ceased, and the snow stopped sifting down. The stars came out, cold and white and still.

When morning dawned there was dazzling brightness over the earth, a new created world, white as the first soul God made.

When Betty awoke she heard Jane singing like a blackbird down in the kitchen. The glare of the sun through the snow-clogged glass blinded her so that at first she could not open her eyes. There seemed to be something electric in the air, something joyous and different. In spite of her firm resolve not to yield to it, not to let anything make her enjoy what this terrible exile had to present in place of the joys she had lost, she found herself hurrying eagerly to get dressed; rushing down the stairs to see what it was all about, healthily hungry and ready for bacon and eggs and toast. Yes, even ready for despised oatmeal or anything that was to be had.

The boys went out with their father immediately after the meal was finished, and Jane was not far behind, in one of the old despised sweaters, and some queer woollen leggings, her feet in goloshes and her hands in an old pair of socks she had found in a knitting bag in the living room. Betty took a broom and followed.

It was very exciting.

Father and the boys had only cleared about a foot from the door yet, and she had to wait until there was room for her to work also. It was most amazing, this great white wall that shut out all sight of the outer world, high as the door, even higher in places, hardly room to get the handle of the shovel out.

Father seemed to know just how to slide the great snow shovel in to take out a mountain of the white feathers and fling it far out of the way, over where the wind had blown a place almost down to the ground. Chris was smaller, not so tall nor stout as Father, yet he was managing pretty well too. And presently Chester got Jane and John to work going toward the back while he and Chris worked toward the front. At last there was a path out into an open place where there were no drifts, and where the snow was only about a foot deep, blown hard and dry and crusty, and they could all come out and stand.

Eleanor put on her fur coat and came too. And there they got their first view of the new white world. They stood in awe and silence and looked, their eyes almost blinded by the glare of the snow. Out across the wide sweep of snow-clad meadow, sloping gently away and down, where gaunt birches waded knee deep, and sometimes almost neck deep in plumy whiteness, and where heavy laden evergreens dipped lacy dark fingers into the foam. They looked to eternal other hills of whiteness just like theirs, hill beyond hill, rising to shadowy mountains, snow capped, and furred with heavy hanging hemlocks.

It is safe to say that none of them save Chester had ever looked on such an awe-inspiring, breath-taking scene before, and they stood and gazed, without even the wish to speak, so beauty-startled were they with the sight. They looked till eyes went blind with the glory of it, and bodies shivered with the clear cold. Yet when they went in they had to come straight out again, as if it would be gone before they could get back. Such wonder! Such appalling beauty! Such spotlessness! So much of it in such vast reaches! Even Chris could hardly keep on working.

"Good night! If some people could see that! If they just could! Why, good night! We might advertise and charge admittance! Oh boy! Wouldn't we get rich quick! Nothing poisonous about that, is there Betty?"

But Betty had gone inside. It was too great! She could not bear it. She felt as if she had been snatched away from the regular commonplace world of reality to which she belonged and set down in a spirit world where she was all out of harmony, and it was choking her. She went in and went upstairs and made all the beds! She actually did, virtuously, without being told, absenting herself from the great world show belowstairs. Not even trying to look through the impenetrable tracing on the window panes.

Till suddenly, reaching her mother's room in her rounds, she came full upon the display of lacy frost work lit up by the full blaze of the winter's sun. She had to stop and exclaim in ecstasy.

Such elfin blades, with fairy towers, and fern work,

127

such carvings and fret work, and little flower faces peering at her here and there from unexpected dells of asphodels—what was that phrase—yes, "celestial asphodels." All the poetry she had ever read came rushing round her asking to be expressed in words for this lovely sight.

One window was thrown up to air the room, and she seemed to be atop of the world as she advanced to close it, and saw the vast whiteness from a new angle. She caught her breath with the beauty, the almost fearsome beauty of it all, caught hold of the window frame to steady herself from the feeling that she was going to fall adown the world.

And as she looked there below her lay a little house half hidden beneath the slope of the hill, a little house with a low hanging roof, a tall chimney wide and generous, and soft lazy smoke like a plume penciling itself against the sky in a little curly smudge.

That must be the house where Aunt Letty lived so long ago, and almost froze to death in a snow storm like this! And here was she, a young girl too, alive and warm and vivid, and not hurt at all by the storm. What would it have been to have lived so long ago and be old fashioned? Wear queer clothes and long hair, teach a country school, build fires, be Victorian, and have family worship every night. Oh Heck! Just think of it!

Betty put the window down with a slam and switched the bed into shape, tucking the old patchwork quilt in viciously, not stopping to regard the delicate stitches of great-grandmother Thornton's sampler, exquisite and microscopically small.

Head up and chest out she stalked into Chris' room at the back of the house, feeling very virtuous that she was making beds without request. Here too she found the window wide and the sun streaming in. The view was entrancing, for there below her, down a sharp incline of whiteness, lay a great smooth table of white, almost round in circumference, and fringed by close crowded trees. Across it, wind blown and smooth as metal, flashed a broad space of silver like a great mirror giving back the sunlight in a flood of blinding light.

Chapter XIV

It was some minutes before Betty's eyes could stand the brightness enough to figure out what it could be, so startling it was, there amid the quiet white hills. A white valley like all the rest, fringed by snow decked trees, except for that flash of silver! It seemed mysterious, uncanny, as if the earth had somehow manifested a new phenomenon.

But of course! It was a lake, round and beautiful, hidden there among the pines, and frozen over likely before the snow began, for where the wind had swept it it was perfectly glassy and smooth. How wonderful! A lake all their own, and frozen like that, so perfectly! At home they had skating for only a week or ten days, or sometimes only a day or two at Christmas, and for the rest of the year they had to go to the rink, and Daddy didn't like that very much. There had always been a fuss if she let it be known she was going. He said it was too public. But skating! There might be compensations after all. Life wasn't quite so poisonous as it had looked before.

She closed the window and made the bed thoughtfully, taking care with the smoothness of each sheet and blanket. Skates! How could they get their skates? It would take perfect ages to send home for them, and maybe the skating would be all gone by the time they got here. In fact, would they ever be able to communicate with the outside world until Spring? She doubted it, all that wilderness of snow, oceans deep and impenetrable. Well, there must be some skates found somehow. Perhaps the attic might yield a store of queer old things that could be made to do.

She went downstairs with her face almost bright.

"Come on out, Betts, it's wonderful!" said Chris, coming in for something to wear on his hands, having hopelessly split the fur lined gloves he had started out with.

Eleanor opened up the trunk of old flannels that had been deposited in the woodshed the night they came and found mittens galore, old and darned and ugly, left-overs from the years, but good and warm and welcome now. Betty, peering out at the tunnel they had already accomplished to the pump, scurried back and donned anything in the way of warm garments she could lay her hands on, not excepting those despised galoshes. She came out in a red sweater, gray cap and scarf, and woollen stockings drawn over her slippers.

As she stepped back to the kitchen she stopped and called joyously, with a ring to her voice that sounded almost like the old time Betty of two years before:

"Oh, Mums! You brought our skates! You old darling! Did you know there is a perfectly precious lake down in the back yard?"

That was a morning of utter joy and excitement. Even Betty forgot that she was an exile and worked away with a broom and a fire shovel till her back ached and her cheeks needed no rouge to make her utterly beautiful.

Eleanor in the kitchen, looking out occasionally from a window pane that Chris had cleared for her, forgot her weariness and anxiety, her tormenting doubt whether they had done right to bring the children away from school just at the critical time of the year with examinations coming on, and Christmas in the offing. She forgot everything but the joy of seeing them all together working away, father and children like so many comrades shoulder to shoulder intent on getting paths everywhere, and making a way of communication with the outside world.

Their voices rang out happily, calling how many feet they had done, and how deep the drift was in his or her particular space. Happy tears welled into her eyes as she turned away and went back to the kitchen, resolved to have a wonderful dinner ready for them when they came in hungry and tired after their task was finished.

She stood amazed for a minute and read the names on the cans and packages and bags. Flour and sugar and corn meal, hominy, rice, oatmeal, and a sack of buckwheat. Tins of crackers and biscuits and cakes, glass jars and tin cans of fruits and jellies, and vegetables. Baking powder, cocoa, chocolate, even some boxes of shredded cocoanut. Bars of chocolate, cans of coffee, boxes of tea, salt and codfish and kippered herring. She could hardly think of anything that she could possibly make that did not have its ingredients all there before her. How had Chester managed it? But of course he had given it into the hands of some clerk to select the things. Poor Chester. He didn't realize how expensive that would be. She ought to have given the order and asked prices carefully, now that they were going to be poor. Well, she would hoard the dainties and deal them out little by little making them last a long time so that more would not have to be purchased again soon.

It was almost pleasant to get back to the kitchen lore of her early married days. She was hampered a little by not understanding the wood range, and constantly forgetting to poke wood down its voluminous throat, which it seemed to devour in a second, and die down in another if she did not poke it in again. It was also bewildering to have to use iron pots and pans instead of her nice smooth aluminum which she doted on at home. But a further search revealed the fact that Hannah had even managed to put in a few of those, saucepans of different sizes, and some of the cake and pie pans. That would make things easier.

Just as she had selected the materials for the meal she was planning and turned to leave the pantry she heard Chester's voice outside the window, as he slid the big shovel into the top wall of the drift that covered the pantry window and came into touch with Chris' shovel on the other side of the drift.

"Hello, Kid!" called Chester. "That you already? Good work! Having a good time?"

"I'll tell the world!" shouted back Chris happily.

She paused and watched through the window. She could just see both their faces through the top pane where the light stole down inside the big drift in a jagged line. They were working away on either side of the drift a foot apart, and the snow was giving way before them. It was hard work too. She knew they had to carry some of it back ten or twelve feet through the narrow passage they had made to get to an open space where they might deposit it.

When she turned back to the kitchen again there came the girls' ringing laughter, Betty the loudest of them all. She and Jane had formed a partnership, pelting John and Doris with snow balls in return for those they had thrown while the girls were shoveling.

Who would have believed that the Betty of yesterday could be this gay creature, playing like a child in the snow!

John had started a snow man out in an open space where the wind had blown the ground almost bare. He was rolling a great ball almost as tall as himself, and now the girls stopped snow balling and helped. When they got it as large as they could roll they made another smaller one and put it on the top of the first for a head. Jane tore some blue woollen balls from the knit cap she was wearing and stuck them in for eyes. Betty fashioned a nose from snow, and found a bit of red ribbon in her pocket which she applied like lip stick. They made arms and put mittens on for hands, and Jane took off her cap and scarf and put them on him, and then they all stood back and shouted for Dad and Mother and Chris to come and see. Altogether it was a wonderful morning, and a great deal of work got itself done.

Hungry as wolves they came in when Eleanor rang the big farm dinner bell, all talking at once, all eager to tell Mother how much each had shoveled.

It appeared they were nearly down to the road that led to the little log house at the turn. When they got there, they would be in touch with the world again, and could arrange for milk to be left at the gate each morning, and the mail and the daily paper to be brought up. But why care, after all? The load of fretfulness and anxiety to get back to the world seemed to have dropped from every shoulder.

"And Daddy," asked Betty, forgetting her recent affectation of calling him by his first name, "is that really a lake down behind the house, and is it truly frozen over, or is it only a mirage? It looks like a sheet of silver in the sun."

"Why, yes, certainly, haven't I mentioned the lake?" asked Chester composedly, helping himself to baked beans—real bean-hole beans from a can, that Eleanor had doctored with molasses and seasoning and butter and browned again in the oven. "Yes, that lake is always great. We boys used to spend every afternoon there until dark when we didn't have chores to do. And sometimes when it was moonlight—"

"Oh-h-h-h-h-hhh!" chorused the excited young people. *"Could we?"*

"We could!" said Chester happily, watching the play of pleasure on Betty's beautiful little face.

Oh, Chester was glad now he had come. He knew he was glad. He felt his prayer was being answered.

"Did you know that Mums brought our skates?" announced Betty with the air of conferring a great secret. "Yes sir, all of them," as Chris turned an eager questioning face.

"How long will it be before we can get down there?" asked Betty. "It looks miles deep in snow."

"Ah, but there's a path if you only know the way. We'll have to do a pretty bit of shovelling and it may be a day or two before we get around to the lake, but we'll get there," promised Chester.

They all slept like logs that night, going to bed at half past eight. Not even Betty made a protest. But she went to the window of Chris' room before she went to her own, and looked out on the luminous valley with its one clear little streak of moonlight from a tiny thread of a new moon, and caught her breath again at the loveliness. Strange, unreal world of beauty. It seemed as if it was all a dream. What a dandy place for a house party. If it wasn't for that old business going punk she would ask Chester to let her invite the whole class up for Christmas week, and they could give a dance, and maybe invite some of the people around the neighborhood if there were any people worth while. What a mess that Chester should have failed! She never thought a thing like that could happen to her, to be the daughter of a poor man and have to live on a farm!

And so in spite of the silver sheen in the valley, and the heap of skates in the woodshed, and the little thread of a new moon hanging over the frozen lake, Betty went to bed with an evil spirit attending, and a grudge against her father growing again in her heart. Also she longed for a cigarette, feverishly, wildly as she lay down on the old cord bed that creaked and groaned even with her light weight. A cigarette! If she could have just one. Here it was two whole days since she had had a smoke, and she hadn't been that long without one for over two years! It was fierce! Perfectly poi— But at that stage Betty fell asleep, for shoveling snow does not tend to make one wakeful.

It took two days to get shoveled down to the lake, because there was so much else to do that they couldn't work at it constantly. It was maddening to have to come in and wash dishes and carry wood. But finally the last step in the steep hill was cut and a path shoveled out on the ice to meet the wind swept silver, and they all raced up to the house to get their skates.

Mother was making doughnuts, and there was a great platter full of the hot delicious circles, freshly powdered with sugar, standing on the table. Good cheer fairly exuded from every face as they stood around eating as many as they pleased, with not a word of objection from Eleanor. She would have to mix up more dough, but after all, why not let them enjoy them while they were hot? The cold air and exercise would help to digest them, and they would likely stay out till all hours now that the ice was ready.

So they ate till they could eat no more, then shouldered their skates and flew down to the ice.

The sun was just sinking behind the farthest mountain, as they came out of the house. It looked like a ball of fire opal against the golden glitter of the departing day. Long ruby rays slithered over the crusty snow. Fine brown pencillings of birch trees made pictures against the distance.

"It looks just like a Christmas card!" said Jane. "Look Betty!" And Betty, pausing on the top of the hill to finish her last bite of doughnut, felt something like a faint thrill of appreciation for the grandeur spread out before her. Then she whirled down to the ice and putting on her skates glided away into the sunset filled with the joy of living, a child on wings flitting over the fairy dazzle of glass as lightly as a bird. Just a happy child, all her tantrums and half developed passions held in abeyance by the pure animal joy of flying along on the ice.

The next day a letter came from Dudley Weston, and two other letters from Betty's best girl friends. Betty was a woman again, with all her pride of self will, all her arrogance and fury at being kept in prison when the world she had left behind her, her world, was swinging on with dizzying whirl without her.

Betty locked herself in her bedroom to read her letters, though everybody but her father and mother were down on the ice, and even they were in conference behind closed doors over some letters they had received.

Betty read Dudley's letter first, with bated breath and eyes that burned hotly.

> "Thorny, old girl;" it began,
>
> I call it pretty lousy of your old man to step in and disconnect you the way he did up at the Tav. I must say I think he owes me several apologies, knocking me stiff right out of the blue that way. If he hadn't been your Dad I'd have knocked him cold

for that, and next time I'll do more than that if you know what I mean. Better warn him!

But anyhow, what's the little old idea doing the vanishing act? I called up your house twice yesterday and nothing doing. Gyp Magilkey says she thinks it's some parent stuff, that your Dad was mad as a hatter up at the High dance, but I told her you wouldn't stand for anybody monkeying with your rights.

Still, if the old man has got you pinned and you can't help yourself, me for the rescue! How'd you like to get married? We might try companion-ate way, it seems to be the latest now—or just go off, that's really less trouble and lots are doing it, though it isn't quite so new. Probably companion-ate would make less kick, it's more formal you know.

But say, we could get away with it in vacation and nobody the wiser, and then sometime if anybody makes a kick about anything, or we want to pull something we could spring it on 'em. Whaddya say? Mebbe I could get Gyp and Sam to come along. They'd do for witnesses. But you must let me know. Make it snappy. I'll have to make arrangements. We could make a getaway after school the Friday before Christmas. Gwen has a house party and all of us are going of course, and nobody would miss us till we were off for fair.

I can't seem to find out where you've gone. Everybody is vague. You send directions and I'll meet you where you say, and when; only don't keep me waiting and spoil the game. Better wire if you accept.

Yours to get drunk,

Dud.

P.S. The play went rotten. They put Sue Rounds in your place, but I kicked and now Gwen's going to get it, but ishkabibble if you wire O. K. I shan't be here to see. Here's hoping, and *MAKE IT SNAP-PY!*

Chapter XV

Mary Magilkey, otherwise Gipsy, had given more gossip.

Betts, you little beast! You're the limit!

Here I give up a perfectly good date to spend the night with you and help you fix up that faun costume so your mother wouldn't find out, and when I get to your house there's nobody but that ugly old woman, and she says she doesn't know when you'll return. She won't even say where you're gone, but I'm sending this through the post office. Of course they'll forward it to you if you're really away for long.

But say, you certainly did one dirty trick leaving before rehearsal. It certainly was a scream. I thought I'd pass out. Sue Rounds volunteered to take your part, said she knew it all. You know she's a wow for learning everybody's part. She's dying to get into a play sometime, and she's just hanging around ready for any little old chance like you handed out to her. But Oh, Boy! If you could have seen her make love to Dud! He glared at her like a jazz pirate and she rolled her eyes and got in that line, you know—'Oh, my dearest love! You have come back to me at last—!' I nearly died! and Lois snickered right out and Miss House shut her lips hard and shook her head severely at her. But Sue went right on with her mushy speech. I thought Dud was going to knock her down, but he caught sight of Housey's face, and grabbed her round the waist like a bag of beans, and said "Come, let's get out of here where we can talk!" and he sounded just like the chief of police come to arrest her. Honest, we all simply screamed and went into spasms and Dud put out his foot and tripped Sue and she fell flat! It was great! Housey finally dismissed the rehearsal and said there 'wouldn't be any play at all if this happened again' etc. you know, like she always does when she's mad. But afterward I heard Dud asking Gwen Phillips to take the part if you didn't come back. He said he'd make it right with Housey. He'd threaten not to act himself. So you'd better get a move on you, Betts. You don't want Gwen to nail him, and she will! I could see she was flattered when he asked her to take the star part with him. You can't trust any man, Betts. Out of sight is out of mind. But perhaps you don't care. Of course, Gwen is giving a house party in vacation and all that,—but perhaps you know. She is going to have a big dance at Shillingsworth's too, and Dud'll probably drive her to that if you don't get back. But perhaps you've already had your invitation.

And oh, yes, Fran's uncle has let her ask the class to a trip on his yacht during Christmas week. You'd better get back. I'm having a couple of new sports things made just for the occasion. And Estelle has a new dress her aunt brought her from Paris. She calls it a 'frock' but it looks like a patchwork quilt and hangs something fearful on her!

Now, darling, write me at once and tell me what you want me to say when Gertie Gates gets to prying about where you've gone and why, and whether it is true that your dad thrashed Dud Weston and told him never to come near you again; and whether you and Dud have really had a fuss; and all that. You know Gertie. Besides, I'm dying of anxiety about you. I shall pass out absolutely if I don't hear by Wednesday. And Precious, one word of advice, Don't let your parents put anything over on you! You're almost of age, and have a *right* to do as you please! *They* did of course!

Passionately,

Gyp.

Frances Allison's letter was brief and to the point.

Betts, old thing:

This is just to let you know that there's a new man in our class. He came the day after you left and he's simply stunning! But he belongs to me, so hands off. He's taken me out twice in his car and it's a humdinger. He lives in the old Foster place and

his uncle is T. Y. Pettingill, the Real Estate man.
They have simply scads of money and he's awfully
generous. I think he would make a wonderful class
president, in case Willie Boyer doesn't get well
enough to come back this year. We really ought to
have somebody who looks the part, don't you
think?

And Betts! He has a cousin coming at
Christmas, a college man. I've seen his picture and
he's almost as good looking. If it's really true as
Gertie Gates is telling round that you and Dud are
sore at each other I'll introduce you to him first and
give him the high sign. So you better hurry home.
Your adoring Fran.

Betty read these effusions through and then turned
back to Dudley Weston's, reading it again with thoughtful brows. Gone was the childlike look, and the glow of
the morning, gone the far view of distant mountains and
sunsets, and the vivid joy of skimming over perfect ice.
Betty was back in her High School days, as if there had
been no interval. Her heart burned hot with pride of
possession, possession of her man,—or what she was
pleased to call a man. A flame of jealousy shot through
her heart at the thought of Gwen Phillips and her house
party. Dud used to go with Gwen down in the Eighth
Grade. She *should not* get him back again!

Nor was Betty averse to attaching the new man from
college, especially if he was good looking. It was just as
well for Dudley Weston to see that he wasn't the only one
that admired her.

All the same Dudley had been fairly white. Hadn't
he asked her to marry him? And that really was as much as
he could be expected to do after her father had knocked
him down. Yes, quite decent, suggesting companionate or
any old thing she chose!

Betty narrowed her eyes and stared unseeing off at
the mountains out of her window, trying to decide which
she would prefer of the three.

It would be thrilling just to go off. She had always
dreamed of that, albeit fearsomely. Some fragment of

139

antiquity, perhaps, still lingered in her blood. One couldn't quite get away from one's stuffy ancestors, and even the psychologists admitted that a certain percentage of your character was inheritance, though not nearly as much as they used to think. The rest was environment, and of course if one had the courage to make's one environment what one wished, why one could be *anything*—almost anything in the universe!

Betty's heart swelled within her, and she rose, her head uplifted, and her soul full of aspiring thoughts. What if she should go off with Dud? Just go off! Still, that was old stuff of course as Dud had said. People had been doing it for centuries. Of course companionate was newer, and nobody in Briardale had tried it yet. It really sounded a lot better than just going off, and made it easier to change around providing things didn't go so smoothly. As for getting married, real downright respectable getting married, of course every girl had that in the back of her mind as she grew up, veil stuff and white satin and orange blossoms. But one couldn't have that and a thrill too, and really nowadays most people would choose the thrill. There really wasn't much you could get a kick out of in a wedding after all. There simply *weren't* any new combinations of colors for bridesmaids unless one dared have them garbed in black velvet with big white horsehair hats trimmed in something severe, perhaps a tail of monkey fur—just one, like a tassel hanging down over one shoulder, and drawn through the hat in a pinched fold—!

Betty narrowed her eyes again and studied the mountain intensely. Of course a bride would have to wear white, and it wouldn't look exactly right to trim it in black even though black and white were awfully smart just now—But stay! Why *did* a bride always have to wear white? Why couldn't the bride wear black? Black velvet, that was it, with a dash of ermine, and the bridesmaids in white organdy. They could still wear the monkey fur tassel on their hats. That certainly would be different from anyone else, and the headlines in the newspapers could read "The Bride in Black"! Black had always been becoming to her and Mums would never let her wear it, she said it was too old for a young girl. Mums was extremely old fashioned. But of course she couldn't pull off any costumes like that if she *were* married at home or in the church. Well one ought to consider all those things, but everything taken into consideration it would really be easier, and she'd get far more of a kick out of accepting Dud's suggestion.

And wouldn't it make a sensation in High School? She could fairly see Miss House's irate complexion turn brick color when the news came out. And wouldn't the girls envy her? Of course she would drive Dudley's car whenever she liked after that, even before she told that she was married. But perhaps after all she and Dudley wouldn't bother to go back to High School. Why should they? Married people didn't need a diploma. It was only a gesture.

Into the midst of her reflections came a clear call for supper, and Betty was hungry. She had been skating all the afternoon and she was ravenous. She went down to the dining room and mingled with the family, taking part in the conversation, and seeming to be just as she had been two hours before, but her mind was running on other things. She was thinking all the time, "What would they say if they knew I was going to be married in a couple of weeks? *Am* I?"

So she toyed with the idea, laughing a good deal with Jane and Chris to cover her self-consciousness, playing paper dolls with Doris most obligingly, and a game of checkers with John on an old checker board he had found in the desk drawer.

"What if I should?" she kept saying over and over to herself. "What if I should? But of course—how could I?"

By the time she went up to bed she had reached the stage of wondering how she could get a telegram off to Dudley Weston. *If* she should decide to do it, how could she send him word without the family becoming aware of it? Of course she might send a letter, but she doubted if it would get by the family censorship. Chester Thornton had told his daughter she was to have no communication

141

whatever, *ever*, with Dudley Weston: that he was not fit
for a decent girl to speak to. If her father should see a
letter addressed to Dudley lying with the letters to be
carried down to the mail when he drove down to the
village as he did almost every morning with the milkman,
he would be sure to destroy it, and forbid her to write
again. Well, she might enclose it to Gyp, or Fran, and ask
them to mail it or give it to Dud, but could she really trust
them with an errand so momentous? If anything
happened that they left it around or told anybody else—
Fran might tell that new man for instance—or Gyp might
think she would steam the letter open and read it or hold it
up to the light and get a few words. Gyp was very curious
and she might think as she was her best friend that she had
a right to find out how matters stood between her and
Dud. No, a letter sent that way was not really quite safe,
and besides, there was Gwen Phillips, and no telling how
much work she might get in on Dudley in the meantime.
Even a day was precious. She really ought to send a
telegram. Dud would be sore if she didn't do as he
suggested, even though it was unreasonable of him. She
must somehow manage. Couldn't she steal out of the
house early in the morning and catch the milkman down
at the foot of the lane? Dad didn't go in town every day.
She could send it tomorrow perhaps.

She lay awake a long time after the family were all
asleep thinking about it, making plans. By this time she
had fully made up her mind that she was going. How
could any girl give up a chance like that?

Having decided to go, Betty now turned her
thoughts to the wording of a telegram.

It must be brief. It must be business like. It must be
misleading to all but the one concerned. Phrase after
phrase formulated itself only to be rejected, but at last she
settled on the following words as covering the case
satisfactorily:

"Will arrive Railroad Station Springfield Massa-
chusetts noon Saturday. Companion preferred."

She solaced her conscience by saying that it would

be easy enough to call it off later if she changed her mind, and so thinking went to sleep.

But she missed her calculation and overslept, and the morning was far on its way before she awoke. There was nothing for it but to get her father to take her with him when he went down to the village next time, trusting to luck to get away and send her telegram.

As she went about her dressing, thinking this all out, she remembered with sudden dismay that she had no money wherewith to send that telegram and how was she to get any? Of course she could send it collect, but that didn't seem just right. Betty was a proud little thing. But at last that problem too was solved.

At the supper table the night before the conversation had run on Christmas, and the prospect of no gifts, each one of the children bewailing the fact that they had not bought nor brought anything that would do for that purpose. Their mother had looked up with a quick smile that nevertheless contained a swift warning look toward their father and said, quite as if it were a usual thing to do:

"We'll have to *make* our Christmas presents this year. I was thinking about that last night. I believe it will be interesting. Just make some little thing, each of you for each of the rest, and we'll give a prize for the most original gift."

"But there's nothing to make them out of," mourned Jane.

"Oh, plenty!" said Eleanor still smiling. "There is a wonderful attic full of beautiful things, and there's all outdoors also. When I was a girl I made a braided rug for my mother for Christmas once, out of old rags that were to be thrown away. She loved it, and I enjoyed the making, too."

"What's out of doors, I'd like to know?" asked Chris.

"Well, pine cones and acorns and acorn cups. We used to make picture frames out of those. And you have your camera. There are plenty of beautiful pictures which some day you can have enlarged. Once my father made

143

me a doll house out of a packing box—"

"Oh—hh!" said Doris looking from one to another of the family hopefully.

Betty remembered this now and turned it over in her mind. It gave her an idea, and one idea begat another. Later when they were washing dishes together she said:

"Mother, could you give me about a dollar or two? I want to get a new thimble. And my toothbrush keeps shedding bristles. I broke my comb too, and I'd like some decent letter paper. I thought I'd ask Dad to let me go along down to the village tomorrow if he goes. I hate to ask him for money, since you say he hasn't any."

"Why, I think I can manage that much," said Eleanor smiling. It seemed a reasonable request. But Betty went up to her room feeling like a liar and a thief. She had done far worse things than that at home sometimes, without being troubled, but somehow this seemed a more flagrant offense because she was deliberately planning to bring trouble and sorrow to her mother and father. Yet she went straight on with her planning.

The next morning Betty went down to the village on a farmer's sleigh, an old farm wagon with runners beneath, and straw for upholstery. Chester went to the hotel to do some telephoning. He told Betty to float around and do her shopping. He pointed out the shopping district, a General Merchandise store, Dry goods and Groceries combined, a Drug store combined with the Post Office, and the railroad station a little further down the street.

Betty went to the last one first and got a time table, to make sure she could reach Springfield at the hour named. She also sent her telegram and discovered the price of a ticket to Springfield. How was she ever to get enough together even for so short a journey? She must hoard her money. Her mother had given her two dollars and there was not much over a dollar left after sending the telegram. She must have some cigarettes, too!

The man in the drug store gave her a sharp look when she asked for cigarettes, and she thought for a moment that he was going to refuse her. But she told him she was buying them for her brother and he finally went and got them. She bought Chris some too. It seemed only fair, since Chris would have done as much for her if he had the chance. Then she went back to the hotel and wrote a letter to Dudley Weston. It had necessarily to be brief lest her father appear before she finished and she wanted to mail it if possible to-day. She wrote:

> Old Thing:
> You've said it! Parent Stuff. Pinned all right. Broke too. All kinds of a time getting wire off. Meet you in Springfield Railroad Station at noon Saturday the 22nd. If school closes early Friday afternoon you ought to make it by then. If you write don't put your name on outside of envelope. Forbidden stuff! Hard going! If you want to send anything make it chocolates with a layer of smokes inside. This is a perfectly poisonous place. Empty as a flask! Be sure to bring Gyp and Sam, or else get Fran and somebody. And let's make it companion-ate. That sounds newer. Don't be late.
>
> Thorny.

Chapter XVI

Betty slipped out and mailed her letter and then came back and sat down in the funny old stuffy parlor and waited. She stared out of the window at the little empty street with its mountains of snow on either side, and its far vista of frozen lake at the end. The lake was surrounded by a huddle of closed summer cottages and boat houses shivering on the bank like worn old ladies in white fur capes and hoods. She was thinking that she had done it now. The word was gone out of her hand that she would marry Dudley Weston. She could not call it back! It was under the United States stamp and seal! It had to go with its message. If she wanted to retract she would have to go back on her word, and there was an unwritten law that one who did that had a streak of yellow. Betty had never showed a streak of "yellow." She was known all over school as a "game kid." She would have to carry it through now, no matter what.

Her cheeks glowed and her eyes shone. It was going to be a lot of fun, anyway, something to break the horrible monotony of this snow bound dump to which they had brought her.

When her father came back to her she was looking almost happy and her cheeks glowed so brightly that he gave a relieved sigh. Betty was standing the exile better than he had dared to hope. Perhaps if they stayed long enough she would forget all about the dreadful things she had left behind her and become again the pure sweet child she had been. If only it might prove that he had not discovered things too late! He had just arranged to have a telephone put into the old house, which would make it possible for him to stay all winter, with only a trip to the office now and then.

"Well, Betty, did you get everything that you wanted?" he asked pleasantly.

Betty looked up, then answered evasively:

"Well, no, not everything. Some things cost more than I thought. I didn't have money enough."

"Not money enough?" he said smiling, and dropped a five dollar bill in her lap. "Run along and get what you want. I want to write a letter and then we'll be ready to go when Mr. Brown comes back."

Betty took the money, her cheeks growing very red, and went slowly over to the store. She would have to get something or her mother would ask about it. She felt as if she were taking her father's life blood in that five dollar bill. She almost ran back to give it to him, and tell him she didn't need the things,—that he had better keep it for necessities,—that she knew he couldn't afford it. Then she reflected that it would go far toward making her journey to Springfield possible; and after all, when she was gone, there would be one less in the family to support.

She bought a twenty-five cent toothbrush, a ten cent thimble, a thirty cent box of letter paper, and came slowly, almost shamedly back to her father, feeling that she ought to give the change back, yet knowing she did not mean to do so unless he asked her.

Chester did not ask for the money. Betty got into the old sleigh and settled down in the straw telling her conscience that she wasn't doing anything criminal. The money would be there in her pocket if either her father or mother asked for it back again. She wasn't stealing it. They had given it to her. She reflected as she drove back to the merry jingle of the sleighbells, that she had done very well to get things so far under way for her going, and she could afford to be nice and pleasant the rest of the time she had to stay. Of course they were going to feel terribly sore at her for a while, and perhaps it was a rather rotten thing for her to do. Yet after all, it was rotten of them to bring her away from all her associates, and park her up in a mountain to die! They had no right! It was her own life, and she had to live it. She was preparing to live it to the limit, and the thought made her fairly sparkle with good will toward her family.

As a sort of expiation she entered at once into plans for Christmas, as soon as she got back to the farm. She instituted an expedition to the attic immediately after lunch in search of materials and professed to have great ideas for what she was going to do. But she said nothing at all about the other ideas she had evolved while hunting through the old trunks and bandboxes and chests. She came down with her arms full of old velvets and satins and silks, but she did not tell about the rose colored taffeta she had found in the depths of the biggest trunk. It had been a part of great aunt Elizabeth Thornton's ancient trousseau. She brought it down wrapped in an old hand embroidered nightgown, of firm fine linen embroidered in delicate vines and flowers. The taffeta was made with a slim fitted waist and a long full skirt, much oh, much like the present day fashion of evening dresses. It had a low round neck and a bertha of priceless old lace. Why

wouldn't it do to take along for a dance frock? She had
nothing whatever fit to appear in before her own world
except the little jersey dress she had worn away from
school that day. She scorned all the sensible garments her
mother had brought along. Of course when she got home,
after the companionate marriage and a suitable interval
for some kind of a honeymoon, depending on how much
money Dud could rake up, she would be able to get into
the house and perhaps find some of her own clothes.
Surely everything must be there just as when they left it.
The house wouldn't have been sold with all their clothes in
it, not so soon anyway. Of course Mother and Dad had
had a lot of conferences behind closed doors, and hadn't
breathed a word. There was no telling what had been
done. Mother looked awfully sad sometimes when she
came out, and once Betty had caught her crying. It was
hard on Mums of course. After she was married and living
in luxury she would invite Mums a great deal to visit her.
Of course she would be living in luxury for Dud's father
was said to be fabulously rich, and he had been awfully
generous with Dud. When he found he was really married
and settled down he would of course likely build him a
house and furnish it. Too bad Dad couldn't get her a
decent trousseau, but going off this way would really let
him out. Nobody could expect him to do anything when
he hadn't been told, and of course he would be sore for a
while. That would be natural, and people wouldn't expect
anything of him till he got over it. Then by that time he
would likely have pulled up in his business, and of course
Dad would come across handsomely with chests of silver
and things as fast as he got into shape. He had always been
generous.

So reasoned Betty as she locked her door against
intrusion, turned her back on great aunt Elizabeth's limp
china doll that she had brought down to dress for Doris
for Christmas, and arrayed herself in the rose colored
taffeta. It certainly was becoming, with its fall of rich old
lace about the shoulders, almost down to the slim little
waist. The skirt was put on to the waist with a cord, and
hung about her deliciously. If she could only manage to

curve up the hem line in front a little, it would make it more chic, but on second thought that might be dangerous, with no long mirror by which to get the effect, and no one to help her pin it up. Besides, there were many dresses made nowadays with straight hems, and it would be charming to say it was being worn just as her great aunt had worn it on her wedding trip! All it really needed was ironing, and she could easily manage to bring up an iron and an ironing board or something and smooth out the wrinkles. This business of making Christmas gifts for each other was going to make it quite possible for her to do a lot of things in privacy without exciting suspicion, because they were all working behind closed doors.

She whirled about to let the rich rosy waves of silk swish around her, and the lace bertha foam around her shoulders. She spread out her young white arms before the old looking-glass where perhaps her old-young aunt had once stood in that same dress. She put her head on one side and sighed happily. It looked as if a real thrill was on the way.

Then she suddenly shivered. It wasn't as warm up in that old Vermont farm house bedroom, heated only by a drum from the sitting room below, as it was in her hotwater heated bedroom at home in Briardale. Prinking and admiring herself might be at the expense of a cold, and she mustn't run that risk now or she might not be able to get away with her program.

So she slipped out of the rosy silk, and folded it safely away in its shrouding of embroidered linen in her bottom drawer, locked the drawer and put the key in her sweater pocket. Then she put on her warm farm garments again and stole downstairs to read by the fire. She had found an old book which was thrilling and wanted to finish it. It told of Lords and Ladies and quaint old times of persecution when knights fought for ladies fair, and love was supreme. The essence of the story somehow chimed in with what Betty was planning to do. She began to idealize the noble Dudley as her rescuer.

Yet she had a very tender feeling toward her mother and the rest of the family. She even laid down her book

149

and went to the kitchen door to ask if she could help her mother when she heard her sigh as she shut the oven door on a couple of big apple pies she had just made.

"No, dear, it's all done now," said Eleanor gently, "but you may set the table if you will. Then everything will be ready for supper and we won't be in such a rush when they all come in."

So Betty set the table, listlessly, boredly, leaving off half the things that go to the making of a smooth and quiet meal, and went back to her book with a conscience at ease. After all, was she not a dutiful daughter, even though she was planning to run away with a man whom her parents disapproved! But then one must live one's own life!

Betty came reluctantly at the third call, in the midst of the most exciting chapter of all, to eat the delicious meal that her mother had prepared. She ate rapidly with enjoyment and was about to excuse herself and go back to her book when her father halted her.

"Sit down, Betty!" he said. His tone was kind but firm. There was a new note in it which Betty in her preoccupation failed to notice.

"Nothing doing, Chester," she said with an impudent laugh, "I'm right in the thrill of my book and I can't wait another minute."

She had not called him Chester since they came to the farm, and somehow with the use of the disrespectful term her old bravado returned. It would not be long now before she was free from this kind of thralldom. She tilted her chin impertinently and turned away from the table.

"I said, 'Sit down,' Betty!" And now there was something unmistakable in his voice, though it was quiet and self-controlled.

Betty flashed at him a defiant look as she took another step toward her book, and then suddenly, she did not quite know why, she came back and sat down, her face overclouded by a sudden sullen anger.

But Chester paid no attention to her attitude. He continued to look at her steadily, with that quality of searching justice in his eyes that made her uncomfortable in spite of her anger. It seemed an age that he looked at her so, until she wished to drop her eyes from that steady glance, but could not do so.

"Betty, while you are in my house—"

Betty gave him a sudden quick startled look. Why did he say "While you are in my house"—as if he knew? Could he possibly have found out? Had he followed her down in the village without her knowledge?

"While you are in my house," went on the steady voice, "you will not call me by that name any more. What began in jest has ceased to be amusing and has become disrespect. It is a part of the disrespect of the age. It is what we came here to get away from. It was perhaps partly our fault that you were allowed to fall into such habits. But it will not be our fault if you continue in them. Your mother and I are determined to undo as far as possible what has been done while we had our eyes shut. Now, I hope that is thoroughly understood—"

His eyes went around the table and searched each young face, with a meaningful glance. There was something about his expression that showed he was not to be trifled with.

"This is something that applies to you all," he added, "a principle that must be observed. We want no more flippant remarks, and no more refusals to do what you are told to do."

Chris turned red and began to put more butter on a piece of bread, though he had seemed to have quite finished his supper. Jane folded her napkin in tiny plaits and affected not to have heard him, but it was plain that each recalled some recent offense, and understood what he meant.

"Excuse me, Mums," said Chris hurriedly stuffing the last bite of bread and butter into his mouth, "I wantta get in that wood. It might snow again tonight and we'd need it."

"There is apple pie—" said Eleanor looking troubled and rising quickly, "and cottage cheese the milkman brought. You like that—!"

She started toward the kitchen.

"Wait!" said Chester in that arresting tone. "Sit down, Eleanor, please. There is something else I want to say first. It is time you children began to help your mother, and to keep her from waiting on you all the time. It is time the work of the house was divided among you, and not all left for your mother to do. I came in here a few minutes ago and found your mother sitting down with a dizzy head, as white as could be, and all in a tremble from cooking all the afternoon. She is scarcely able to sit up at the table now and yet you have all let her wait on you hand and foot, and you were going to let her continue to do so. Eleanor, can't someone else get that pie? You sit still. Betty, get the pie!"

"For Pete's sake, aren't we ever going to have a maid again?" said Betty impudently.

"Perhaps not," said Chester coolly. "Betty, get the pie!"

"Well, if we weren't in such a poisonous dump you might get some kind of a job somewhere and *get* a maid!" said Betty furiously and flounced out to the kitchen.

Eleanor cast a reproachful look at her as she went. Betty felt fiercely glad as she picked up the pie and came back, glad that they had given her occasion to rebel? Life seemed once more all wrong and the only way to right it was to accept Dudley Weston's rescue. She gave her conscience a slap and told it to be quiet and she carried the pie in and put it down in front of her mother with a thump.

"You may bring the pie to me," said Chester, noticing how tired Eleanor was looking.

Betty slammed the pie in front of her father.

"I thought children of respectable families were supposed to be sent to school," she said as she slumped into her chair again.

"Perhaps we are not a respectable family," said Chester eyeing the pie. "I have had strong suspicions during the last week that we were not. Jane, will you get me a knife and some plates?"

"Well, aren't we going to school any more?" asked John eagerly as if he personally would be quite willing to dispense with that conventionality.

"Certainly," said Chester evenly. "There are several different kinds of schools. I felt that a change would be most salutary at this time. You are about to engage in a course in domestic science and agriculture."

"Agriculture?" asked Chris contemptuously. "At this time of year?"

"At this time of year," said Chester. "Wood cutting and carrying has a large part in the winter work of the farmer. In the interim it will not hurt you boys to get a little touch of domestic science along with your sisters. To that end we are all going to wash the dishes tonight and put them away. Tomorrow I am expecting a man to put in our telephone, and after that I shall be busy most of the mornings and afternoons, but after five o'clock I shall expect to do my part toward the running of this house with the rest of you, and I shall expect each one of you to do your share without complaint. I believe Mother has some plan for division of labor and she will tell you about it tomorrow. But I want you to understand there is to be no shirking. I brought you up here partly to give you an understanding of some of the hardships of the world of which you have so far seen very little, and they can only be understood by experience. Therefore we are going to have experience."

"Great Cats!" said Chris.

"I abominate housework!" said Betty wrathfully, "I don't see any sense in people with brains having to do it, either."

"Were you under the impression that you had brains?" asked her father half amusedly.

Betty flushed angrily and swallowed her last bite of pie before answering. Then she arose haughtily, gathering up her dishes with the air of a degraded princess:

"Well, if this sort of thing is going on," she said as she opened the kitchen door with her pile of dishes, "I for one shall leave!"

"Indeed!" said her father calmly. "Just where would you go?"

"There are plenty of places I can go!" she tossed her head mysteriously. "Lots of girls are leaving home today, getting jobs and things like that. I don't blame them either

153

if this is the sort of parents they have to endure!"

With that Betty went out and shut the door behind her. A moment later they heard her stamping noisily up the narrow back stairway.

Chester opened the door into the hall and his voice met her as she reached the door of her own room:

"Betty, you may come down at once. Your part of the evening's work is not done."

Betty came down, her eyes stormy. Silently she went about doing what she was told to do, and doing no more. Silently until she was dismissed she remained, and when the lamp in the kitchen was put out she rushed up to her room and had it out with herself, telling herself that she was glad she had sent word to Dudley. Such antique oppression was not to be borne. Then she cried a little, angry tears of self pity, to think that her proud family had come to such straits as this. But it was not for the sake of the family she cried, but for her own. She was full of self pity. And she began to think hard thoughts against her heretofore indulgent father. What could have come over him to act this way, after all his years of kindness? He surely must be losing his mind!

But Chester Thornton was not losing his mind, heavy though his heart might be. As he worked away at the great banks of snow that hindered their moving about and down to the road as they would, his thoughts were busy trying to discover wherein the fault lay that his children who had apparently started out so well in life had run amuck of all the modern trash and eagerly embraced it. Perhaps he was trying to blame some one else, for what he was slowly coming to see had been at least partly his own fault.

His full enlightenment came the evening he found his mother's old Bible, with a few faded words from her own trembling hand written on the fly leaf.

To my children,

I leave this old Book as the best heritage I can give. Study it carefully and you will find the way to peace and righteousness and happiness as I have

done. If there is ever anything wrong with your
lives, come back to this Book as if it were a looking
glass, and it will clearly show you what is the
matter. And when you are lost in the World it will
guide you home.

Mother.

The tears rolled unexpectedly down Chester's
cheeks when he read that. His mother's message across
the years, like a voice from the grave showing him what to
do! As if he had put to her the very questions that had
been troubling him and she had handed him this book as
an answer!

He read until far into the night. Read until Eleanor
came down in dressing gown and slippers with a worried
look upon her face and asked what was the matter.

The strange part of it was that the first page he had
opened to, had been the story of Eli's two sons who were
misbehaving and the curse that God told Samuel to bring
upon Eli.

He had begun to read the story because it had been
one that his mother often read to him and his brothers
when they were little children, sitting on their low stools
about their mother's knee on Sunday afternoon. The
child Samuel! How well he remembered what charm it
had for him at five years old! But the story itself had
grown vague, and its meaning utterly obscured. The part
that Eli and his two profligate sons played in it began to
appear like writing that has been done in invisible ink and
brought near the fire. Eli stood out a picture of himself,
Eli, who meant to be a good man, but who had been too
indulgent with his children! His heart burned within him
as he read, and ever he could hear the sweet voice of his
mother through the words. No, it was not as it had seemed
at first, a miracle, that the worn old book should have
fallen open at the third chapter of first Samuel. Often and
often had it lain open there upon her knee while they
listened entranced to the story.

And now as he read the once familiar sentence
against the old easy-going father-priest the words stabbed
themselves into his heart, and it was as if his own name

155

were substituted for Eli's, and his own neglect became a sin, heinous as Eli's.

> In that day I will perform against Eli all things which I have spoken concerning his house: when I begin I will also make an end. For I have told him that I will judge his house for ever for the iniquity which he knoweth; because his sons made themselves vile, and he restrained them not. And therefore I have sworn unto the house of Eli, that the iniquity of Eli's house shall not be purged with sacrifice nor offering for ever.

Over and over he read the awful words of the Lord God, and as they forced their way into his soul he seemed to be being judged of the Lord Himself, for the iniquity in his own household.

Back to the years of the babyhood of his little children he was carried, when he stood beside the pink and blue laced and beribboned cribs and watched the tiny buds of life unfold in beauty with such high hopes of what their lovely lives would be. All his own faults and follies were to be carefully erased from them, all guards and helps put about them to direct them into perfection. Perfect they had come from God, and perfect they should grow up to show what perfection in men and women could be. No children had ever been so fair and sweet and promising as his.

How hard he had worked during the years to make the home a fitting background for their youth, to pile up money wherewith to lavish upon them all the best that the world could give. Early had he sought out the best institutions of learning and carefully arranged that their initial education should be such as to prepare them for the requirements of the great Universities which he had chosen. Never had they asked for anything that other children had but he had given it if he could, and if he could not he generally managed soon to make it possible. He had ever been their comrade, playing with them when he could, taking time as often as possible for extended holidays, or at least sending them and their mother on holidays. He had chosen the best church in town, that is, the church where the best people, the really cultured, educated, refined people went. He had insisted that they be identified with its activities, although now he recalled that Betty's sole effort in that line had been the playing of the star part in a great religious pageant wherein she had posed as some indefinite, angelic, personified principle looking more than angelic, and receiving enough praise to turn any girl's head. Jane, too, had done a little childish act, a feather dance, between parts. After all, had that sort of thing helped them heavenward? Yes, too, he remembered now a carnival held in the Public Hall of Briardale, for the benefit of the new church Community Hall which they were trying to build. Betty had entered into the drive for raising funds enthusiastically. She had presided over a fountain of lemonade dressed in some queer fantastic garb of a heathen goddess. He remembered she had been barefoot, and that he had protested, but the committee had carried the day, saying she wouldn't look the part if she wore shoes. Oh, his children had always looked the part in whatever they had done, even church work. But what had been the matter?

They were all members of the church, the whole family, himself an elder. They entertained the session once a year, royally; he always contributed generously, loaned their car, and sent flowers and cake to whatever was going on. They even sang in special choirs on occasion, and helped decorate the church for holidays and holy days. And yet, they had made themselves *vile!* That phrase kept repeating itself over and over in his weary brain. "Thy sons have made themselves vile! Thy house shall not be purged by sacrifice nor offering for ever!" He had forgotten Eli. He seemed to hear the words spoken to himself. *Thy* sons! *Thy* children! At times it came over him with overwhelming shame.

So, to-night, when Betty had gone upstairs and all was still a kind of gray ashen look came over the father's face. He was hearing those words again, "Thy children have made themselves vile! Thy house shall not be purged with sacrifice nor offering for ever!"

Chapter XVII

Eleanor had gone up early to bed with the younger children. She looked utterly worn out. Chester knew that the scene at the supper table had not rested her. These things pierced her like a sword. Eleanor loved peace, and loved to see the children happy. It distressed her beyond measure to have dissension. He could see that every word that Betty spoke had hurt her.

Chris was in the woodshed with a lamp on the high shelf by the door pounding and sawing away at a doll house he was trying to make for Doris for Christmas. He seemed to be fairly interested and that was something to be thankful for. Jane had locked herself in her room professing to be working at Christmas presents also, and there was no longer need to keep up an appearance of cheerfulness. Chester slumped in an old rocking chair by the stove, the gray look overspreading his face like a fast traveling cloud that was blotting out the light.

He sat for a long time with his elbows on his knees and his face buried in his hands, seeing things he had never seen before, feeling his need of something that he had never missed before, feeling his utter helplessness, unable to bear the weight of his little girl Betty's defection.

The chair in which he sat had been the one in which his mother had rocked her babies long ago. She had put those gentle loving arms around them; he could feel the frailty of them now, so slender and so warm and so tender, and yet so strong, holding his little hot body when he had a fever, her fingers touching the burning forehead, so cool, so dear! He had felt so safe in her arms, his little gentle frail mother! If he only could go to her now, kneel before this same chair, put his aching head in her lap and pour out his troubles!

And she had sent him word down through the years to go to the Book she had left, for guidance! Well, he had gone and it had only brought him condemnation. Utter, hopeless condemnation! He groaned aloud, and Betty lying wide-eyed above the big old base burner with its upstairs drum to warm her room, heard the groan through the echoing stove pipe, and stared and shrank. Was that her Dad, groaning like a woman? Heard and despised him for it. Heard and hardened her fierce rebellious young heart. He had no right to act like that! He had no right to be so old-fogyish, and care that way about things nobody else believed in any more!

Half an hour later as she lay in her bed, still staring at the dark ceiling, still thinking bitter thoughts about him she heard his footsteps coming slowly up the stairs. He stopped at her door and opened it gently, listened a moment and spoke:

"Betty, are you asleep?"

Betty stirred and coughed. She could not think how to reply. Something in her soul refused to let her answer directly.

He came over beside the bed and touched her gently on the forehead.

"Betty, little girl," he said, and his voice was very tender, the way she remembered it when she was a tiny child, "Your father loves you!" His voice was wistful. "I've been thinking about it child, and I'm afraid I haven't been the right kind of a father to you!"

Of all things! What a horrible thing to say! That was sob stuff! That was against the code. Her father talking *mush* like that!

"Shall we begin again, little girl, and try to straighten things out, try to understand and help each other?"

"Don't!" said Betty jerking away from his touch, "Don't!" in a sob that was almost a scream, and burst into angry hysterical tears, flinging herself as far away from him as she could get and letting the great sobs rack her slim young body.

Her father stood there in the dark room, with the light from the hall casting a long bright finger sharply on the floor through the crack under the door. He waited hoping she would turn back, perhaps answer him, when the storm of tears should have past. But the shaking sobs went on, and presently he went round to the other side of the bed, and stooping kissed the bit of hot wet forehead between the guarding fingers, and so passed out of the room.

And Betty lay and sobbed and hated her father for bringing back that awful feeling of the presence of God in the room, God standing out there in the middle of the dark room, condemning her! God!—and there *wasn't* any God! Everybody said so nowadays. Just everybody!

She cried the harder. She felt that she would like to take poison or something just to show them how she hated it all. There was a fierce resentment in her wild uncontrolled nature. She had her own life to live and they should not hinder her. She felt if this kind of thing went on that she would not be able to go away with Dudley Weston. And yet she *would!* Nothing should hinder her now! This was a perfectly awful place, all shut in by fierce cold and snow, and God out there in the middle of the room looking at her in the dark. God! when there really *wasn't* any God at all!

The next day the morning mail brought trouble. A telegram which had been put in the mail and brought up by a neighbor passing that way. There was word from the bank. Chris had forged a check for two hundred dollars! Chris was closeted with Chester for two hours in the little room off the sitting room. He came out at last with red rims around his eyes, and a more shamed look than ever on his hard young face, came out hastily and hurried into the woodshed where he was heard for a long time chopping kindling.

Eleanor had been openly weeping, and nothing was said about the new regime of work. Indeed Eleanor made no move toward getting the midday meal. She went to her room and lay down with the door shut. Jane, loitering to ask a question about something she was trying to sew for one of the boys for Christmas, thought she heard a sob, and came away.

"Oh, Heck!" she said turning a hand spring on the kitchen floor for Doris' benefit; "I wish we could go home. This place is rotten!"

Chester went down to the village, walking because there was no conveyance at this hour. The gray look on his face had deepened perceptibly. He seemed twenty years older. It was nearly four o'clock when he came back, everybody was hungry and nobody knew what it was all about. Chris had gone out to the barn after he finished chopping the wood, and remained there. He did not come back to the house till his father came home. He slipped in then, and up to his room like a rabbit trying to get by without notice.

Betty came down about noon and began a few works of virtue. Everybody had gone crazy. They should see that she was sane.

She washed the dishes and straightened the dining room. Then she made some toast and scrambled some eggs for the children. That was about the extent of her culinary knowledge. She had never had time to learn anything more. There had been too many dances and High School plays and basketball games.

She felt most virtuous when she had finished. She reflected that it would be good to leave a sweet savor of good works behind her when she went. She had a generous forgiving spirit toward her family this morning. They never had been young—at least it was so long ago. And anyhow, life had scarcely been worth living in their day. Such prudish impossible notions! She wondered what could be the matter with Chris? But even Jane's most accomplished snooping failed to make plain the cause of Chris' depression, and when she finally made bold to waylay him on the stairs during one of his restless excursions out to the barn, and ask him what was "eating" him he pushed her roughly aside and said:

"Aw, nothing! ! Shut up, won't ya? Yer a pain in the neck! A fella can't take a step without finding you under foot!"

The telephone had been installed and Chester Thornton retired into the library and carried on long conversations with "long distance." But the room was not under any of the bedrooms, nor near any of the stove pipes which carried sound so beautifully, and not one word of the low voiced communications leaked out to the curious children. Nor did the heavy oak doors that shut their father and their brother in give away any secrets.

Chris slid in furtively, and stayed hours with his father. An occasional tinkle of the telephone bell gave sign that something important must be going on. When the two came out for meals Chester was grave and preoccupied, and Chris wore a white frightened look.

Nor was Eleanor any more communicative. When Jane who was the boldest of the group essayed to question her, she answered, "Oh, just business. You wouldn't understand."

Three days like this went by, depression in the very atmosphere, Eleanor giving a low voiced question when Chester came to meals, or maybe a mere lifting of the eyebrows, that seemed to mean "Have you heard yet?" and Chester answering by a mere negative movement of his eyes, scarcely perceptible.

It was terrible! Betty wished she had said she would come at once to Briardale. She could have sold something—her watch perhaps—her precious platinum watch! Anything to get away from this terrible place! It seemed as if the judgment day was about to dawn upon them all.

To add to the general gloom there was a thaw, and mist and steam began to ascend to a gloomy threatening sky with intermittent sunshine. Nobody went down to skate, nobody went down to the village. The sled that Chris and his father had found and had been repairing for family coasting stood dismantled in the woodshed with one runner off. There was nothing left for Betty to do but dress Doris' doll, and bungle up an outfit for herself from the old chests in the attic. Betty did a great deal of ransacking in those days, unearthing some most interesting garments. Her mother was entirely too preoccupied to notice when she asked if she might have them, so Betty had a free hand with several rare old dresses, and prinked and pinned and cut and slashed to her heart's delight. Jane, meanwhile, was also conjuring Christmas presents out of old things from the attic. And occasionally Betty, between costumes, worked a while at Doris' doll, making many lace ruffles on green silk for its party dress.

Doris and John were the only really happy members of the family. They made endless snow men and snow houses and snow forts, and revelled in the great out of doors, coming in with rosy cheeks and shining eyes to get a handful of unguarded cookies, or doughnuts, when driven by hunger, and back again to the fray.

But at last there came a day a little after noon when the door of the closed room suddenly opened and Chris came out with his old brisk manner. Not closing the door carefully with that funeral-in-the-house air that he had been doing.

Betty was in the dining room setting the table for lunch because she was hungry and hoped it would bring her mother downstairs to suggest something about lunch if she jingled the dishes loud enough.

Betty had a strong conviction that her mother was up in her bedroom most of the time praying. Not that Eleanor had heretofore been given to much obvious prayer, but Jane had burst into the room one morning and found her kneeling by her bed, and reported that her face was all red and tear-stained. Eleanor always came downstairs with that wistful unhappy look in her eyes that Betty naturally connected with prayer. Why should one pray unless one was in a terrible strait? What could be the matter? Business couldn't be so awful that they would feel it like that! Why, one could always get a new business if the old one failed. And besides, what could Chris have to do with that? He was too young to help in business.

Betty heard Chris come out of the old library and go upstairs with a spring, two steps at a time. He sounded almost as if he were whistling. Yes, that was a whistle. He was stamping around his room and opening and shutting closet doors and bureau drawers, and *whistling!* Betty drew a sigh of relief.

Then Eleanor came swiftly down the stairs and went in to the library, just as Chester was coming out. His face looked as if a great burden had rolled off from his shoulders, and Betty heard her mother exclaim, "Oh, thank the Lord!" and then she saw her put her face down on her husband's shoulder and cry. Betty hurried into the kitchen and stood looking out of the window at the distant mountains overhung with clouds, and just as she was watching, the sun burst through and sent golden bars down through the purply gray and blue of the sky.

Then Chris came clattering down the back stairs and greeted his sister for the first time in four days.

"Hello, Betts!"

Betty turned a disturbed face on him:

"What's the matter, Chris—For Pete's sake tell me!" she pleaded.

"Absolutely nothing!" declared Chris joyously. "Everything O. K. *Absolutely!* Say, Betts! Aren't there any doughnuts left or something? I'm holla as a log, an' I gotta beat it down ta the village with a business letter fer Dad. It's gotta go on the next train. Get me something, can'tya? Something I can take in my hand. Where's the rest of that apple pie, that'll do. And gimme a hunk of cheese! Thanks awfully. Dance at yer wedding and all that sorta thing!"

He was gone into the front part of the house. She could hear him breezing into the library and calling out excitedly to his father in his old confident tone.

But Betty stood still in the pantry, the dish cloth she had been holding in her hand dropped to the floor. Now why did Chris say that about dancing at her wedding? She felt weak and upset. Of course Chris hadn't an idea about her plans. He just said it. It didn't mean a thing. But it certainly did make her head reel.

Well, it was a relief to have the atmosphere cleared again, of whatever it was. She almost felt like singing herself, or whistling or something. Perhaps she didn't want to go away. But of course that was nonsense. She must. She had promised. But now she could show Mums the doll's dress. It certainly was pretty. Mums would like it. And she had made it all herself.

It was like having life freed from some great obstruction. Now things could go sparkling on like a

164

stream in the summer sunshine.

Jane appeared at the door, her face full of satisfied curiosity.

"Oh, Betts! You've dropped the dish cloth! That means company, and we're going to have it. The minister from that funny little white church down in the village, with the sharp steeple and the big bell in a square box under it, is coming to call. He just telephoned and Daddy said it was all right to come. He's coming *this afternoon!*"

"Oh Heck!" said Betty ungraciously. "Let's go down and skate!"

"We can't!" said Jane. "Daddy said the ice is all slushy on top. He says we'll get our feet awful wet. And he says if it'll only be a nice still night and turn cold without any wind that the ice'll be good again."

"Jane, have you heard what's been the matter? What's Chris been up to?"

"Oh, that!" said Jane nonchalantly. "Didn't you find that out yet? You aren't very keen, Betts. It's something about Jim Disston's Packard that Chrissie has been buying with some money that wasn't his, or a check or something."

"For Cat's Sake! I thought Chris had more sense!" said Betty looking off at the hills with her cheeks growing red. What would they all say when it was discovered that she had run away and got married?

"Well," she went on after a minute, "we can go somewhere when that minister comes. I've had all the glooms I can stand for one week. When we see him coming we'll beat it out the back door and run down the hill out of sight. Get your coat and galoshes and leave them down in the kitchen so you won't have to go back after them."

There was no opportunity however to disappear when the minister arrived, for he came walking up the snowy lane with no sleighbells to announce his coming.

Betty and Jane had been kept busy all the afternoon in the kitchen. Eleanor had come out with her face wreathed in thankful smiles and put the finishing touches to the lunch that Betty had prepared, and immediately after lunch she challenged them to help her do some baking.

It really was almost interesting, with their mother in such a mood, to put on big aprons and roll up their sleeves and learn how to make real pies and cookies and biscuits. Betty made a cake, too, chocolate layer, with the black butter frosting, and it turned out wonderfully. She was so proud of it that her eyes took on their old childish shine, and her cheeks were glowing, and when Chris came in from his long walk of six miles, hungry as a bear, he stood in the door and admired it.

"Oh, Boy!" he said licking his lips eagerly. "Oh Boy! Some cake! When ya going to give us a sample Betts? You don't mean you made it all by your lonesome? Sure 'nough? No kiddin'?"

Suddenly the home seemed dear. Just because she had contributed to its comfort. She had forgotten that she was leaving it so soon. She had a choking feeling in her throat as if she were going to cry.

"Well," she said to herself, "at least we won't starve. Mums always said people had to learn cooking before they got married. I guess I'll try pie. Though I don't really suppose I'll ever have to cook. The Westons have plenty of servants, more than we ever had. But it's likely I might have to tell a servant how to make a chocolate cake some day. Anyhow it's fun!"

And right at that point the minister walked into the kitchen!

"Excuse me!" he said, "I knocked several times but nobody seemed to hear, so I just followed your voices. My name's Dunham. Is this Mrs. Thornton?"

Eleanor dried her hands and greeted the minister, introducing the children.

"Shall we go into the sitting room?" she said preparing to lead the way.

"Well, it smells mighty good out here," said the minister looking around with a twinkle in his eyes. "I'd be entirely satisfied to sit right down here and let you go on with your work."

Jane slid up to him in her elfish way and presented a plate of hot cookies just out of the oven, that she had been helping to make, and they each took a cookie and went munching into the sitting room.

The minister won Betty's heart by pausing at the table where she had just finished icing her wonderful chocolate cake.

"Well, that certainly is a cake to be proud of!" he said. "Are you the cook that made that work of art?"

Betty swelled proudly, and forgot that she had meant to be haughty and superior if any minister tried to make up to her.

Chester appeared on the scene with a hearty welcome and Chris entered a moment later with an armful of wood. He had just finished building up the fire on the hearth and the flames snapped and roared up the great old chimney with old time good cheer. Betty slid into a chair, pleased, interested, just tired enough with her cake making to be glad to sit down and listen.

She saw Chester turn to Chris with a quick flash of anxiety: "Did you make the train my boy?" he asked in a low tone. "I didn't know you had got back."

"I sure did!" said Chris with a proud ring to his voice. Betty looked up at him wonderingly. It seemed almost as if Chris had added a year or two to his voice, it sounded so manly. She caught a quick glance of relief from her father, before he turned back to talk with the minister. How glad Chester had looked! Did he care so much about what Chris did as all that? He would care a lot about her too. It was a rotten deal she was going to hand him! But why did she have to keep thinking of those things all the time? There was a whole week before she had to go, and she wanted to enjoy it as much as she could. She must keep such thoughts out of her mind or she would be turning "yellow," and that would never do. She would lose all her reputation at school for being "hard boiled" and she was very proud indeed of that, though it must be owned that she had a very vague idea of what it really was intended to mean.

The minister had beautiful silver hair, and keen blue

eyes that could either twinkle or look straight through one. His cheeks were rosy like two winter apples, and his shoulders were sturdy as if he knew how to carry burdens as well as stand in the pulpit.

He showed at once that he had a sense of humor by telling two or three stories that fascinated the children and sent them off into peals of laughter. Betty found herself wondering why a perfectly good fine gentleman like that wasted himself in being a minister, it seemed such a slow profession.

He spoke of his son as being away studying for the Christian ministry, and Betty thought:

"Oh, how poky! How perfectly poisonous for any man to wish that on a young man. Just burying him alive! What a rattling shame!"

"David is coming up at Christmas to see us," said David's father, beaming with pleasure at the idea. "His mother and I can hardly wait for the time to come! He can't get here till Christmas day, probably, and he may be delayed a day or so later on account of having to take some services for a fellow student who is ill, but you understand, Christmas doesn't occur for his mother and me till he gets here! I'd like him to meet you. There aren't so many young people around in the winter months, all off to college or a job in the city somewhere you know. David is a great man for sports. He just revels in them while he's home, and the snow is fine this winter."

"Our young people have been trying to fix up an old sled for coasting," said Chester heartily, "perhaps your son will come up and join them. The old hill out behind the house used to be something worth while."

"I'm sure he will if you'll let him," beamed the father. "He has a sled that he thinks is rather fine, a 'humdinger' I think he calls it. Perhaps you'll let him bring it up."

"What a bore!" thought Betty. "Of course he's just a country clod. But then, I'll be gone, and it won't matter!"

Chester was quite eager about it. He was saying that his children had been somewhat lonely since they came. Now how did Chester know that? They certainly didn't want any native talent around. Still, the old man was kind of a good sport. The son might not be so bad. Only any young man in this age that would submit to having himself made into a minister was simply off the map so far as she was concerned. She let the conversation drift past her while she began to think about Dudley Weston and wonder why she hadn't heard from him again. Surely Dud couldn't back out now, after having asked her to marry him! No, Dud was game! He wouldn't stand her up.

When her thoughts came back to the room again the minister was talking about skiing, describing a great meet over at Brattleboro.

"David has always been interested in it," said David's father. "When he was quite a little lad he got hold of a pair of skis and he used to drive his mother almost insane jumping off mountains and disappearing and turning up on the top of another somewhere."

"Oh, can he do that?" said Betty suddenly before she realized she was saying it. "I should think that would be a real thrill! I'd do anything in the world if I could learn."

"Well, it's a thrill to watch it," said the father, "and David is rather a wonder at it. I have no doubt he'll teach you if you ask him," smiled the minister. "He's taught a great many."

"I shall certainly ask him," said Betty eagerly, and then remembered, she wouldn't be there when David came! What a shame. Perhaps she could get Dud to come back after a few days and visit, and they would try it together. That would be a great stunt! Dudley was always ready for anything new. That was one reason why she liked Dudley better than most of the other boys, because he never stopped at anything she proposed and then always went her one better in proposing something still more daring.

When Betty came back to the conversation again from her thoughts, her father was proposing a most astounding thing. He had actually asked this apple cheeked minister, this native of the backwoods, to open a school there at their house for them! Of course the man talked very well, and probably knew something about stuffy old theological books, but not anything modern. Ministers had to be pretty well educated or people wouldn't call them to churches, but imagine an old fossil like that who didn't know any of the up-to-date ideas, of course, trying to teach them anything! Why, even Doris would know more of what was going on in the world to-day than he would be likely to know.

But Chester seemed to be in earnest. He was even getting it down to the number of hours a week. They were talking about how in Scotland the minister always used to be the teacher of any higher education. Chester was saying that he wanted his children to get back to the good old ways. He was actually talking about Latin and Greek! Greek! Imagine it! That would be a scream! What would Dud and the girls think if they heard of it, Betty Thornton studying Greek!

Chester and the minister talked on, speaking of literature, how rotten the books of to-day were. What did an old fossil like that know about the books of to-day? He couldn't possibly have heard of some of the Russian novels they had to read in lit. class. He would probably be horribly shocked even to know what they were! Imagine!

"I think perhaps I could spare the time," the minister was saying. Great Cats! Was Dad actually going to try to pull off a thing like that? Well, she was thankful she was out of it.

"There is no book like the old Book," the minister was saying. There was almost what one might describe as a glow of tenderness in his voice.

"If people would really study the Bible more they would find in it a liberal education. They would find wonders in it that have never yet been revealed. But they are being discovered now. It is marvellous how the scriptures have been opened up in even the last ten years. Discoveries, history, the shaping of nations, archaeology, are all giving keys to that which has long been locked away from the knowledge of man, and it will not be long before the world is startled into knowing that the old despised Book has all the time contained the germs of all knowledge."

What a scream he was. The idea of talking about archaeology! When every one knew that they were digging up bones of extinct animals that were living millions of years ago, just perfectly proving that the Bible was all off, and evolution was the only thing. But of course, a minister had to pretend to believe all those things or he wouldn't be paid his salary.

Thus irreverent youth kept up a running comment.

But what was this that her father was saying?

"I would like my children to study the Bible too. Yes, that is the very thing! I would like them to know all there is to know about the Bible!"

For Pete's sake! Was Chester really going to try to put a thing like that over on the kids? Study the Bible! And with that old fossil! Wasn't this the limit? Well, she would be off in a few days and give them something else to think about!

But the minister was speaking to Betty, and Betty could not help liking his pleasant pink smile.

"I shall have to tell David what wonderful chocolate cakes you make up here. I am sure he will be knocking at your door the very first day he gets home! He's great for chocolate. His mother can hardly keep up with the demand while he's home."

But Betty hardened her heart against the thought of a David who would let himself be wished into a minister, and she secretly hugged the thought that she would be gone when David arrived.

Chapter XVIII

The house took on a very different atmosphere now. Chris went around whistling everywhere and keeping up at least a show of work. The woodboxes overflowed with wood, and the fires were always replenished when he was about. Also he wore a more manly, respectful air toward his father and mother, as if somehow they had plucked him from some danger and he was grateful. If Betty had not been so occupied with her own affairs she would have wondered about it. As it was he was a very pleasant brother to have around, developing a gallantry altogether new, and an anxiety to please everyone that was most delightful. He had taken Betty into his confidence, and she spent one whole afternoon making lace curtains for the doll house out of a piece of old net she found in the attic, papering the different rooms, and glueing together the minute stairs that Chris had sawed out. It really was becoming tremendously interesting, this getting ready for a home-made Christmas.

The still clear cold came down as Chester had predicted it would, and the lake became a glassy sea, spreading like silver in the sun. Then the days were all too short for the wonderful skating, and they went down after supper once or twice, father and mother and all, and it was fun to watch the parents glide away together like two young people, Eleanor, after the first wild clutch and flounder getting her girlish poise and sailing off with fair rhythm.

It was great fun, the whole family skating together! It seemed as if time had given them a reprieve and they were all children together. There were times, hours together, when Betty forgot her contempt of the country, and her plans to get out of it, and enjoyed everything wholeheartedly.

Christmas would fall on Tuesday this year.

It was the Thursday before Christmas that they went out to get the tree, Betty with the rest, and Eleanor along on the bob sled to help pick it out.

The air was clear and keenly cold, but the dryness made it most exhilarating. The white clad mountains with their fringe of evergreens looked like vast Christmas cards in the distance, and even Betty felt a new kind of Christmas excitement in the air. There had been days when she wept and mourned for her class plays and her dances and her giddy little friends, but she was fast becoming interested in the new vast world to which she had been transplanted. If it had not been for Dudley and what he would think of her, and the howl that would arise from those of her friends to whom he had undoubtedly by this time confided their plans, she would have been glad to forget him and enter heartily into the holiday.

But a troubled mind is not a mind at rest, and Betty was ready at the slightest inconvenience to burst into contempt or fury and visit her scorn on her family.

It was an afternoon to remember. The tramping over the crisp crust of the snow to find the particular tree that would just fit into the place in the big sitting room where Father remembered the tree always used to stand; the glitter on the snow as they stood around while Father and Chris took turns cutting down the tree; the resinous smell of the chips as they flew from the axe; the plumy sweep of the spruce boughs, as the tree finally toppled, and bowed its lovely tip slowly, almost with a sweep of pride to the ground. All those things were photographed on Betty's mind, and something like a plaintive song in her heart kept going over and over, "You're going away! You're not going to be here to see this tree all decked out with paper ornaments and popcorn, and cheap home-made stuff!" And something hurt at the thought.

"Sob stuff!" said Betty to herself turning sharply on her heel and walking away from the rest, determined not to think about it. She had her life to live! She had her life to live! They had no right to hold her here in this poisonous dump!

Mother opened a basket of lunch she had brought along and they all ate raisin gingerbread as they rigged the tree on the sled. Then all hands took hold to pull it home, everybody but Eleanor who walked smiling beside the tree, and looked as young as any of them. Once Betty turned around and caught a glimpse of her mother's face looking so pleased, and full of delight, and it came to her suddenly as a new thought that Mums must have been a very pretty girl indeed! Would she look mature and serious all the time after she had been married for a while? Well, perhaps, but she doubted it. She didn't intend to work as hard as Mums had done. She would lie in the lap of luxury.

They carried the tree home with much shouting and laughter and made a ceremony of getting it set up. There was a great bundle of hemlock branches Chris had cut and lashed to the tree with a piece of rope, and Betty took pleasure in decorating the room with these, putting them over pictures and windows and on the mantel.

Dan Woolley from the next farm brought in the mail just as they were sitting down to a belated supper. There was a letter for Betty. She hid it in her pocket and did not open it until she had a chance to run upstairs while the others were lingering at the table, excusing herself to go after her apron.

It was from Dudley. She had recognized it, though he had evidently tried to disguise his handwriting. It was brief and to the point:

> Old Girl:
>   O. K. You've said it! Suits me! We'll paint the town red! Sam and Gyp have renigged! Too much pull for Gwen's shindig! But I know another kid in New York and he can get a girl easy enough. Don't you be late. We might want to take in Gwen's ourselves later. We better get tied in New York if you think that's necessary. If you keep me waiting I'm off you for life.
>
>   Dud.

It wasn't exactly the kind of letter a bride would expect to receive from her lover two nights before she expected to be married, but it stirred Betty with a strange excitement. Perhaps there was beneath it all in her heart a trace of unrest and disappointment at the lack of something, call it romance if you like—Betty termed it "thrill"—something which the world for generations has taught its children to expect of love and courtship. But Betty reflected as she stuffed the precious missive into her pocket, that this was a frank and progressive age and she was a modern girl. There was no mushy stuff nowadays, everything was matter of fact. She had prided herself on attaining that attitude for the past two years and this was no time to retract. She was going out into the world on her own, and she must be firm and carry the thing through gallantly.

She came flying downstairs with her eyes feverishly bright and her cheeks aglow, and offered to do the dishes all by herself. Chester looked up with a pleased smile.

"It agrees with our Betty up here," he said happily. "Look at her cheeks, Eleanor. She doesn't need any rouge or lipstick now. That was the way nature meant to have the cheeks painted."

Betty caught her breath and hurried into the kitchen with a pile of plates. Something in her father's tender glance made her suddenly vaguely afraid, a wild homesick throb of fear, or was it only that she was so excited? But she mustn't let things get her this way. She had to carry this thing out right, and she mustn't let Dud see she had wavered.

They all insisted on helping with the dishes however. They would not leave her alone a minute. And afterward they went into the sitting room and sat around the fire, with the lamp in the hall so that they sat only in the fire light with the soft glow over the crisp resinous spines of the great beautiful tree, the sweet piney smell mingling with the fragrance of wood smoke. Betty was stabbed with a sudden throb of the dearness of her family that she never had suspected before. She realized that she would never forget that moment.

They sang Christmas carols for half an hour, and then suddenly Chester stood up and said:

"I think we'll have to thank our heavenly Father tonight!" His voice was almost wistful as he looked around in the firelight and smiled, and before Betty realized they were all kneeling again with the shadows playing over them while Chester brought them each to the Father's notice in words that were matchless for tenderness and pleading. It seemed to Betty that she could not stand it. For there was God standing out there in the room again, looking at her, and there was her father telling God all about her in such tones as if he could see Him. See a God who was not! Poor old-fashioned Chester! And she was planning to steal out of the house tomorrow toward morning when they were all asleep and run away to be married! It was awful! If she had only known her father would do that queer absurd thing again she would have slipped off before they sang, said she was sleepy or something.

She stole a quick glance around to see if there was a way open to the stairs, that even now she might disappear. She saw her father, with the glow of flickering light on his graying hair, and over his tired face, her father in that humble attitude, and she shrank from it. If only she had not looked! For she knew again that this was something she would never forget, and she did not wish to remember it. It was something that paralyzed the spirit that was driving her on into life, something that disarmed her and made her weak and humble, something that would reach out clinging hands and try to keep her from going.

The day had been full of eager plans and mysterious secrets. Mrs. Woolley had sent down a can of mince meat. She said it was made after Mr. Thornton's mother's own recipe, and no mince pies could beat old Mrs. Thornton's.

Betty and Jane had made molasses taffy and had great fun pulling it and cutting it into neat shapes and arranging it on wax paper. Mrs. Woolley sent down some cranberry jelly; and the turkey, a great twenty-pounder, was from a near-by farm, also sent as a love gift in memory of the departed grandmother who had been a blessing to the whole neighborhood. The house had been full of good spicy smells, and laughter from morning to night, and Betty had worked harder than any of them, her conscience driving her most mercilessly.

"For I won't be here long to help," she said to herself a hundred times.

"Why Betty is waking up, the dear child!" thought Eleanor, and Chester's pleased smile was constantly upon her, making Betty almost writhe as she met it, for she kept hearing in contrast her father's stern voice as it had sounded that night he took her away from Dudley Weston. And now another day would bring that hard look back to his face.

"But he will forgive me all right when it's all over," promised her heart gaily whenever she faltered; and she had filled the hours so full that there was no more time to think.

All this went over in Betty's mind while her father prayed and when she rose from her knees she hurried up to her room, not daring to stay around the fire and talk any longer. She had yet her little gifts to tie up. The quaint old china doll in its modern up to date green silk was already reposing in a box for Doris. She was leaving her string of coral beads which she had had on the day she left Briardale, for Jane. Jane loved them, and she could think of nothing else. She had bungled a necktie out of an old piece of silk for Johnnie, hemstitched a handkerchief each for Eleanor, Chester and Chris out of a piece of fine linen from the attic, and embroidered initials on them. It was all she knew to make.

After they were all tied and labelled she looked at them unhappily and reflected that if Dud brought money enough along she would buy some really nice things for them in New York and send them up after she was gone.

There remained yet a note to write. Young girl elopers always wrote notes to their angry parents. The only trouble was hers were not angry just now, and she had been having a really wonderful time for the last two or three days. Still, she had a duty to herself. She had her life to live.

So she bolstered up her failing courage.

There was a pleasant bustle in the air next morning when she awoke, and it seemed unreal that she was planning to go away. The very smells in the house made her tingle with excitement. Wood smoke stealing deliciously up through the cracks around the old stove pipe. Scent of pine tree, fragrant from its recent living in the great out of doors, odor of hemlock mingled with other faint suggestions of sage; onion; thyme and sweet marjoram, pickles and cloves and spice. It wasn't at all the time to leave home, Christmas! Christmas belonged to home and mother and father and the children. But of course,—she was going out into the world now to make her own Christmas,—and it was too late to draw back.

Betty sprang up and dressed quickly. So much conscience as she still retained told her that at least she must do all she could for the common good this last day.

She came down with docile conscious air, but everybody was too busy and too eager to notice her much.

Someone brought the morning mail, it might have been the milkman on his way home from his route. The neighbors did such kindly things. Betty was wiping the dishes at the time. She looked fearfully toward the pile of letters half hoping there would be one from Dudley calling off the wedding. If Dudley should want to put it off till after Christmas she wouldn't feel half bad, she told herself.

But there was no letter for Betty. There was one for Chester however, something about Chris, it seemed, for Chris and his father retired to the library and read it. Chris came out smiling and went whistling back to his work. Whenever he spoke his voice was so glad it sounded almost like singing. Betty looked at him curiously once or twice and thought how dear he suddenly seemed. Betty could hardly understand herself all that day. Sometimes she wanted to cry. Even when they all went down that afternoon to skate for a couple of hours, her heart seemed in her throat.

Night came and the sitting round the fire. Betty couldn't stand that. Chester was telling a long story about his boyhood, the night of a blizzard when there was a little sick lamb, and he and his brother Clint had to dig a tunnel to the barn and bring it in the house and feed it with warm milk in a bottle. Next there would come some singing and then perhaps another prayer. If she had to kneel through another prayer she would scream! She simply could not carry that picture of her father on his knees away with her into the world. It would spoil everything.

So she slipped to her mother's side and whispered that she was very sleepy and must be excused to go to bed.

178

Everything was all ready for her flight. Her own little suitcase that she always carried when she went to visit some girl for the week end was all packed in the closet hidden under an old sweater beside her little overnight bag, also fully packed. A coil of clothes line was tied through their handles. She meant to let them down through the window after the family came upstairs, and have them already there for morning.

Quickly she undressed, and put on the frail under garments she meant to wear on her trip, scorning the heavy flannels her mother had brought along, which she had gladly been wearing to keep out the unusual cold.

Then she put on the heavy flannel nightgown over her underwear and crept into bed shivering. Coming as she had from the warm cheery room downstairs the room seemed colder than usual, even with the stove pipe hot enough to burn to the touch. A rim of light around the stove pipe seemed to bring her in close touch with the room below.

Yes, she was right, she had come away just in time. They were singing that queer old song that Chester loved, just because his mother used to sing it, likely:

> *"Rock of ages, cleft for me,*
> *Let me hide myself in Thee,*
> *Let the water and the blood*
> *From Thy riven side which flowed,*
> *Be of sin the double cure,*
> *Save me from its guilt and power."*

Rocks and blood! A queer old song. How could Chester bear to sing it. Sin! As if anybody believed in it any more. There wasn't any such thing. Sin was supposed to be something that God had said you mustn't do, and if there wasn't any God, if there was only a force of Nature or whatever you called it, what bunk it all was, and why did anybody want to put anything like that over on the world anyway in the first place?

Betty covered up her ears and shut her eyes trying to draw her spirit away from the consciousness of it all, but

179

the words sang clearly up the old stove pipe and seemed not to mind the bed quilts at all.

> *"Nothing in my hand I bring,*
> *Simply to Thy cross I cling,—"*

As if a cross could do anything for anybody! Such superstition!

> *"Naked come to Thee for dress,*
> *Helpless look to Thee for grace;*
> *Foul I to the fountain fly;*
> *Wash me Saviour or I die."*

There! There was that horrid word, "foul." Chester had used that when he spoke of Dudley. He said he was a foul-mouthed rascal! Betty shivered again, and drew her head farther under the bedclothes. Foul! That meant unclean. Dirty! That was ridiculous! Just because people were frank, and spoke of things that everybody knew. Just because they happened to be younger than a few other people, they were called dirty! Well, that wasn't fair! That was injustice, and the young people of to-day were not taking anything like that handed out to them. Not on your life, thought Betty!

There, there was that other horrid verse, the worst of them all,

> *"While I draw this fleeting breath,*
> *When my eyelids close in death!"*

A shudder passed over her and she put her fingers in her ears. But still there came faintly, because she had to listen in spite of herself, the words,

> *"When I soar to worlds unknown,*
> *See Thee on thy—"*

She stuffed the blanket into her ears, but she knew the rest was "judgment throne," and she hated it! Why did she have to be judged? Just because she was following out her nature! She didn't! She wouldn't! And she didn't want to hide in any Rock no matter how many Ages it had lived and fooled people.

The singing died away, and now she had to listen again, and she heard them kneeling down. She might as well have stayed, for she could hear every word that Chester said. And Great Cats! He was praying for *her*. By *name!* "Our little Betty!" He had no right! He had no *right!* "Give her a meek and quiet spirit. Help her to learn to do right!"

This was the limit!

And there were tears on her face, very wet tears, that made the sheet and pillow damp and would not stop. Oh, she was frantic! This was poisonous! Perfectly poisonous! Would Chester never stop? It would have been almost better if she had stayed down. He would not have made it so personal then. But if he had she would have cried right there before them all, and that would have been awful! Nobody cried any more. It wasn't the thing to do at all. Everybody would howl if they knew she cried at old sob stuff like that! And the strange part about it was that she hadn't gained a thing by coming upstairs, for there was God, out here in her bedroom looking at her, just the same as He had done downstairs when she knelt with the rest. God! Just an idea! But there He stood looking at her with such strange wistful, almost loving eyes, the way Chester looked at her sometimes, only more so. And she couldn't get away from Him even with her eyes shut. She couldn't get away from Him even with all the bedclothes over her head. Well, she would get away from Him when she went with Dudley, that was certain. Dudley hadn't much in common with God!

Now they were rising from their knees, and the vision of God was gone. She felt great relief, and turned over her pillow, arranging the spot where her tears had wet the sheet so Eleanor would not feel it if she came in to say good night. She lay down and tried to breathe very regularly, her face turned away from the door. They were coming up now. Chester was banking down the fire on the hearth, and locking the door. The key turned with a grating sound. She had meant to put a drop of oil in that lock and had forgotten it.

She could hear Jane tiptoeing by the door, and now Eleanor opened it softly and looked in. Her father was coming up the stairs with the lamp in his hand. She could see the flare of the light on her opposite wall through the fringes of her lashes.

"She seems to be sound asleep," she heard Eleanor say in a whisper. "Poor child, she was tired! I guess I won't go in, it might waken her!"

She closed the door softly, and Betty missed her mother's kiss.

Cautiously she stole out of bed and lifted her window. The night air bit at her thin garments like ice. The old-fashioned catch slipped from her excited fingers once and the window slid down with a thump. She held her breath but no one seemed to notice. She could hear her mother talking in low tones in the room across the hall. She tried the catch once more and this time it held and the cold air poured in about her again, bitterly, romping with the flannel nightdress and chilling her bare feet.

She went softly to the closet, brought out the suitcase and bag, let them down till they touched on the crisp snow below and slid a little way catching in the stalks of a tall old lilac bush. She looked at them for an instant half frightened. There they were! They had started! And soon she too would be on her way, very very early in the morning.

She cast a fearful eye at the sky. It was clear as a bell. The stars seemed larger than she had ever seen them before, and a new moon hung like a silver boat in a sapphire sea. Across the distance the mountains were dimly shadowed against the night. It was a wonderful scene, almost terrible in its cold sparkling beauty. There was one star that was larger than the rest, looking down straight at her. It seemed to pierce her like an eye. She remembered that idea of God coming into her room and watching her, and she turned quickly away from the window and crept into bed, pulling the clothes over her head again. She must get some sleep. This was no way to pull off a stunt. What would Dud think of her if he knew? It was weird. It was perfectly fusty.

She deliberately set herself to go to sleep, but sleep seemed far from her. She seemed to be holding her body up from the bed, holding her breath, somehow imagining that her secret would make itself known if she breathed aloud.

Chester and Eleanor were still talking. She could hear their pleasant tones. It was good to go away when they were happy. Perhaps Chester had had some good word about business.

Then she remembered that she had meant to put the rest of her clothes by the bed so that she would make less noise getting off when the time came, and she slid out in the cold air again and brought her dress, the pretty jersey dress she had worn to school the last day, and her slippers, and placed them on a chair by the bed. She went back to the closet and got her fur coat and hat, and on second thought her goloshes and put them where she could reach them without moving about on the floor, for she did not trust the old flooring. Some boards creaked horribly under the least step.

All these excursions with the window open chilled her to the bone and she crept back to bed with her teeth chattering, and finally fell asleep.

Chapter XIX

It was still dark with the stars shining when she awoke, but she could see a streak of dawn over against the horizon, and she knew it must be getting toward day. She listened and presently the old clock in the hall that

Chester had put in running order the first day they arrived, chimed out four.

Betty had heard that four o'clock was the time that sleep was the deepest, so she had chosen that hour for her going.

It took all the courage she had to even reach out into the cold and pull in her dress under the bed clothes. She had not realized it would be so cold. She ought to have closed her window.

Neither was it an easy thing to put on her dress under the bed clothes without making the bed creak wildly in the still old house. The clock had struck the half hour before she was really ready, hat on, fur coat buttoned. She stuffed her slippers inside her galoshes and stole out upon the floor in her stocking feet. Slowly she reached the door, step by step, with intervals between, lifted the latch with infinite pains, released it as carefully, and moved with almost fairy tread into the hall, down the stairs, half leaning on the railing and sliding down. It seemed an age till she reached the door, and another till she had slid back the rusty old bolt, turned the key and was out at last with the door shut behind her.

She stopped an instant and listened. The house was as still as if it were empty. The branches of the maple tree stirred with the wind and hit against the upper hall window, clashing like sabres. They startled her. Surely, some one would waken at that sound! But all was silent.

The stars were still out, though the sky was paling, and off to the East a rosy light was appearing now. She must get on her way at once.

She had put on her slippers and galoshes before she opened the door. She stepped out upon the snowy path and her footsteps crunched, like the little lumps of confectioner's sugar under the rolling pin when she was making that butter icing for the cake yesterday. She only dared take one step at a time, and wait between lest some one would waken and hear her.

Slowly she made her way to the side of the house where the bags waited under her window, reached out on the smooth crust for the end of the rope which she had purposely flung as far toward the path as she could from her window, and drew it toward her. The bags were caught in the lilac but she finally managed to free them and draw them slowly toward her. At last she was out on the open path that led to the lane.

She drew a long breath when she finally turned into the lane and the shelter of the thickly grouped birch trees. She was hidden now by the shadows at least and no one could see her here from the house. She would have to make a detour around the log house by the highway, but she had planned that all out. Besides, no one there would be up yet, and she felt reasonably sure that she would beat the milkman down by a full hour at least. No one else would know her, and anyway, by the time they could get word to her people she would be safely hidden in the station, or in the train if it was on time.

But it was hard walking on the rough snow, with baggage to carry, and the three miles to the village loomed ahead like a trip around the world. Her back soon ached, her arms grew heavy, her feet were very cold and her hands in their thin kid gloves were frozen numb. She had to stop several times and take off her gloves and put her hands inside her fur coat to get any feeling into them at all. She wished she had brought her mittens along, but it was too late to go back now. So she wound a couple of handkerchiefs around her hands over her gloves and took up her heavy suitcase again. If she had only brought that rope along she might have dragged it on the snow, but that was now too far away.

She tried walking on the crust of the snow, but in places it was soft and once she went through and floundered around getting snow inside her clothing until she was most uncomfortable. She wished she had worn her thick underwear until she got to the station at least. She might have thrown it away afterwards. She had no idea it would be so mortally cold at this hour in the morning.

She was on the verge of tears when at last she staggered into the highway, and began the long hard walk down the hill. If it had been up hill she could not have managed it, for the suitcase and even the little overnight bag were growing heavier every minute.

The thread of a moon like a silver boat hung low in the sky now, almost over the brink of the horizon, just tilted a little lazily, as if its work for the night was done, and it was about to drop over into another world to rest.

The woods on either side of the road seemed dense and full of awful shadows. One could almost expect bears or bandits to walk out of them at any minute, and behind her she kept imagining a continual procession of people coming on to catch up with her, but she made her painful way mile by mile, and saw not a soul. Once off in the distance she heard sleigh bells, but they stopped soon, and the next time she heard them they were farther away.

Unmolested she came at last through the woods, and down into the still sleeping village. She drew a deep breath and put down her burdens on the outskirts of town, to rest and warm her hands inside her coat. Her feet were numb, and when she tapped them on the snow to try to get up a circulation they stung painfully. She wished she had worn her heavier shoes, or brought the warm woollen stockings her mother insisted upon her wearing for skating.

As she walked down the village street the frozen lake with its huddle of cottages and boat houses had turned to pink and gold, and a new world burst upon her jaded sight. She had never seen such early morning before. It was lovely. But she was by this time too frightened and too tired to appreciate it.

She was petrified with anxiety when she found the station was not open. Off in the distance about two blocks she saw a light in the kitchen of a house. She might go there and get warm, but they would ask questions and besides, she might miss the train. So she settled down on her suitcase on the sheltered side of the station, covered her feet as much as possible with her coat, and waited for the day to break and the train to come.

It came at last and she had to get on without buying a ticket, for the station agent was just taking down his shutters as the train crawled round the curve, and there was no time for tickets.

It rather frightened her to see how little money she had left after paying her fare to Springfield. For the first time it occurred to her to wonder what she would do if Dudley did not keep his contract.

But she was too weary and too sleepy to think long about anything just now. It was warm in the car, too warm, and she soon curled up in the corner of her ill-smelling seat and went sound asleep.

Back at the farm things had been happening also.

Eleanor was putting a pan of muffins in the oven when the telephone rang. Jane was setting the table.

"I don't see why Betty can't come down and do this," Jane complained. "It's her turn to set the table."

"Never mind this time," said Eleanor, "she can take two turns the next two days. I wouldn't waken her this morning, she seemed so very tired last night. Go tell Daddy his phone is ringing."

Jane called up the stairs to her father, and Eleanor came to the kitchen door with a troubled look.

"Don't make a noise, Janie dear. Really it isn't kind. Betty was not feeling well last night."

"Oh, rats!" said Jane crossly, "perhaps I wasn't either. Betts just lies down on her job every time and you let her! I'm sick of it. When are we going back home? I want Hannah! This is a heck of a life!"

"Janie!" said Eleanor in dismay, tears sounding in her voice. "Why, Jane dear, I thought you liked it here! You've seemed so happy, and have been working so well."

"Oh, it's all right!" shrugged Jane. "When everybody works together I don't mind, but when Betts gets this Princess complex it makes me tired! Who crowned her I'd like to know?"

But Eleanor had no chance to answer that. Chester came out of the library excitedly:

"It's too bad, Nell, but I've got to go back home to sign some papers. There isn't time to get them here and back again, and it involves a great deal of money. But it

187

can't be helped. Can you get along without me for a couple of days?"

"Oh, Chester!" gasped Eleanor in dismay, feeling as if the earth were reeling under her. "And Christmas—The children—!"

"I know! It's too bad! But I hadn't any choice. I'll make it back before Christmas Day is over if it's a possible thing. We'll make it up to them somehow—!"

"Now Daddy, I think that's *rotten!*" burst out Jane. "No Christmas! And you gone! I wish I was *de-e-e-ead!* Well I *do!*" and Jane broke into a torrent of angry tears and flung herself down on the couch shaking with sobs.

Chester turned impatiently toward Eleanor, looking suddenly gray with anguish.

"It can't be helped!" he said almost hoarsely in his excitement. "I've got to go, Eleanor. Can you come upstairs and help me a minute? John Dowley is going to stop for me and run me down to the train. I just telephoned him. There's barely time for me to catch it. Could you put some buttons in a clean shirt for me, Eleanor?"

"But you must sit down and eat something first," began Eleanor.

"I haven't time I tell you!" said Chester excitedly, and tore up the stairs, "I can get something on the train."

"Get up Janie, and make some coffee quick for Daddy!" called Eleanor as she vanished up the stairs.

"Good night!" said Chris appearing at that moment from the wood shed where he had been getting an armful of wood. "What's eating you Jay? This certainly is some house!"

Jane sat suddenly up and glared at her brother, eyes blotched with tears, lips puckered with disappointment, shoulders shaking with more sobs:

"Daddy's got to go back home! He won't be here for Chris-s-s-muss!"

"Dad going home!" exclaimed Chris, turning suddenly white and frightened. "W-w-w-what for?"

"Oh, I do-no!" bawled Jane. "Some old papers he's gotta sign. I think this earth is a horrid old place. This Christmas 'll just be *l-l-l-l-ost!* That's what it'll be! I w-w-w-ish we could *all* go home and get back to real life again!"

But Chris was up the stairs three steps at a bound, and made no reply. He appeared at his father's door white and anxious.

"What's the matter, Dad?" he asked, a note of almost fright in his tone. "Anything more about that check?"

Chester paused one instant to take in the look on his son's face and flashed him a smile.

"No, son, all right. This is the office. A contract that I have to sign, and something about a loan that has to be put through early Monday morning. There isn't time to get the papers here for signature and back again for Monday. You look after Mother and the kids, won't you son? Sorry about Christmas, but I may get back before the day is over. You do what you can to make up. You're the man of the house."

"Yes sir!" said Chris looking pleased and relieved. "Yes *sir!*"

The next ten minutes were strenuous. Chris went to the attic for his father's suitcase and manifested a man's intelligence in getting the right things together to put into it. Eleanor sewed on a missing button and hunted clean collars and cuff links. Even Jane roused herself, sobbing, with the tears still blurring her eyes and poured a cup of coffee for her father, creaming and sugaring it just as he liked it, and making two dainty sandwiches for him to eat on the way.

It seemed no time at all till Chester was striding from the door, too hurried even to kiss them, calling back directions, and waving good-bye in the early morning sunshine, as the old farm sleigh bumped its way over the ruts and out down the lane.

The family turned back to the house that seemed suddenly deserted and empty.

"Aw Gee!" began Chris, and then caught a glimpse of Eleanor wiping a furtive tear from her eye, and changed his tone. "Say, Mums, you go sit down and eat a good breakfast. You've been on the double jump ever since you got up. Here, Janie, you put back those muffins in the oven and get 'em hot. Let's all sit down and eat. That'll make the time go. And while we eat let's plan some surprise for Dad when he gets back. Say, Mums, can't we put off Christmas till Dad gets here? Make it daylight saving or something,—just set back the clock a coupla days or something? What say? 'Nobody round here'll know what we're doing, so we can't be interrupted by any nosey people that wantta know why we're doing it. Just pretend it isn't time yet. How'll that do?"

His voice was cheerful and even enthusiastic, and Eleanor stifled the sigh that was in her heart and smiled.

"Surely!" she said. "Why not? This interruption was something we couldn't help so we might as well make the best of it."

Jane looked up hopefully.

"Do you think Daddy will bring some candy or something back with him?" she asked.

"Well, I'm not sure," said Eleanor hating to spoil the child's ray of hope. "You know Daddy will be very busy every minute he is there, no time to go out and buy anything, even if he could afford it—"

"Oh, I forgot the old money!" said Jane disconsolately. "Won't he ever have any money again?"

"Why, I hope so," said Eleanor trying to banish the fear that clutched at her own heart. "I haven't talked about money to your father since we have been here. The doctor told me he ought to get away from everything for a little while and have a real rest. I thought the main thing was to be cheerful. But I imagine there must be some hope somewhere for the business or he would not be going down to sign a new contract, although it may be just something about settling up with their creditors. I didn't have time to ask him. But such things don't really matter, Jane dear, if we are all together and all well. We'll pull out of the troubles. Let's just get ready for Daddy's home coming and make him have a good time so he will forget if he has had any business troubles while he was gone."

"But what shall we do?" asked Jane mournfully. "We're all ready for Christmas now."

"How about popcorn balls?" said Eleanor brightly. "Would you like to make some of those? And we must string a lot of popcorn for the tree, and cut out things to put on it. Oh, there's a lot to do. There'll hardly be time to get it all done. Here, John, you and Doris eat your breakfast and begin to shell the popcorn. The milkman brought a lot of it over yesterday. And Chris, there's an old popper hanging in the woodshed. You might try scouring it a little. I think it would be all right if some of the rust were rubbed off."

"Oh, how darling!" said Jane, sunshine coming back into her face, as suddenly as it had gone. "Shall I go wake up Betts? She'll like making popcorn balls, I'm sure."

"No, don't wake up Betty yet," said Eleanor. "Let her sleep till she feels like herself again. She'll feel more like working if she's had her sleep out. Let's get everything ready first, the table all cleared off, and the dishes washed. I thought about making some cookies in the shape of stars, too."

"Fine!" said Chris. "And Mums, how about me cutting out some tin stars from the tomato tops for the tree."

"Why that's a wonderful idea. I was wondering how we were going to get something silver on it."

"And say, muvver," put in Doris, "couldn't you make some gingerbread men with currants for eyes, like the story in my reader at school?"

"I think I could," laughed Eleanor, her heart growing lighter as she saw each one of the children beginning to take hold of the idea of a delayed Christmas. Now if only Betty would be as cheerful, everything would be all right. She dreaded Betty's coming down, lest she would cast discouragement and blight upon all the others. She decided to let Betty sleep as long as possible.

Meantime the horse that John Dowley had hastily harnessed to take Chester to the early morning train was racing down the road with a wicked stride as if he rather enjoyed the errand, and his sleigh bells jingled a merry tune in the frosty air.

191

"Stand a pretty good chanct of makin' her," said John Dowley as he wrapped the reins around his big sheepskin mitten and gave the secret cluck to his horse that let him know he might go his best pace.

"I'm afraid not, if my watch is correct," said Chester taking it out again and looking at it anxiously as if it might have something encouraging to say about it. "Is this train ever late?"

"Times it is," said John Dowley, "when ther's a blizzard up state. But we'll make her."

The horse skimmed over the rough road, and the sleigh bumped along, almost upsetting at times, and then righting itself amazingly. Chester sat grimly in his seat holding on to the sleigh, and trying to plan what he should do if he missed the train. There was scarcely a chance in a hundred that he could make home in time if he had to wait for the noon train, and there were no intermediate trains this time of year. Besides, that noon train was a way train and stopped at every crossroad and watering trough as it were.

They had climbed the hill now and were coming down the other side. The little village lay spread out before them, the station a mere red dot at one side. The sun on the lake flashed back at them dazzling their eyes. The black gash in the whiteness of the landscape that was the railroad track wound away in the distance, and at the extreme end there was a plume of smoke.

"She's on her way!" said John Dowley with set lips. "But we'll make her."

"Is that the train off there?" asked Chester with anxious eyes watching the little plume of smoke pause, spume up again and begin to move.

"That's her!" said John Dowley. "She's stoppin' at the Crossin'! Up Blackie, we gotta make her!"

The horse seemed to understand and plunged on, and Chester went through the mental process several times of gripping his suitcase and sprinting for the train at the last minute.

The train came on, and was lost to view as the sleigh dashed into a little wood, but they could hear the whistle, shrill and defiant, echoing among the hills. Chester's heart beat fast, and he felt as if he were running with the horse.

The train was just screaming into town as they rounded the corner by the little white church and took the short cut back of the stores to the station. But some one had left a truck across the road, and Blackie had to turn out for it and wallow a wild minute or two to get around it. Chester's heart sank once more. It seemed hopeless now, and no use to get out and spring, for the drift was too deep to run in. Then Blackie righted herself, pulled free of the snow and was off again. John Dowley stood up in the sleigh and gave her the reins, and truly the horse seemed to understand.

The train was just pulling out of the station as they drew up at the far side, out of sight of the engineer who might have waited if he had known. Chester sprang from the sleigh, suitcase in hand, just as he had planned, and sprinted for the slowly receding end of that train. Almost he lost his footing on a spot of ice, but caught himself, and whirled on, catching the last car and reeling to the step with something of his boyhood's agility.

It took him several seconds on that bottom step before he could gather breath to pull himself up and into the car. He dropped into the last seat and sat back relieved. It was not so much that last few feet of sprinting that seemed to have taken the strength from him. It was the whole tempestuous episode, the having to leave Eleanor and the children just before Christmas, the terrible need of getting that train because of the crisis that had arisen at home; the agony of watching that little plume of smoke coming nearer and nearer, and only one brave horse to bridge the distance. It seemed to him he would never forget the sound of that fiendish whistle, as the train began to gain on them, as if it knew it were racing with humans.

In due time Chester's mind calmed, and he got out his papers and began to do some important figuring, while station after station slipped by without his notice.

And all the time, in the second car ahead, curled up fast asleep in her seat, his daughter Betty rode.

Chapter XX

At Springfield he looked up, got out his watch, and the time table to see if they were on time. Well pleased that they were, he glanced out again, and watched the crowds idly. As the train started on, he noticed a pretty girl who looked extremely like his Betty, standing on the platform. If he hadn't just left Betty at home in her bed asleep, he would have been almost startled, this girl looked so much like her. Dressed as Betty did at home, too. A fur coat just like hers and a little black hat. He turned his head to watch her, keeping up the illusion pleasantly. She walked like Betty too, carrying a little suitcase, with her small head tilted proudly, and her back straight as a pipe stem.

The girl disappeared into the station and Chester went on with his figuring and thought no more about it. In due time he arrived in New York making perfect connection with his home train. He was filled with satisfaction at the way things were coming out.

Meantime, back at home the family were making popcorn balls and gingerbread men and tin stars and cookies. They were busy and happy, and did not even notice when a few lazy flakes began to come down.

It was not till they had cleared off the things and began to get lunch that Chris looked up.

"Aw! Gee! Look, it's snowing again! Now we'll havta sweep off that lake, it'll spoil the skating! Gee, I hope it don't snow all night. I don't know how we'll manage to get the lake clear without Dad!"

"Never mind," said Eleanor soothingly, casting an anxious glance at the sky. "It doesn't look so very dark. Perhaps it won't snow long. Doris, you may go and waken Betty now. Lunch is all ready to put on the table."

But Doris came back with word that Betty wasn't there.

"Oh, you're a baby!" said Jane speeding past her. "She's in some other room. She's probably gone in my room to borrow something."

"No, she isn't, Janie," cried Doris aggrieved. "She isn't anywhere. I looked in all the rooms!"

"She's probably up in the attic getting some more stuff for Christmas presents," said Eleanor setting a steaming dish of potatoes down beside another of creamed codfish. "Come, get up in your chair and put on your bib, Doris. We want to eat while the things are hot."

But Jane came flying back wide-eyed.

"She isn't anywhere, Mums. I don't think it's fair. We thought she was asleep and here we did all the work, and she's probably off hiding reading an old book or something."

"Aw, she's in the attic," said Chris. "Call her, can't you? I'm holla as a log. Let's get ta eating."

"I went up in the attic," affirmed Jane. "I looked behind all the trunks and everything. I bet she's gone skating all alone. I say that's no fair. Let's eat all the lunch up—!"

"Mercy!" said Eleanor, "I hope she hasn't gone skating alone. Your father said yesterday there was a hole in the ice. It might not be safe—!"

"Aw, her skates are here, Mums! She couldn't have gone skating. Run back Jane and look again. You'll find her. Call. Tell her about the popcorn balls. That'll bring her. Hurry!"

"I tell you I looked everywhere, and I'm not going to look again!" said Jane sulkily. "Betty won't come for me anyway, ever. She thinks she's too big to mind me!"

Then suddenly Eleanor dropped the dishcloth she was holding and sped up the stairs. A strange premonition had come to her. Something had happened to Betty!

Chris found his mother, five minutes later, sitting by the bureau in Betty's room crying, a letter lying on the floor by the chair. Eleanor's face was covered by her apron, and she seemed to be stifling great sobs which shook her whole body. Chris had never had anything hurt him so as it did to see his mother cry like that, as if everything was lost. He went over and put his arms around her, gathered her up like a little child, and sat down on Betty's bed with her still in his arms, his little mother!

And suddenly all the bad wild careless things he had ever done rose up and stood around him to shame him, and his face grew red and shy. He patted his mother awkwardly, and tried to think what Dad would have done if he had found her instead. He was the man of the house now. He shook off the condemning past and rose to meet his manhood.

"Wha's z' matter, Mums?" he crooned shyly. "Don' cry, Muth! I say, Muth, wha's z' matter? Tell a fella, can't ya? Aw, c'mon!"

For answer Eleanor suddenly buried her face in her boy's neck and cried the harder, and Chris' eyes went wildly round the room wondering what he should do next? What did men do when women cried? He had always been the one to be comforted before. How did they do it? He had done his awkward best, and it did no good—

"Muth—!" he said helplessly, almost reverting to the uncomforted one himself, feeling baby enough at this minute to cry himself and seek comfort from her.

Then suddenly his anguished wandering gaze touched the letter lying on the floor. Betty's handwriting! Why had Betty written a letter?

Some vague fear menaced his further peace. He strained his eyes and tried to read the words, but only one here and there was readable from the crumpled paper lying so far away. "Christmas," he saw, and "poisonous." "Perfectly poisonous" that must be. It would be if Betty wrote it. And, was that Dudley? Yes, that was a W after the Dudley. What had Dud Weston been doing? That *mutt!* Thought he was king! What did Betts see in him? Was that last word "Good" or "Goodbye"?

"Muth!" he cried in alarm. "Muth, where's Betts?"

"She's gone!" said Eleanor with a quick little sob that sounded like a knife.

Chris' arms went round his mother tighter, protectingly, and his mouth shut in a thin firm line that made him look like his father.

"Now, look here, Muth, be sensible! Betts can't

196

have gone far. We'll get her. Where's she gone?"

"She says she's gone to get married," said Eleanor, in smothered sobs, as if the son who was comforting her were older than herself. She seemed to be utterly dazed at the thought. "There's her letter, read it," and she motioned toward Betty's note lying on the floor.

"Good night!" said Chris in horror. "Here, I'll put you on the bed, Muth! You lie still and let me han'le this! Good night! Why Muth! Betts is only a child! A mere child!"

He laid his mother gently on the rumpled bed that Betty had deserted at dawn, and snatched up the letter, reading it with a deep frown on his young face.

"Old Dears!" it read,

"I shall simply pass out if I stay in this poisonous dump any longer, so Dud and I have decided to tie up. You needn't feel bad, because we were going to do it anyway as soon as Commencement was over, and this will help out a little in one way for nobody will expect Dad to give me a wedding if I just go off. We're thinking of making it companionate, so if things don't go right we can just quit any time. That ought to make Mums feel better about it, but I'm sure you'll like Dud all right when he's really in the family. I'm sorry about Christmas, but I'll have plenty of money of course when I'm married, and I'll send some real presents when I get somewhere. Till then these things can do. Bye Bye. Let you know later when we get our plans made. Have a good time.

Betty."

Chris cast a pitying eye towards his mother and tried to speak, but his voice choked up! He cleared his throat and tried again.

"I say, Muth, that's a rotten deal! Betts oughtta be whaled when we get her home again. She's a little fool! That's what she is. What she sees in that Dud Weston! He's just a loud mouthed boob! She thinks she'll have plenty of money when she marries him! I *see* her! Why, that poor fish is always broke! His dad gives him a smaller allowance than we get, and he's always spent it two or three months ahead. He goes around borrowing off the fellas. He borrowed two bucks off me just last week. I'll bet a hat he borras the money to get married. That kid'll find out whatta bad egg he is soon enough if she ever marries him! But we won't let 'er. We'll get busy, Mums, and stop it! Don't you worry, Mums, she can't uv got far. How long d'ya 'spose she's been gone? He couldn't 'a come way up here after her. He doesn't know the way. She musta walked ta the village 'n less she got the milkman to take her. Wait! I'll phone up there and see."

"Wait! Chris!" said his mother suddenly sitting up and wiping her eyes. "We mustn't tell people! Not yet—anyway! We don't want anyone to know what a wild thing Betty is trying to do. We'll have to look out for your sister's reputation, you know dear."

"Don't you worry, Muth! I'll be discreet all right. We gotta find out something to start on. We gotta work fast you know. I'll just ask the milkman if my sister caught him all right or did she havta walk all the way to the early train, see? That'll make him think we were in on it."

"He'll think it very strange that we let her go down the lane alone so early in the morning."

"Well, let him think! I'll tell him the kid woke up early and slipped off so not to wake us up! See? I'll fix it up. Don't you worry. No, Muth!" as she started to go downstairs with him, hindrance in her very attitude, "You lemme handle this! Dad said I was to be the man of the house. Now, you jus' stay here, an'—an' well, you jus' stay here an' *rest!* Now I'll han'le this all right. We haven't any time to waste, you know."

Eleanor sank back on the pillow with a quivering, sob.

"All right, Chris. But you be very careful what you say, and *hurry!* I'll stay here and pray!"

"Aw! Now, *Muth!* It isn't as bad as that! You don't havta *pray!* I'm handling this all right, an' we're gonta get *results* right off the bat! You just wait, and *rest!* Take a good *rest!* Then you'll be all ready to make it nice for Betts when she gets back, or bawl her out!" he added under his breath.

Chris went downstairs in three leaps, and she could hear his voice in the library below talking in low grown-up tones.

But Eleanor was praying even while she held her breath to listen. She might be able to tell from the sound of Chris' voice what replies he had received.

It was fully five minutes before Chris returned.

His face was grave and thoughtful and there was not so much assurance in his voice as when he went downstairs.

Eleanor rose on one elbow and eyed him eagerly, a new dependence in her voice:

"Did she go with him?" she asked in a sharp frightened voice. Little Betty! Her little daughter, guarded all her life, at least supposedly so, out alone with a strange milkman at four o'clock in the morning!

"They don't know," said Chris evasively. "He ain't got back yet. He was going over across the mountain to buy a couppla cows he heard of, and he won't be back till night. Whaddya say, Muth, I hire a car down ta the village an' chase after him? I cud catch him in no time with only that team he drives, and then like as not Betts hired him to take her some place to meet Dud Weston, an' I'd catch her before she met him, see? And bring her back."

"No!" said Eleanor sharply. "You mustn't leave here. You know your father said you mustn't even go down to skate while he was gone. He wanted you here! I should die if I didn't have you here. This is terrible! And besides, Chris, that would be a wild goose chase. You don't even know that Betty is with him, and while you were gone something might turn up that would tell us where she really is."

"But I've got a hunch she's with the milkman. Right now. See? At least I think it's worth trying."

"Look here, Chris. That is not to be thought of. We can't waste time going off on a hunch. And if you are going to do crazy things like that I can't trust you to manage for me. You can probably telephone and get that milkman by this time at the place where he was going. His wife will know where to telephone. Besides, I don't believe Betty has driven across any mountains in that old milk

GRACE LIVINGSTON HILL

sled. She may have gone down to the village, but Betty would have been too impatient to ride a longer distance that way. She turned up her nose yesterday at having to ride in a sleigh like that with only straw on the floor for a seat. The thing to do is to find out if she went on the train. We must telephone to the station."

"I've already done that," said Chris in a half offended tone. "The only morning train was the one Dad went for. There isn't another till two o'clock. The station wasn't open till eight o'clock so they don't know whether any girl took that early train or not. But anyhow if Betts was on that train Dad'll see her. Dad'll take care of her. We'll likely get a telegram from Dad pretty soon saying she's along with him and for us not to worry."

Eleanor caught at the idea eagerly, but she did not feel like relaxing activities.

"We could send a telegram to that train, Chris!" she said brightening. "We could let your father know. He'll understand just what to do—"

"Now, look here, Muth!" exclaimed Chris raising his voice. "You don't understand about things. You gotta let me han'le this. Dad's train musta got away off we don't know where, an' what's the use o' bothering Dad? He left me in charge an' I'm gonta handle this. If Dad knew Betts had gone off with that half baked simp he'd go off his nut. You know how crazy he was with that trouble about me, and Betts means ten thousand times more to him than I ever did—!"

"Chris!"

"Yep! she does! She's a girl! I don't mind. But she does. And he'd hafta give up that 'mportant business he was going down to tend to and go traipsing off no one knows where. And you know he said he simply had ta be down home tonight! And what could he do anyhow? I ask you? Could he do more'n we're doing? You don't seem to realize she started from here! She didn't start from down there! And he'd hafta come back here, and then where would his 'mportant business be, I ask you? And mebbe, if he knew what Dud had done, leastways what he was gonta do, he go an' kill Dud, or hit his Dad or something awful! You know how Dad is about Betts! You know he'd

200

be awful angry. No. Muth, the thing for us to do is get busy, and right now I'm gonta get a long distance in for Dud Weston. If he's home I'll talk to him kinda like I wanted him to do a favor for Betts or something like that, see? And then I'll find out where he's gonta be tonight, an' then I'll send the p'lice to arrest him, see? Or something, so if Betts has gone down to Briardale ta meet him we'll stand her up! See?"

"But Chris, you don't even know that Dudley is at home. If he's meeting Betty somewhere, or if he came up here after her—!"

"I'll eat my hat if Dud Weston ever took this long trip after Betts. He'd make her come somewhere. He's the laziest cuss in Briardale. However, I'll find out. I gotta buddie at home that's a regular sleuth fer finding out things. I'll put him onta this job by phone—"

"But Chris, you mustn't let people in Briardale know about your sister—why it would be simply awful—! We must stop it before they ever get married! We *must!* And then there will be nothing for them to gossip about. You mustn't tell any boy about your sister's private affairs—!"

"There you are again, Muth. It's evident you don't trust me. *I* wouldn't tell anything about my sister! I'd just let that fella know I wanted ta get pointers on Dud Weston. Now, Muth, I gotta get that call in fer Dud. It's our best bet ta find out first whether he's at home 'r not. If he is, we got plenty o' time ta let Dad know before he gets there, and he can get Betts before she sees him. He can nail Dud before he goes to meet her. See?"

"Oh!" groaned Eleanor, sinking down on the edge of the bed again. "Oh, I'm afraid it will *kill* your father!"

"That's it, Muth, we gotta get this thing in hand before Dad has to know. And I gotta get busy. Muth you sit down and write out what Betts had on so's I can give a description if I hafta have her paged ur anything at a station ur hotel."

"But how do I know what she had on?" groaned the mother.

"Look in her closet and see what's she left behind!" said the practical boy. "Did she wear her new fur coat?"

Given something practical to do Eleanor went to work, taking out the things in Betty's closet, running up to the attic to see which suit case she had taken, writing down a probable description.

Jane appeared at the head of the stairs, looking silently in on her mother as she wrote.

"Aren't we ever going to have lunch?" she asked, "I'm starved. What are you and Chris fighting about?"

"Oh, Jane!" said her mother, her eyes filling with tears again, "You don't know what a dreadful thing has happened, dear."

"Sure, I do!" said Jane, "I'm not dumb. Betts is a selfish thing, that's what she is. She doesn't care whether we any of us have any Christmas or any good times any more or anything." Jane was winking back the tears and her voice sounded suddenly like a sob at the end of her sentence.

Eleanor turned and caught Jane in her arms, and realized suddenly that it had been a long time since she had held Jane so. Her little girl had somehow grown hard and unloving and had not wanted petting. But now suddenly Jane buried her face on her mother's shoulder and cried like any little dear girl whose good times were spoiled and who wanted to be comforted.

"Darling," said Eleanor, "Never mind Christmas. We'll make all that up afterward if we can only find Betty. My dear, your sister is in great danger!"

"Well, she put herself there, didn't she? If she hadn't a wanted to she wouldn't have, would she? I wouldn't fuss about her. Let her go. We can have a better time without her. She always wanted the best things anyway, and she's been as cross as two sticks ever since she came. She hated this place, and she wasn't going to get over it. She told me. And she didn't like ta work. It wasn't fair, and then she always got the biggest pieces of pie—I'm glad she's gone," and Jane shook the long dark forehead curl out of her eyes and glared up fiercely through her tears.

"My dear, my dear! What a terrible state of things between two sisters. But you must not talk that way. Even if Betty has done wrong and been selfish, now she is in great danger. We must do all we can to find her, and there will never be any happiness in this house till she is found. We love all our children. Now, Jane, dear, stop crying and stop thinking hard thoughts against Betty, and try to help me. Think! Did you ever hear Betty say anything about where she would go if she went away? Did she ever say she wanted to go?"

"I'll say she did!" said the little girl, "She couldn't get done talking about it. She told me once she was going ta write ta Dudley Weston and get him to rescue her from this poisonous dump. That's just what she said. She said Dudley would lie down and let her walk over him if she asked him."

"Have you any idea how she was planning to go? Did she suggest any way when she talked with you?"

The little girl shook her head.

"No, but you might find something in her drawer, some letter, or in some of her pockets. She had a letter from Dudley one day. I saw his name signed, just as I came into her room, I was looking over her shoulder, and I saw it. It said "Yours ta get drunk. Dud" and I was going to read more only she turned around and saw me and she was awfully sore at me, and said she'd tell you and Daddy if I didn't keep out of her room. But she hid the letter in her pocket. Why n't ya look?"

Jane went over to the bureau and began to rummage.

"What's this?" she asked taking up the package Betty had left with her name on it. She broke the string and opened the paper.

"Her coral beads!" she said. "Well, she never liked them herself, she needn't think she's done anything great! But they always looked better on me than they did on her. I think she's just too mean for anything, anyway, to spoil all our Christmas,—and Daddy gone too. It's desperate!" and Jane broke down and cried again.

Eleanor was looking through the things in the closet, and she stopped and gazed at her little girl in dismay. Such deep rooted hardness between two sisters! How had it come about? So unloving, so selfish, both of them! Why hadn't she known how things were going? Why hadn't she seen it before and done something to bring about a sweeter life in the home? Oh, she had been wrong! It had been her own fault! This must be a punishment for her own neglect.

But she had thought she was doing everything for them! They were being educated in the best of schools, with the most expensive teachers, and that class at the woman's club had said that children must not be fussed over and noticed in every little wrong thing they did.

Suddenly she came on a couple of letters in Betty's old sweater pocket and brought them out to the light. They were only from Betty's girl friend Gipsy, but they shed a good deal of light on Betty's associates, and opened Eleanor's eyes to a number of things more than any amount of club lectures could have done.

She was sitting in a daze of sorrow looking at them when Chris came back. Word had come back from the Weston home that Dudley was away at a week end party down at the shore.

"So that's that!" said Chris frowning thoughtfully, "Mebbe he's there, and mebbe he isn't. If I only knew where that house party was, whose house—Aw! this is the limit, living away off up here! If I knew who was giving it, might be Gwen or Fran or Gip Magilkey. 'F I only knew, I might telephone there and ask to speak to Dud. Maybe that's where Betts was going to meet him."

"Oh!" said Eleanor looking up from her daze of trouble, "Why it must be Gwen's house party. This letter I found in Betty's pocket speaks of a house party at Gwen's, and a dance at Shillingsworth's. Isn't that the dancing pavilion down at Lancet Beach?"

"It sure is," said Chris excitedly, "Let me see that letter!"

He glanced through Gipsy's effusive epistle, flung it back into his mother's lap with a contemptuous "Say, isn't that just like *a fool girl!*" and went off down stairs again. Eleanor felt a thrill of hope. Perhaps after all Betty was only going down to that house party and didn't really mean to get married. Perhaps she only said that to throw them off the track, and worry them so they wouldn't make a fuss about the party afterwards.

But in half an hour Chris came back with a really anxious look on his face.

"I had Gwen on the wire all righty," he said slumping into a chair near his mother, "But she didn't know a thing about Dud,—said he promised to be there last evening to help put up laurel, but he hadn't turned up and hadn't sent any word. I asked who else was there, letting on I was a friend of Dud's and might wantta speak to 'em. They named over all Betts' class but they didn't say a word about Betts so they can't be expecting 'em back there. So that's that! I'm up a tree! Where's Jane?"

"I sent her out with the children. She's so forlorn I thought it would do her good to get a little air. Don't you think we ought to try finding out about Daddy's train? Couldn't we wire him now? He ought to be getting into the city in an hour or so, and I wouldn't know where to reach him after he once gets off the train. The office will be closed you know, and he didn't have time to tell me where he would be—"

"I been keepin' the wires hot," said Chris efficiently. "I got the list of towns that early train stops at, and I've phoned three or four, but none of 'em have seen a girl of Betty's description. I was thinking of trying Springfield next, only that's not far enough away. Dud would never have come way up there for Betts. He wouldn't have gas enough. He never has any gas left in his machine. Always hasta borrow ta get anywhere. Bah! But I gotta wire in now for tha conductor of the early train. He'll know if a girl got on that early, and where she was going to."

"Why yes," said Eleanor, "Why didn't we think of that before? Of course he would."

Jane appeared in the doorway with the twins behind her.

"I went down to the log cabin," said Jane solemnly, "and asked 'em if they had heard a queer sound in the night like anyone going down the lane or anything, or may'ze early this morning, but they said no, they didn't hear a thing, that it mighta been a rabbit I heard, and the sick man said it couldn'ta been anything 'cause he's most always awake nights, and he'd a heard it if it hadaben. But I found some tracks!"

"Tracks!" said Chris eagerly, "What kinda tracks?"

"Tracks in the snow, 'bout the size of Betty's galoshes, where she musta broken through the crust of the snow."

"Where?" Chris was out following her like a real detective.

The tracks left the beaten path and went in a detour across the fields, giving wide berth to the log cabin, and ending abruptly in a stretch of crust that was thicker than the rest because it was in a sheltered nook where the sun could not reach it, and was strong enough to bear the weight of a light person. Chris tested it, and then walked all around it searching till he came to the tracks again, several rods ahead on the southern slope of the hill, and followed them down till they ended in the highway. But they unmistakably turned toward the village. That was plain. He felt sure that they were Betty's.

Chris hurried back to the house to tell his mother, and just as he entered the door he heard the telephone ringing.

It was an answer to his telegram to the morning train conductor. Yes, a young girl of Betty's description had boarded the train at the village station that morning. She was all alone and had paid her way as far as Springfield.

"Well, we got something at last!" said Chris as he hung up the receiver. "Gee! I never thought she'd be so near as that. I wish I'd telephoned there first! Good night! She's had time to make a great getaway. What time is it, five o'clock? Well, I can find out where she bought a ticket to from there, anyhow, or if she didn't buy one I'll have her paged! I can find out if she was alone when she bought her ticket too. Well, we're getting on!"

Chapter XXI

When Betty got out of her train at Springfield and disappeared into the station she found that it was half past ten o'clock. That was three quarters of an hour later than the time table had said it would be and she sighed contentedly. Three quarters of an hour less to wait for Dudley.

She looked around eagerly. Perhaps he was even here already. Unconsciously she straightened her hat, and tried to blink the sleep out of her eyes, for she had just wakened from one of the soundest sleeps she ever had, and might have been carried on beyond this station if it had not been for the kindness of the conductor who wakened her and helped her out.

As Dudley did not seem to be anywhere in immediate view Betty sought and found the ladies' waiting room, and began to repair the damages of travel. Her small vanity case which she had been carefully hoarding during the days at the farm did heavy duty, for Betty felt that she was getting back into her own world again and must look her best. Perhaps she applied a trifle more lip stick and rouge than was usual with her, for now there was no disapproving parent's eye upon her, and she experienced a daring delight in making her lips and cheeks as vivid as she had always longed to have them. She knew that her special type needed just this touch—at least that was what Dudley Weston had told her,—to make her look distinguished and interesting. She surveyed her finished result with real pleasure. She really had a wicked look as she turned from the smoky little mirror in the Ladies' Room and picked up her suit case to go back into the Main Waiting Room. She hoped Dudley would come soon. She was deadly hungry, but of course it wouldn't do to eat before he came, for he might come any minute now.

She selected a seat where she could see all doors of entrance, and settled down to wait, with the clock in full view.

She had just thirty-seven cents left after paying her fare to Springfield, and after waiting an hour with no results she walked over to the news stand and purchased a five cent card of chocolate and a five cent package of peanut butter cracker sandwiches.

She ate them hurriedly, prepared to hide them at once should Dudley enter either of the doors, for she did not want him to see that she had been eating and not waiting for him. But when she had finished eating she seemed hungrier than before. The minutes dragged themselves slowly by, and at last the great clock hands in the station pointed to twelve, and various whistles and bells in the town set up a screeching and clanging to call attention to the fact that it was high noon.

Betty's cheeks grew hot at the thought that in a few minutes she would be actually off on her wedding trip with Dud. As each moment passed by she found her heart beating more wildly.

A sudden rush of memory made her think of her mother and father, her brothers and sisters. Queer she felt this way. She had not expected any such softness as this. If Dud would only come! Well, she would have something on him now, if he was late. He was always saying girls were late!

But the next half hour slipped away, slow throbbing minute by slow throbbing minute, and no Dudley.

Betty began to grow angry. Dudley had no right to keep her waiting so long! When she had come as far as this, and kept her agreement she had a right to expect him to be there! It wasn't gallant in a bridegroom to keep her waiting. He really ought to have been there before her. He should have been there at early dawn to make things right!

Still, of course he might have had an accident with his machine, a flat tire or something. Betty was not given to fears. She did not begin to think of anything like a real accident, until the clock hands pointed to quarter past two. Then she got up with her suit case in her hand and walked briskly to each of the doors and windows in turn and looked out. Finally she went out and walked around the outside of the station, scanning each car parked in the block, but there was nothing like Dudley's loud combination of colors in the whole collection. Then she went back nervously and took her seat again, fearful lest he might have come and gone away mad because she was not right there to his first glance as he entered the station.

Her eyes were beginning to burn with constantly watching the opening doors, and scanning the windows of the station. Her cheeks felt as hot as their color, and her lips felt cracked and fairly bleeding from her long walk in the wind in the morning. She felt dizzy and sick and her head ached with great throbs. Dudley was spoiling it all!

Her hunger had long ago turned to a gnawing faintness as the afternoon wore on, and she began to wonder what she should do if Dudley did not come before night. How long could she go without food? What a fool she had been not to bring more than just the two or three tiny sandwiches she had managed to slip in her suit case the afternoon before. It would have been easy to bring along plenty without exciting suspicion in the least. Doughnuts and cookies, and gingerbread. There was always plenty on hand. Jane delighted to try her hand at the new things she had been learning how to make. How good it would be to walk into the dining room now and sit down to a good meal! If only nobody knew that she had gone away!

A train came rushing up and they called out its stations. It was the train that went back to the little village below the farm. If she had the money she could get on it and go back. It would serve Dudley Weston right, keeping her waiting so long! She would have been almost willing to do it now, she was so angry with Dudley for being late. Yet of course she couldn't because she had no money!

She walked restlessly to the door and watched the people get on. No one would know her of course. She would not know any of the passengers, yet it was comforting somehow to feel that that train was going back to where she had come from, back where mother was, and home, and Christmas.

A sudden compunction assailed her for having gone away before Christmas. Of course she might have waited.

Probably if she got on the train now and told the conductor she hadn't money enough to get home but would send it to him he would likely let her ride. She could give him her wrist watch as surety. But she wouldn't do it of course.

The train began to move and she looked around again hastily to see if Dudley was coming. There was no Dudley and she took a couple of steps toward the last car which was moving past her more rapidly now. And then she saw that she couldn't get on it even if she wanted to, it was moving too rapidly. It had gone past her the full length of the car.

She turned with a long drawn sigh, half wishing she had got on. The deadly thought assailed her that perhaps Dud would stand her up! Perhaps he would not come at all. Perhaps he had gone down to Gwen's house party! And she like a fool was sitting alone in a strange station, moneyless and hungry, and utterly out with her family, while he danced the giddy hours away with Gwen!

Furious she walked crisply across the station and out the opposite door. If she had only done something to get some more money! If she could sell her watch now, for instance, and hire a taxi—no it was too far for a taxi—but she could telephone home at least. Perhaps, if she asked them, they would reverse the call and let her talk to her father! That would be the last resort! Poor Dad. He would be furious of course, but the approaching evening and the hunger and the anger were making her almost willing to stand his fury, if only she might get back to her own bed, something good to eat, and peace and safety! Out on her own, with nothing to do but wait in a station for somebody who did not come! Running away wasn't all it had promised to be.

During the little moment in which she had entered the train shed, and gone through to the opposite side of the station, the night seemed to have come down. It startled her to look out upon the square and see the lights springing up on all sides, see the streets dim away vaguely into twilight, and the sky dark, with little occasional flakes drifting slowly, lazily down.

Her mind went back to the drive they had had in the snow when they came up to the farm and she shuddered at the thought that this might be another night like that, with Dudley and his crazy roadster wallowing through the drifts.

She scanned the sky anxiously, and then stepped back quickly into the shadow as a car came swooping up toward the station, with the air of intending to drive right up on the platform and go inside the door.

The car stopped a few feet from where she was standing, and she heard a girl's voice laughing raucously:

"Well, so long, Buddy! Thanks for the buggy ride! I'll love you always for this day! You saved my life, I'll tell the world! If I'd had to come on the train I'd uv been bored to death. I only wisht you was going the rest of the way!"

"Same here, darling! But no chance! I gotta skirt inside here, sore's a boil by this time. You'n I lingered a little long over our dinner. I'm late by just five hours! Sorry, but it can't be helped. 'Nother time possibly. Ef you come down my way again call me up an' I'll show you a wild night! So long, Peachy. I won't forgetya!"

The young man got out and stood beside the girl for an instant, then laughingly stooped and kissed her, and she slapped him smartly on the face and giggled, saying:

"Oh, go long, Buddy, that's one too many," and disappeared laughing into the dusk.

The young man turned and came face to face with Betty trembling with anger. Her little delicate face was white beneath its make-up, and the white light of an electric arc suddenly leaping up shone upon her.

"Hello, Betts!" said Dudley easily. "On time after all! I wasn't counting on that! First time in yer life! Well, couldn't be helped. Had two flat tires and a blow out! Got a leak in the radiator, and water in the carburetor, and came through three thunder storms and a fog. Gosh but it's a heck of a journey! Hadn't been you, Thorny, I'd uv turned back! Think you're worth it?"

211

Betty, furious with anger, tottering fatigue and hunger, perceived that Dudley had been drinking. Not enough to be stupid or angry, only enough to be loud mouthed.

"For mercy's sake, Dud, hush!" she said as she saw some passing people turn to look at them. "Lock your car and come let's get some dinner. I'm starved! I'm just about to pass out! I've waited for you ever since noon!"

"Good night! Thorny, I've just finished a meal! Couldn't eat another bite 'f I was to be 'lectrocuted for it. You run along an' get a bite while I get gas. We gotta beat it! I promised Gwen we'd be down ta th' house party soon's we could make it. Run along. Make it snappy. We oughtta get outta here!"

Betty's heart sank and her fury rose. She was so angry that she wanted to cry. She was so tired and hungry that she wanted to run home. Dudley had been eating a good dinner with that other awful girl! He had not cared that she was waiting, hungry, anxious! And now he wanted her to go and eat alone! When she had waited all day! And he was not offering to pay for it either! And she had but twenty-seven cents!

Yet, with all her despair and poverty she would not tell Dudley that she did not have money! Some terrible sense of pride descended upon her. She would rather starve than ask Dudley for money. She would not put herself in his power to that extent. Some thing innate told her that as soon as she did she would cheapen herself to him. She had always held him in her power, had carried a high hand, and ordered him around. To tell him now that she was penniless would be to change their relations, to put herself in his power.

She was trying to think what to do, whether she could get enough to satisfy her hunger out of twenty-seven cents.

"Oh," she said coldly, "I see! You preferred to have dinner with that girl! Perhaps I had better go back to my home and you can marry her!" and she turned as if to go away, carrying her little head haughtily, holding her suit case with a firm grasp, though the hand that held it trembled with weariness.

"Heck! Thorny, You're the limit! Didn't I come all this way after ya? What more da ya want? There's plentya girls I cud get, you know darn well—!"

He was talking very loud now, and people were turning again to look at them. Betty shrank into her shadow and protested.

"Hush, Dud. You're making yourself a spectacle," she said in a low tone. "See those people are coming this way just to listen."

"What's the dif?" said Dudley, speaking still louder. "It's none of their darn business! You're jealous, that's what's the matter, jus' plain jealous! Jealous of that poor little kid that I picked up on a lonely road, walkin' to Springfield jus' 'cause she didn't have the money! If you're going to develop a complex like that I better beat it!"

Betty was about to tell him he had, with her heart full of fury and her lips shaking so that she could scarcely speak, when suddenly a voice arrested them both, startling into their controversy like a voice of authority.

"Paging Miss Betty Thornton!" it said in the tone of a monotonous giant doing his duty, "Miss Betty Thornton of Briardale Pennsylvania will please come to the telephone in the office!"

The door of the station had swung wide, and the great megaphone which was located on the wall opposite seemed to be directed definitely at them. They started toward one another in a common fear, and Betty found herself clinging to Dudley's hand and trembling like a leaf. It was as if she had been caught and shamed before the whole world.

And while they stood, silent, listening, the monotonous voice went on again:

"Paging Miss Betty Thornton of Briardale Pennsylvania. Please come to the telephone in the office."

Suddenly Dudley Weston came alive.

"Get in there, quick!" he said roughly and pushed her toward the car, fairly lifting her into the seat and slamming the door.

"They're after us, Thorny! We gotta beat it!" he breathed, and flung himself around to his own seat starting the car with a jerk, and dashing out among the

213

taxi cabs with a vehemence that set up a commotion among drivers and traffic police.

Betty was trembling still. She looked back and some one swung wide the door of the station again, and the sonorous voice pursued them: "Paging Miss Betty Thornton of Briar—"

The car swung around a corner and the voice was lost in the multitudinous noises of the city. Betty felt as if she were being snatched from a helping hand that had been reached out to save her. She knew in her heart that if that voice had come a few minutes sooner, if it had come while she was sitting alone and forlorn in the station, she would have answered it, gladly, and flown back to home and mother; or if it had come even afterward when she saw Dudley with that unspeakable girl, she would have turned and fled to the call as to a city of refuge.

As they turned another corner, barely escaping a crash with a big car, and reeled into line among the traffic, Betty clutched wildly at her companion's arm, and cried convulsively:

"Take me back, Dudley, take me back at once. I've got to answer that telephone call! I've got to, don't you see? Someone might be sick or dead!"

"Let 'em die, then!" said the boy roughly. "You left 'em, didn't ya? Well, then don't go whining back. I got ya and you're mine now! Shut up and leggo my arm! How cun I drive with you pulling my arm like that? You little fool you. You're yella, that's what you are! I useta think you had nerve, but you haven't any more pep than a mouse. Get over there!" and he shoved her roughly to the other side of the seat.

Betty froze into dignity.

"Dudley Weston, don't you *dare* touch me again!" she cried furiously, "And you take me back at once! I've got to answer that call. Take me back, I say! Or I'll jump out right here in traffic and then you'll be responsible!"

For answer Dudley replied:

"Help yerself! You're Thorny all right!" and stepped on the gas, making the pedestrians scuttle to left and right wildly to get out of his way, and a traffic whistle pursued them as they vanished into the distance.

Betty sat back in her seat furious and helpless, the cold air keeping her alive, and driving back the deadly faintness that assaulted her now and again. She shut her lips tight and sat silent and angry, mile after mile, with Dudley driving hard and fast.

How he got through the thick of the city without being arrested was nothing short of a miracle. Betty kept hoping he would be arrested and then she might escape.

She was not frightened, for she was used to Dudley's wild driving, she was merely hungry and tired and angry, furiously angry. This was no romantic marriage as she had fancied it, driving like mad away from all that had hitherto been comforting, driving into an unknown night with an ungallant knight who swore at her every time he escaped running down a trolley car, or colliding with a truck; with an empty stomach and another girl in the background who had dined with her beloved, a blowsy girl too, with a loud voice and bad English, and a sneer on her unwholesome face. To think he would care to stop for that girl—eat dinner with her—when he was on the way to meet his bride! Well, she wasn't sentimental, but this was the limit!

Chapter XXII

Farther and farther from the city they drove, out into the empty country, with snow on the ground and snow beginning to come down from the sky now in earnest, in lazy whirls, and fantastic drifts, that gave a sense of power, terrible power, power to come down in flocks and droves pretty soon if it chose.

They were out in the country now with no moon, no stars, black leaden sky over head, and only the light of the

snow to guide them. There were occasional woods, dark
as velvet, and only the streak of their own lamps to break
it, and in one of these Dudley suddenly brought the car to
a dead stop, so suddenly that it almost threw her off the
seat.

"Now!" said the gallant young bridegroom, "if you
wantta jump out here's a good place to try it. You get out
and walk back, and I'll go on to Gwen's house party. I'm
sick of a grouch! You've lost yer nerve! Get out!"

For one angry instant Betty was on the point of
obeying. She put out her hand to open the door, and
looked out to the blackness of the woods, with the one
gash of white where the lamps shone ahead, and she
thought of the lamps going on without her. Only the little
red taillight at the back, winking, winking, in the distance
and vanishing, and she shuddered. Her voice broke, and
tears came into her throat and eyes, angry tears that those
gallant young eyes tried to conquer, and failed.

"I'm hungry!" wailed Betty like a frightened little
child. "I'm not grouchy. I'm just-just-tired and hungry! I
haven't had any-any-l-l-lunch, nor d-d-dinner!" Her voice
was coming through real sobs now—"and you-you-you-
b-b-b-rought that g-g-gr-rlll!"

"Oh! Gosh! Yes, I thought that was it! Jealous little
cat you are! Anything I hate is a snivveling woman!
Anything I hate is a jealous little cat! I never thought you
were like that! I wouldn'ta come if I had! I'd a sight rather
stayed at Gwen's, only I had given my word of honor—"
he swaggered.

"I'm not jealous!" said Betty suddenly straightening
up and dashing the tears away from her face, her nervy
look coming back into her eyes, "You think I'd be jealous
of a thing like that? Fat, and dowdy! She hadn't a bit of
style! She was common! Very common! How could I
think of being jealous of a thing like that? Why, she had
dirty finger nails, and looked as though she'd never had a
shampoo or a marcel. Her hair hung round her face like a
row of pins in a paper. No, I'm not jealous! I'm just
disappointed in you, Dudley Weston."

"I'll say you are! I'll say you're a peach! I'll say

you're a pippin! You're the bees knees and then some. I drive thousands of miles after you just to rescue you from a cruel family, and give up all my fun, and my midyear exams, and all my chance of graduating, and feeling I have an education, and what for? I ask you? Just to get my eyes scratched out by a jealous little cat!"

Betty withdrew into her corner and closed her lips in a hard little line. This was a new Dudley! How she hated him! Was this what she was marrying?

"Well, are you going to get out?" asked Dudley loftily, after a long minute's silence.

"No," said Betty composedly in her very best princess style, "Not in a place like this, of course."

"All righty!" said Dudley preparing to start the car. "Last chance now ur never!" and they shot out into the road again and dashed through the night, but neither spoke for a long time.

At last after what seemed to Betty like an eternity wherein she had been regretting everything she had ever done since she was born, Dudley handed her a flask.

"Here!" he said though still gruffly, "Put yerself around some of this. It's a wow! I got it on the way up. It oughtta bring ya outta yer grouch ef anything will. If it don't I'm done!"

She perceived that Dudley was making a drunken attempt to make up with her, and she took the flask eagerly and tipped it up to her lips.

The flask had apparently been recently replenished for it was nearly filled, with some hot stinging liquor that was new to Betty and burned her throat as she swallowed it. Immediately a sense of comfort pervaded her, and the clamor in her stomach was warmed and soothed.

"Hot stuff!" said Dudley leaning over and taking the flask as she handed it back, a little frightened at the new feeling of exhilaration that began to tingle all over her tired body. Dudley took great swallows of the liquor and the smell of it filled the car with a queer sickening odor.

Dudley took a long drink and then lurched over with his arm around Betty and kissed her. The smell of his

217

breath was hot and heavy. Betty felt a dizzy disgust at his touch.

"Hurry up, Dud," she said, trying to get her old imperious tone back again. "Let's go! I want some dinner and then I'll feel all right!" What was the use in quarrelling with Dudley? It was too late. She must make the best of things and get her old control over him.

"Awwright ole girl! Jus' you shay!" said Dudley starting the car again with one arm still around her, crushing her to him.

Dudley drove wildly as usual, and by and by they came to a town and a gas station.

"Gotta get gas, ole girl!" he said affably, "Shay, you got any dough? I haven't got mush more'n 'nough to pay fer gas. That darned kid pinched it off me. She gave me a lotta sob stuff about her folks turning her out, an' her not having any place ta go, till I shelled out all I had."

"Dudley! Do you mean we haven't any money? Why, what are we going to do? Do you mean you gave that girl all the money you had when you were coming to marry me?"

She was both frightened and angry again, and her voice had a helpless note in it.

"Oh, tha's all right, kid," he said comfortingly, "Got nough to get gas, and I'll telephone to the ole man and get him to wire me some money awwright! Donchoo worry, kid!"

"But I'm hungry!" said Betty beginning to cry now without realizing it.

"That's tough luck, Kid, but it won't take so long now ta get ta N'York. Are you broke too?"

"I've only got twenty-seven cents!" said Betty with a quiver.

"That's awwright!" soothed Dudley, "Getta good meal fer that!"

So while Dudley bought gas and a package of cigarettes Betty climbed out and spent twenty-five of her twenty-seven cents in a cup of bitter coffee, a box of stale crackers and an overripe banana.

"Have a cigarette!" said Dudley graciously as she got back into the car.

Betty took it eagerly and tried to get the usual thrill out of smoking, but somehow everything seemed to have gone stale like the crackers. All she wanted in the world was to lie down and go to sleep.

They dashed on through the night, passing villages and larger towns more often now and shooting through their quiet streets or noisy thoroughfares alike regardless of life or limb.

"Oh, Dud, I wish you wouldn't drive so fast through these towns! We might get pinched!" said Betty after a peculiary narrow hairbreadth escape.

"'Smatter of you, Thorny?" enquired the gallant youth, "getting soft? Losing yer nerve? Thought you liked a kick. This is nothing. Only fifty-five. Let's make it sixty." He stepped on the gas and the car lurched out around a curve and almost into a staid old Ford driven by an elderly man.

Betty caught her breath and looked back expecting to see the Ford on its side, but her escort gave her far too much to think about and she had to turn back and forget the old man and the Ford.

"Goin' to take a short cut," said Dudley swerving into a rough asphalt road that looked as if it were utterly out of repair.

"Oh, I wouldn't Dud, not to-night!" cried Betty, "What if you should get a flat tire! What if we should have a blow out! Let's take the regular road!"

"Oh, I know you wouldn't. You'd wantta be all night and all next day on the road. You're yella, that's wha's the matter with you. A fella I met tol' me this was a good road. I'm tryin' it, see? Take another drink! Brace ya up. Look at me! I'm not afraid to take a chance. You gotta keep up your end ur we can't make a go of it. Why, Thorny, you useta be a tough little egg. Wha's eatin' ya?"

"I think we'd get there quicker if we kept to the good road," answered Betty sulkily. "You make me tired the way you act."

"Oh, I do, do I? I make you tired, do I? Well, just for that we're goin' this road, see? An' we'll take it at seventy-five if I like. Or ninety, maybe. Wantta see me take this road at ninety an hour?"

That was a night to be remembered.

The rough road proved to be anything but a short cut. Mile after mile they careened along, over breaks that seemed like ditches, through snow that had blown in the way and never been cleared. Traffic had gone around the drifts but Dudley went straight through and nearly stalled his engine. Twice he had to get out and work at the machinery with cursing lips and uncertain fingers. Then Betty discovered that though the flask had been emptied much to her relief several miles back, Dudley had more of the queer tangy sickly smelling liquor in the back of his car, and each time he got out he replenished the flask.

He offered it to her every time he drank, but she refused. She had heard about drugged hooch that made people very sick, killed them sometimes, and to-night she somehow felt a strange reluctance to take a chance.

"Where did you get it, Dud?" she asked after the fifth refusal, and his accompanying jeer at her new principles. "It tastes queer. Maybe it's poisoned."

"Great Cats!" said Dudley. "I musta made a mistake an' brought along yer grandmother! Letcha off at the next town an' ya can walk back. Didn't know ya'd gone on the water wagon."

"Oh, cut it out, Dud!" said Betty trying to assume her old superiority. "You're not pleasant!"

"Pleasant! Pleasant! I like that! When I came all the way—"

And so it went on, hour after hour, as the night waned, and morning began to dawn. Betty thought it never would end.

"Where are we going, Dud?" she asked at last wearily. "I'm just ready to pass out. Aren't we ever going to get there? This road is so humpy my back aches."

"Get there! Get there!" repeated Dudley drunkenly. "All you care is get there! Whaddaya think of me? I drove all last night—"

Betty looked at him in the early dawn of the cold cheerless morning. His face was flushed in blotches, his eyes were blood shot, his collar awry, his hair dishevelled, his lips swollen. He had a wild look about him. She wondered why she had ever called him good looking. She shuddered and drew herself away, a feeling of utter disgust coming over her. She used to think it was manly to get a little drunk. But Dudley was more than a little drunk. He was beside himself, and he was driving like a madman. He was talking like a madman, swearing at her in the intervals.

"Tied to a skirt! That's what it is to be tied to a skirt!" he said. "Get me away up here, outta my way! Make me shpend all my dough gettin' gas. Then make a fuss about a little bitta road. Awright! We'll try another road—!"

Suddenly, without any warning, he deliberately turned the car to the left. The road sloped down abruptly to another highway several rods below the one they were on.

Dudley had been drinking at intervals all night, but the last drink had been deeper and longer than all the rest, inasmuch as he had recently refilled his flask from the mysterious supply in the back of his car, and now he seemed to be utterly beyond reason. Betty had never seen him like this. She had never seen anyone quite so drunk and wild and angry as Dudley was now. Probably it was a combination of exhaustion from long driving, and over stimulation from the bad liquor. He seemed quite like an insane person.

Betty, forgetting all her pride in being hard boiled, and daring anything, was frightened beyond anything she had ever felt before. She cried out, and sprang forward at the same time, trying to lay hands on the wheel and turn the car back into the road before it should be too late, but Dudley was only infuriated by this. He turned like a wild beast and glared at her, striking her hands from the wheel with a paralyzing blow, and then dealing a stinging slap across her mouth and another over her eyes, till she huddled speechless with fear in her corner of the car too

221

frightened to think. The last vision her eyes had caught as they received the blinding blow was a rim of crimson disk like a great fire opal, coming up above the distant mountain.

Dudley had begun to brake, and had caught the wheel once more, but the car was beyond his control. Betty in her blindness and horror and pain could feel it hurtling down the sudden grade, could realize what it meant, had time to wonder what the swift end would be, and then to suddenly feel the eye of God upon her,—God, standing down there in the Valley, watching them come, knowing what was happening to them, knowing she had brought this all on herself, and yet looking at her in that same yearning way, as if He would have saved her from it if she had but let Him! God! Why, *God* could save her even yet, couldn't He, if He was a God?

"Oh, God!" she cried. But the awful execrations of Dudley as he tried to direct his car into the road, drowned out her voice. Had He heard? Had God heard?

And then the car turned over and all was blotted out.

Chapter XXIII

Back in Vermont there was consternation when the word came that the young woman who had answered the description of Miss Thornton, and who had been seen by several employees of the railroad in the station during the day, was not to be found. She had been paged for half an hour and had not been found.

"I knew I ought to have telegraphed your father the first moment we found she was gone!" cried Eleanor with a gasp of fear. "He will never forgive me! Our little girl gone and I didn't let him know! And now it is getting dark, and where can she be?"

She dropped down on the hard old davenport in the library and buried her face in her hands.

"Oh, good night, Muth! We're doing the best we can! If Betts was really in Springfield she can't be so far away from here yet! Likely she's gone to a hotel. I'll phone all the hotels and find out! You know we can get a detective in Springfield and get right on the job, if you're willing!"

"No," said Eleanor springing to her feet. "I must tell your father before we do another thing. He will likely be in the home office by this time. If he caught that train this morning he would have gone right on through. Call up the office—"

"But it's Saturday. The office is closed."

"Somebody might be there. Try it. Your father would be there I'm sure if he has reached the city."

So Chris tried the office.

But only the janitor answered. Yes, the office was closed. No, there wasn't anybody there! No, Mr. Thornton hadn't been in that day. Mr. Thornton was out of town for an extended stay.

"I toldya, Muth," said Chris turning to his mother triumphantly, "Now you lemme handle this—"

"No, Chris. You must get the telegraph office and send a telegram to the train. If your father had to stay over in New York—I've been thinking it over and I believe he said he might have to stop there to see a man—but if he did stay over he would have taken the four o'clock from the Pennsylvania station. That's the train he always takes when he goes to New York. You must send a telegram to him on that train. That will get him before he reaches home and he will have time to think up what to do."

"Great Cats, Muth, what can we say in a telegram that won't publish the whole thing to the world? He won't understand without a whole letter. Now I ask you, what can he do away off there?"

"Your father always knows what to do," said Eleanor firmly. "This is no time to worry about the world,

223

but anyhow nobody on the train will know anything about us. Here's a telegram I've written out. Send it quick and then get Mr. Chalmers' number and ask for him. I want to talk to him. We can confide in him. If he isn't home get some other member of the firm. I've *got* to have help at once!"

But Chester did not get Eleanor's telegram. He was not on the four o'clock train from New York. He was speeding across his home city in search of a man who was about to leave for a Christmas vacation, and was a very important factor in the contract which was to be signed. He had no time to send telegrams, nor receive them, and when later he remembered to send a message it merely read: "Business well in hand. Probably shall reach farm Monday night. Will keep you informed." But the message gave no clue to his whereabouts at the time.

The messages to the members of the firm brought equally poor returns, for everyone seemed to be off somewhere on this last Saturday before Christmas, and the message Eleanor left at each point "Please have Mr. Thornton call up his wife as soon as he comes in" lay scattered about Briardale and the city like so many useless fragments. Chester took no time to go anywhere except where he was obliged to go, and the small amount of sleep he snatched was taken at a little inconspicuous hotel where he happened to be when he got done Saturday night, and where he had never stayed before.

So the night came down, the awful first night of Betty's absence, and still they had managed to get no clue.

Eleanor walked up and down her room, or stared out of the window at the slow moving flakes that wavered past the window, and thought and shuddered and blamed herself. And then she walked again, and thought of the Child Psychology class and the things the teacher had warned them against. What utter folly they all seemed now, and how well she had followed their lead! "Let a child express itself."

Well, Betty was expressing herself!

Not once had they told the eager mothers what to do

if a child went wrong and brought life-long sorrow upon herself and her family! They had said if a child used bad words, you must not notice it. It was a phase. It would pass. They had said if a child rebelled against you, you must turn his attention to something else, sooth and engage him elsewhere, lead him to view the question from a pleasanter standpoint. But not once had they said anything about teaching your children right and wrong, teaching them to obey, to respect law and order. No, they had rather decried that attitude. No parent had a right to put limits upon his children. Who was to say what was right, or wrong? The child's own inner sense would ultimately determine those things and so allow the young nature to develop without being warped, or hindered, or misshapen, or biased according to ancient inherited dogmas and superstitions. Oh, she knew the phrases by heart! But they none of them helped in this terrible crisis. They had never told her what to do when a child had gone wrong.

Well, right or wrong, Betty was gone. Where? The mother shuddered and knelt by her bed with wordless prayers upon her lips.

In the early dawn of the Sabbath morning Betty came to her senses with a breath of cold air blowing in her face. Somewhere in the air there was the vanishing sound of a crash and there seemed to be splinters of glass all about her for when she put out her hand feebly, she touched something sharp and brittle that crushed under her fingers, and afterwards there was blood on her hand and face.

There were two men standing over where she was huddled, and presently they loosened the thing that confined her, and lifted her out into the cold morning, stinging sharply on her cheeks, snow falling in great splotches on her forehead and eyes.

There was a large car standing a few feet away and they opened the door and put her on the back seat, tenderly, as though there was something sad and terrible about it. Then they went back and left her there alone. She watched them idly, apathetically, from the window of the car, licking the snow from her lips where it had fallen, and wondering what it was all about. She could see the two men working, bending over in the snow, lifting something, pulling, lifting again, and then they came toward her bearing something between them. They stopped and shook their heads and looked toward her, and laid it down, gently, oh, very gently, almost reverently. She wondered! Why, it looked like Dudley! Where—! How! Where was she?

The two men came and asked her if she could sit up. It had not occurred to her that she was lying down until then. She said yes, and her voice sounded weak and far away, with a tremble in it. She wondered what was the matter with her.

The men lifted her into the front seat and tucked a rough blanket around her. They went back and picked up the thing that looked like Dudley and brought him and laid him in the back seat of the car, being very careful about it. She caught a glimpse of his face. It was ghastly, and streaked with blood. One arm hung limply down and his hand was bleeding too. Was there a cut across his cheek? She might have turned to look again, but she felt so weak and tired, and somehow her soul was revolted with the sight of him. She tried to shake off the daze and think back. Where had they been? What had happened? How had they got here in the road? She looked over to the broken car, scattered on the roadside, its gay painted body splintered like a child's toy, its fenders ripped off and bent out of shape. How long ago was it that she and Dudley had been careening down that hill?

She closed her eyes with the dizzy memory and swooned away.

A long time afterward, it seemed, she came to herself again, and they were driving along a smooth road. There was snow only at the sides of the road now. The road way was clear and there were many cars coming and going, and houses and other buildings along the way.

The two men were talking. One of them was driving the car, and the other sat in the back seat with the thing

226

that was Dudley, holding him. She was glad she could not see behind her. She did not have to look. It sent a great wave of sickness over her to think of it. She heard the men saying something about a hospital. The nearest hospital.

"It might be a question of minutes whether the lad lives or dies," one said. "He's pretty far gone!"

Something froze within her. Suddenly the whole ugly business flashed across her consciousness. She and Dudley had been running away to get married, and they had come to this! And perhaps Dudley would die! Then would she be a murderer? And have her picture in the paper! And a terrible trial! And all the family have to come and hear the whole thing told out! They would tell how she had dropped her suit case out of the window and stolen out of the house, before daylight. They would have great big headlines in the newspapers. "HIGH SCHOOL SENIOR RUNS AWAY WITH YOUTH WHO DIES IN SMASH-UP!" Father and mother would be dragged through all that!

She thought of herself as she had been the night of the last High School dance, dressed in her rose petal taffeta. Betty Thornton, the star pupil of the school, the acknowledged beauty, the belle of the school! Herself, Betty, come to this!

She began to watch the way with a wild fascination. Dared she jump out and run away? Oh, she must not go to a hospital and have them ask her questions. She must never never be discovered! And yet! Could a Betty Thornton run away? When she had let Dud get into this mess, she would have to stand by!

She must have swooned away again, for the next time she knew anything the car had stopped in the din of a city street. In the distance was the outline of tall buildings against the sky and in the immediate foreground loomed a many storied brick building which she seemed to understand was the hospital.

Some men in white linen coats hurried out and two others came with a stretcher. She heard one of the men in the car say: "I thought we'd never get to New York with 'em! This here lad is far gone!"

So they were in New York at last! This was the way they had arrived! They had meant to be married in New York, and now Dudley was dying, dead perhaps already! It was ghastly! It couldn't be real! It must be she was asleep, dreaming. Perhaps she was really back in her bed at the farm having the nightmare!

The men in the linen coats had opened the car door and stepped in. They were lifting out Dudley, and laying him on the stretcher. She tried to keep her eyes shut, but something made her look, and as she looked Dudley moaned, moving his swollen, cut lips. There was more blood on his face. It was horrible!

She closed her eyes and dropped her head sideways on the back of the seat, and listened as they carried the stretcher with its ghastly burden up the steps and into the great building.

A hand touched her forehead, and then another hand was laid firmly about her shoulders. She looked up and saw a white-robed nurse looking at her kindly.

She looked down startled and saw a stretcher waiting to take her into the hospital. There was a smear of blood on one edge. She started to her feet in fright.

"Oh, no! I can walk!" she said. "Let me go home!"

"Are you able to walk?" asked the nurse kindly, and helped her out of the car.

Betty's feet felt strange and weak. Her knees trembled. She stood uncertainly. One of the helpers came forward and put his arm about her, and the nurse helped her on the other side; so she walked, tremblingly, up those awful steps and into that grim building where they had taken that huddled form that was Dudley. Would she have to look at him?

The nurse put her into a wheeled chair and pushed her down a long hall to an elevator. They went up several flights and she was wheeled down another hall to a little white room where they made her lie down on a white iron bed.

"But I've got to go—" protested Betty as she sank back on the pillow.

"The doctor must examine you," said the nurse,

unfastening her coat and taking her hat off.

An interval followed in which Betty drowsed and realized nothing. Then a doctor and another nurse came in and gave her a thorough examination, looking for broken bones.

"Does that hurt?" they asked her.

Betty assured them that it did not, although she had not much of an idea what it all meant. She had a feeling that she must please them all so that they would go away and let her alone and she might steal away from them. It was terribly hot around her now, and she was one big ache from head to foot.

"Mainly shock," she heard the doctor say. "Keep her quiet. Give her some nourishment. I've left a prescription—"

The doctor went out and the nurse gave her something in a spoon.

"I must get up," said Betty trying to lift her head from the pillow.

"You'll have to have something to eat," said the nurse crisply, "I'll bring it."

Betty reflected that she was faint. Perhaps that was the reason her legs felt so weak, and her arms and hands when she lifted them. It would be better to wait for breakfast. It wouldn't take long, and she remembered that she had no money.

The nurse brought hot milk and fed it to her in a spoon. It tasted good. She wondered that she had always despised hot milk.

Memories were beginning to flit into her mind. The morning she started. The place she had left her galoshes under a seat in the station in Springfield. Would they be there when she got back?

In a minute now when the nurse went out she would put on her slippers and her coat and hat and slip out. Nobody would know. They would think she was a visitor. The nurse had put her coat and hat in that queer long wardrobe at the foot of the bed. It would be easy to get away. And she would go to Aunt Florence's. Aunt Florence would help her. She wouldn't have to tell—

everything. She could make up some kind of an excuse for being in New York alone. She would think about it later when she got a little rested.

She closed her eyes and took the last few spoonfuls.

"Now," said the nurse setting the cup and spoon down on the little stand by the bed, "you haven't told me your name yet. We have to have the name and address to keep our records."

Betty kept her eyes closed and breathed steadily. She didn't want to answer that question. Perhaps the nurse would think she was asleep.

The nurse brought her pad and pencil, and said:

"Now, what did you say your name was?" But Betty did not hear her. She seemed to be lying in her bed upstairs at the farm, with her father down stairs praying, and God standing out there somewhere in the room watching her.

The nurse went out in the hall.

"She dropped off to sleep before I got her address," she said, to the head nurse. "Now, what'll I do? The doctor told me to phone her folks."

The head nurse consulted the card the doctor had given her:

"Better let her sleep," she said. "What her folks don't know won't hurt them, and the doctor's got her marked up as just needing to rest before she goes home."

So Betty slept.

From time to time the nurses flitted in and out of the little room where she had been taken for examination. They took her temperature, and they gave her medicine, and even fed her a few mouthfuls of broth, and still Betty slept.

She slept all through the long Sabbath day, while her mother was agonizing at the farm unable to get in touch with her father, while Chris kept the wires hot telephoning and telegraphing in various directions, while the children sat around disconsolately trying to amuse themselves, and Jane stood at the window and watched and grew strangely silent and mature.

It was Monday morning, bright and shining when

Betty awoke. She found that she had been undressed and put to bed regularly. She stirred and found that she was able to move. She got up and stood upon her feet. They were shaky, but they would hold her. She could walk as well as ever.

She was nearly dressed when the nurse came in with her tray.

"Well!" said the nurse. She was a new one that Betty had not seen before, "Good morning. You're up already! And ready for the day. I hear you're to be dismissed this morning if you haven't any temperature. The doctor comes in about ten o'clock and he'll look you over and then I guess they'll let you go if he doesn't find any complications. I guess you'll be glad."

Betty smiled shyly.

"You're fortunate!" said the nurse, "The young man that was brought in same time as you hasn't got conscious yet."

A horror filled Betty.

She did not feel like eating the breakfast that was spread before her, hungry as she was. She tried to ask a question but it stuck in her throat.

"Is he—Then he isn't—He's-a-live yet?" she asked with blanching face.

"Oh, yes, he's alive. But he's got a fractured leg and arm, and a fractured skull. They don't know but they may have to trephine. They've sent for his folks. They found his driver's license and got 'em on the phone. The doctor wouldn't let anyone wake you. He said you'd be all right after you woke up but you needed an unbroken rest."

Betty tried to eat a little of the fluffy omelet but another question was sticking in her throat. Ought she to go and see Dud? Would they let her? It wouldn't be quite white not to even ask about him. He had been unspeakable. It made her shudder to think of that terrible ride. She felt as if she never wanted to see him again. But she didn't want to run away and leave him. If he was dying she couldn't run away. Even if they thought she was the cause of his death! Even if they had her arrested for murder, she had no right to run away. It was yellow to do it. Something fine in her nature would not let her go without making some effort to help. She would have to stick by.

"Would they—" she paused to gather words— "could I go in and see him?"

"Oh, yes, I guess you could," said the nurse, "I could ask the head nurse. It couldn't do him a mite of harm I shouldn't think. He isn't conscious. Of course his folks aren't here yet—"

But Betty had to get to the bottom of this. She must know just how far she ought to be expected to go.

"Would I be allowed to—to—help him—any?"

The nurse gave her a keen look.

"What relation are you to him?" she asked curiously. "You ain't his sister, are you? You don't happen to be married to him, do you? You look awful young for that."

"Oh, no!" said Betty quickly, her cheeks growing scarlet, "I'm just a—just a—just an acquaintance. We were out taking a—a—ride together!"

"Mercy goodness!" said the nurse aghast. "An' you were out at that time in the morning!"

Betty's cheeks flamed hotter.

"Oh, no," she said quickly, "It was early evening when we started," and then she realized that she was only making things worse.

"Good night!" said the nurse, "Then you musta lain on the roadside pretty near all night before anyone found you."

Betty looked down at her tray and poured cream on the dish of oatmeal.

"It was—pretty awful—I guess!" she essayed, "I don't really remember much about it after the car began to go down the hill."

"Well, don't talk about it," said the nurse, "You'd best forget it as soon as you can. You've got to live, and you can't keep yourself upset remembering things like that. I guess you could go in and look at him, but they won't let you stay. He's too sick. They won't let even his mother stay in the room when she comes. She'll mebbe

232

take a room near here, but they don't let folks stay in the room much when a patient is so bad."

Betty brightened.

"You don't think I—that is, perhaps it would be polite for me to stay around till he was better. It doesn't seem just right to go off and leave him alone."

"Oh, my land, child! He ain't alone. His folks phoned for him to have a special nurse, two if necessary, and they're coming on this morning too. They'll be here by noon or a little after. And even if you wanted, there wouldn't be any place for you to stay except the little sun parlor down the hall, and that's always full with visitors. This room is engaged for to-day. A girl. Operation. Appendicitis! She'll be in along about three o'clock. The hospital's awful full now. You'd a been put in the ward if you'd been a regular case, but they had two women dying there last night and one was hollering to beat the band. The doctor thought it would be better for you to rest in here, being as this wasn't occupied till to-day."

Betty shivered and drew a deep breath of thanksgiving. She had never realized before what depths of horrors there were that one might escape. She took another bite of the oatmeal and cream.

"I ought to pay something for all you've done for me here," she said thinking aloud, rather than talking. "But I haven't got my pocket book with me. I guess it got lost in the snow."

Betty remembered the meagre two cents left in her pocket book and wondered if that had been a lie. "I'll have to send something back when I get home."

"Oh, that'll be all right, I'm sure," said the nurse smiling, "But don't your folks know about your accident? Aren't they coming to see you?"

"Why—my people—" Betty hesitated, "my people are out of town," she finished glibly, "and it wasn't worth while to worry them you know. I—am—going to my aunt's. She didn't know just what day I was coming, so of course she won't worry."

"Well, that's fortunate, now isn't it? I always feel so sorry for the folks that have to worry. What pretty hair you have. It's naturally curly isn't it? I always say that people that have naturally curly hair have the advantage of everybody else. Now, if you've finished your breakfast, I'll see if they will let you look at your friend—"

She went out with the tray and Betty felt suddenly cold and frightened and very young. Oh, if she only didn't ever have to see Dudley Weston again looking that way! It was too horrible! Why did people have to die anyway? What an awful world it was!

The nurse came back with permission for Betty to go to Dudley's room, and in fear and trembling she followed the nurse.

"He won't know you, you know," the nurse whispered as she opened the door, and Betty took a deep breath and stepped within the threshold casting frightened eyes at the bed.

But there was nothing of Dudley Weston there on the bed to recognize save the tip of his chin with the cleft in it, the cleft that used to make him so good looking. His hair had been cut away and his head and face were swathed in bandages. Some of them were soaked in blood. His hands were bound up in gauze also, and one arm was in splints. There was a weight hanging at the foot of the bed from under the bedclothes, which the nurse explained sepulchrally was put there to keep the broken bone in place and stretch it so that if he got well one leg would not be shorter than the other.

If he got well!

She shivered at the thought of Dudley, bound up that way, with all those terrible possibilities hovering over him. Dudley, the lithe, the athletic, the best dancer and tennis player in High School. Dudley who was planning to be a polo player! Dudley whose pride was his grace of movement, his incessant activity! What if he should never walk again! What if one leg should be shorter than the other, like the Boyd boy who had to walk with a crutch! She could not picture Dudley a cripple.

Dudley was turning his head monotonously from side to side, and babbling strange sentences that were utterly unintelligible. He frightened her, and made her feel as if she were back in the car going down that steep incline, while he shouted awful curses at the brakes! She began to cry softly, and hid her face in her handkerchief, her little crumpled dirty handkerchief that had done over duty for the last forty eight hours.

The nurse put her arm about her and led her from the room.

"I wouldn't feel so bad," she said comfortingly. "He might get well after all. The doctor said he had a chance."

A chance! Only a chance!

"If I only hadn't gone with him!" Betty sobbed, unaware that she was revealing herself.

"Well, now I wouldn't blame myself," soothed the nurse, "you know we can't help these things. What was to happen has to happen, I always say, and no good comes of blaming anybody. Like as not some other girl woulda gone if you hadn't uv."

Betty thought of the loud coarse common creature at Springfield, and owned to herself that this was probably true. Dudley Weston would always find a girl, of some kind. Yet she felt herself judged guilty by some finer moral judgment.

"You'd better lie down a while now," said the nurse. "I'll just spread up the bed, and you can take a nice nap. You need it after going in there. It's kind of a strain, and you're sort of shaken up. You'll have plenty of time for a good rest before the doctor makes his rounds, and like as not he'll dismiss you."

Betty submitted to having her shoes taken off, and being put to rest under a blanket. But as soon as the nurse's footsteps had died away down the hall she slipped up again and put on her shoes and her hat and coat. She did not want to wait for that doctor and more questions. She wanted to get away without having her name taken. She was fairly in a panic about it. It seemed as if her full senses had just come back to her. Also, she wanted to get away from Dudley in the room down the hall, moaning and turning his head from side to side. If she could do nothing she must get away. She could telephone afterward and find out how he was, but she must go quickly. If his father and mother were coming they would look after him.

She stole to the door and listened. There seemed to be nobody in the immediate vicinity of her room just then. There were two nurses down at the end of the hall talking but their backs were turned. There was only an old colored woman with a mop and pail just going into the room next to hers.

She glanced down the hall in the other direction. The stairs were only a few feet away, with the elevator next to them, and the incessant bell sounding mysteriously in the passage. It seemed a propitious time to make an escape.

With another quick look around she opened the door, crossed the hall like a wraith, and slid into the stairway.

The stairs were white marble, a few steps and then a turn to a landing, then a few more steps and another turn. She was out of sight from the floor above in a moment.

Her knees felt shaky yet, but her fear of being held up and made to tell her name and address gave her strength to go on, down and around, turn after turn, floor after floor. She had no idea she had been brought up so far in that wheeled chair in the elevator.

But at last she came to a hall that had a great arched doorway to the street, and a row of patients sitting in line waiting to see the doctors.

She gave them one quick wild glance and hurried past them out through the door, into the noise and bustle of the street. No one had seemed to notice her, no one had tried to detain her, or seemed to realize that she was a patient escaping before she had been dismissed, but she felt as if an army with banners were pursuing her.

At the first corner she turned and walked rapidly, feeling a little easier. Then suddenly she stopped, realizing that she did not know the name of that hospital. She could not send them money for what they had done for her, and she could not find out how Dudley was unless she knew where he was.

It took courage, but she turned back and went

almost to the door till she was able to read the name on the great brick building. Then she walked to the corner on either side and read the signs of the streets, and memorized them. She started on again not caring which way she went only to get out of that region. She kept repeating the names of the streets and the name of the hospital like a charm, and feeling very noble and satisfied with herself that she had compelled herself to go back and read that name.

Chapter XXIV

But after she had walked a good many blocks she suddenly began to feel very tired, as if she must sit right down on a doorstep and rest. She must get to Aunt Florence's at once and try to think what to do next. If she only had some money she could telephone Aunt Florence to come after her, but two cents wouldn't buy anything! Not anything! But a newspaper. And what would she want of a newspaper.

Well! She might buy a newspaper and look at the want advertisements, and get a job. If she didn't feel so shaky all over that might be quite a thrill, something with a kick in it to tell forever after. Something she could even tell to Dudley with pride!

But somehow when she came to think about any kind of a kick she felt no enthusiasm. Her pep was all gone. She didn't seem to want anything but a bed to lie down upon. Perhaps she ought to have stayed longer in the hospital. She could have closed her eyes and pretended to be asleep if they came around asking for her name again. But then if Mr. and Mrs. Weston came in the room to see her they would know her. She wouldn't have to speak, or even look at them. They would know her at once and would probably telegraph Dad and Mother, and there would be a mess in no time. No, she must fight this thing out with dignity. Having swung off from home she could not go back crestfallen and become subject to her parents again. That would be too humiliating!

So she began to take account of numbers, and discovered that she was walking down town instead of uptown where Aunt Florence lived. Fortunately she knew Aunt Florence's address, away up in the hundred and eighties, on Riverside Drive. And this was only in the forties! It was going to be a long walk! Oh, if she had only had a few pennies that she might take the bus!

After walking what seemed like weeks to her weary soul, she began to feel uneasy. Things did not look natural, and when she tried to cut across to where it seemed to her the right street ought to be, there loomed the Park, wide and white and interminable. At last in desperation she went to a policeman.

It was quite against her ideas of what was proper for a modern young girl to have to ask advice from a policeman, but she was desperate, and little chills were beginning to creep down her back, and up her ankles, clad only in their thin silk stockings, with thin little slippers on her feet.

"Yer wy off, Miss," said the policeman, red haired and blue eyed and brusque, eycing her trim little figure in its fur coat and modish little hat. "Ye mustav come up the wrong side of the pahk! Plenty of um does. You jus' stan' heah till a bus comes along goin' that wy, and you git on an' it'll tak' ye within' two blocks uv yer house."

"Thank you," said Betty looking dismayed, and hesitating at the curb.

"Right here, Miss. I'll put ya on the right bus. Ya can't miss it."

Betty turned her big beautiful eyes upon him and seemed ready to cry.

"But—I've spent all my money," she said childishly. "I'll have to walk. Couldn't you tell me which way to walk?"

He looked her over thoughtfully from the crown of

238

her pretty hat which was pretty in spite of being somewhat battered, to the tip of her little scuffed patent leather slipper. He cast his blue eye at the lowering sky and flicked a lazy snowflake from his sleeve.

"It's a good two mile, Miss," he said. "Hundred and eight-third street. You can't make it across the pahk 'fore the storm breaks. We're due for more snow this afternoon. I better lend it to ya. I got a goil myself ya know. The bus oughtta be comin' any minute. Heah she comes now. I'll jus' speak a woid to the driveh—He'll put ya off at the right place—"

The bus was bearing down upon her as he spoke, and before she had time to protest he had signalled it, and pressed a quarter in her hand.

"Oh, thank you," said Betty, "but won't you give me your address so I can return it? I couldn't let you—"

"Just bring it next time ya come this wy," he smiled, "ask ennybody fer Pat."

He smiled and winked, and Betty found herself seated in the coach, with the conductor ringing up her fare.

Oh it was good to sit down and rest, to close her eyes, and forget just for an instant what an awful situation she was in. What would Dad and Mother say if they knew?

But it would be all right when she got to Aunt Florence's. Aunt Florence wouldn't ask too many questions. She was a good sport. She wore imported hats and frocks, and wasn't as strait-laced as Mother. She was Mother's youngest brother's wife, and Mother didn't quite approve of her, but Betty admired her with her whole soul. Aunt Florence belonged to the smart set of New York and went to night clubs, and never had a dull day. Betty had longed to visit her, but Dad and Mother had always managed to have a good excuse for declining all the New York invitations she had received.

It came to her as she rode along, through the white streets blurred with the scurrying flakes coming down closer together now, that she must arrange some tale to tell Aunt Florence before she reached the house. Well, why couldn't she just say that she was bored to death up there at the farm and took a notion to run away and spend Christmas in New York? From what she knew of Aunt Florence she would laugh and pinch her cheek, and maybe tell her to run and telephone to the folks so they wouldn't be scared, and say she was going to keep her the rest of the winter!

What a great thing that would be! To stay with Aunt Florence all winter during the gay season in New York, and go to night clubs and plays and parties with her! My! That would be worth even the accident. Why hadn't she thought of just running away to New York? She could have pulled that off without Dudley Weston's help and then all this awful mess wouldn't have happened.

And if she stayed the rest of the winter in New York why then everything would be quite smoothed over by Spring and Daddy would likely be only too glad to have her come home and to go back to Briardale too if she made that a condition of returning. Daddy would get over his social purity complex and maybe learn a thing or two in the bargain!

Betty's spirits were quite revived by the time the conductor motioned to her that she had reached her corner.

She got out in the falling snow, and even enjoyed the refreshing bite of the flakes on her cheeks as she walked the few steps to her aunt's number.

As she stood waiting for the door to be opened she looked around with growing elation. The tall buildings filled her with joy. Apartment houses loomed in the background, and mansions were all about her. Her heart began to swell within her. She had heard that a famous Moving Picture actress, of New York and Hollywood, owned the house two doors from here. Which was it, she wondered, up, or down?

Then the door was opened grudgingly by an elderly woman in working garb.

Betty lifted her voice eagerly:

"Is my aunt—I mean is Mrs. Cassatt in?"

"No, Mrs. Cassatt ain't in."

Betty's face fell.

"Oh,—well,—I'll just come in and wait for her then. When will she be back?"

"Mrs. Cassatt has gone to Palm Beach," said the woman freezingly. "She won't be back till Spring."

Betty exclaimed in dismay.

"Oh, what shall I do? I've come to make her a visit. I didn't know she was going away. She said I was to come any time I liked."

"Did you send her word you was coming, Miss?" asked the woman cruelly calm, eyeing her battered hat, and the torn place on her fur coat.

"Why, no," said Betty, "I came in a great hurry, and I was going to surprise her!"

"She's been gone two weeks," said the woman. "There ain't anybody here but the caretakers."

"Well, I don't know what I'm going to do," said Betty. "You see I've spent all my money. I haven't enough to get back home, and besides I've lost my suit case on the way. I wonder if you could lend me some money till tomorrow. I could return it right away you know."

The woman's eyes narrowed.

"That's a common dodge for beggars," she said. "You can't pull one like that off on me!"

Betty's cheeks flamed and her eyes flashed.

"I'm not a beggar!" she said haughtily, "I'm Mrs. Cassatt's niece, Betty Thornton from Briardale, Pennsylvania, and we are spending the winter up in Vermont at my father's old home on the Thornton farm."

"I never heard of no such people," said the woman dryly her eyes hard and amused.

"Well, at least you can let me come in and telephone to my father to wire me some money, can't you?"

"We've had our orders to admit no one, Miss!" said the woman curtly.

"Well, what am I to do?" asked Betty with her princess air.

"It's none of my concern, Miss."

Betty stood stormily trying to think what to do.

"At least you can go in and telephone for me, then,

can't you? Just say that Betty is here without money and will they tell her what to do, or wire some money or something. I can sit on the front steps till they come for me if you won't let me in the house. The number is—"

But the woman interrupted:

"No, Miss, I won't do no telephoning for ye. I got no time to fool with beggars of any kind, and as for that old gag you can't fool me. You're just tryin' to get into this house, and you ain't going to do it. As for settin' on the steps, just try it and I'll hand you over to the p'lice quicker'n you can think. Now, you better be moving on or I'll call the dog out. He's a p'lice dog and he's fierce. He don't like strangers!"

Betty tried to maintain her dignity, though the tears were very near to falling.

"I shall take care that my aunt knows how I was treated at her house when I was in trouble," she said as she whirled about and walked unsteadily down the steps.

"Help yerself," called the woman disagreeably, "I'm doing my duty, and ef you was doin' yours you wouldn't be here."

With which wholesome truth she slammed the door and locked it noisily.

Betty walked out into the fast falling snow, and stared up and down the street, wondering what she should do now. She looked across the Drive at the torpid black river with its border of dirty drifts, and wished she dared fling herself over one of those cliffs and down into the icy depths below. What was life worth any way?

But life still had a hold on Betty, much as she might toy with the idea of youthful suicide. And when a big bus lumbered down and paused at her very side she remembered the change from her quarter still in her purse, and climbed on board. At least she could not continue to stand on the sidewalk in the snow.

As she settled back in her seat she realized that her feet were wet and her throat was beginning to burn roughly. Now she was getting a cold she supposed. She must get somewhere out of the cold. There were chills going down her back again, and her limbs ached like the toothache. Her head ached and her eyeballs burned, and her soul burned with humiliation. To think she had been called a beggar, and openly suspected of being a thief! Betty Thornton! How mortified Daddy and Mother would be!

And now she must sell her watch. It was the only thing about her that was worth much, but where should she go to sell it?

Following an impulse she got off the bus in the shopping district and went into one of the largest department stores.

In the jewelry department where she made her request they eyed her suspiciously again. Betty flamed gorgeously as she looked the two men clearly in the eye while they took her watch and examined it.

She needed no rouge to make her cheeks vivid. The snow and the excitement and embarrassment had painted them crimson.

"Whose watch is this? Where did you get it?" asked one of the men.

"It is a very valuable watch," added the other man.

Betty looked up and tried to smile engagingly but only succeeded in looking frightened.

"It is mine. My father gave it to me. You'll find my name Elizabeth Thornton on the back of it. I wouldn't want to sell it permanently, you know. I wouldn't part with it for anything, but I spent all my money and I must get enough to get home. I just want to leave my watch as security, and I'll be glad to pay something extra for your trouble you know."

The two men looked at one another meaningfully, and handed her back her watch.

"We don't purchase second hand jewelry," said the first man.

"You'd have to go to a pawn shop for that," said the second.

"Oh," said Betty pitifully, "where is one? Could you send me to a respectable one? I thought they were all quite common places."

The two men did not smile.

243

"There is one around the corner, two blocks over and then turn to your right a block," said one of the men after a due pause. "It doubtless is common. But it is a pawn shop."

They bowed and left her standing amid the gorgeous display of jewels and silver and platinum, her little watch in her hand.

Slowly Betty walked out of the great store, the two men standing together at a distance and following her with hard suspicious eyes, like the Pharisees in sacred paintings.

Her feet were wet and cold. It seemed as if the bones were breaking in places when she walked. Her back ached and her head was whirling and dizzy. The oatmeal and the egg she had taken at the hospital were long ago forgotten. Her stomach was empty and she felt faint, but she was not hungry. She felt her throat growing sore again as she went out into the wet snow. She heard people saying that it was going to be a white Christmas, and wasn't it nice to have the fresh snow for tomorrow.

Christmas! Tomorrow was Christmas! And she was wandering about New York alone!

Of course she could always go back to that hospital, if she could walk there, for now she had not the price of another bus ride left. Yes, she could go back and grovel before Mr. and Mrs. Weston, and disgrace her family forever. She could go back, and perhaps they would be glad to have Dudley marry her. She had heard that they said they wanted Dudley to marry young. She shuddered. She did not want to marry Dudley. She never wanted to see him again. That ride had cured her. She would never, never willingly go near him again. There were unspeakable things he had said and done on that awful ride that were burned into her memory and would always be there. She felt she would never be really happy again in this world. Yes, she could go back to the hospital and borrow money from Mrs. Weston. But she would rather go over to one of those looming cliffs across the river and fling herself in than that!

Having uttered that fiercely in her heart she went

out into the snowy avenue, garlanded with holly and mistletoe, bordered with hemlocks and spruce and pine, filled with happy people going home with last packages. Christmas cheer on every hand and only Betty Thornton left out!

She turned around the corner and sought that pawn shop.

And then they gave her only ten dollars for her watch, her precious platinum watch with the little diamonds set about it. Would she ever see it again? Betty Thornton pawning her watch, her last year's Christmas gift from her father, to get money to go home!

"And when he had spent all. And when he had spent all!" Where had she heard that phrase and why did it keep ringing over and over in her head now?

It had grown very dark while she was in the pawn shop. The old man with a hooked nose and a scraggly beard had kept her waiting a long time before he told her what he would allow her on the watch, and when she faltered and told him it was very valuable and ought to bring more than that he swept it aside and told her he had more watches now than he knew what to do with, and people never came back for the things they pawned anyway. So she told him hastily that she would accept it, and that she meant to send for her watch the very next day after Christmas!

When she came out of the shop the lights bewildered her and she took the wrong turn and wandered eight or nine blocks out of her way before she discovered it. Frightened she turned back again. She began to remember how her mother was afraid to have her out alone at night in city streets and a queer kind of fright took possession of her. Betty Thornton, the little hard boiled high school sport, was frightened all alone by herself in New York! She tried to shame herself out of it, but the tremor remained until at last she straggled into the great station, too weary to hardly drag one foot after the other.

It was unfortunate perhaps that she should have gone to the restaurant before finding out what a ticket to the village below the farm would cost. But she was ready to drop with faintness, and felt that food was the first consideration.

And then she was too weary to eat what she had ordered. She could only eat a little of the soup. When she tried the chocolate ice cream and the cocoanut cake which she had ordered, she found them too sweet and the cold sent shivers down her back again. Her feet felt wet and cold, and her throat was decidedly sore now. Sore she was from head to foot, with a blinding headache.

When she gave up trying to eat and went to buy a ticket she found to her horror that she had not money enough to take her home.

She spread her money out before the ticket agent. There was a long line of impatient travelers behind her waiting their turn.

"That's all I have left," she said. "How far will it take me?"

The man counted it with a practiced eye.

"Take you to Weldon," he said. "That's thirty miles this side Wentworth."

The woman behind Betty reached out a gloved hand with a twenty dollar bill clutched in it and waved it impatiently at the man behind the window:

"I want to get that next train!" she said in a loud tone.

"All right!" said Betty wearily, "I'll go to Weldon."

She had to wait nearly an hour for the next train. When she finally crept into a stuffy seat in the common car and curled up with her head on the window seat she was too tired to think at all. She just wanted to keep still and try to endure the terrible pain in her back and the terrible ache in her head, and the great mountain of a lump in her throat when she swallowed.

Fitfully she slept, apathetically she endured the hard seat, and the twist that came in her neck and shoulder from lying down against the window sill, the chill that came from the crack under the window.

As the night went on the car grew very cold. If it had not been for her fur coat she would have perished. She was too far down in the depths of weariness and despondency to question what she should do in the morning. She had not even enquired what hour her train reached Weldon. It is doubtful if she would have taken in the added catastrophe if she had known it was due there at four o'clock in the morning.

However, a kindly hot box delayed the train an hour and a half, and it was not until half past five that a long-suffering conductor hunted her up and shook her gently, though gruffly, telling her it was time to get out.

She stood dazedly on the platform of the little closed station and watched her train amble away into the white darkness of the chill before the dawning. When its last red twinkle died into the darkness she turned around and looked about her.

Everything was still and dark. There seemed to be no one about anywhere. White arc lights blazed overhead with that appalling brilliance that lights can assume about a deserted station in a lonely spot at unearthly hours. Little white houses with green shuttered windows huddled along a straggling street. The snow had fallen anew here too, for all the trees were outlined in white velvet, and stood out against the dark like nerves of a skeleton. There was almost an uncanny stillness over the white dark world. And not a soul in sight!

Betty tried the door of the station. It was locked. Dim lights were burning inside. Perhaps someone slept there. But though she pounded on the door till her knuckles ached it brought no response. The telegraph instrument clicked away to itself "Cluck-cluck-cluck! Cluck!—Cluck!" Like a deaf old man who was snoring and would not listen. A little mouse inside ran across the station floor, and its plush feet echoed like a clatter in the empty room. It was weird.

In despair she turned away and walked to the end of the platform.

There was an arc light here, and a sign post. She came nearer and read it. "Wentworth 41 miles!" A finger pointed out through the village on a road well-rutted by vehicles.

247

Chapter XXV

She looked back at the station glooming in the dark, with no seats offering friendly help. Not even a packing box to sit on! What should she do? She couldn't stand here till daylight. One lonely place was no better than another. Why not start on? She would be warmer than standing here in the wind.

So with feet that were stiff and sore from her day's walking, with flimsy slippers that were scarcely more than half dry, with silk stockings of gauzy film, she stepped out into the snow and started on her journey. Forty-one miles! And then three on top of that to the farm! Would she be able to make it? Oh, if she only had her galoshes that she left behind the scrap basket in the waiting room in Springfield, years and years and years ago!

The new fallen snow was soft and feathery, and the track had not yet been beaten through it. As she put her foot down, it would sink in some places up to her ankles. The slipper was low cut, and the snow rushed in beneath her instep, and nestled about her foot with a chilling embrace that was sickening. She became more conscious of her sore throat, and her aching head, and with a wild thought of plunging through and getting somewhere quickly she started to run.

But running in a rough road was a most uncertain matter, and more than once she lost her footing and fell. Once she pitched sideways into a drift and plunged her arms into the snow bank beyond their depth. It was not easy to rise again, and when she did so she found there was snow inside her sleeves and up her arms.

The hour too was almost uncanny, gray dawn fighting with the rising day, the streets of the little town deserted as if the inhabitants were long dead. She rose and fled along once more, now gaining a footing on a sidewalk which offered firmer walking. Here she could stamp the snow out of her shoes and shake it out of her sleeves. She even stood on one foot at a time, and took off her slippers and emptied them, brushing off the snow from her icy

248

feet. That made her feel a little more comfortable. And so she hurried on.

But even the sidewalks came to an end very soon as the houses grew fewer and farther apart. At last she came to the beginning of the open country again. The sidewalk ended abruptly, in a great drift of snow like a barrier which must be breasted before she could get into the road again. She was in despair. How could she go on? Her feet were fearfully cold, and if they got wet again they would surely freeze stiff.

She retraced her steps till she came to a house where the way had been cleared in front of a gate to the road, and a stepping stone bridged the curb. She stood poised an instant before stepping out again into that horrible cold mass, and tried to think of something she might do to keep her feet from actually freezing. If she only hadn't been too proud to wear her galoshes!

She was wearing a scarf of soft silk, long and wide, and very gauzy in texture, painted over with flowers. It had been a gift on her last birthday, and in her extravagant love of show she had been wearing it to school the day she was taken away. She looked at it now, dubiously, her lovely scarf! But it must be sacrificed. She would freeze if she did not do something.

Ruthlessly she unwound it from her neck and tore it in two. Then sitting down on the horse block, with a furtive glance toward the still-sleeping frame house set back from the road, she took off her little slippers and carefully wound each foot with the scarf. It took several experiments before she was able to get her foot back into her slipper with the added folds of silk, but at last she stumbled up to her feet again and started on. For a little while she did feel more comfortable, although the lumpy folds of silk made it hard to walk. But her feet were getting so numb now that a little thing like that did not seem to matter so much.

She had gone what seemed to her about ten miles, stumbling and falling, slipping back each step sometimes, till it seemed she made little progress, when she came at length to another sign post. Eagerly she read the mileage. "Wentworth, 39 miles." All this long cold terrible way and she had gone but two miles! How could she ever get there? Her feet were absolutely numb now. They were so cold that stinging pains were going up her limbs. She had a feeling that presently her feet would be frozen solid like icicles, and perhaps snap off at some careless step, and leave her lying there in the road with no one to know.

All at once home and mother and father and the children loomed large and dear in her life. Suppose she should die there in that lonely road, and not be found for days, and word never even got to her people that she had died. Strangers would pick her up and take her to the morgue!

She shuddered and plunged forward again with a sickening feeling that she must, even though it was no use. Every step she got nearer to Wentworth meant that much more chance that they would at least know sometime that she had tried to come home.

A wind had risen, gradually, blowing the snow around, and flinging it into her face sharply, stingingly. It bit into her like venomous insects, and added one more source of discomfort.

She had reached the top of a hill where the fields on either hand were wind-swept and barren, and where the snow had drifted over the fence tops, and obliterated the lines of it completely. It had even eddied across the road, obliterated the tracks of the last few weeks, and wiped out the way for some distance into a smooth blanket of deep white. She paused at the brow of the hill and looked across in new dismay to the vague lines of snow capped fences in the distance and tried to determine just where the road might be.

She took a few steps forward, and found that the drifts were not so deep but that she could plunge through provided she kept in the track of the road, but the least misstep brought her down in snow beyond her depth. Then she would look back and try to get her bearings again, but the downward trend of the road had carried her out of vision of the fences behind, and she had nothing to guide her except that vast expanse of whiteness ahead going down to the valley, with vague tracings like quiltings in a patchwork of snow fields.

Nevertheless she tried bravely to stumble on, frightened and weary. It seemed as though her heart was a pump that would not work, and her breath hurt in her breast, and stung maddeningly in her nostrils, as she labored.

The snow was growing deeper now, and she realized that she must be off the road again, or else the drifts were deeper. How was she ever to go on? Her feet felt like leaden weights, and once or twice when she fell she stayed down in the snow for a moment to rest, and get her breath again. The pain in her throat was like a knife cutting when she tried to swallow, and her head ached as if it were going to burst. The tears were rolling down her cheeks, blinding her at times, yet she was not conscious of crying. Once she put up her hand to see why her cheeks were so cold, and found the tears frozen on her lashes, and her face.

It was just then, bewildered and frightened, that a new predicament arose. She had stepped into snow a little deeper than she had yet found, and her numb feet refused to lift themselves and go another step. It was as if they had suddenly been turned to stone, loaded with lead, and all the efforts of the brain and heart could not make them take another futile step in that deadly white way.

Crying out at last with a weak little bleat like a lost lamb, Betty leaned forward with her hands against the snow to make one last effort and plunged forward, her arms sinking in to the shoulders. Snow inside her sleeves, snow inside all her garments, snow against her bare flesh! Snow that felt warm like a blanket compared to the chill of her flesh! Good snow! Kind snow! She lay upon it like a tired child in the arms of a great mother.

She thought of the stories she had read of quicksands and people sinking to their death. But this was not quicksand. It was more like a mammoth feather bed in which she was sinking, sinking down, and would soon be out of sight. If she opened her eyes she could look across the snow, and down to those interminable white fields stretching their vastness away to the rim of the world, and no help anywhere. She had taken herself out of the realm of her family, the only ones in the wide world who really loved her! Betty! A lost lamb on the snowy mountain.

The gray morning came up, with a sullen sky, the morning that was to have been Christmas Day, and Betty Thornton lay out alone on a billow of snow slowly freezing to death.

She had read that people freezing to death did not suffer pain. It was true then. She was satisfied to lie here and rest. The things that hurt, her chilled feet, the aching in her back, and the pull on her tired limbs and heart, were gone. Even the sting of the cold in her nostrils was not so bad when she did not have to breathe much, and her throat did not hurt so much if she did not try to swallow. She would go to sleep a little while, and perhaps when she wakened the sun would shine and the snow would be melted at least enough to show her the way.

She closed her eyes with a little sob, and let her body rest down in the feathery bed of snow, and suddenly she could hear the family singing the old song, down in the living room of the farm house. Chris' baritone, and Daddy's tenor. Jane singing alto and Mother carrying the soprano all alone, her voice sounding weak, and trembling like a sob in the end of the words, and Betty not there to help! She tried to open her lips and sing. Perhaps they would hear her and come to help her out. But when the sound came out in a little cracked squeak her throat hurt her so terribly that she had to give it up. But what were those words they were singing, the words she had formed with her lips but could not utter?

"While I draw this fleeting breath,
When my eyelids close in death,
When I rise to worlds unknown,
See Thee on Thy judgment throne—"

Then she was dying. This was almost her last breath! Her eyelids were closing in death, and she was going to an unknown world. There would be a judgment throne, and she would be tried for all the things she had done that were wrong and for all the things she ought to have done that were right. And God would be there!

Suddenly she knew that God was there now, out there in the white fields just beyond; that He had been out there all the time looking at her in His kind sad way, watching how far she had gone away from home. She had thought to get away from Him but she had only got away from those she knew and loved, and God who frightened her had come along. She could not get away from God!

She could hear her father praying now with agonized tones, kneeling on the snow out there, with his head bowed and tears in his voice, or was it in the living room at the farm he was kneeling? She was not sure. It was not at home in Briardale, she was sure of that, for he never prayed in Briardale except sometimes in church, a very formal polite prayer that had not seemed like prayer at all, and had not bothered her in the least. But he was praying now, in tones that tore her young heart: "Oh God, find my little Betty! Save my little Betty!" she could hear it over and over again, with the tears in his voice, and her mother sobbing in between; Jane sobbing too, and Chris wiping his eyes—and even little Doris and John crying, kneeling there beside the old davenport and crying, or was it out in the snow? She could not tell. Strange that she could see them all so plainly, hear them too, and she could not make herself known to them. But perhaps she was already dead. Her feet were dead, anyway. It was a long time since she had felt them at all. And there was something packed away inside her lungs that made it hard to breath. It hurt like a knife now when she tried.

And God was out there yet. She had not opened her eyes but He was there! Yes, she must be dead already, and this was the judgment God had come for. So, there *was* a God after all! The teachers in High School had not known. Was Dudley dead too? Did he know too that there was a God? Would they be judged together for what they had tried to do?

It was just then, perhaps, that Betty suddenly grew up, and became a woman.

Chester had not received any of the frantic messages that were sent to him. He had not gone to the places where he might reasonably have been supposed to go. He had found one or two important matters that must be attended to at once, and he had used every minute of time and attended to them, with the one object in view, to get back to the farm Monday evening and spend Christmas eve with his family. He had not even taken time to call on the phone, he was going back so soon. Instead he took the time to purchase gifts—not the gifts he had planned for them on that evening when he had first known of his new prosperity, but sensible things that could be used on the farm, and make the winter in the cold and isolation a delight. He telephoned an order for skiis, and snow shoes and a new kind of sled for coasting and some better skates and warm sweaters, and a lot of games that could be played indoors on stormy days. He bent his every energy to getting back, that this Christmas might yet be one of the happiest that they had ever spent together.

He reached the farm about nine o'clock Christmas eve, and burst into the door with a shout of welcome.

They all came rushing to meet him, Eleanor with tears upon her face, eager expectancy in her look.

"Oh, have you found her?" she cried as he stooped to kiss her. "Where is Betty? Didn't you bring her back with you? Oh, *couldn't* you bring her back? Was it too late?—"

She looked with blank eyes past him to the closed door where no Betty stood as she had hoped.

"Bring her back!" said Chester. "Back from where? Has Betty gone down to the village alone at this time of night? Surely you didn't let her go alone!"

It was a long time before they could make him understand, and finally Chris had to break in:

"Now, Muth, dear—" he said gently, "you just wait, and let me han'le this! I'll tell Dad. He left me in charge—!"

And so they finally made the whole terrible story clear.

It appeared that they had done every one of the things that he suggested eagerly as the story was unfolded. Yes, they had telephoned this one and that,—yes, they had wired to all the stations. Yes, they had—

He walked the floor in his first frantic realization of the truth that Betty had been gone three days and no word had come from her. It was too late to hope to stop the folly of a marriage. Too late to do anything but try to find her and keep her from further folly if possible.

"It is all my fault!" he exclaimed as he wheeled at one end of the room and started pacing back again, "I have not been the right kind of a father! I have not watched my children! I am like Eli. My children have become vile and I have not restrained them! It is my fault and now my punishment has come!"

"Oh, but I am her mother!" broke out Eleanor, sobbing as if her heart would break. "I have not been the right kind of a mother—"

"Stop!" said Chester pausing before her and laying his hand on her bowed head. "You have been a wonderful mother! You have not gone out into the world to know the world as I have. You did not know—"

"Oh, I knew," said Eleanor, "but I did not believe it was true. I didn't think such things could ever happen to us. I thought people were exaggerating! Oh, if I could *only* go back and have Betty in my arms again, a little baby, I would do so differently. Those people who are teaching child psychology don't know. They ought to be told that they are doing mothers harm—!"

"They are blathering idiots!" said Chester viciously, "but that does not let us out. We were brought up in the fear of the Lord, you and I, and somehow we have failed to hand it on to our children. They have lost the sense of sin! They have lost the sense of right and wrong. I saw that the night I went out after Betty! I saw that when I found Jane dancing a vulgar dance in a drug store for the edification of a lot of dirty minded fellows. I saw it later when the letter came—"

255

He became aware of Chris' miserable eyes upon him, and little Jane's dark head down upon the arm of the davenport as she huddled in its corner, her eyes smoldering with unhappiness.

"But we must not think of that now. We must do something! You have been wonderful, Chris, I'm proud of you. But now I think that we cannot any longer keep this thing quiet. I will try to get in touch with Mansfield, our New York man who handles all the office detective work. Perhaps he can think of something else to do. Chris, you say you tried to get in touch with the Westons, how lately?"

"This afternoon," said Chris, comforted that his father was satisfied with his action. "They are gone to New York, but the servant didn't know the address."

"Well, I'll get Mansfield at once if I can. It's a bad night, Christmas eve, to expect to get anybody, but we'll be able to find out something. Perhaps they'll broadcast it to-night, though I'm afraid it is too late to get in now."

"Oh, Chester!" wailed Eleanor. "Must we do that?"

"I'm afraid we must, dear, if we want results. But I'll see what Mansfield says—"

"But Chester, you must have some supper," Eleanor sprang up and went toward the kitchen.

"No, Eleanor, I couldn't eat!" said Chester. "Not now. You go to bed. You look completely exhausted. I'll come up and tell you what he says when I get him."

"But just a cup of coffee—!"

"No, Eleanor. Not now. I couldn't swallow it. I'll get something when I want it."

Chester went into the library and shut the door. They heard the telephone ringing now and then, they heard Chester's low voice talking, and then long silences. The household settled to sleep at last feeling the burden of responsibility rolled from their shoulders to a certain extent, feeling greatly comforted to have the husband and father at home again and undertaking.

But Chester, in the room below as he waited for his man, who was reported to be out of town for a few hours, was kneeling beside his mother's old rocking chair, praying. By his side on his father's desk the old Bible was spread open, for Chester had been reading the word of God concerning Eli, trying to find some hope for his own sin. And when he could not find it he bowed in deep anguish, and prayed "Oh, God, forgive me! Have mercy upon me a sinful father, that I have not seen nor known what was coming to my children, and have not restrained them. Oh, God, have compassion on my little Betty! Oh, God, *find* my little Betty! *Save* my little Betty!"

Chapter XXVI

Out across the miles of snowy fields the echo of that prayer hovered in the air as it went up to the throne of God, its wave lengths lingering about through the gray dawn, while the father knelt and poured out his heart in the same words again and again: "Save my little Betty! Oh God, *find* my little Betty!" From heaven's broadcasting station perhaps that prayer went back till Betty's heart tuned in and heard,—Betty, lying in the cold white snow, listening to her father's prayer that had gone up to God and was sent back to her. Betty, finding God still following her, standing apart, across the snows of Christmas morning!

All had gone blank out there on the snow. Betty could no longer hear her father's voice in prayer. She felt alone, forsaken! But God was still there. She could not rise nor look, for her body seemed to have gone dead, but she knew He was there.

Suddenly a hand touched her on the shoulder. She was surprised. She opened her eyes and saw a face bending over her, and two pleasant eyes looking into hers.

"Are you God?" she thought she heard her own voice ask, her little frozen voice.

"No," said a kindly voice, "but I'm God's child! What are you doing here, little sister?"

"My feet are dead," she answered out of the case of fire and ice in which her body seemed to be fastened. "I think perhaps they are broken off."

He stooped and lifted her in strong arms and she felt the sucking bed of snow release her from its deadly hold.

She was too tired to look up, except for a glance at the kindly face and the pleasant eyes upon her, eyes that looked as though the sunshine was in behind them somewhere.

There was an old Ford standing out there in the road about a rod from the place where she had fallen. She wondered how it had got there without her hearing it. He put her in the back seat, brushing the snow from her garments. He unwound the tattered silk about her ankles, that had slipped down farther and farther until they were mere ribbons cluttering about her feet.

"You poor kid!" he said as he unfastened the little inadequate slippers, "You poor kid! Your feet must be frozen!"

"Oh, are they there yet?" said Betty rousing from the stupor into which she had immediately sunk, "I thought they were broken off!"

He cast a furtive anxious glance at her flushed face, and caught the hoarse rasp of her voice as she coughed. He took off his big driving gloves and took her cold, cold feet in both of his warm hands and rubbed them.

"You poor kid!" he said gently.

She laughed hoarsely.

"I ran away to get married!" she said laughing again deliriously, "and I left my galoshes in the station!"

He gave her a quick keen glance.

"Where do you live, little girl? Who are you?" he asked in a quiet voice, not at all as if it mattered or were anything to make her excited.

"I'm Betty Thornton," she babbled, "I live in Briardale when I'm home, but we're spending the winter at the old farm beyond Wentworth. I'd better get out and go on. I'm on my way home. It's getting late and my head is hot and my feet are cold, or else it's the other way around."

The young man looked at her anxiously as he took out a suit case and began to search for things.

"How long have you been on the way?" he asked pulling out a pair of long gray woollen golf stockings and drawing them over her feet.

"Since the stars came out," said Betty unintelligibly. "The car rolled down the hill and the glass broke, and there was one star God had in His hand! God was there!"

She looked at the young man anxiously as if she wanted to be assured that she was right.

"Yes, God is always there," affirmed the young man quietly. "Now, drink this coffee. It's still hot."

He unscrewed the top of a thermos bottle and poured out the last few swallows of coffee. He tipped the little metal cup to her lips and she tried to swallow, but the knife was there in her throat.

"There's ice in my throat," she explained looking at him wildly, "I shall have to wait till it melts."

"Drink the rest of this. It will help to melt the ice!" he urged and Betty swallowed again, obediently, and sank back on the folded coat he had laid under her head.

She did not open her eyes when he tucked the robe about her. She felt herself sinking into a deep place now that was as hot as she had been cold a little while before. She was thinking that God's child had kind eyes. They were nice eyes. They comforted her. She liked to hear him say "Poor kid!"

While Chester was still upon his knees crying to God, confessing his sin, and praying for mercy on his child, the shabby Ford turned into the lane and ploughed its way up to the old farm.

Betty's mother was the first one at the door.

She had come down stairs to prepare breakfast, anxious for her man, tiptoeing about lest she waken him, not daring to open the library door lest she disturb him, yet anxious to know what he had done during the night.

The throb of the car roused the house. Chris was

down almost at once, and Jane, calling from upstairs at the window:

"It's Betts, Muth! But that's not Dudley Weston with her! Who can it be?"

Eleanor did not hear Jane. She had flung wide the door and with her hand fluttering to her throat was standing wide-eyed looking out, her intuition telling her that this was no ordinary news which was about to be revealed.

"While they are yet speaking I will hear," was the promise that Chester Thornton had read as he knelt before the old Bible.

He was still praying "God, find my little Betty!" when John flung the library door wide and called excitedly:

"Dad, come quick! Betty's come home and she's awful sick!"

They carried Betty upstairs to her bed in the bright Christmas morning, for the clouds had cleared and the sun was sparkling over everything, but Betty did not recognize it. She tossed on the big cool bed, and thought it was a field of snow. She looked in her mother's face and did not know her. Two white robed nurses presently took up their station around her bed, and two noted physicians from New York came in consultation with the little country doctor from Wentworth, and all that skill and science could do were being done for Betty Thornton.

Down stairs the Christmas tree, partly decked in its tin stars and paper frills, stood neglected and desolate. The children stole by it without looking. It seemed a desecration now to think about Christmas with Betty so sick.

The white haired minister drove up every day in his son's Ford to find out how the little patient was doing. Once or twice he came up into the room and knelt beside Betty's bed and prayed, while her mother wept outside the door, and her father stood beside her, his arm about her, and a look of utter anguish on his face. The minister's son did not come in. He did not want to intrude, but he always asked anxiously, "How is she?" when his father came back to the car.

The Christmas season passed without a celebration. Anxiety held the household in its grip. Even John and Doris learned how to sigh, and one day Eleanor caught Jane at the window crying.

"Betty had no right!" she explained when her mother asked what was the matter. "She had no right to spoil Christmas for us all. She oughtta uv thought of other people a little!"

"Hush, darling," said her mother. "If Betty will only come back I think perhaps she'll understand that now—"

"Come back?" said Jane with a quick catch of alarm, "won't she come back?"

"We hope so, darling, but the doctor isn't sure!"

"Well, why did she have to do something to upset everybody else. If she wanted to be silly she'd oughtta have found some way that wouldn't hurt her family."

"When people do wrong, Janie dear, they never do it alone. They always bring consequences on other people. We're all bound up in the bundle of life together, and a man or woman or girl or boy can't sin in any way without hurting others."

The day came when Betty turned feverish eyes upon them all and demanded:

"Where is God's child? I want to see him."

And for hours she kept asking the same question.

They did not know what she meant, and they sent for the old minister, who knelt beside her bed and prayed.

She stared at him with eager eyes.

"You are nice," she said looking at him intently, "but you are not the child of God. He warmed my feet and brought me to my father's house. I want to see him. I want to ask him a question."

"Ah!" said the minister smiling kindly, "I think it is my son David that you mean. He is a child of God. I will send for him!"

And that night David Dunham left his studies in a far city, and journeyed up to Vermont in answer to his

261

father's call, but he did not borrow his roommate's Ford this time. He caught the fast express, and was at home as soon as steam and rail could bring him.

"Well, little sister," he said sitting down beside the bed, and taking her little hot hand in his, "I am the child of God you sent for. What can I do for you?"

. She turned her restless eyes upon him and her voice was full of pleading:

"Oh, won't you ask God not to judge me for letting Dudley take that drive?"

"And who is Dudley?" asked David Dunham kindly.

"Dudley is the boy I was going to run away with, and he wouldn't have got killed if I hadn't gone."

There was great distress in her voice. Chester and Eleanor looked at one another in dismay. This was the first they had heard of Dudley. Had Dudley been killed? What terrible experience had their beloved child been passing through without them? Or was this some wild raving of delirium?

The anxious young voice went on:

"Won't you tell God not to look at me? He keeps looking at me all the time. He thinks I'm unclean! He thinks I'm foul! My father said so. And He keeps looking at me all the time. Won't you tell Him to stop?"

David Dunham turned his clear eyes on the little sick girl. He took hold of the little hot hand that Betty held out pleadingly, with his big cool grasp, and spoke quietly, commandingly, to her:

"Listen, little sister! Didn't you know that Jesus Christ has opened a fountain for sin and for uncleanness? Long ago He shed His blood to make a fountain to wash away our sins. He wants to make you clean, little sister, that's why He is looking at you."

"But I'm afraid of blood!" she cried clinging to his hand. "There was blood on Dudley Weston's head and face. There was blood on the stretcher they carried him on—I couldn't wash in blood!"

"This is Christ's blood, little sister. It is not human

blood. Human blood could not wash us from sin, but Jesus' blood can wash us whiter than snow!"

"Oh, did you have to be washed too? Is that why you look so much like God?"

"I certainly did, little sister. We all have to be washed."

"But won't it hurt?" Betty's eyes were full of fear.

"I'll say it won't!" said the young man with a light in his face. "You just ask Him, and it's done, just like that!"

"You ask Him, won't you? I'm afraid."

David Dunham knelt by the side of the bed, the little hot hand still in his, and began to pray:

"Oh, God, our Father, in the name of Jesus, who died to make us clean from sin, please wash this little girl, and make her free from sin forever. Put her behind the blood now, and make her Thy child! Wash her and make her whiter than snow, for Jesus' sake who loved her and died for her—"

When the prayer was ended she looked in his face eagerly.

"Is that all? Is it done?" she asked.

"Yes, it is done. You can trust Him to take care of all the rest."

"Then I'm going to sleep," she said with a sigh, "I was afraid to go to sleep before."

Her hand still in his she closed her eyes, and lay quiet.

Suddenly the big troubled eyes opened again.

"I ought to go back and tell Dudley—" she said anxiously. "Dud doesn't know, and he's a *mess!*"

"Dudley shall be told—" promised Dunham quickly, and the white lids fluttered down, content.

For a long time David Dunham knelt beside the bed with Betty's hand lying lightly within his own, his head bowed, his eyes closed. And Betty fell into the first natural sleep she had had since he brought her home.

The doctor had waved them all away, and told them that if she could sleep a few hours there was hope, so the house was still as still could be. When Dunham at last

263

came down stairs, his face wearing the look of one who had just had audience with the King, Chester met him with extended hand.

"I can't thank you enough," he said, his voice unsteady with feeling. "You've saved our little girl's life the doctor tells me. I shall never forget it. You are a wonderful young man."

David returned the hand clasp warmly.

"Don't say that, Mr. Thornton," he answered, "Say we have a wonderful God! It was God who reached down and gave peace to your little girl."

"It was you who made her ready to receive it."

"No," said David, "it was the Holy Spirit. He only used me as a humble instrument. And now, Mr. Thornton, who is this Dudley? I promised I would see him."

Chester's face grew hard.

"He is a vile little beast who is trying to lead my daughter astray," answered Chester fiercely. "It is his fault that she is lying there. I would rather have nothing to do with him. He is not worth it. I hope that Betty may never see his face again!"

"I surmised as much from what she told me on the way home, although I do not think she knew what she was saying," said Dunham. "But still, I'd like to keep my promise. Could you give me his address? I shall not of course mention you in the matter. I would do it wholly on my own initiative."

"Thank you," said Chester, "that's good of you of course. I would really prefer not to have our family drawn into the matter at all. I do not know yet just how far Betty has involved herself. Of course she was not able to give any connected account of herself. She has been in delirium ever since you brought her home."

"I surmised from phrases she kept repeating on the way home that there had been some sort of an accident, and that the young man was in a hospital, either dead or dying. She kept saying over and over the name of the hospital and the street it was on. I am sure it must be in New York."

"You don't say!" said Chester startled. "That's awkward! I suppose somebody ought to find out. They are neighbors of ours in Pennsylvania, but people whom we don't much care for. We have not had much to do with them. I wonder if they know where their son is? I don't want to be unchristian of course, but really the boy has been unspeakable, and I would like to spare Betty any connection with the matter if I could. However, we must not be inhuman—"

"Suppose you let me inquire into things," offered Dunham. "I am a stranger, and can find out how things are before you make any move."

"Thank you! I'd be grateful for that," said Chester bowing gravely, trying to keep the anger out of his voice. "You can't understand, perhaps, how bitter I am toward the young man who led my daughter into a situation like this. Or, if she was partly to blame, as I am afraid she was, who allowed her to go through this awful experience, who has compromised her—"

"I can understand!" said David quickly, "I'd like to go out and thrash him this minute myself. But it seems as if perhaps God may have taken it out of our hands and is dealing with him Himself."

Chapter XXVII

David did not lose time in locating the hospital where Dudley Weston was. It had been easy for Betty had babbled the name and the streets over and over on the way home as if it had been a lesson she was conning and David had written them down lest it might be important later. He enquired about the young man, and found that he had just passed through an operation on the skull which they hoped was going to be successful; that he was doing as well as could be expected considering the injuries he had sustained, and that his parents were with him. David asked how soon he might receive visitors and was told that it would be at least a week before anyone outside his family would be admitted.

"And now," said David as he turned away from the telephone, to face Chester who had been sitting near, "I guess there isn't anything to do but pray about it for a while. I'll just ask guidance. And when he's able to see me I'll run down to New York and try to get a heart to heart talk with him. I shouldn't think there was any obligation upon you to do anything just now either, Mr. Thornton. Your daughter is too ill for you to have time or thought for anything else. The lad is evidently being cared for, and in need of nothing that we can do at present. Besides, you're not supposed to know what has happened. I should think you might well afford to wait until your daughter is able to tell you more about the situation, I'll keep you informed of what I may discover. And the way will open up. It always does, when we put the problems in His hands."

"I'm afraid I've never got in the habit of that," said Chester humbly. "It's going to be hard to have any sympathy whatever with such a young viper as that boy is."

At the doctor's request David Dunham stayed at the farm until Betty had passed the crisis and was decidedly on the way to improvement. He said that he did not care to risk having David away if she should suddenly ask for him, that he had been more valuable than any medicine. So David stayed, although it meant hard work when he got back to make up for lost time.

But Betty did not ask for him again. She did not even seem to remember anything about what had passed between them when she finally woke up one morning with a weak smile and looked intelligently into her mother's face. She was almost like a baby for a few days, only able to smile a little and lift her hand a few inches to sign what she wanted. She seemed too weak and tired for words, a frail sweet shadow of the Betty that had been. She crept slowly, hesitantly back to life again. And after a few days, when it was a thoroughly established fact that she was going to get well, David Dunham went back to his studies.

On his way he stopped over in New York, and sought out the hospital. Somehow he managed to get an interview with Dudley Weston. Under guidance of the Lord, with Spirit-given tact, and preparation on his knees, the young man waited until a favorable opportunity presented itself, with the elder Westons both away for the afternoon. In fact it developed that they were not especially devoted to wasting much time in whiling away the weary hours of their only son while he stayed in the hospital.

It was like David Dunham to hunt around until he found an old school mate who had gone into medicine and was serving an apprenticeship in the very hospital where Dudley had been taken. Having reestablished his old friendship with the young interne by a few minutes talk, and well knowing that an interne has no time for company, he said he would just stroll through the halls and wait around till his friend had some time off and they could go out together for lunch. There was a lad up in the private ward to whom he was taking a message. No, he wasn't a personal friend, in fact wasn't known to the young man, but he had a reason for wanting to meet him. Was there any way he could be casually introduced? The name was Weston, Dudley Weston.

The doctor eyed him curiously.

"Sure," he said, "I'll take you up. But you won't like him. He's not your kind, Dave! He's the very devil!"

"So I have been told," said David calmly.

They went up to the fourth floor, and the doctor knocked at Dudley Weston's door and went in.

"Hello, Weston, how are you?" greeted the doctor with his best hospital manner. "I want to take your temperature, if you don't mind."

"Just had my temperature taken half an hour ago," growled Dudley Weston turning a frowning face and glaring at the door.

"Well, this is special," said the doctor getting out his

thermometer. "I want it for my report, see?"

David stood just without the doorway, studying the lad.

Dudley Weston's handsome countenance was still adorned with strips of plaster, and a cigarette was trickling out of one corner of his sensuous lips. The recent suffering through which he had passed had not sweetened either his temper, or his expression.

"What the devil do you want to annoy me for?" said Dudley. "I should say it was your business to get your figures from the nurses, and not bother me again. Well, stick her in and get it over with."

The doctor got out his thermometer talking as cheerfully as if he had been received with the utmost courtesy.

"Having a tough time of it, aren't you Weston? I brought a friend along with me, thought he might amuse you a few minutes till I get off duty. He's the best man on skis I know outside of the regular professionals."

The frown which had been gathering like a quick storm on the boy's face, was held in abeyance.

"Skis?" he said with a quick ungracious look, which nevertheless gave permission to David to enter.

So David, with his ready smile and his quick charm got entrance to Dudley Weston's room, and for half an hour sat and talked.

They spoke of several men who were noted in the various sports, and David knew them all, some of them being personal friends of whom he related little amusing incidents. Suddenly he turned to the invalid and said:

"I wonder if you know my best friend, the Lord Jesus Christ?"

Dudley Weston only stared, and his face grew hard and cynical.

"What are you?" he asked insolently. "A sky pilot? No real man would swallow that bunk!"

"I'm sorry," David answered gravely, "It's evident you don't know Him or you wouldn't talk that way. But there was a time when I didn't know Him either. I met Christ and He forgave my sins, and washed me in His blood, and taught me that the existence I had led before wasn't real living at all. And I've found He is so wonderful that I want everybody I meet to know Him."

Dudley regarded his visitor with a supercilious smile:

"I pass," he said flippantly. "He's not my type. I prefer to keep my sins. Better snap out of it. Life is too brisk to put on that sob stuff and talk tommyrot like that!"

David took out a card.

"Sorry," he said pleasantly, "I'd like you to know Him. If you ever feel differently let me know. Here's my address. I'll be glad to introduce you."

"Not here!" said Dudley with a shrug of his one good shoulder. "Speed for mine! Have a drink, Dunham? I've got some of the real thing in that bureau drawer in a flask. Be glad to have you try a pull at it."

"Thanks, no," said David evenly, "I wouldn't get a bit of kick out of it. That's not my speed you know."

There was a twinkle in his eyes, but his mouth looked strong and had a firm set. Dudley eyed him for an instant half inclined to think he was being laughed at, but a diversion occurred.

There came a knock at the door, bold and assured, and without waiting for invitation two girls entered, showily and scantily attired. They were heavily painted and carried an atmosphere of scent,—one would hardly call it perfume,—that was as loud as their voices.

"Hello, Dud!" they called as they entered, "Got company? I thought you said you were all by your lonesome."

"So I was, Peachy. This is a new importation. Shows what I've come to. Make you acquainted with the parson. He's been trying to save my soul but somehow it didn't take. Dunham, meet Peachy and Pearl. Now here's two girls that are just my speed. Sit down and have a little chin with us. Perhaps you'll get a kick out of it. Peach, get the flask, you know where it is, and let's have a regular time. Sit down, Parson! Get acquainted with the ladies!"

"Thank you," said David gravely, looking them

over without a flicker, "But I'm afraid they wouldn't care for my line. I'll be going now, but remember, my offer holds good to the end."

He was gone; the three sending peals of laughter after him were not quite certain whether he had been kidding them or not. Had there, or had there not been a twinkle in his eye as he said it?

"Whaddee mean, his line, Dud?" asked Peachy, "Whadya let him go for? He's a good looker if he is a parson."

"Well," said David to himself as he walked down the street and drew a long breath, "that's done—or—is it? The incident is closed, my promise is fulfilled, and if I'd done it on my own initiative I'd think I'd made a mighty bungle of it, but I've that promise, 'Ye have not chosen me, but I have chosen you.' I'll just roll the burden of it on Him now. Perhaps in Eternity I'll know. But anyhow, I had to go."

A little later he added to himself, "The little girl was right. He certainly is a mess! Poor child! How did she come to get mixed up with him?"

Chapter XXVIII

Betty crept slowly back to life, but there was about her something childlike and dependent, something sweet and new and yielding that the old Betty had not known. Eleanor felt as if she had her baby back again. Betty smiled when anything was done for her, and showed almost none of the old impatience and irritation if she had to wait for something. And yet withal she seemed reserved and more mature, as if life had hit her hard and taught her something.

She talked very little and said nothing at all about her recent experience. They did not even know if she remembered it, or if it might not have been mercifully blotted out of her mind.

They rejoiced with trembling however, and thanked God for her present gentleness. They were constantly fearful of possibilities in the future when Betty would be well again. When Dudley Weston should be well, perhaps, too. What would be the next move? There would have to come a day in the near future of course when Betty must be questioned about her escapade. That is, provided she did not volunteer information. God grant there might not have to be any more terrible revelations!

So Betty came back from Death's door, and the day arrived at last when she was to be brought down stairs for the first time.

It had been Eleanor's plan for her not to get up until after the midday meal but Betty suddenly roused to interest and begged to be taken down stairs in the morning. This was rather a complication because Dr. Dunham was coming for the first lesson with the children. Eleanor had arranged to have them use the living room for a school room, and the couch that Betty was to lie on was in that room.

"I'm afraid it will tire you, dear, the whole morning long and you having to listen."

"No, it will not tire me, Mums," said Betty, with more vigor than she had shown since she went away.

"If I get tired I'll just shut my eyes and pretend I'm not there. I'm tired of being away off here. It's time I got well!"

So they yielded to her urgency and Chester carried her down stairs and established her on the couch by the fireplace, somewhat apart from the little circle around the big table. There was a blackboard at the other end of the room, and on the table was a pile of beautiful new Bibles in soft leather bindings.

The new teacher was already in the room and greeted Betty pleasantly but did not act as if she were a member of the class, and the room settled down to business.

"Now," said the teacher when Eleanor had tiptoed out of the room, and Chester had retired into the library, "friends, we're going to try out a new kind of school, you and I. We're going to study history, literature, biography, biology, geology, chronology, astronomy, theology, geography, philosophy, and a lot of other ologies, with maybe a touch of mathematics here and there, but we're going to study it all out of one Book.

"We may bring in other books occasionally as side lights, but the whole study is to centre around one Book. And if there is any difference of opinion between other books and other people and *our* Book, *it* is to be the criterion, because its Author is the only writer in the universe who can possibly know the *truth* about any of the subjects named! The reason that He is so well informed is that He is the Originator of them all, and that His name is God!

"I hope that as we go on with our study you will find that none of the subjects I have mentioned are really separate subjects, but are merely classifications of one great theme, which together explain life.

"Now if you can bring to this study a belief in the Book which we are to take up, you will be able to enter deeper into the things of which it tells. But if not you will only see the things which are on the surface. I do not mean an intellectual belief that comes from being convinced that the Book is logically true, I mean a *will* to accept every statement the Book gives. If you can do that you will have a key which will unlock a great many secret and beautiful treasures of knowledge and wisdom which have been placed there for only those who believe. And if you can do that honestly I can promise you that the proof of its truth will later be shown to you.

"I cannot do this for you. You will have to do it for yourselves. But you will be well repaid if you exercise this act of the will and come to your study believing the Book comes from God, and giving it opportunity to prove itself true. But even if you are unwilling to do this, the Book can show you many wonderful treasures and delights if you will give yourselves to a study of it. It is up to you, my friends, how much you get out of what we are about to do."

Betty was listening with closed eyes. No one was

noticing her, but she did not miss a word.

At this stage Jane raised her hand.

"How can we believe that, when *anybody* might have written it?" she asked pertly.

The teacher smiled.

"You think anybody might have written it?" he asked pleasantly. "Try it and see. A great many have tried to write something like it and failed. But yes, Jane, you *can* believe it in spite of any doubts you may have, if you *will* to do so. People easily believe much more foolish things than that. You can say, 'I'm going to take this Book with a mind open to receive every word it says as absolute fact, and let it prove itself to my reasoning powers as I study, and begin to understand.' You have no right to doubt a book until you know what it says. The Bible is able to prove its truth to you if you will give it a chance to reveal itself to your spirit. You can't just understand the Bible with your mind alone, your spirit must enter into it, because it is written for your spirit to understand. If you were to try to get at the Bible through your body alone, if you were to take it and eat it and try to get it into your system in that way, you would not get anywhere with it. And why do you expect to understand it merely through your mind alone?"

Jane giggled.

"And now," said Dr. Dunham, "I am going to tell you a little story I once heard a great teacher tell that will illustrate one way we know the Bible is true. We will suppose a man in England makes his will. He leaves his property in trust for a good many years until it shall accumulate interest enough to amount to a certain very large sum. At that time it is to be divided between all his descendants who are then living. A copy of this will is filed with the English Government at the time of the man's death, perhaps in some court house or Government building in England. After a few years have passed one of this man's sons decides to move to Spain. He desires to give his children the benefit of his father's will so he gets a copy of it, and takes it with him to Spain. There it is translated into Spanish and put on file, perhaps with the Spanish Government. Another son moves to Germany, and he gets a copy of the will in German. Later another goes to Itlay and the will is translated into Italian. Another to India, and perhaps another somewhere else. Each takes a copy of the will in the language of the country to which he is going, filing it for use of their descendants. Then one day a great fire destroys the building in which the original will is filed. The will is burned. At last the day comes when the property has reached the sum named in the will and the heirs make application to have it divided. But the original will is gone and what can they do? They get together the wills that have been translated into the different languages, and compare them. In this way they get an accurate copy of the original will, and by it the court divides the property. Now just such a thing happened with the Bible. We have not the original manuscripts on which the men wrote who were taught of God what to write. But as the years went by those original manuscripts were copied and recopied into many languages and scattered over the whole earth; scholars who have devoted their lives to the study have gathered these different copies and compared them. They find that they all agree! Here is a book,"—he held up a little brown volume, "which tells about this investigation. It is written by one of the greatest scholars in the world, who has devoted forty-five years to looking into this matter. You will be interested to study this some time. It was written to show that from the standpoint of a scholar we may know that we have the original word of God as it was given to Holy men of old, moved by the Holy Spirit. That is what we call 'inspiration.' We shall talk of that later.

"Now, will you open your Bibles to the first chapter and the first verse of the first book, called Genesis, and we will have our first geography lesson."

There was a little rustle of excitement as the new Bibles were opened.

"Christopher, will you read the first verse?"

Chris read, almost embarrassedly:

"In the beginning God created the heavens and the earth."

The old minister interrupted him:

"You will remember we are going to take up our study of this Book with the idea of accepting all its statements and giving it a chance to prove them true. We must therefore if we are to get anywhere accept this as a fact."

Jane began to be restless. Her lip curled a trifle.

"What is it, Jane?" questioned the keen eyed old teacher.

"Our teacher at school says that isn't so!" said Jane importantly. "She says God didn't make the earth or anything. She says it just developed out of matter and that there isn't any God, only just a force that makes things grow. She says that nobody believes that any more, only ignorant people."

"Shut up, Jane, that's not polite!" admonished Chris in the tone of a mentor.

"Let her speak," said the teacher. "We want to understand all these things and get them cleared away out of our minds. Now, Jane, your teacher is wrong! There are a *great many* famous scholars who believe in God and His Book with all their hearts. One of them is coming to visit me this winter. He is the author of this brown book I showed you. Perhaps I can introduce him to you. He is considered by everybody to be the greatest living authority on ancient languages. He has spent many years in trying to find out these things, and he probably knows more than your teacher in school ever heard of. He has personally read all the ancient manuscripts, and has given his whole life to this study. He knows forty-eight ancient languages, and in over twenty he can talk and write as well as read. He has written two remarkable books about the Bible showing that it is true, which some day I hope you'll read. And after you have read them you may like to send copies of them to your teacher to read."

"But now suppose we get back to our study of the statement that God made the heavens and the earth out of nothing, for that is what the word 'create' in the Hebrew means, 'to make out of nothing'."

The children looked wisely incredulous, but waited.

"Now, we do not know how many ages ago that was," went on the wise pleasant voice, "but it was

275

thousands, perhaps millions of years—"

"Why," broke in Betty, before she realized she was speaking, "Why, I thought all people who believed in the Bible thought the earth was made only about five or six thousand years ago, and that it was all made in six days. And that *couldn't possibly* be you know for there are all those fossils and buried things that took simply ages to get that way—"

The teacher smiled leniently:

"There is room for all that, Betty, between the first and second verses of Genesis. We have been talking about what is sometimes called the pre-Adamite creation. Jane, will you read the second verse?"

Jane read:

"And the earth was without form and void; and darkness was upon the face of the deep. And the Spirit of God moved upon the face of the waters."

"Now," said the teacher, "in the Hebrew which is the language in which this Old Testament was originally written, that word that has been translated 'was' means 'became'. It doesn't mean that it *was* so in the first place, but that it *became* so after it was created on account of some great disaster or cataclysm resulting from God's wrath. There are some words which translated into other languages lose much of their strength, and this is one. The verse should read 'And the earth *became* without form.' There are passages in Isaiah and Jeremiah which have reference to this very thing having happened to 'the world that then was' as it is called. Jane, I've given you the Isaiah reference to read, and Christopher may take the one in Jeremiah. I'll give Doris and John each something to look up also. It is very interesting to study about the destruction of this first creation because of sin and how God had to make the world over again. Now, Jane, will you read?"

The morning flew away before any of them realized it, and Betty did not want to go back to bed again when the class was over. She even sent Jane down stairs that afternoon for one of the new Bibles and got her to make a copy of all the references that she might look them up again.

"It's going to be kind of fun, I believe," vouchsafed Jane when she brought the Bible.

"I never heard anything like it," said Betty. "I don't believe they know these things in school. I wonder if he knows what he's talking about?"

"Well, he sure has a good line and is interesting," said Chris who was standing in the doorway, "but maybe it's all just bologny!"

That was the beginning of a new order of things.

The children took hold of their studies with avidity, and worked and played happily. They seemed to forget the life from which they had been so summarily withdrawn.

Betty grew stronger every day now and came regularly to the classes. Her father had been fearful that she would rebel against studying with the minister, but she went into the work without any question.

Chester and Eleanor looked on with delight. What a miracle had been wrought! Even Doris and John were eager and interested and went about conning Bible verses and vying with one another as to who could learn the day's portion first. All of them seemed simply fascinated by the new study. Even Chester and Eleanor began to drop into the classes.

"I had no idea what the Bible was like," said Chester humbly one day. "I have brought my children up in ignorance. They are simply little heathen. I am not much better! And I thought I knew the Bible well!"

"Well," Chester heard Chris say to Betty one day, "I don't know whether the old man has got the right dope or not, but it's darned interesting anyway. That about the pyramid being all told about in the Bible was great! Gee I'd like to go over to Egypt and see that thing and crawl all through those passages. He says he's got a model of it, he's going to bring it over and show us."

The clear cold weather had settled down upon them now, and the children spent many happy hours upon the ice or coasting down the old hill; coming in with faces glowing, healthy appetites, and minds alert for study. Even Betty took her part now again in the sports and seemed to be getting fully back to normal once more.

Eleanor and Chester watched her with growing delight and began to hope that her fearful experience was not to be so disastrous after all. Yet nothing had been said between them yet about her running away. Chester and Eleanor were both afraid to disturb the happy calm which seemed to have settled down upon the old farm, and decided to let well enough alone, and just ignore the circumstance for the present. Betty was noticeably maturing day by day.

One day Mrs. Dunham fell ill however, and the lessons had to be interrupted. She was so ill that after a few days they sent for her son and David came swiftly in answer to his mother's call.

When she grew better Dr. Dunham came down with a heavy cold brought on by weariness and loss of sleep during his wife's illness, and David lingered on a few days longer.

It was at his father's request that he came up to the farm to conduct the classes for a time or two.

"Davy has one or two new discoveries in archaeology I want the children to hear about," explained the old minister when Chester came up one morning to see how he was getting on, "I want David to tell them too, about the prophecies, and the way they are being fulfilled over there in Europe to-day by the lining up of the nations, that shows the Coming of the Lord cannot be far away. He has a new book on the Chronology of the Bible that I want him to show them. It makes things very clear. It's a kind of key to some of the sealed passages in Daniel. We must have it for reference. You know the Bible says that in the time of the end they shall be unsealed and the wise shall understand these things, but none of the wicked shall understand."

"I never noticed that passage before," said Chester humbly. "I'm learning a lot this winter, including what a miserable father I have been."

"But Thornton, it's wonderful how your children are taking hold of this study," went on the teacher. "It's given me an idea. I wish I was young and had money. I'd start such a school with the Bible as the basis of all studies.

I understand there are several now, here and there with much the same idea back of them."

"Well, why not come down to Briardale and start it there," said Chester. "I would dare to take my kiddies back home if I had such a school to send them to. We could have a winter school in Briardale and a summer one up at the farm. I believe I could get some other men to join with me and finance the thing, if only I could show them the result of it on my children. What do you say? Will you do it?"

"But there's my church," smiled the minister.

"Let some young man just starting take the church for the winter months," said Chester, "and you and David come and help me start a school in Briardale. You need to get busy out in the world. This is no time to hide away a wise man of God in the wilderness like this. Look at my children! Think what was happening to them! And there are millions of others in their condition."

"Not every father is awake to the condition of things," said Dunham.

"Well, I'll admit God sent me an eye-opener," said Chester, "but there must be a few others who are worried about the state of things. I'll see what I can stir up."

David came up to the farm for a few days and began to teach more wonders to the eager students. He was "David" to them all now.

He took them out and taught them to use their skiis, and they were wild with delight. They skated and coasted and had wonderful times together after the lessons were over, and then they came in and helped Eleanor cook and wash dishes.

One day Jane expressed their feeling:

"I'll say I'm glad daddy kidnapped us all and brought us up here, aren't you Betts?"

And Betty with a smiling face owned she was.

Betty had received David shyly, almost silently at first, but after they had played together out of doors for a few days she began to talk with him a little more naturally. He wondered if she remembered any of the things she had said to him in her delirium. But one day when they had been coasting together and he was helping her up the hill again she suddenly turned to him and said:

"Did you mean all those things you told me while I was sick, or did you just tell me that to quiet me?"

"I certainly meant every word," he said with a glad ring to his voice. "I have been wondering if you remembered."

"Oh, I couldn't forget that!" said Betty earnestly. "It had been so awful having God looking at me all the time. I could see just what He thought of me. But isn't He going to bring it all up sometime and judge me for it?"

"No, He says in His word that He'll forgive your transgressions and remember them no more."

"But it will always be there," said Betty sadly. "There'll always be those things that I have done! I'll always be unclean!"

"What God has washed cannot be unclean. 'As far as the east is from the west so far hath He removed our transgressions from us,'" quoted David.

She was silent for a long time and then she said timidly, as though she were not sure she ought to say it:

"But *you* will always think of me that way—as—unclean!"

"I will always think of you as the little girl who is saved!" he said reverently and his voice had a glad ring in it.

"Oh, will you!" she exclaimed with a light coming into her eyes. "I'm so glad! But oh! I wish I'd never known Dudley Weston!" She pressed her fingers over her eyes and gave a little shiver of horror at the remembrance.

When David Dunham went back to his work he wrote to Betty every few days and life began to take on a new look. She was no longer the haughty princess in exile. She walked the earth as if it were paved with flowers and all day long she was singing.

Plans for the new Bible school went forward rapidly. Chester took a trip home and found three or four more men whose children were disappointing them. They were dubious, it is true, as to whether anything about the Bible could ever touch their young outlaws but they were willing to be convinced and Chester brought three of them up to the farm when he came back, along with Hannah who said she was homesick for her family. When the three fathers had listened in on the Bible studies for several hours they marvelled and went away thoughtfully to tell others. And so the scheme for a Bible School grew.

The Spring came on and the snow melted at last. Arbutus and mountain laurel appeared and the earth took on a loveliness that even surpassed the grandeur of the winter whiteness.

Chester went back home for part of each week now as the business claimed more of his time. But the family had elected to stay at the farm till summer was over. So the Bible lessons went steadily on. As the Book opened its treasures to them the children changed and grew thoughtful and lovely of attitude. Eleanor was expressing this to their teacher one day and he smiled and said:

"The Lord has promised that his word shall not return unto Him void but shall accomplish that whereunto He sent it. Your children are growing wise in the deepest lore of the ages. I think they are going to be among the wise, Mrs. Thornton."

As the summer drew to a close the plans for the new school began to mature. Money had been forthcoming. A building had been secured. The Dunhams promised to undertake and had found several other fine wise spirits for teachers. Word had gone forth that the school would be open for students in the fall.

The exile was over.

The Thorntons were going back to Briardale again but they were all reluctant to leave the farm, and talked eagerly of their return next summer.

David had come up to help his father pack and spent much time at the farm. He and Betty were standing one day on the brow of a hill. The frost had already begun to fling scarlet banners of loveliness over the world in preparation for another winter. Betty's face was tender as she looked across the misty purple of the mountains.

"It's going to be queer going back," she mused, "I almost dread it. There won't be any of my old friends who will be in sympathy with me. I shall be practically alone. There are some I wish I never need see again. I'm glad the

Westons have moved to New York. But Gyp and Fran will not understand. I used to be proud of being hard-boiled and they will think I am crazy. I shall be separated from everybody."

"That's the history of every child of God," said David quickly. "'Come ye out from among them and be ye separate.' The church is a body of called out ones. He has called us to be a royal generation, kings and priests unto Him. Isn't that good enough, Betty?" He looked at her earnestly, reaching out and gathering her hand into his. "You are very precious to me, Betty. I have loved you ever since I found you like a little lost lamb in the snow. Do you think you could ever love me? Do you think after the school is on its feet and things straighten out that you and I could go together through life? Could you love me, Betty?"

Betty lifted wondering startled eyes that filled with humble tears.

"Oh, David," she said sadly, "I love you. Yes I love you. I didn't know there was anything like love before. I thought it was all bunk. But David, I'm not good enough for you. I'm—" she caught her breath in a sob and laid her face against his shoulder, "I'm *unclean!*"

"Whom Jesus Christ hath cleansed is not unclean, Betty darling! 'The King's daughter is all glorious within.'" And he laid his lips reverently upon hers and drew her close to his heart.

The next day the Thorntons went back to their home to begin a new life. As they drove up to the house they saw a beautiful blue Mermaid Eight standing at the door.

"That," said Chester to Betty, "is by way of a birthday present. I saw how things were going and I thought I'd like to get it in before it had to be a wedding gift."

The End